THE
COMPLETE
CRIME
STORIES

THE

COMPLETE

CRIME

STORIES

JAMES M. CAIN

MYSTERIOUSPRESS.COM

OPEN ROAD

INTEGRATED MEDIA

NEW YORK

Cover design by Neil Alexander Heacox

978-1-5040-1132-7

Published in 2015 by MysteriousPress.com/Open Road Integrated Media, Inc.
345 Hudson Street
New York, NY 10014
www.mysteriouspress.com
www.openroadmedia.com

CONTENTS

JAMES M. CAIN

Introduction
By Otto Penzler

James M. Cain, the quintessential hard-boiled writer, claimed he didn't know what the term meant, and he wasn't alone. So what is it? They are realistic works of fiction in the sense that people who go out to get a private investigator license are hired to solve crimes, even if they are committed by tough guys (who, in fact, commit most violent crimes), which is more than the village vicar or the head of the gardening club can say. Since they are not part of an official police force, they have a lot more freedom to get information in whatever manner works best for them. This is true only in fictional accounts, of course.

The reason Cain never wrote a detective novel is that he didn't like the notion of a criminal being caught in a neat ending with all loose ends tied together. His stories are mainly concerned with murder and love, and are told primarily from the criminal's point of view.

Born in Annapolis, Maryland, in 1892, he was the son of James William Cain, a professor, and Rose Mallahan Cain, an opera singer. James also wanted a career in opera until he was told emphatically (by his mother) that he didn't have the voice for it. His father later became president of Washington College in Chesterton, Maryland, where James received his bachelor of arts degree in 1910 at the age of eighteen, and a master's degree in 1917 after teaching mathematics and English at the college for four years.

Eschewing a promising academic career, Cain decided to become a reporter and worked for the *Baltimore American* and the *Baltimore Sun*, with time out for two years in the Army during World War I. He was encouraged by H.L. Mencken in Baltimore and later by Walter Lippman at the *New York World*, where he wrote political columns of a relatively uncontroversial nature. There were so many taboos, Cain said, that as an independent columnist "all you could condemn was the man-eating shark, and all you could praise was your favorite flower."

His magazine articles and short stories began to appear in the 1920s and he started to write screenplays in Hollywood in 1931 and continued to write them with increasing success, both artistically and financially, for seventeen years. He became a best-selling author with his first novel, *The Postman Always Rings Twice* (1934).

As a California writer, Cain inevitably faced comparison with Dashiell Hammett, Raymond Chandler, and, to a lesser degree, Ross Macdonald. They are "tough guy" writers in the same way that John Steinbeck, Ernest Hemingway, Horace McCoy, and B. Traven were. The noted critic Edmund Wilson called Cain and his peers "poets of the tabloid murder" because they forced a new style of literature to be taken seriously.

Cain broke precedent with past literary works by producing a sensationally popular novel (later a play and twice a motion picture) in which both leading characters are repulsive. After the success of *The Postman Always Rings Twice*, he repeated the formula in *Double Indemnity* (1943). Displaying exceptional psychological insight in these and other works, such as *Serenade* (1937) and *Mildred Pearce* (1941), Cain was able to uncover and articulate the beginnings of the thought processes leading to the entangled schemes that ultimately result in the commission of murder.

Whereas Hammett and Chandler wrote about good/bad, soft/tough detectives who tried to unravel the messes that someone else caused by a violent or greedy act, Cain created two-dimensional characters interested only in themselves and who were motivated by their lust for money or sex or by some form of snobbery. They are flawed as characters because they are too thoroughly evil and Cain shows them no mercy. He is, as David Madden wrote in his biography, "the twenty-minute egg of the hard-boiled school."

Although Cain wrote eighteen novels, he was essentially a short story writer, especially if one remembers that most of his novels were really novellas, extremely compact, coming in about half the length of conventional novels. *Postman* was only 35,000 words, *Double Indemnity* only 29,000, and his best-selling *The Butterfly* (1947) was so slim that Cain added a twelve-page introduction to try to give it a bit more heft. He edited an anthology, *For Men Only* (1944), in the introduction to which he extolled the virtues of the short story: "It is greatly superior to the novel, or at any rate, the American novel. It is one kind of fiction that need not, to please the American taste, deal with heroes. Our national curse, if so perfect a land can have such a thing, is the 'sympathetic' character . . . The world's greatest literature is peopled by thorough-going heels."

Cain's literary style is a paragon of spare prose. In the wardrobe of literature, he is a thong. Along with George V. Higgins and Ernest Hemingway, Cain was identified by Elmore Leonard as one of his greatest literary influences. When you read these wonderfully taut stories, you will see that he followed Leonard's advice long before it was given—Cain left out the parts that people tend to skip.

THE
COMPLETE
CRIME
STORIES

THE BABY IN THE ICEBOX

Of course there was plenty pieces in the paper about what happened out at the place last summer, but they got it all mixed up, so I will now put down how it really was, and 'specially the beginning of it, so you will see it is not no lies in it.

Because when a guy and his wife begin to play leapfrog with a tiger, like you might say, and the papers put in about that part and not none of the stuff that started it off, and then one day say X marks the spot and next day say it wasn't really no murder but don't tell you what it was, why, I don't blame people if they figure there was something funny about it or maybe that somebody ought to be locked up in the booby hatch. But there wasn't no booby hatch to this, nothing but plain onriness and a dirty rat getting it in the neck where he had it coming to him, as you will see when I get the first part explained right.

Things first begun to go sour between Duke and Lura when they put the cats in. They didn't need no cats. They had a combination auto camp, filling station, and lunchroom out in the country a ways, and they got along all right. Duke run the filling station, and got me in to help him, and Lura took care of the lunchroom and shacks. But Duke wasn't satisfied. Before he got this place he had raised rabbits, and one time he had bees, and another time canary birds, and nothing would suit him now but to put in some cats to draw trade. Maybe you think that's funny, but out here in California they got every kind of a farm there is, from kangaroos to alligators, and it was just about the idea that a guy like Duke would think up. So he begun building a cage, and one day he showed up with a truckload of wildcats.

I wasn't there when they unloaded them. It was two or three cars waiting and I had to gas them up. But soon as I got a chance I went back there to look things over. And believe me, they wasn't pretty. The guy that sold Duke the cats had went away about five minutes before, and Duke was standing outside the cage and he had a stick of wood in his hand with blood on it. Inside was a dead cat. The rest of them was on a shelf, that had been built for them to jump on, and every one of them was snarling at Duke.

I don't know if you ever saw a wildcat, but they are about twice as big as a house cat, brindle gray, with tufted ears and a bobbed tail. When they set and look at you they look like a owl, but they wasn't setting and looking now. They was marching around, coughing and spitting, their eyes shooting red and green fire, and it was a ugly sight, 'specially with that bloody dead one down on the ground. Duke was pale, and the breath was whistling through his nose, and it didn't take no doctor to see he was scared to death.

"You better bury that cat," he says to me. "I'll take care of the cars."

I looked through the wire and he grabbed me. "Look out!" he says. "They'd kill you in a minute."

"In that case," I says, "how do I get the cat out?"

"You'll have to get a stick," he says, and shoves off.

I was pretty sore, but I begun looking around for a stick. I found one, but when I got back to the cage Lura was there. "How did that happen?" she says.

"I don't know," I says, "but I can tell you this much: If there's any more of them to be buried around here, you can get somebody else to do it. My job is to fix flats, and I'm not going to be no cat undertaker."

She didn't have nothing to say to that. She just stood there while I was trying the stick, and I could hear her toe snapping up and down in the sand, and from that I knowed she was choking it back, what she really thought, and didn't think no more of this here cat idea than I did.

The stick was too short. "My," she says, pretty disagreeable, "that looks terrible. You can't bring people out here with a thing like that in there."

"All right," I snapped back. "Find me a stick."

She didn't make no move to find no stick. She put her hand on the gate. "Hold on," I says. "Them things are nothing to monkey with."

"Huh," she says. "All they look like to me is a bunch of cats."

There was a kennel back of the cage, with a drop door on it, where they was supposed to go at night. How you got them back there was bait them with food, but I didn't know that then. I yelled at them, to drive them back in there, but nothing happened. All they done was yell back. Lura listened to me awhile, and then she give a kind of gasp like she couldn't stand it no longer, opened the gate, and went in.

Now believe me, that next was a bad five minutes, because she wasn't hard to look at, and I hated to think of her getting mauled up by them babies. But a guy would of had to of been blind if it didn't show him that she had a way with cats. First thing she done, when she got in, she stood still, didn't make no sudden motions or nothing, and begun to talk to them. Not no special talk. Just "Pretty pussy, what's the matter, what they been doing to you?"— like that. Then she went over to them.

They slid off, on their bellies, to another part of the shelf. But she kept after them, and got her hand on one, and stroked him on the back. Then she got ahold of another one, and pretty soon she had give them all a pat. Then she turned around, picked up the dead cat by one leg, and come out with him. I put him on the wheelbarrow and buried him.

Now, why was it that Lura kept it from Duke how easy she had got the cat out and even about being in the cage at all? I think it was just because she didn't have the heart to show him up to hisself how silly he looked. Anyway, at supper that night, she never said a word. Duke, he was nervous and excited and told all about how the cats had jumped at him and how he had to bean one to save his life, and then he give a long spiel about cats and how fear is the only thing they understand, so you would of thought he was Martin Johnson just back from the jungle or something.

But it seemed to me the dishes was making quite a noise that night, clattering around on the table, and that was funny, because one thing you could say for Lura was: she was quiet and easy to be around. So when Duke, just like it was nothing at all, asks me by the way how did I get the cat out, I heared my mouth saying, "With a stick," and not nothing more. A little bird flies around and tells you, at a time like that. Lura let it pass. Never said a word. And if you ask me, Duke never did find out how easy she could handle the cats, and that ain't only guesswork, but on account of something that happened a little while afterward, when we got the mountain lion.

A mountain lion is a cougar, only out here they call them a mountain lion. Well, one afternoon about five o'clock this one of ours squat down on her hunkers and set up the worst squalling you ever listen to. She kept it up all night, so you wanted to go out and shoot her, and next morning at breakfast Duke come running in and says come on out and look what happened. So we went out there, and there in the cage with her was the prettiest he mountain lion you ever seen in your life. He was big, probably weighed a hundred and fifty pounds, and his coat was a pearl gray so glossy it looked like a pair of new gloves, and he had a spot of white on his throat. Sometimes they have white.

"He come down from the hills when he heard her call last night," says Duke, "and he got in there somehow. Ain't it funny? When they hear that note nothing can stop them."

"Yeah," I says. "It's love."

"That's it," says Duke. "Well, we'll be having some little ones soon. Cheaper'n buying them."

After he had went off to town to buy the stuff for the day, Lura sat down to the table with me. "Nice of you," I says, "to let Romeo in last night."

"Romeo?" she says.

"Yes, Romeo. That's going to be papa of twins soon, out in the lion cage."

"Oh," she says, "didn't he get in there himself?"

"He did not. If she couldn't get out, how could he get in?"

All she give me at that time was a dead pan. Didn't know nothing about it at all. Fact of the matter, she made me a little sore. But after she brung me my second cup of coffee she kind of smiled. "Well?" she says. "You wouldn't keep two loving hearts apart, would you?"

So things was, like you might say, a little gritty, but they got a whole lot worse when Duke come home with Rajah, the tiger. Because by that time he had told so many lies that he begun to believe them hisself, and put on all the airs of a big animal trainer. When people come out on Sundays, he would take a black snake whip and go in with the mountain lions and wildcats, and snap it at them, and they would snarl and yowl, and Duke acted like he was doing something. Before he went in, he would let the people see him strapping on a big six-shooter, and Lura got sorer by the week.

For one thing, he looked so silly. She couldn't see nothing to going in with the cats, and 'specially she couldn't see no sense in going in with a whip, a six-shooter, and a ten-gallon hat like them cow people wears. And for another thing, it was bad for business. In the beginning, when Lura would take the customers' kids out and make out the cat had their finger, they loved it, and they loved it still more when the little mountain lions come and they had spots and would push up their ears to be scratched. But when Duke started that stuff with the whip it scared them to death, and even the fathers and mothers was nervous, because there was the gun and they didn't know what would happen next. So business begun to fall off.

And then one afternoon he put down a couple of drinks and figured it was time for him to go in there with Rajah. Now it had took Lura one minute to tame Rajah. She was in there sweeping out his cage one morning when Duke was away, and when he started sliding around on his belly he got a bucket of water in the face, and that was that. From then on he was her cat. But what happened when Duke tried to tame him was awful. The first I knew what he was up to was when he made a speech to the people from the mountain lion cage telling them not to go away yet, there was more to come. And when he come out he headed over to the tiger.

"What's the big idea?" I says. "What you up to now?"

"I'm going in with that tiger," he says. "It's got to be done, and I might as well do it now."

"Why has it got to be done?" I says.

He looked at me like as though he pitied me.

"I guess there's a few things about cats you don't know yet," he says. "You got a tiger on your hands, you got to let him know who's boss, that's all."

"Yeah?" I says. "And who is boss?"

"You see that?" he says, and cocks his finger at his face.

"See what?" I says.

"The human eye," he says. "The human eye, that's all. A cat's afraid of it. And if you know your business, you'll keep him afraid of it. That's all I'll use, the human eye. But, of course, just for protection, I've got these too."

"Listen, sweetheart," I says to him. "If you give me a choice between the human eye and a Bengal tiger, which one I got the most fear of, you're going to see a guy getting a shiner every time. If I was you, I'd lay off that cat."

He didn't say nothing: hitched up his holster, and went in. He didn't even get a chance to unlimber his whip. That tiger, soon as he saw him, begun to move around in a way that made your blood run cold. He didn't make for Duke first, you understand. He slid over, and in a second he was between Duke and the gate. That's one thing about a tiger you better not forget if you ever meet one. He can't work examples in arithmetic, but when it comes to the kinds of brains that mean meat, he's the brightest boy in the class and then some. He's born knowing more about cutting off a retreat than you'll ever know, and his legs do it for him, just automatic, so his jaws will be free for the main business of the meeting.

Duke backed away, and his face was awful to see. He was straining every muscle to keep his mouth from sliding down in his collar. His left hand fingered the whip a little, and his right pawed around, like he had some idea of drawing the gun. But the tiger didn't give him time to make up his mind what his idea was, if any.

He would slide a few feet on his belly, then get up and trot a step or two, then slide on his belly again. He didn't make no noise, you understand. He wasn't telling Duke, "Please go away"; he meant to kill him, and a killer don't generally make no more fuss than he has to. So for a few seconds you could even hear

Duke's feet sliding over the floor. But all of a sudden a kid begun to whimper, and I come to my senses. I run around to the back of the cage, because that was where the tiger was crowding him, and I yelled at him.

"Duke!" I says. "In his kennel! Quick!"

He didn't seem to hear me. He was still backing, and the tiger was still coming. A woman screamed. The tiger's head went down, he crouched on the ground, and tightened every muscle. I knew what that meant. Everybody knew what it meant, and 'specially Duke knew what it meant. He made a funny sound in his throat, turned, and ran.

That was when the tiger sprung. Duke had no idea where he was going, but when he turned he fell through the trapdoor and I snapped it down. The tiger hit it so hard I thought it would split. One of Duke's legs was out, and the tiger was on it in a flash, but all he got on that grab was the sole of Duke's shoe. Duke got his leg in somehow and I jammed the door down tight.

It was a sweet time at supper that night. Lura didn't see this here, because she was busy in the lunchroom when it happened, but them people had talked on their way out, and she knowed all about it. What she said was plenty. And Duke, what do you think he done? He passed it off like it wasn't nothing at all. "Just one of them things you got to expect," he says. And then he let on he knowed what he was doing all the time, and the only lucky part of it was that he didn't have to shoot a valuable animal like Rajah was. "Keep cool, that's the main thing," he says. "A thing like that can happen now and then, but never let a animal see you excited."

I heard him, and I couldn't believe my ears, but when I looked at Lura I jumped. I think I told you she wasn't hard to look at. She was a kind of medium size, with a shape that would make a guy leave his happy home, sunburned all over, and high cheekbones that give her eyes a funny slant. But her eyes was narrowed down to slits, looking at Duke, and they shot green where the light hit them, and it come over me all of a sudden that she looked so much like Rajah, when he was closing in on Duke in the afternoon, that she could of been his twin sister.

Next off, Duke got it in his head he was such a big cat man now that he had to go up in the hills and do some trapping. Bring in his own stuff, he called it.

I didn't pay much attention to it at the time. Of course, he never brought in no stuff, except a couple of raccoons that he probably bought down the road for two dollars, but Duke was the kind of a guy that every once in a while has to sit on a rock and fish, so when he loaded up the flivver and blew, it wasn't nothing you would get excited about. Maybe I didn't really care what he was up to, because it was pretty nice, running the place with Lura with him out of the way, and I didn't ask no questions. But it was more to it than cats or 'coons or fish, and Lura knowed it, even if I didn't.

Anyhow, it was while he was away on one of them trips of his that Wild Bill Smith, the Texas Tornado, showed up. Bill was a snake doctor. He had a truck, with his picture painted on it, and two or three boxes of old rattlesnakes with their teeth pulled out, and he sold snake oil that would cure what ailed you, and a Indian herb medicine that would do the same. He was a fake, but he was big and brown and had white teeth, and I guess he really wasn't no bad guy. The first I seen of him was when he drove up in his truck, and told me to gas him up and look at his tires. He had a bum differential that made a funny rattle, but he said never mind and went over to the lunchroom.

He was there a long time, and I thought I better let him know his car was ready. When I went over there, he was setting on a stool with a sheepish look on his face, rubbing his hand. He had a snake ring on one finger, with two red eyes, and on the back of his hand was red streaks. I knew what that meant. He had started something and Lura had fixed him. She had a pretty arm, but a grip like iron, that she said come from milking cows when she was a kid. What she done when a guy got fresh was take hold of his hand and squeeze it so the bones cracked, and he generally changed his mind.

She handed him his check without a word, and I told him what he owed on the car, and he paid up and left.

"So you settled his hash, hey?" I says to her.

"If there's one thing gets on my nerves," she says, "it's a man that starts something the minute he gets in the door."

"Why didn't you yell for me?"

"Oh, I didn't need no help."

But the next day he was back, and after I filled up his car I went over to see how he was behaving. He was setting at one of the tables this time, and Lura was standing beside him. I saw her jerk her hand away quick, and he give me the bright grin a man has when he's got something he wants to cover up. He was all teeth. "Nice day," he says. "Great weather you have in this country,"

"So I hear," I says. "Your car's ready."

"What I owe you?" he says.

"Dollar twenty."

He counted it out and left.

"Listen," says Lura, "we weren't doing anything when you come in. He was just reading my hand. He's a snake doctor, and knows about the zodiac."

"Oh, wasn't we?" I says. "Well, wasn't we nice!"

"What's it to you?" she says.

"Nothing," I snapped at her. I was pretty sore.

"He says I was born under the sign of Yin," she says. You would of thought it was a piece of news fit to put in the paper.

"And who is Yin?" I says.

"It's Chinese for tiger," she says.

"Then bite yourself off a piece of raw meat," I says, and slammed out of there. We didn't have no nice time running the joint *that* day.

Next morning he was back. I kept away from the lunchroom, but I took a stroll and seen them back there with the tigers. We had hauled a tree in there by that time for Rajah to sharpen his claws on, and she was setting on that. The tiger had his head in her lap, and Wild Bill was looking through the wire. He couldn't even draw his breath. I didn't go near enough to hear what they was saying. I went back to the car and begin blowing the horn.

He was back quite a few times after that, in between while Duke was away. Then one night I heard a truck drive up. I knowed that truck by its rattle. And it was daylight before I heard it go away.

Couple weeks after that, Duke come running over to me at the filling station. "Shake hands with me," he says, "I'm going to be a father."

"Gee," I says, "that's great!"

But I took good care he wasn't around when I mentioned it to Lura.

"Congratulations," I says. "Letting Romeos into the place seems to be about the best thing you do."

"What do you mean?" she says.

"Nothing," I says. "Only I heard him drive up that night. Look like to me the moon was under the sign of Cupid. Well, it's nice if you can get away with it."

"Oh," she says.

"Yeah," I says. "A fine double cross you thought up. I didn't know they tried that any more."

She set and looked at me, and then her mouth begin to twitch and her eyes filled with tears. She tried to snuffle them up but it didn't work. "It's not any double cross," she says. "That night I never went out there. And I never let anybody in. I was supposed to go away with him that night, but—"

She broke off and begin to cry. I took her in my arms. "But then you found this out?" I says. "Is that it?" She nodded her head. It's awful to have a pretty woman in your arms that's crying over somebody else.

From then on, it was terrible. Lura would go along two or three days pretty well, trying to like Duke again on account of the baby coming, but then would come a day when she looked like some kind of a hex, with her eyes all sunk in so you could hardly see them at all, and not a word out of her.

Them bad days, anyhow when Duke wasn't around, she would spend with the tiger. She would set and watch him sleep, or maybe play with him, and he seemed to like it as much as she did. He was young when we got him, and mangy and thin, so you could see his slats. But now he was about six years old, and had been fed good, so he had got his growth, and his coat was nice, and I think he was the biggest tiger I ever seen. A tiger, when he is really big, is a lot bigger than a lion, and sometimes when Rajah would be rubbing around Lura, he looked more like a mule than a cat.

His shoulders come up above her waist, and his head was so big it would cover both legs when he put it in her lap. When his tail would go sliding past her it looked like some kind of a constrictor snake. His teeth were something to make you lie awake nights. A tiger has the biggest teeth of any cat, and Rajah's must have been four inches long, curved like a cavalry sword, and ivory white. They were the most murderous-looking fangs I ever set eyes on.

When Lura went to the hospital it was a hurry call, and she didn't even have time to get her clothes together. Next day Duke had to pack her bag, and he was strutting around, because it was a boy, and Lura had named him Ron. But when he come out with the bag he didn't have much of a strut. "Look what I found," he says to me, and fishes something out of his pocket. It was the snake ring.

"Well?" I says. "They sell them in any ten-cent store."

"H'm," he says, and kind of weighed the ring in his hand. That afternoon, when he come back, he says: "Ten-cent store, hey? I took it to a jeweler today, and he offered me two hundred dollars for it."

"You ought to sold it," I says. "Maybe save you bad luck."

Duke went away again right after Lura come back, and for a little while things was all right. She was crazy about the little boy, and I thought he was pretty cute myself, and we got along fine. But then Duke come back and at lunch one day he made a crack about the ring. Lura didn't say nothing, but he kept at it, and pretty soon she wheeled on him.

"All right," she says. "There was another man around here, and I loved him. He give me that ring, and it meant that he and I belonged to each other. But I didn't go with him, and you know why I didn't. For Ron's sake, I've tried to love you again, and maybe I can yet, God knows. A woman can do some funny things if she tries. But that's where we're at now. That's right where we're at. And if you don't like it, you better say what you're going to do."

"When was this?" says Duke.

"It was quite a while ago. I told you I give him up, and I give him up for keeps."

"It was just before you knowed about Ron, wasn't it?" he says.

"Hey," I cut in. "That's no way to talk."

"Just what I thought," he says, not paying no attention to me. "Ron. That's a funny name for a kid. I thought it was funny, right off when I heard it. Ron. Ron. That's a laugh, ain't it?"

"That's a lie," she says. "That's a lie, every bit of it. And it's not the only lie you've been getting away with around here. Or think you have. Trapping up in the hills, hey? And what do you trap?"

But she looked at me and choked it back. I begun to see that the cats wasn't the only things had been gumming it up.

"All right," she wound up. "Say what you're going to do. Go on. Say it!"

But he didn't.

"Ron," he cackles, "that's a hot one," and walks out.

Next day was Saturday, and he acted funny all day. He wouldn't speak to me or Lura, and once or twice I heard him mumbling to himself. Right after supper he says to me, "How are we on oil?"

"All right," I says. "The truck was around yesterday."

"You better drive in and get some," he says. "I don't think we got enough."

"Enough?" I says. "We got enough for two weeks."

"Tomorrow is Sunday," he says, "and there'll be a big call for it. Bring out a hundred gallon and tell them to put it on the account."

By that time I would give in to one of his nutty ideas rather than have an argument with him, and besides, I never tumbled that he was up to anything. So I wasn't there for what happened next, but I got it out of Lura later, so here is how it was:

Lura didn't pay much attention to the argument about the oil, but washed up the supper dishes, and then went in the bedroom to make sure everything was all right with the baby. When she come out she left the door open, so she could hear if he cried. The bedroom was off the sitting room, because these here California houses don't have but one floor, and all the rooms connect. Then she lit the fire, because it was cool, and sat there watching it burn. Duke come in, walked around, and then went out back. "Close the door," she says to him. "I'll be right back," he says.

So she sat looking at the fire, she didn't know how long, maybe five minutes, maybe ten minutes. But pretty soon she felt the house shake. She thought maybe it was a earthquake, and looked at the pictures, but they was all hanging straight. Then she felt the house shake again. She listened, but it wasn't no truck outside that would cause it, and it wouldn't be no state-road blasting or nothing like that at that time of night. Then she felt it shake again, and this time it shook in a regular movement, one, two, three, four, like that. And then all of a sudden she knew what it was, why Duke had acted so funny all day, why he had sent me off for the oil, why he had left the door open, and all the rest of it. There was five hundred pound of cat walking through the house, and Duke had turned him loose to kill her.

She turned around, and Rajah was looking at her, not five foot away. She didn't do nothing for a minute, just set there thinking what a boob Duke was to figure on the tiger doing his dirty work for him, when all the time she could handle him easy as a kitten, only Duke didn't know it. Then she spoke. She expected Rajah to come and put his head in her lap, but he didn't. He stood there and growled, and his ears flattened back. That scared her, and she thought of the baby. I told you a tiger has that kind of brains. It no sooner went through her head about the baby than Rajah knowed she wanted to get to that door, and he was over there before she could get out of the chair.

He was snarling in a regular roar now, but he hadn't got a whiff of the baby yet, and he was still facing Lura. She could see he meant business. She reached in the fireplace, grabbed a stick that was burning bright, and walked him down with it. A tiger is afraid of fire, and she shoved it right in his eyes. He backed past the door, and she slid in the bedroom. But he was right after her, and she had to hold the stick at him with one hand and grab her baby with the other.

But she couldn't get out. He had her cornered, and he was kicking up such a awful fuss she knowed the stick wouldn't stop him long. So she dropped it, grabbed up the baby's covers, and threw them at his head. They went wild, but they saved her just the same. A tiger, if you throw something at him with a human smell, will generally jump on it and bite at it before he does anything else, and that's what he done now. He jumped so hard the rug went out from under him, and while he was scrambling to his feet she shot past him with the baby and pulled the door shut after her.

She run in my room, got a blanket, wrapped the baby in it, and run out to the electric icebox. It was the only thing around the place that was steel. Soon as she opened the door she knowed why she couldn't do nothing with Rajah. His meat was in there; Duke hadn't fed him. She pulled the meat out, shoved the baby in, cut off the current, and closed the door. Then she picked up the meat and went around the outside of the house to the window of the bedroom. She could see Rajah in there, biting at the top of the door, where a crack of light showed through. He reached to the ceiling. She took a grip on the meat and drove at the screen with it. It give way, and the meat went through. He was on it before it hit the floor.

Next thing was to give him time to eat. She figured she could handle him once he got something in his belly. She went back to the sitting room. And in there, kind of peering around, was Duke. He had his gun strapped on, and one look at his face was all she needed to know she hadn't made no mistake about why the tiger was loose.

"Oh," he says, kind of foolish, and then walked back and closed the door. "I meant to come back sooner, but I couldn't help looking at the night. You got no idea how beautiful it is. Stars is bright as anything."

"Yeah," she says. "I noticed."

"Beautiful," he says. "Beautiful."

"Was you expecting burglars or something?" she says, looking at the gun.

"Oh, that," he says. "No. Cat's been kicking up a fuss. I put it on, case I have to go back there. Always like to have it handy."

"The tiger," she says. "I thought I heard him, myself."

"Loud," says Duke. "Awful loud."

He waited. She waited. She wasn't going to give him the satisfaction of opening up first. But just then there come a growl from the bedroom, and the sound of bones cracking. A tiger acts awful sore when he eats. "What's that?" says Duke.

"I wonder," says Lura. She was hell-bent on making him spill it first.

They both looked at each other, and then there was more growls, and more sound of cracking bones. "You better go in there," says Duke, soft and easy, with the sweat standing out on his forehead and his eyes shining bright as marbles. "Something might be happening to Ron."

"Do you know what I think it is?" says Lura.

"What's that?" says Duke. His breath was whistling through his nose like it always done when he got excited.

"I think it's that tiger you sent in here to kill me," says Lura. "So you could bring in that woman you been running around with for over a year. That redhead that raises rabbit fryers on the Ventura road. That cat you been trapping!"

"And 'stead of getting you he got Ron," says Duke. "Little Ron! Oh my, ain't that tough? Go in there, why don't you? Ain't you got no mother love? Why don't you call up his pappy, get him in there? What's the matter? Is he afraid of a cat?"

Lura laughed at him. "All right," she says. "Now you go." With that she took hold of him. He tried to draw the gun, but she crumpled up his hand like a piece of wet paper and the gun fell on the floor. She bent him back on the table and beat his face in for him. Then she picked him up, dragged him to the front door, and threw him out. He run off a little ways. She come back and saw the gun. She picked it up, went to the door again, and threw it after him. "And take that peashooter with you," she says.

That was where she made her big mistake. When she turned to go back to the house, he shot, and that was the last she knew for a while.

Now, for what happened next, it wasn't nobody there, only Duke and the tiger, but after them state cops got done fitting it all together, combing the ruins and all, it wasn't no trouble to tell how it was, anyway most of it, and here's how they figured it out:

Soon as Duke seen Lura fall, right there in front of the house, he knowed he was up against it. So the first thing he done was run to where she was and put the gun in her hand, to make it look like she had shot herself. That was where he made *his* mistake, because if he had kept the gun he might of had a chance. Then he went inside to telephone, and what he said was, soon as he got hold of the state police: "For God's sake come out here quick. My wife has went crazy and throwed the baby to the tiger and shot herself and I'm all alone in the house with him and—*oh, my God, here he comes!*"

Now that last was something he didn't figure on saying. So far as he knowed, the tiger was in the room, having a nice meal off his son, so everything was hotsy-totsy. But what he didn't know was that that piece of burning firewood that Lura had dropped had set the room on fire and on account of that the tiger had got out. How did he get out? We never did quite figure that out. But this is how I figure it, and one man's guess is good as another's:

The fire started near the window, we knew that much. That was where Lura dropped the stick, right next to the cradle, and that was where a guy coming down the road in a car first seen the flames. And what I think is that soon as the tiger got his eye

off the meat and seen the fire, he begun to scramble away from
it, just wild. And when a wild tiger hits a beaverboard wall, he
goes through, that's all. While Duke was telephoning, Rajah come
through the wall like a clown through a hoop, and the first thing
he seen was Duke, at the telephone, and Duke wasn't no friend,
not to Rajah he wasn't

Anyway, that's how things was when I got there with the oil.
The state cops was a little ahead of me, and I met the ambulance
with Lura in it, coming down the road seventy mile an hour, but
just figured there had been a crash up the road, and didn't know
nothing about it having Lura in it. And when I drove up, there
was plenty to look at all right. The house was in flames, and the
police was trying to get in, but couldn't get nowheres near it on
account of the heat, and about a hundred cars parked all around,
with people looking, and a gasoline pumper cruising up and down
the road, trying to find a water connection somewhere they could
screw their hose to.

But inside the house was the terrible part. You could hear
Duke screaming, and in between Duke was the tiger. And both
of them was screams of fear, but I think the tiger was worse. It is a
awful thing to hear a animal letting out a sound like that. It kept
up about five minutes after I got there, and then all of a sudden
you couldn't hear nothing but the tiger. And then in a minute that
stopped.

There wasn't nothing to do about the fire. In a half hour the
whole place was gone, and they was combing the ruins for Duke.
Well, they found him. And in his head was four holes, two on each
side, deep. We measured them fangs of the tiger. They just fit.

Soon as I could I run in to the hospital. They had got the bullet
out by that time, and Lura was laying in bed all bandaged around
the head, but there was a guard over her, on account of what Duke
said over the telephone. He was a state cop. I sat down with him,

and he didn't like it none. Neither did I. I knowed there was something funny about it, but what broke your heart was Lura, coming out of the ether. She would groan and mutter and try to say something so hard it would make your head ache. After a while I got up and went in the hall. But then I see the state cop shoot out of the room and line down the hall as fast as he could go. At last she had said it. The baby was in the electric icebox. They found him there, still asleep and just about ready for his milk. The fire had blacked up the outside, but inside it was as cool and nice as a new bathtub.

Well, that was about all. They cleared Lura, soon as she told her story, and the baby in the icebox proved it. Soon as she got out of the hospital she got a offer from the movies, but 'stead of taking it she come out to the place and her and I run it for a while, anyway the filling-station end, sleeping in the shacks and getting along nice. But one night I heard a rattle from a bum differential, and I never even bothered to show up for breakfast the next morning.

I often wish I had. Maybe she left me a note.

PAY-OFF GIRL

I met her a month ago at a little café called Mike's Joint, in Cottage City, Maryland, a town just over the District line from Washington, D. C. As to what she was doing in this lovely honkytonk, I'll get to it, all in due time. As to what I was doing there, I'm not at all sure that I know as it wasn't my kind of place. But even a code clerk gets restless, especially if he used to dream about being a diplomat and he wound up behind a glass partition, unscrambling cables. And on top of that was my father out in San Diego, who kept writing me sarcastic letters telling how an A-1 canned-goods salesman had turned into a Z-99 government punk, and wanting to know when I'd start working for him again, and making some money. And on top of that was Washington, with the suicide climate it has, which to a Californian is the same as death, only worse.

Or it may have been lack of character. But whatever it was, there I sat, at the end of the bar, having a bottle of beer, when from behind me came a voice: "Mike, a light in that 'phone booth would help. People could see to dial. And that candle in there smells bad."

"Yes, Miss, I'll get a bulb."

"I know, Mike, but when?"

"I'll get one."

She spoke low, but meant business. He tossed some cubes in a glass and made her iced coffee, and she took the next stool to drink it. As soon as I could see her I got a stifled feeling. She was blonde, a bit younger than I am, which is 25, medium size, with quite a shape, and good-looking enough, though maybe no raving beauty. But what cut my wind were the clothes and the way she wore them. She had on a peasant blouse, with big orange beads dipping into the neck, black shoes with high heels and fancy lattice-work straps, and a pleated orange skirt that flickered around her like flame. And to me, born right on the border, that outfit spelled Mexico, but hot Mexico, with chili, castanets, and hat dancing in it, which I love. I looked all the law allowed, and then had to do eyes front, as she began looking, at her beads, at her clothes, at her feet, to see what the trouble was.

Soon a guy came in and said the bookies had sent him here to get paid off on a horse. Mike said have a seat, the young lady would take care of him. She said: "At the table in the corner. I'll be there directly."

I sipped my beer and thought it over. If I say I liked that she was pay-off girl from some bookies, I'm not telling the truth, and if I say it made any difference, I'm telling a downright lie. I just didn't care, because my throat had talked to my mouth, which was so dry the beer rasped through it. I watched her while she finished her coffee, went to the table, and opened a leather case she'd been holding in her lap. She took out a tiny adding machine, some typewritten sheets of paper, and a box of little manila envelopes. She handed the guy a pen, had him sign one of the sheets, and gave him one of the envelopes. Then she picked up the pen and made a note on the sheet. He came to the bar and ordered a drink. Mike winked at me. He said: "They make a nice class of business, gamblers do. When they win they want a drink, and when they lose they need one."

More guys came, and also girls, until they formed a line, and when they were done at the table they crowded up to the bar. She gave some of them envelopes, but not all. Quite a few paid her, and she'd tap the adding machine. Then she had a lull. I paid form my beer, counted ten, swallowed three times, and went over to her table. When she looked up I took off my hat and said: "How do I bet on horses?"

" . . . You sure you want to?"

"I think so."

"You know it's against the law?"

"I've heard it is."

"I didn't say it was wrong. It's legal at the tracks, and what's all right one place can't be any holing outrage some place else, looks like. But you should know how it is."

"Okay, I know."

"Then sit down and I'll explain."

We talked jerky, with breaks between, and she seemed as rattled as I was. When I got camped down, though, it changed. She drew a long trembly breath and said: "It has to be done by telephone. These gentlemen, the ones making the book, cant have a mob around, so it's all done on your word, like in an auction room, where a nod is as good as a bond, and people don't rat on their bids. I take your name, address, and phone, and when you're looked up you'll get a call. They give you a number, and from then on you phone in and your name will be good for your bets."

"My name is Miles Kearny."

She wrote it on an envelope, with my phone and address, an apartment in southeast Washington. I took the pen from her hand, rubbed ink on my signet right, and pressed the ring on the envelope, so the little coronet, with the three tulips over it, showed nice and clear. She got some ink off my hand with her blotter, then studied the impression on the envelope. She said: "Are you a prince or something?"

"No, but it's been in the family. And it's one way to get my hand held. And pave the way for me to ask something."

"Which is?"

"Are you from the West?"

"No, I'm not. I'm from Ohio. Why?"

"And you've never lived in Mexico?"

"No, but I love Mexican clothes."

"Then that explains it."

"Explains what?"

"How you come to look that way and—and how I came to fall for you. I am from the West. Southern California."

She got badly rattled again and after a long break said: "Have you got it straight now? About losses? They have to be paid."

"I generally pay what I owe."

There was a long, queer break then, and she seemed to have something on her mind. At last she blurted out: "And do you really want in?"

"Listen, I'm over twenty-one."

"In's easy. Out's not."

"You mean it's habit-forming?"

"I mean, be careful who you give your name to, or your address, or phone."

"They give theirs, don't they?"

"They give you a number."

"Is that number yours, too?"

"I can be reached there."

"And who do I ask for?"

" . . . Ruth."

"That all the name you got?"

"In this business, yes."

"I want in."

Next day, by the cold gray light of Foggy Bottom, which is what they call the State Department, you'd think that I'd come to my senses and forget her. But I thought of her all day long, and that night I was back, on the same old stool, when she came in, made a call from the booth, came out, squawked about the light, and picked up her coffee to drink it. When she saw me she took it to the table. I went over, took off my hat, and said: "I rang in before I came. My apartment house. But they said no calls came in for me."

"It generally takes a while."

That seemed to be all, and I left. Next night it was the same, and for some nights after that. But one night she said, "Sit down," and then: "Until they straighten it out, why don't you bet with me? Unless, of course, you have to wait until post time. But if you're satisfied to pick them the night before, I could take care of it."

"You mean, you didn't give in my name?"

"I told you, it all takes time."

"Why didn't you give it in?"

"Okay, let's bet."

I didn't know one horse from another, but she had a racing paper there, and I picked a horse called Fresno, because he reminded me of home and at least I could remember his name. From the weights he looked like a long shot, so I played him to win, place, and show, $2 each way. He turned out an also-ran, and the next night I kicked in with $6 more and picked another horse, still trying for openings to get going with her. That went on for some nights, I hoping to break through, she hoping I'd drop out, and both of us getting nowhere. Then one night Fresno was entered again and I played him again, across the board. Next night I put down my $6, and she sat staring at me. She said: "But Fresno won."

"Oh. Well say. Good old Fresno."

"He paid sixty-four eighty for two."

I didn't much care, to tell the truth. I didn't want her money. But she seemed quite upset. She went on: "However, the top bookie price, on any horse that wins, is twenty to one. At that I owe you forty dollars win money, twenty-two dollars place, and fourteen dollars show, plus of course the six that you bet. That's eighty-two in all. Mr. Kearny, I'll pay you tomorrow. I came away before the last race was run, and I just now got the results when I called in. I'm sorry, but I don't have the money with me, and you'll have to wait."

"Ruth, I told you from the first, my weakness isn't horses. It's you. If six bucks a night is the ante, okay, that's how it is, and dirt cheap. But if you'll act as a girl ought to act, quit holding out on me, what your name is and how I get in touch, I'll quit giving an imitation of a third-rate gambler, and we'll both quit worrying whether you pay me or not. We'll start over, and—"

"What do you mean, act as a girl ought to act?"

"I mean go out with me."

"On this job how can i?"

"Somebody making you hold it?"

"They might be, at that."

"With a gun to your head, maybe?"

"They got 'em, don't worry."

"There's only one thing wrong with that. Some other girl and a gun, that might be her reason. But not you. You don't say yes to a gun, or to anybody giving you orders, or trying to. If you did, I wouldn't be here."

She sat looking down in her lap, and then, in a very low voice: "I don't say I was forced. I do say, when you're young you can be a fool. Then people can do things to you. And you might try to get back, for spite. Once you start that, you'll be in too deep to pull out."

"Oh, you could pill out, if you tried."

"How, for instance?"

"Marrying me is one way."

"Me, a pay-off girl for a gang of bookies, marry Miles Kearny, a guy with a crown on his ring and a father that owns a big business and a mother—who's your mother, by the way?"

"My mother's dead."

"I'm sorry."

We had dead air for a while, and she said: "Mr. Kearny, men like you don't marry girls like me, at least to live wit them and like it. Maybe a wife can have cross eyes or buck teeth; but she can't have a past."

"Ruth, I told you, my first night here, I'm from California, where we've got present and future. There isn't any past. Too many of their grand-mothers did what you do, they worked for gambling houses. They dealt so much faro and rolled so many dice and spun so many roulette wheels, in Sacramento and Virginia City and San Francisco, they don't talk about the past. You go tot admit they made a good state though, those old ladies and their children. They made the best there is, and that' where I'd be taking you, and that's why we'd be happy."

"It's out."

"Are you married, Ruth?"

"No, but it's out."

"Why is it?"

"I'll pay you tomorrow night."

Next night the place was full, because a lot of them had bet a favorite that came in and they were celebrating their luck. When she'd paid them off she motioned and I went over. She picked up eight tens and two ones and handed them to me, and to get away from the argument I took the bills and put them in my wallet. Then I tried to start where we'd left off the night before, but she held out her hand and said: "Mr. Kearny, it's been wonderful knowing you, especially knowing someone who always takes off his hat. I've wanted to tell you that. But don't come any more. I won't see you any more, or accept bets, or anything. Goodbye, and good luck."

"I'm not letting you go."

"Aren't you taking my hand?"

"We're getting married, tonight."

Tears squirted out of her eyes, and she said: "Where?"

"Elkton. They got day and night service, for license, preacher and witnesses. Maybe not the way we'd want it done, but it's one way. And it's a two-hour drive in my car."

"What about—?" She waved at the bag, equipment, and money.

I said: "I tell you, I'll look it all up to make sure, but I'm under the impression—just a hunch—that they got parcel post now, so we can lock, seal, and mail it. How's that?"

"You sure are a wheedling cowboy."

"Might be, I love you."

"Might be, that does it."

We fixed it up then, whispering fast, how I'd wait outside in the car while she stuck around to pay the last few winners, which she said would make it easier. So I sat there, knowing I could still drive off, and not even for a second wanting to. All I could think about was how sweet she was, how happy the old man would be, and how happy our life would be, all full of love and hope and California sunshine. Some people went in the café, and a whole slew came out. The juke box started, a tune called *Night and Day*, then played it again and again.

Then it came to me: I'd been there quite a while. I wondered if something was wrong, if maybe *she* had taken a powder. I got up, walked to the café, and peeped. She was still there, at the table. But a guy was standing beside her, with his hat on, and if it was the way he talked or the way he held himself, as to that I couldn't be sure, but I thought he looked kind of mean. I started in. Mike was blocking the door. He said: "Pal, come back later. Just now I'm kind of full."

"Full? Your crowd's leaving."

"Yeah, but the cops are watching me."

"Hey, what is this?"

He'd sort of mumbled, but I roared it, and as he's little and I'm big it took less than a second for him to bounce off me and for me to start past the bar. But the guy heard it, and as I headed for him he headed for me. We met a few feet from her table, and she was white as a sheet. He was tall, thin, and sporty-looking, in a light, double-breasted suit, and I didn't stop until I bumped him and he had to back up. Some girl screamed. I said: "What seems to be the trouble?"

He tuned to Mike and said, "Mike, who's your friend?"

"I don't know, Tony. Some jerk."

He said to her: "Ruth, who is he?"

"How would I know?"

"He's not a friend, by chance?"

"I never saw him before."

I bowed to her and waved at Mike. I said: "I'm greatly obliged to you two for your thoughtful if misplaced effort to conceal my identity. You may now relax, as I propose to stand revealed."

I turned to the guy and said: "I am a friend, as it happens, of Ruth's and in fact considerably more. I'm going to marry her. As for you, you're getting out."

"I am?"

"I'll show you."

I let drive with a nice one-two, and you think he went down on the floor? He just wasn't there. All that was left was perfume, a queer foreign smell, and it seemed to hang on my fist. When I found him in my sights again he was at the end of the bar, looking at me over a gun. He said: "Put 'em up."

I did.

"Mike, get me his money."

"Listen, Tony, I don't pick pockets—"

"Mike!"

"Yes, Tony."

Mike got my wallet, and did what he was told: "Take out that money, and every ten in it, hold it up to the light, here where I can see. . . . There they are, two pinholes in Hamilton's eyes, right where I put them before passing the jack to a crooked two-timing dame who was playing me double."

He made me follow his gun to where she was. He leaned down to where she was. He leaned down to her, said: "I'm going to kill him first, so you can see him fall, so get over there, right beside him."

She spit in his face.

Where he had me was right in front of the telephone booth, and all the time he was talking I was working the ring off. Now I could slip it up in the empty bulb socket. I pushed and the fuse blew. The place went dark. The juke box stopped with a moan, and I started with a yell. I went straight ahead, not with a one-two this time. I gave it all my weight, and when I hit him he topple over and I heard the breath go out of him. It was dark, but I knew it was him by the smell. First, I got a thumb on his mastoid and heard him scream from the pain. Then I caught his wrist and used my other thumb there. The gun dropped, it hit my foot, it was in my hand. "Mike," I yelled, "the candle! In the booth! I've got his gun! But for Pete's sake, give us some light!"

So after about three years Mike found his matches and lit up. While I was waiting I felt her arms come around me and heard her whisper in my ear: "You've set me free, do you still want me?"

"You bet I do!"

"Let's go to Elkton!"

So we did, and I'm writing this on the train, stringing it out so I can watch her as she watches mesquite, sage, buttes, and the rest of the West rolling by the window. But I can't string it out much longer. Except that we're goof happy, and the old man is throwing handsprings, that's all.

Period.

New Paragraph.

California, here we come.

TWO O'CLOCK BLONDE

My heart did a throbby flip-flop when the buzzer sounded at last. It was all very well to ask a girl to my hotel suite, but I was new to such stuff, and before this particular girl I could easily look like a hick. It wasn't as if she'd been just another girl, you understand. She was special, and I was serious about her.

The trouble was, for what I was up to, man-of-the-world wouldn't do it. From the girl's looks, accent, manners, and especially the way she was treated by the other guests, I knew she was class. So I guess 'gentleman' would be more like what I was shooting for. Up until now I'd always figured I was one, but then—up until now—I'd never really been called on to prove it.

I had one last look at my champagne and flowers, riffled the Venetian blind to kill the glare of the sun, her pale face, dark hair, trim figure, and maroon dress making the same lovely picture I had fallen for so hard. Everything was the same—except the expression in her eyes. It was almost as if she were surprised to see me.

I managed a grin. "Is something wrong?"

She took her time answering me. Finally she shook her head, looked away from me. "No," she said. "Nothing's wrong."

I tried to act natural, but my voice sounded like the bark from a dictating machine. "Come in, come in," I said. "Welcome to my little abode. At least it's comfortable—and private. We'll be able to talk, and . . . "

She looked at me again and broke out a hard little smile. "Tell me," she said, "does the plane still leave at two?"

That didn't make any more sense than the fact that she'd seemed surprised to see me. I'd told her quite a lot more, about the construction contract and how I had closed it, with the binder check in my pocket, and other stuff. But a nervous guy doesn't argue. "I thought I explained about that," I told her. "The plane was booked up solid, and I'm grounded here until tomorrow morning. The home office said to see the town. Have me a really good time. I— thought I'd do it with you."

"I am indeed flattered," she said.

She didn't sound flattered, but I asked her once more to come in, and when she made no move I tried a fresh start. "Don't you think it's time you told me your name?" I asked.

Her eyes studied me carefully. "Zita," she said.

"Just Zita? Nothing more?"

"My family name is Hungarian, somewhat difficult for American. Zita does very well."

"Mine's Hull," I said. "Jack Hull."

She didn't say anything. The burn was still in her eyes, and I couldn't understand it. After the several chats we'd had in the dining room and the lobby, while I waited for lawyers, contractors, and the rest during the week I'd been here, I couldn't figure it at all. There wasn't much I could do about it, but there's a limit to what you can take, and I was getting a burn myself.

I was still trying to think of something to say when the door of the elevator opened, and out stepped a cute blonde in a maid's uniform—short skirt and apron and cap, and all. I'd seen her once or twice around the hotel, but I'd paid no attention to her.

She smiled quick at me, but gasped when she saw who I was talking to. "Mademoiselle!" she said, in the same accent as Zita's. "*Mademoiselle!*" Then she bobbed up and down, bending her knees and straightening them, in what seemed to be meant for bows.

But if Zita minded her being there, she didn't show it at all. She said something to her in Hungarian, and then turned back to me. In English, she said, "This is Maria, Mr. Hull—the girl with whom you have the date."

"I have the—*what?*"

"Your date is with Maria," she said.

I stared at her, and then at Maria, and then at Zita again. If this was a joke, I didn't feel like laughing.

"I heard Maria's telephone conversation with you," Zita said. "I did not know it was you then, of course, but I heard her repeat your room number." She smiled again. "And I heard her say something about wine."

"Listen—" I began.

"Wine . . . " she said. "How romantic."

"I ordered the wine for you," I told her. "My date was wit you, not with—"

"Yes, the wine," she said. "Where was it to be served? On the plane perhaps? It leaves at two, you said, when you told me good-bye a little while ago. You made me feel quite sad. But at two o-clock, with a smile, comes Maria."

I knew by then what had happened, and how important it is to get names straight before you phone—and to make sure of the person you're talking to before you do any asking. It put quite a crimp in my pitch, and I guess I sounded weak when I go the blueprints out and tried to start all over again.

"Please," Zita said. "Don't apologize for the maid. She is very pretty, Mr. Hull. *Very* pretty."

I opened my mouth to say something, but she didn't wait

to hear it. She went off down the hall, switching her hips very
haughtily. She didn't stop for the elevator, but left by way of the
stairs.

I looked at the blonde maid. "Come in, Maria," I said. "We've
got a little talking to do."

I had some idea of a message, which Maria could deliver when
the situation cooled down a bit. But by the time I'd closed the
door and followed Maria into the living room, I'd closed the door
and followed Maria into the living room, I'd come to the conclu-
sion that a message was not such a good idea. So I got my wallet
out, took out a ten, and handed it to Maria. "I'm sorry," I told her,
"that we had to have this mix-up. I think you see the reason. Over
the telephone, to an American, one accent sounds pretty much
like another. I hope your feelings aren't hurt, and that this little
present will help."

Judging by her smile, it helped quite a lot. But as she started
toward the door, something started to nag at me. "What a minute," I said. "Sit down."

She sat down on the edge of my sofa, crossing her slim legs
while I cogitated, and trying to tug the short skirt down over her
knees. It was quite a display of nylon, and it didn't make it any
easier for me to think. She was an extremely well-built girl, this
Maria, and she had the legs to go with the short skirt. I looked the
other way, and tried to figure out this point that had popped into
my mind.

"There's an angle I don't get, Maria," I said. "What was she
doing here?"

"You mean Mademoiselle Zita?"

I turned around to face her. "What did she come here for?"

"Didn't she tell you?"

"Not a word. Listen, I can't be mistaken. She knew romance
was here—with wine ordered, who wouldn't? But she didn't know

I was here. Until she saw me, I was just Mr. X. Why would she buzz Mr. X?"

I closed my eyes, working on my little mystery, and when I opened them Maria was no longer a maid making a tip. She was a ferret, watching me in a way that told me she knew the answer all right, and hoped to make it pay. That suited me fine. I got out another ten.

"Okay," I said. "Give."

She eyed my wallet.

She eyed my ten-spot.

She picked it up.

"It baffles me," she said.

"Listen," I told her. "I'm paying you."

She walked to the door and opened it part way. She hesitated a moment, and then pushed the door shut again and walked back to where I was standing. She looked me straight in the eye, and now she was smiling. It wasn't an especially pretty smile.

"Well?" I said.

The door buzzer sounded.

"Heavens!" Maria whispered. "I mustn't be seen here I'd compromise you, Mr. Hull. I'll wait in the bathroom."

I may have wondered, as she ran in there, just what compromising you, Mr. Hull. I'll wait in the bedroom."

I may have wondered, as she ran in there, just what compromising was. But as I stepped into the foyer I was thinking about Zita. I was sure it was she, back to tell me some more.

I turned the knob, and then the door banged into my face. When the bells shook out of my ears, a guy was there. He stood in the middle of the living room floor, a big, think-shouldered character in Hollywood coat and slacks.

"Who the hell are you?" I asked him. "And what the hell do you want?"

"My wife's all I want, Mister. Where is she?"

"Wife?"

"Quit acting dumb! Where is she?"

I heard the sharp sound of high heels on the floor behind me. "But, Bill!" Maria said. "What is this?"

I looked around at Maria—and got one of the biggest jolts of my life.

She didn't have a stitch on, except those nylons and that little white cap on her head.

"You damned tramp!" Bill yelled, and made a lunge at her.

I took a seat by the window and watched them put on their act—he chasing her around, she backing away—and I woke up at last to what I'd got my foot into. When Maria had gone to the door and opened it part way, it had been a signal to this big bruiser. She couldn't have been wearing anything under her maid's uniform, or she couldn't have gotten so naked so fast. And now I was the sucker in a badger game, caught like a rat in a trap. This pair had me, and unless I wanted he house detective, and maybe even the police, all I could do was grin and kick in when the bite was made.

When the ruckus began to slacken off a bit, I said, "Okay, Bill, I get it. I don't have to be hit with a brick. What is it you're after? Let's hear your pitch." I hadn't seem any bulges on him as he circled around, and it seemed to me that a gun was the last thing he should have if his caper went slightly sour and he had to face some cops. I couldn't be sure, of course, but by then I didn't much give a damn.

But all he did was blink.

"What're you after?" I asked him again.

"Dough, Mister. Just dough."

"How much?"

"How much you got?"

I took out my wallet, squeezed it to show how thick it was, and began dealing out tens, dropping them on the cocktail table. When I'd let eight bills fall, I stopped. "That'll do it," I said.

"Hey," he said, "you got more."

"I think you'll settle for this."

"And what gives you that idea?"

"Well," I said, taking my time, "I figure you for tinhorn chiselers, a pair that'll sell out cheap. It's worth a hundred—this eighty and the twenty I already gave her, when I'm sure she'll tell you about—to get you out of here. I'll just charge it to lessons in life. But for more, I'd just as soon crack it open. You want this money or not?"

It wasn't all just talk. From Maria's eyes as she watched the bills, I knew that for some reason they worried her. She looked at them a second, and then said to me, "Will you please bring me my uniform, Mr. Hull? Like a nice fellow?"

I didn't know why I was being got rid of, but when I went into the bedroom and had a peep through the crack in the door, Maria was down on her knees at the table, holding my tens to the light, looking for the punctures that are sometimes put on marked money. Bill was grumbling at her, but she grumbled back, and I heard her say, "Mademoiselle Zita."

When I heard Zita's name, I saw red. I made up my mind I'd get to the bottom of this if I had to take the place apart piece by piece. The big problem was how. I sat down on the edge of the bed, and the more I thought about it the madder I got. I glared down at Maria's uniform lying there on the bed beside me, and called her a few choice names under my breath. And then, still glaring at the uniform, I suddenly knew I had it. That uniform was going to be good for something besides showing off Maria's legs.

I grabbed the uniform off the bed, went to the window and threw it out. Then I went back to the sitting room. Maria was still on her knees at the table.

"Lady," I said, "if you want a uniform, you tell Mademoiselle Zita to bring it up here. Call her, and make it quick. Somebody else won't do. I want to talk to *her*."

"Oh," I said. "That."

"Give it to me!" she said. "You took it. You—"

"Well, no, Maria, I didn't," I said. "Not that I wouldn't have taken it. Not that you misjudge my character. I'm just that greedy. And just that mean. I didn't remember it, that's all."

"Ah!" she said. "Ah!" She was standing with her feet spread apart and her hands on her hips. I'd never seen a nude woman so completely unconscious of her body as this one was.

Bill came over from the window and slapper her—to make her pipe down with the racket, I suppose—and suddenly I realized I'd pulled a damn good stunt. It was now a question of who was trapped. All three of us were, of course, except that I didn't care any more if the cops barged in or not. I didn't care, but *they* did.

"Get on that phone," I told Maria, "because you don't get out till Zita comes—unless you go with the cops."

"Call," Bill told her. "You got to."

He went to the phone in the foyer, put in the call, and gave Maria the receiver. She talked a long time in Hungarian, and then she hung up and came back into the living room. "She'll be here," she said. "She'll bring me something to wear. And now, Mr. Hull, give me that money you threw out with my—"

I clipped her on the jaw, and I didn't pull the punch. Bill caught her as she fell, which was his big mistake. I dived over her head and got both hands on his throat, and we all went down together.

I didn't hit him, or take time to pull the girl away, or anything of the kind. I just lay there, squeezing my fingers into his windpipe, while he clawed at my hands and threshed. I let him thresh for one minute, clocking it by my wristwatch, which was as long as I figured him to last.

When he'd quit threshing, and lay there as limp as Maria was, I let go and dragged him away from her. I reached in his pocked and got my eighty dollars, and then I massaged his throat to give him a chance to breathe.

His fact was almost black, but he began to fight for air, sounding like a windsucker horse.

I went over a Maria and aimed a kick at her bottom.

It gave me some satisfaction, sinking my toe in like a kick from the forty-yard stripe, and listening to her groan. I did it again, and when she sad up I said, "Once more, baby—what did Zita come here for? You ready to talk about it?"

She opened her mouth to answer me, but then she saw Bill lying there and she gave a yelp and scrambled on all fours to him to help him.

I had to slap her around a little more to get it through her head that I was the most important guy in this room. And I had to ask her a question.

"Come on," I said. "Let's have it. What was it she came about?"

"To—warn you." Maria said. "I knew she was becoming suspicious of Bill and me, and . . . "

She moistened her lips and turned to look at where Bill was still sleeping with his noisy gasps.

"The rest of it!" I said. "And hurry!"

She shrugged. "I phoned Bill right after I talked to you, so that he'd know where to come. I spoke softly—but even so, perhaps Mademoiselle Zita overheard enough to put two and two together."

"You said she came here to warn me," I told her. "Why didn't she go ahead and do it?"

She shrugged again. "You ask her."

She moved over and took Bill in her arms, and I didn't try to stop her. I watcher her stroking his face, and I was so surprised to see that a ferret like her could love that I was a second slow on the buzzer when it sounded abruptly.

I was a little groggy from all my exertion by then, but I staggered into the foyer, closed the living room door, and opened the one to the hall.

Sure enough, Zita was there again. She was holding a dress folded across her arms.

I jerked the dressed away from her. "Come in, Zita," I said. "Come in and join our fouled-up little party. We're having one hell of a time here, Zita—thanks to the warning you didn't give me."

I took a breath, and was all ready to start in on her again, when she took a step toward me and fired a slap that stung clear down to my heels. Her eyes sparkled with anger.

"What did you expect?" she said. "You dated my maid! *My maid!*"

I stepped out of range and thought over what she'd just said. It could explain a lot, the warning she had expected to give some poor boob in this suite, and the warning she didn't give when she saw that the boob was me.

The way she'd reacted when she knew it was I who had made the date with Maria was just feminine enough to be compatible with linking me pretty well.

All at once, bill started that wind-sucking sound in the living room again, a truly frightening sound. Zita grabbed the dress away from me, brushed past me, and went in there.

It wasn't more than a minute before Bill went staggering out, and after him Maria, zipping up the dress in back and crying.

Zita came out of the living room and walked up to me slowly. She apologized then for having slapped me, and I apologized for having spoken so roughly to her, and she nodded at me and I nodded at her.

Pretty soon we were both smiling, and there didn't seem to be much point in doing any more apologizing.

And so that was that. Starting from that moment, things moved along very smoothly, and Zita's Hungarian accent never gave me a minute's trouble.

It didn't, that is, until a few afternoons later when we were faced with the novel situation of the bridegroom having to ask the bride what he should fill in under: WOMAN'S FULL NAME— PLEASE PRINT.

THE BIRTHDAY PARTY

He bounced the tennis ball against the garage with persistence, but no enthusiasm. He would have gone swimming, but Red would be there, and he owed Red ten cents. Red drove the ice-cream truck evenings, and so swam in midafternoon; debtors, therefore, used the creek mornings, late afternoons, and, if there was a moon, nights. Between times they passed away the hours bouncing tennis balls against garages.

He bounced the ball with sudden zeal. There had come a call from the house: "Burwell!" It was repeated, twice, and then amended: "Burwell Hope!"

He slowed the tempo. "You call me, ma?"

"I don't see why you can't answer when I call."

"I was practicing strokes," he told her.

"Well, don't stand there yelling so the whole neighborhood can hear you; and, besides, I don't think that's any place for practicing strokes. It makes an awful noise and I don't wonder people are annoyed."

He slouched slowly into the house, practicing a trick that involved mashing the ball into the ground, hitting it with the edge of the racket as it sprang up, and catching it in the pants pocket as it bounced waist-high.

"Have you bathed?"

"It's too hot to bathe now. I'll be all perspired up again. I'll bathe after supper."

"You ought to bathe now."

"It's too hot."

"Did you black your shoes as I told you?"

"Not yet."

"Not yet, what?"

"Not yet, ma."

"Well, there's the pen and ink; sit down and write the card now so I can wrap it up. I've got a minute now and I don't want to have to think about it later."

"Wrap what up?"

"Burwell, how many times have I got to tell you you must stop this habit of asking useless questions? It's annoying, and you have to stop it. Marjorie's birthday present, of course. I can't wrap it up until I have the card, and you're giving it to her, so you have to write the card."

"I'm not giving it to her. I don't even know what it is."

"It's a very nice bottle of perfume. Want to see it?"

"Phooie!"

"Stop—using—that—word!"

"I don't want to see it."

"Very well. Then as soon as you write the card you can black your shoes."

"What for?"

"Will you stop asking those useless questions! For the party, of course. Didn't I tell you? Answer me. Didn't I tell you not two hours ago that Mrs. Lucas stopped by, told me they were giving a little surprise party for Marjorie tonight because it's her birthday, and that she especially wanted you to be there? Didn't I tell you that?"

"I'm not going."

"You're—"

"Sure, you told me, but I never said I would go."

"Why, Burwell Hope, the very idea. And after Mrs. Lucas said she especially wanted you to go. And after I made a trip down-town to buy a nice present. Why, I never heard of such a thing. All her friends are going. Spencer, and Jackie, and Junior LeCrand, and—"

"Bunch of sissies."

"Is every boy a sissy that has some kind of manners and does what his mother tells him to once in a while without always hav-ing to argue?"

"I'm not going."

"What will Marjorie think?"

"Marjorie Lucas. The belle of Home Room Twenty-nine."

"Why do you always have to be so mean to Marjorie? What has she ever done to you?"

"The face that only a mother could love."

"I haven't time to stand around and argue with you. You write the card right now—'Happy Birthday to Marjorie from Bur-well'—and then you go out and black your shoes. They're on the back porch, and there's a new can of blacking in the things that came up from the market."

He wrote the card, then went out on the back porch and looked at his shoes. Then he looked at the sun. Then he looked at the sun again, making certain calculations based on its position in the heavens and its relation to the general progress of the after-noon. Then he drifted into the backyard, took his swimming suit off the line, and slipped quickly through the hole in the hedge.

The creek was deserted, but damp spots on the boat landing

showed that Red, to say nothing of his more solvent customers, wasn't long gone. Burwell peeled off his clothes, had a moment of wild determination to go in naked, but compromised on trunks, without shirt. The water felt queer, and all his tricks seemed shriveled: He kept opening his mouth to yell, "Hey, look at this one," but there was nobody to look. He tried a back dive, but all he got out of it was a pair of smarting shins, where they slapped the water as he came over. He tried a feat of his own, for which he imagined he had acquired quite a local reputation: to go down under and stay down under, with only his feet sticking out; but something seemed to be wrong with it. As a rule, he could stay down under at least five minutes—or, at any rate, so he frequently asserted, in the absence of any watch to time him, and in the absence also of any knowledge that even one minute is a prodigious time for holding the breath; but now, for some unexplainable reason, he was no sooner down than he had to come up again, puffing grievously.

Treading water, about to try again, he felt a tingle in his back: somebody, he knew, was watching him. This time, as he lazily flipped himself under, all was as it should be. He stayed down at least ten minutes, crossing his feet as they stuck out in the air, wiggling his toes, sending up bubbles, and in other ways putting in subtle artistic touches. When he came up he tossed the hair out of his eyes nonchalantly and breathed through his nose—to conceal the puffing, and to show that, staggering though the performance might be, it had been done with ease.

Marjorie was on the boat landing. "Hello."

"Hello."

"My, but you scared me."

"Me scare you?"

"I thought something had happened to you. When I saw your toes wiggle I thought something had you. I thought I would die."

"Oh, that. That wasn't nothing."

He put his face in the water and blew through his mouth, at the same time uttering loud noises. He conceived this to be a peculiarly terrifying experience for the beholder.

However, she didn't seem to be paying much attention. "I wish I could go in."

"Well, come on."

"I didn't bring my suit."

He became a steamboat, churning up a great deal of foam, but stopped when she wandered into the canoe house. When she came out she had his swimming shirt.

"Are you going to be wearing this?"

"Only sissies wear shirts."

"I could pin it at the bottom. It's pretty big for me, and I could pin it so it would be all right."

"I don't mind."

She went back into the canoe house again, and he began doing all his tricks, one after the other. Presently she came out, a bit suggestive of diapers and safety pins here and there, but in the main clad neatly in a one-piece bathing suit, made of his shirt. He let go with a jackknife; then climbed out with an air of triumph mixed with boredom.

She climbed down the cleats and felt the water with one toe.

"What's the matter? You scared?"

"I'm not scared. But I always like to know if it's cold or not."

"You're scared."

"Well, I always am. A little."

"If you're scared, you've got to dive in."

"I'm going to."

"Well, why don't you?"

"I'm going to. In a minute."

He had a moment of vast, soul-warming contempt, but it congealed within him to a drop of bitter, cruel gall. She was climbing the piling. He watched her, stunned, saw her poise far above his head, then go off and cut the water so cleanly that only a high spurt of foam marked her entering it.

Nobody had told him that little girls dive better than little boys. Nobody had told him that little girls could possibly do anything better than little boys. All he knew was that he had never had the nerve to climb the piling and dive off, and here she had done it; and not only done it, but done it, apparently, without even knowing that it was hard.

He jumped up, as soon as her head came out of the water, and yelled at her: "So you think you're smart, hey? That's nothing. I can do it too. I've done it plenty of times. I can even do a back dive from up there."

"Can you really?"

She said it with honest admiration, and he climbed up. But when he got there a sick feeling swept down his throat and into his stomach. It was higher than he imagined. It was higher than he had ever imagined anything could be. The water was way, way down, far removed from anything that he could possibly dive into.

He tried to get set for a dive, but couldn't even stand up. All he could do was squat there, holding the tops of the piles with his hands, and gulp.

"If you're scared," she said, "you've got to dive in."

The ancient apothegm, quoted so blandly by himself not two minutes ago, was spoken innocently, yet it floated up from the water with a terrible mockery.

"Who's scared?"

"Well, my goodness, anybody can be scared."

"I'm not scared. I'm just taking it easy."

"It just comes from being dizzy."

"Why don't you kick your feet when you swim? That's no way to swim. Why don't you kick your feet like I do?"

"I can't swim very well, but I like to dive."

"Well, anybody can dive. Swimming's the important thing. If you can swim good you might save somebody from drowning, but what good is diving?"

"Maybe if you sat down on the big pile and then let go, it would be like jumping off."

"Who's asking you?"

She climbed up beside him. "What makes you dizzy is looking down. Why don't you look up at the sky and try it? like this."

She threw back her head, gripped the pile with her toes, stiffened, sprang. But he didn't see her swash into the water. The pilings shuddered so sickeningly from her leap that he had to clutch them tight with his fingers, looking cravenly into the cracks of the wood. When the swaying stopped he looked up at the sky and tried to stand. He couldn't. She climbed up there again. This time she turned her back to the water, leaned out. He knew it was a back dive, but he didn't see that one either. She stretched herself out on the boat landing to rest, and there was nothing he could do but climb down. He was panting when he reached her, not from exertion, but from rage.

"I know what you're doing here. I know why you're not home. It's your birthday, and they're giving you a surprise party, and they ran you out of the house so you wouldn't see them getting ready for it. Yah! Got run out of the house. Yah!"

"I knew it all the time, but I think it was mean of you to tell me."

"Whole lot of cake and stuff coming in and they didn't want you to see it. Bum old cake from the bakery."

"It's not bum old cake. It's a special birthday cake with my name on it in icing."

"How do you know?"

"I peeped and saw it. It's going to have candles on it and they're going to bring it out in front of everybody and then I'm going to cut it."

"Old stale cake they had left over from last week and then they put your name on it in icing."

"It is not."

"Phooie!" He spat in the water and sat there laughing, mumbling, and shaking his head, as though the ignoble tricks of the whole human race were quite beyond him.

She sat up and began to fluff out her hair. "Are you invited, Burwell?"

"Wouldn't you like to know?"

"I kind of said one or two things so they wouldn't forget to invite you."

"Wouldn't you like to know?"

"Are you coming?"

"Is that a laugh! Is that a laugh!"

"I don't see anything funny."

"Am I coming? Say, is that a laugh! Me come to a bum birthday party with a lot of sissies and an old stale cake the bakery couldn't give away but your old man came and bought it cheap and had your name put on it in icing. Well! Is that a laugh!"

"Aren't you really coming, Burwell?"

"Who, me?"

"I was going to give you the first piece of cake."

"That stale stuff."

"Tell me, Burwell. Why aren't you coming?"

"Phooie! I'm busy."

"How do you mean, busy?"

"Don't you wish you knew? Don't you wish you knew?"

She looked at him and he had a sensation of having to think fast. "Are you really busy, Burwell?"

"Sure, I'm busy."

"Doing what?"

"Why—I got to work."

The agreeable degree of her astonishment surprised even him. "Have you got a job, Burwell?"

"Sure I got a job."

"What kind of a job? Tell me."

"Helping Red."

Now this wasn't true. The only relation it had to truth was that he had been considering a plan whereby he would offer to help Red for a night or two, in return for the extinguishment of the ten-cent debt. But actually he had made no such offer, and whether he would ever make it was problematical for Red was a brisk young man, rather hard to talk to, despite his professional affability.

"Honest?"

"Busy guy these days. Me go to a party? Say, is that a laugh!"

"I haven't seen you with Red."

"I'm inside the truck."

"What doing?"

"Oh, lot of things."

"Tell me."

"Well, I pass out the stuff to him. Drive the old bus, so he don't all the time have to be jumping in and out, saves him a lot of time. Keep things going. Ring up the cash. Lot of things."

"Do you get paid for it?"

"You think I'm doing all that for nothing?"

"Well, I didn't know. I thought he might just give you ice cream. You know. A free cake if you wanted it."

"A fat chance."

"When did you start?"

"Oh, I don't just remember. I've been at it quite a while. Maybe a week."

"Just think! And I didn't know a thing about it."

He rather fancied his new job now. As a matter of fact, the truck had a wheel that had always taken his eye; it was a big, horizontal wheel, something like the wheel on the rear end of a hook-and-ladder, and there now leaped into his mind a picture of himself behind it.

"Say, you ought to see me in there, swinging her around corners, dodging traffic, shooting her up beside the curb, ringing the bell—I forgot that. I'm the one that rings the bell."

He acted it out, his feet hanging over the water, his hands caressing the wheel. He shifted gears, pedaled the brake, sounded the bell, pulled up short just in time to avoid a collision with a lady pushing a gocart containing an infant, went on with a noble, though worried, look on his face. A captious listener might have reflected that evening was a strange time for infants to be abroad in gocarts; might have taken exception, too, to a certain discrepancy between the critical situations in which this ice-cream truck seemed always to find itself, and the somewhat innocuous tinkle of the bell which accompanied its doings. However, his listener wasn't captious. She gazed at him with wide-open eyes, and a rapture so complete that all she could think of to say was an oft-repeated "My!"

They took turns dressing, and as they started home he glowed pleasantly under her admiration. Yet admiration, even now, was not quite enough. He craved definite superiority.

"Beat you to the edge of the woods."

"No you can't."

She started so suddenly he was taken by surprise, and as she raced ahead of him he had one twinge of fear that she not only could dive better than he could, but run faster. But the distance was in his favor. She tired, and as he clattered past her he had at last what he had craved all afternoon: the hot, passionate feeling that he was better than she was; that from now on she must be his creature, to worship him without question, to look on from a distance while he dazzled her with tricks. It was short-lived. He felt a jolting, terrible pain in his face, having tripped on the wet bathing suit and slammed down in the road, the dust grinding into his mouth, the little stones cutting his cheek. He set his jaws, closed his eyes, screwed up his face in an agony of effort not to cry.

"It's all right, Burwell. You're not hurt bad. You're just scratched up a little bit. Here, I'll wipe it off for you."

He felt the wet bathing suit wiping his face, then the soft dry dabs of her handkerchief. The effort not to cry was becoming more than he could stand. He clenched his fists.

"Open your mouth and close your eyes, I'll give you something to make you wise." A quick, warm little kiss alighted on his mouth, stayed a moment, pressed hard, and then left.

A wave of happiness swept over him. The strain eased, he hadn't cried. He opened his eyes. She was gone.

They were at supper when he got home, and his mother jumped up when she saw him. "Mercy, Burwell, what on earth has happened to you?"

"I fell down."

"Mercy! Mercy!"

"I'm all right."

"Are you sure? My, I'll have to put something on your face before you come to the table."

"I don't want any supper."

She felt his brow.

"I'm going to bed."

"I don't think he has any fever."

"I'm all right, but I'm going to bed."

However, at this point Liza, the cook, appeared with a platterful of sliced watermelon, then hastily backed out: "Ah thought you-all was th'oo."

His eye caught the wet redness, and he couldn't shake it out of his mind. "Well, maybe I could eat a little bit."

"Then sit right down, and I'll put something on your face later."

He sat down, and permitted himself to be coaxed into eating three pieces of fried chicken, two new potatoes, four ears of corn on the cob, a dish of pickled beets, and two big slices of watermelon.

While he was putting this away, his mother kept up a sort of running soliloquy: "I wonder if I ought to let him go to that party tonight. It seems a pity to have him miss it, and yet—we'll see."

It annoyed him that his mother seemed to have forgotten he didn't want to go to the party, and discussed it as though it were something he had been looking forward to for his whole life. However, there was nothing to do but fall in with that view of it, and dodge the main issue, if possible.

"It's all right. I don't mind. I'm going to bed."

"Did you shine your shoes?"

"No'm, I was going to, but—I fell down."

"Well, I'll shine them. You keep quiet after supper, and then we'll see."

"It's all right. I don't want to go."

"Why, Burwell! You know you want to go."

"I do not! I'm going to bed!"

He had overplayed it, and he knew it. At his insistent shout his father, who had been eyeing him narrowly for some time, suddenly spoke: "Burwell."

"Yes, sir."

"What's this about the party?"

"Nothing."

"When you get through supper you're to shine your shoes. You're to bathe and dress. When you're ready, come to me, and we'll get some collodion on that face so it'll have a beauty suitable to the festivities. Then you're going to the party."

"Yes, sir."

Bathed, shined, dressed, and patched, he started out, but he was in no hurry to get there. He was troubled, and he fingered the birthday present in his pocket most uneasily. How to explain his absence from his job wasn't what bothered him. He already had a plan that would take care of it handsomely. He was at an age when it would be sufficient to say, "Yah, were you kidded! Did you bite! Yah!" and this would settle anything. But somehow he didn't like it. He didn't know it, but what ailed him was that he had already tasted triumph, or anyhow some sort of triumph, and what he craved now was humility, the sweet sacrifice of love: the sensation of being unselfish, and noble, and wan about the eyes.

He loitered outside the billiard hall watching the mysterious business of white balls clicking against red; scuffled past the picture show, examining all the posters; dillied and dallied, but after a while he had it. He would put the first plan into effect almost as soon as he got there, but he would combine it with another plan, to be uncorked later. After Marjorie had had an hour of moping brokenheartedly trying to be gay with her guests, he would call her aside and tell her the truth, or what at the moment seemed to be the truth. He had worked for Red. He had helped him on the truck; had helped him for two weeks, as a matter of fact; and all because he knew that tonight would be her birthday, and he wanted to give her something out of his own money, and—well, here it is. Then she would know she had cruelly misjudged him, and they would sit there in the shadows, happy, but in a soft dreamy way, since she would be aware at last of his lofty nature.

So it was quite dark when he got there and the party was in full swing out in the backyard. The yard had been strung with lanterns, and as he slipped back of the house he could see them all out there dancing on the clipped grass, to the radio. He paused in the shadows and looked for Marjorie. She wasn't there. He kept looking and looking, and then a sound caught his ear, so close he jumped. He turned, and found himself looking in the dining-room window. In front of it on a small table, not three feet from him, was the big cake, with Marjorie's name on it, the unlit candles spaced around its edge, with one in the middle.

And approaching that cake, in the dark room, was Marjorie. She got to it, picked up the knife, hesitated. Then he felt creepy at the enormity of the thing she was about to do. She was cutting the cake that was to be carried out before the guests as the grand surprise of the evening.

He was numb with shocked astonishment as he saw the knife go in twice, saw Marjorie pick up the wedge of cake in her hands and hurry out of the room. He was still staring at the mutilated cake when he heard a step, saw her run out of the front of the house, flit down the lawn to the pillar of the driveway, and wait. Then shame, panic, fear, and love shot through him in one terrible stab. He crept to the edge of the porch. He slipped the present under the rail. He ran blindly to the street, into the night.

From the distance, up the street; came the bell of the ice cream truck.

BRUSH FIRE

He banged sparks with his shovel, coughed smoke, cursed the impulse that had led him to heed that rumor down in the railroad yards that CCC money was to be had by all who wanted to fight this fire the papers were full of, up in the hills. Back home he had always heard them called forest fires, but they seemed to be brush fires here in California. So far, all he had got out of it was a suit of denims, a pair of shoes, and a ration of stew, served in an army mess kit. For that he had ridden twenty miles in a jolting truck out from Los Angeles to these parched hills, stood in line an hour to get his stuff, stood in line another hour for the stew, and then labored all night, the flames singeing his hair, the ground burning his feet through the thick brogans, the smoke searing his lungs, until he thought he would go frantic if he didn't get a whiff of air.

Still the thing went on. Hundreds of them smashed out flames, set backfires, hacked at bramble, while the bitter complaint went around: "Why don't they give us brush hooks if we got to cut down them bushes? What the hell good are these damn shovels?" The shovel became the symbol of their torture. Here and there, through the night, a grotesque figure would throw one down, jump on it, curse at it, then pick it up again as the hysteria subsided.

"Third shift, this way! Third shift, this way. Bring your shovels and turn over to shift number four. Everybody in the third shift, right over here."

It was the voice of the CCC foreman, who, all agreed, knew as much about fighting fires as a monkey did. Had it not been for the state fire wardens, assisting at critical spots, they would have made no progress whatever.

"All right. Answer to your names when I call them. You got to be checked off to get your money. They pay today two o'clock, so yell loud when I call your name."

"Today's Sunday."

"I said they pay today, so speak up when I call your name."

The foreman had a pencil with a little bulb in the end of it which he flashed on and began going down the list.

"Bub Anderson, Lonnie Beal, K. Bernstein, Harry Deever . . . ." As each name was called there was a loud "Yo," so when his name was called, Paul Larkin, he yelled "Yo" too. Then the foreman was calling a name and becoming annoyed because there was no answer. "Ike Pendleton! Ike Pendleton!"

"He's around somewhere."

"Why ain't he here? Don't he know he's got to be checked off?"

"Hey, Ike! Ike Pendleton!"

He came out of his trance with a jolt. He had a sudden recollection of a man who had helped him to clear out a brier patch a little while ago, and whom he hadn't seen since. He raced up the slope and over toward the fire.

Near the brier patch, in a V between the main fire and a backfire that was advancing to meet it, he saw something. He rushed, but a cloud of smoke doubled him back. He retreated a few feet, sucked in a lungful of air, charged through the backfire. There, on his face, was a man. He seized the collar of the denim jacket, started to drag. Then he saw it would be fatal to take this man through the backfire that way. He tried to lift, but his lungful of air was spent: he had to breathe or die. He expelled it, inhaled, screamed at the pain of the smoke in his throat.

He fell on his face beside the man, got a little air there, near the ground. He shoved his arm under the denim jacket, heaved, felt the man roll solidly on his back. He lurched to his feet, ran through the backfire. Two or three came to his aid, helped him with his load to the hollow, where the foreman was, where the air was fresh and cool.

"Where's his shovel? He ought to have turned it over to—"

"His shovel! Give him water!"

"I'm gitting him water; but one thing at a time—"

"Water! Water! Where's that water cart?"

The foreman, realizing belatedly that a life might be more important than the shovel tally, gave orders to "work his arms and legs up and down." Somebody brought a bucket of water, and little by little Ike Pendleton came back to life. He coughed, breathed with long shuddering gasps, gagged, vomited. They wiped his face, fanned him, splashed water on him.

Soon, in spite of efforts to keep him where he was, he fought to his feet, reeled around with the hard, terrible vitality of some kind of animal. "Where's my hat? Who took my hat?" They clapped a hat on his head, he sat down suddenly, then got up and stood swaying. The foreman remembered his responsibility. "All right, men, give him a hand, walk him down to his bunk."

"Check him off!"

"Check the rest of us! You ain't passed the P's yet!"

"O.K. Sing out when I call. Gus Ritter!"

"Yo!"

When the names had been checked, Paul took one of Ike's arms and pulled it over his shoulder; somebody else took the other, and they started for the place, a half mile or so away on the main road, where the camp was located. The rest fell in behind. Dawn was just breaking as the little file, two and two, fell into a shambling step.

"Hep! . . . Hep!"

"Hey, cut that out! This ain't no lockstep."

"Who says it ain't?"

When he woke up, in the army tent he shared with five others, he became aware of a tingle of expectancy in the air. Two of his tent mates were shaving; another came in, a towel over his arm, his hair wet and combed.

"Where did you get that wash?"

"They got a shower tent over there."

He got out his safety razor, slipped his feet in the shoes, shaved over one of the other men's shoulders, then started out in his underwear. "Hey!" At the warning, he looked out. Several cars were out there, some of them with women standing around them, talking to figures in blue denim.

"Sunday, bo. Visiting day. This is when the women all comes to say hello to their loved ones. You better put something on."

He slipped on the denims, went over to the shower tent, drew towel and soap, stripped, waited his turn. It was a real shower, the first he had had in a long time. It was cold, but it felt good. There was a comb there. He washed it, combed his hair, put on his clothes, went back to his tent, put the towel away, made his bunk. Then he fell in line for breakfast—or dinner, as it happened, as it was away past noon. It consisted of corned beef, cabbage, a boiled potato, apricot pie, and coffee.

He wolfed down the food, washed up his kit, began to feel pretty good. He fell into line again, and presently was paid, $4.50 for nine hours' work, at fifty cents an hour. He fingered the bills curiously. They were the first he had had in his hand since that day, two years before, when he had run away from home and begun this dreadful career of riding freights, bumming meals, and sleeping in flophouses.

He realized with a start they were the first bills he had ever earned in his twenty-two years; for the chance to earn bills had long since departed when he graduated from high school and began looking for jobs, never finding any. He shoved them in his pocket, wondered whether he would get the chance that night to earn more of them.

The foreman was standing there, in the space around which the tents were set up, with a little group around him. "It's under control, but we got to watch it, and there'll be another call tonight. Any you guys that want to work, report to me eight o'clock tonight, right here in this spot."

By now the place was alive with people, dust, and excitement. Cars were jammed into every possible place, mostly second-, third-, and ninth-hand, but surrounded by neatly dressed women, children, and old people, come to visit the fire fighters in denim. In a row out front, ice-cream, popcorn, and cold-drink trucks were parked, and the road was gay for half a mile in both directions with pennants stuck on poles, announcing their wares. Newspaper reporters were around too, with photographers, and as soon as the foreman had finished his harangue, they began to ask him questions about the fire, the number of men engaged in fighting it, and the casualties.

"Nobody hurt. Nobody hurt at all. Oh, early this morning, fellow kind of got knocked out by smoke, guy went in and pulled him out, nothing at all."

"What was his name?"

"I forget his name. Here—here's the guy that pulled him out. Maybe he knows his name."

In a second he was surrounded, questions being shouted at him from all sides. He gave them Ike's name and his own, and they began a frantic search for Ike, but couldn't find him. Then they decided he was the main story, not Ike, and directed him to pose for his picture. "Hey, not there; not by the ice-cream truck. We don't give ice cream a free ad in this paper. Over there by the tent."

He stood as directed, and two or three in the third shift told the story all over again in vivid detail. The reporters took notes, the photographers snapped several pictures of him, and a crowd collected. "And will you put it in that I'm from Spokane, Washington? I'd kind of like to have that in, on account of my people back there. Spokane, Washington."

"Sure, we'll put that in."

The reporters left as quickly as they had come, and the crowd began to melt. He turned away, a little sorry that his big moment had passed so quickly. Behind him he half heard a voice: "Well, ain't *that* something to be getting his picture in the paper?" He turned, saw several grins, but nobody was looking at him. Standing with her back to him, dressed in a blue silk Sunday dress, and kicking a pebble, was a girl. It was a girl who had spoken, and by quick elimination he decided it must be she.

The sense of carefree goodness that had been growing on him since he got his money, since the crowd began to jostle him, since he had become a hero, focused somewhere in his head with dizzy suddenness. "Any objections?"

This got a laugh. She kept her eyes on the pebble but turned red and said: "No."

"You sure?"

"Just so you don't get stuck up."

"Then that's O.K. How about an ice-cream cone?"

"I don't mind."

"Hey, mister, two ice-cream cones."

"Chocolate."

"Both of them chocolate and both of them double."

When they got their cones he led her away from the guffaw-
ing gallery which was beginning to be a bit irksome. She looked
at him then, and he saw she was pretty. She was small, with blue
eyes, dusty blonde hair that blended with the dusty scene around
her, and a spray of freckles over her forehead. He judged her to
be about his own age. After looking at him, and laughing rather
self-consciously and turning red, she concentrated on the cone,
which she licked with a precise technique. He suddenly found he
had nothing to say, but said it anyhow: "Well, say—what are you
doing here?"

"Oh—had to see the fire, you know."

"Have you seen it?"

"Haven't even found out where it is, yet."

"Well, my, my! I see I got to show it to you."

"You know where it is?"

"Sure. Come on."

He didn't lead the way to the fire, though. He took her up the
arroyo, through the burned-over area, where the fire had been yesterday. After a mile or so of walking, they came to a little grove of
trees beside a spring. The trees were live oak and quite green and
cast a deep shade on the ground. Nobody was in sight, or even in
earshot. It was a place the Sunday trippers didn't know about.

"Oh, my! Look at these trees! They didn't get burnt."

"Sometimes it jumps—the fire, I mean. Jumps from one hill
straight over to the other hill, leaves places it never touched at all."

"My, but it's pretty."

"Let's sit down."

"If I don't get my dress dirty."

"I'll put this jacket down for you to sit on."

"Yes, that's all right."

They sat down. He put his arm around her, put his mouth
against her lips.

It was late afternoon before she decided that her family might be looking for her and that she had better go back. She had an uncle in the camp, it seemed, and they had come as much to see him as to see the fire. She snickered when she remembered she hadn't seen either. They both snickered. They walked slowly back, their little fingers hooked together. He asked if she would like to go with him to one of the places along the road to get something to eat, but she said they had brought lunch with them, and would probably stop along the beach to eat it, going back.

They parted, she to slip into the crowd unobtrusively; he to get his mess kit, for the supper line was already formed. As he watched the blue dress flit between the tents and disappear, a gulp came into his throat; it seemed to him that this girl he had held in his arms, whose name he hadn't even thought to inquire, was almost the sweetest human being he had ever met in his life.

When he had eaten, and washed his mess kit and put it away, he wanted a cigarette. He walked down the road to a Bar-B-Q shack, bought a package, lit up, started back. Across a field, a hundred yards away, was the ocean. He inhaled the cigarette, inhaled the ocean air, enjoyed the languor that was stealing over him, wished he didn't have to go to work. And then, as he approached the camp, he felt something ominous.

Ike Pendleton was there, and in front of him this girl, this same girl he had spent the afternoon with. Ike said something to her, and she backed off. Ike followed, his fists doubled up. The crowd was silent, seemed almost to be holding its breath. Ike cursed at her. She began to cry. One of the state police came running up to them, pushed them apart, began to lecture them. The crowd broke into a buzz of talk. A woman, who seemed to be a relative, began to explain to all and sundry: "What if she *did* go with some guy to look at the fire? He don't live with her no more! *He* don't support her—never *did* support her! She didn't come up here to see *him;* never even knew he was *up* here! My land, can't the poor child have a good time once in a while?"

It dawned on him that this girl was Ike's wife.

He sat down on a truck bumper, sucked nervously at his cigarette. Some of the people who had guffawed at the ice-cream-cone episode in the afternoon looked at him, whispered. The policeman called over the woman who had been explaining things, and she and the girl, together with two children, went hurriedly over to a car and climbed into it. The policeman said a few words to Ike, and then went back to his duties on the road.

Ike walked over, picked up a mess kit, squatted on the ground between tents, and resumed a meal apparently interrupted. He ate sullenly, with his head hulked down between his shoulders. It was almost dark. The lights came on. The camp was not only connected to county water but to county light as well. Two boys went over to Ike, hesitated, then pointed to Paul. "Hey, mister, that's him. Over there, sitting on the truck."

Ike didn't look up. When the boys came closer and repeated their news, he jumped up suddenly and chased them. One of them he hit with a baked potato. When they had run away he went back to his food. He paid no attention to Paul.

In the car, the woman was working feverishly at the starter. It would whine, the engine would start and bark furiously for a moment or two, then die with a series of explosions. Each time it did this, the woman would let in the clutch, the car would rock on its wheels, and then come to rest. This went on for at least five minutes, until Paul thought he would go insane if it didn't stop, and people began to yell: "Get a horse!" "Get that damn oil can out of here and stop that noise!" "Have a heart! This ain't the Fourth of July!"

For the twentieth time it was repeated. Then Ike jumped up and ran over there. People closed in after him. Paul, propelled by some force that seemed completely apart from himself, ran after him. When he had fought his way through the crowd, Ike was on the running board of the car, the children screaming, men trying to pull him back. He had the knife from the mess kit in his hand. "I'm going to kill her! I'm going to kill her! If it's the last thing I do on earth, I'm going to kill her!"

"Oh, yeah!"

He seized Ike by the back of the neck, jerked, and slammed him against the fender. Then something smashed against his face. It was the woman, beating him with her handbag. "Go away! Git away from here!"

Ike faced him, lips writhing, eyes glaring a slaty gray against the deep red of the burns he had received that morning. But his voice was low, even if it broke with the intensity of his emotion. "Get out of my way, you! You got nothing to do with this."

He lunged at Ike with his fist—missed. Ike struck with the knife. He fended with his left arm, felt the steel cut in. With his other hand he struck, and Ike staggered back. There was a pile of shovels beside him, almost tripping him up. He grabbed one, swung, smashed it down on Ike's head. Ike went down. He stood there, waiting for Ike to get up, with that terrible vitality he had shown this morning. Ike didn't move. In the car the girl was sobbing.

The police, the ambulance, the dust, the lights, the doctor working on his arm, all swam before his eyes in a blur. Somewhere far off, an excited voice was yelling: "But I *got* to use your telephone, I *got* to, I tell you! Guy saves a man's life this morning, kills him tonight! It's a *hell* of a story!" He tried to comprehend the point of this; couldn't.

The foreman appeared, summoned the third shift to him in loud tones, began to read names. He heard his own name called, but didn't answer. He was being pushed into the ambulance, handcuffed to one of the policemen.

COAL BLACK

From up the entry came a whir, the blackness was shot with blue sparks, a cluster of lights appeared and approached. Lonnie opened the trap and the motor passed through. He closed the trap, sat down, and wished he was a motorman. Then he debated whether to eat one of his remaining sandwiches, but decided to wait awhile. Then he whistled "In the Shade of the Old Apple Tree." It was one of the three tunes he knew, so he whistled it again. Then he just sat there, and found this pleasant. Of course, *you* might not have found it pleasant to be alone in a tunnel so dark its coal walls sparkled by comparison, with only a carbide lamp to see by and nothing whatever to keep you company. But *he* minded neither the dark nor the solitude: he was so used to both that he hardly noticed them.

As for the tunnel, it had its points. It was always the same even temperature, winter or summer; the air was fresh, the intricate system of blowers and traps taking care of that. He had helped dig it, shore it, and wire it, so that it seemed a part of him—as the whole mine did for that matter. For this was the only world he had known in all his nineteen years; and he was just as at home in it as you are in your world, and found it just as familiar, just as real, just as satisfying to the soul.

After a while he heard something on the other side of the trap. Instinctively he looked at the rails. If a rat scuttled by, that meant run for his life; for a rat knows, before anybody else knows, when something is about to crack, and it is time to move, and move fast. But no rat appeared, and in a moment he got up, opened the door in the center of the trap, and peered through. At first he saw nothing. He unhooked the lamp from his hat and shot the light around. Huddled against a toolbox, her face smeared with coal dust, her dress torn so that in places her skin showed through, was a girl he judged about sixteen. She stared at him, then began to whimper:

"I'll go away, honest I will, if you just show me the way out. I don't mean nothing. I just come in to peep."

"Who let you in here?"

"Nobody. I hid in a car."

"Where? You mean you hid in it outside?"

"I don't know. Yes, of course it was outside. I hid in it, and then the train ran a whole lot further than I thought it was going to. And then I slid out. And then my matches give out, and it was dark and I got lost. And then I kept falling down, and—oh my, look at my dress! Please show me how to get out. I want to go home."

"Where you live?"

"In the north end of town."

"I never seen you before."

"We just moved in. My father, he enlarges pictures. We move from one town to the other. I wanted to see a mine. Please show me how to get out."

"Set down."

She sat down dejectedly beside the trap, and he pondered. You see, it's bad luck for a woman to enter a mine, and whenever this happens, the mine has to be "blown out," as it is blown out when somebody gets killed; that is, all hands have to quit work for the day, lest some dreadful catastrophe ensue. The trouble was that this was the first day's work the mine had had in two weeks, and the last it would have for an indefinite period; indeed, all they were doing now was loading empties for the tipple, so the men could have a little work and stray orders could be filled. If he reported this, and they blew the mine out, it might go hard with this girl; for desperate housewives, counting on a full day's pay to replenish empty shelves, might not be amused if they found they had been cheated by a ninny who merely wanted to peep.

On the next creek a woman who had dashed into a drift to say something to her husband had been so badly beaten she had to be taken to a hospital.

"You know what it means? A woman in a mine?"

"Yes; but I didn't mean nobody to see me."

"Ain't no way you can get out. I can't leave this here trap, and that place you come in, it's at least two mile away, and you can't find it, and anyway you got no light. Ain't no way you can get out, except we wait till quitting time, and then I take you out by the old drift mouth."

"All right."

"You got to stay hid. You heard what I said? They find you in here, something's going to happen to you. And they find out I let you stay, something's going to happen to *me*, too. After they turn me loose, I can't work in this mine no more, and maybe I can't work in *no* mine."

"Somebody's coming."

"In the toolbox—quick!"

She climbed in the toolbox, and he closed the cover, wedging a stone under it so she could have a little air. He sat down and with elaborate nonchalance resumed his rendition of "In the Shade of the Old Apple Tree." Han Biloxi was approaching. Of course, all

that was visible was a bobbing point of light; but to Lonnie a
bobbing point of light had special and personal motions, so that
he knew it was Han Biloxi without knowing how he knew it or
even wondering how he knew it. When Han was within hailing
distance he stopped whistling and yelled, "Yah, Han!" There was
no answer. Han came on, and when his face could be seen, it was
grave. "All right, kid. We're blowing out. Jake's train is on the main
tunnel, third entry down. He'll hold for ten minutes."

"Blowing out? What for?"

"Eckhart got it."

"*What?*"

"Rolled ag'in' the rib."

" . . . When?"

"Just now. I seen it myself. Car jumped the switch and got
him. He didn't have a chance."

"Gee, I rode in with him."

"You got ten minutes."

Han stepped through the trap, went on to notify miners far-
ther up the entry.

Lonnie lifted the toolbox cover. "You heard him?"

"Yes."

"All right. Now you see what you done!"

"Please don't say that."

"He's dead, ain't he?"

"You don't have to put it on me."

"I'm putting it where it belongs."

She stood up, climbed out of the box, and faced him. "It's
not true. Just because I'm in here, it don't mean that's why he got
killed. I won't believe it!"

"Whose fault is it?"

"All right: What are you going to do now?"

"I got to go out on Jake's train."

"And leave me in here all alone?"

"I got to go on Jake's train. If I don't show up, they start looking for me. If they don't find me, they think something happened to me."

"And no light. And pitch dark."

"Nobody asked you in here."

"My, but you're hateful."

She turned her back to him, and the nape of her neck looked disturbingly childish. He felt a twinge of guilt. She walked around, shaking her head angrily, and then dashed for the toolbox. She didn't have time to climb into it. She crouched behind it as six or eight miners, following Han Biloxi, stepped through the trap in gloomy silence.

Lonnie called to Han: "Tell Jake not to wait for me. I'm going out by the old drift mouth."

"What's the matter—you crazy?"

"There's a roll of wire up there I want. I'm making myself some rabbit traps. Maybe catch something while we're laid off."

"Come on, boy—stop acting like you got no sense. Whoever hear'n tell of that, going through all them old dead entries just to get a roll of wire? Can't you go up there tomorrow, from the outside?"

"I want the wire tonight."

"Cut the jawing and let's go."

"That's right; if the kid's crazy, let him do what he wants—and come on, let's get out of here."

They went on, their footsteps growing fainter, the splotches of light contracting until they were a small cluster of luminous blurs, when abruptly they disappeared.

She stood up. "My, but it's lonely in here!"

"Come on."

He picked up his lunch bucket and they started down the entry.

He led the way on the footpath beside the track, she stumbling along behind. When they had gone a short distance he glanced back, and was just in time to see her reel and wave crazily with her arms to keep her balance. Like a cat striking at prey, he batted her arm down, and she fell, snarling. "What you hit me for? I'm doing as good as I can. That lamp, it don't give me no light. You can see, but I can't."

"Watch that wire."

"What wire?"

"The feed wire—can't you see it? Up there on the side, at the top of the rib. That's why I knocked your arm down. You touch that thing, it'll kill you so quick you won't even know what hit you."

"Oh."

"We better walk on the track, if that's how careless you are. If you can't see behind, walk up beside me. And anyway, why didn't you say so?"

Side by side they walked between the rails, stepping from one slippery metal tie to the next. He put his arm around her to steady her, and unexpectedly found himself touching her bare flesh. Hastily he shifted his grip, taking her arm. He began trying not to think how soft her skin was, and how warm.

Soon he turned into another entry, and abruptly the top dipped. The height of a mine tunnel depends on the thickness of the coal from which it is dug. The seven-foot seam they had been in now thinned to less than five feet, so that it was impossible for them to stand. He went along at a sidewise shamble, his back bent to clear the top; for low entries were an everyday affair to him and he slipped through them without effort. But she kept bumping her head, and presently broke into hysterics. "I can't stand it no more! I got to stand up! It's pressing down on me! And my back hurts!"

"Ain't much more of the low top. Set down a few minutes, then you won't feel that way."

They sat down, she panting and convulsively straightening her aching back. He didn't look at her. But he was thoroughly aware of her now—of every detail of her slim shape, of those places where her dress was torn, of the heady, sweetly sensuous scent that hung about her. Presently they went on. The top lifted, and he turned again. She gasped at what she saw.

A dead entry is indeed a terrifying spectacle, and could serve as a chamber in some horrible inferno. Untended by man, the top erodes from the air and forms great blisters, like the blisters on paint, except that each blister is five or six feet across and five or six inches thick. The blisters then crack and fall, piece by piece, to the floor, which is thus covered with jagged shards of stone that look like gigantic shark teeth. Add that one touch can bring a blister crashing down; that the fragments underfoot can cut through the thickest shoe; that wiring, timber, rails, and all other signs of human activity have long since been removed; and that in fact nothing human ever comes here—and you can form some idea of what the abandoned parts of a coal mine are like. They proceeded slowly, hugging the wall, he ahead, she at his heels, holding tight to his denim jacket. Then they turned into another, worse than this, and then into still another. They had gone only a short distance in this when there was a report like a cannon shot and the lamp went out. She screamed.

"It's all right. Some top fell down, that's all. Stick close to the rib, like I do. It generally falls in the middle."

"Is the lamp busted? Why did it go out?"

"Air. Concussion blew it out."

"Please light it. The dark scares me so."

"Sure."

He had, in fact, already unhooked the lamp from his hat and

was banging the flint with the palm of his hand. Sparks appeared, but no light. She moaned: "I knew it was busted."

"It ain't busted. Carbide needs water, that's all."

He opened his lunch bucket, to pour in water. Then he remembered he had drunk all his water. He waited, hoping a few drops might still be left. Nothing happened.

He closed the bucket, set it down, puckered his lips, preparatory to priming the lamp with spit. Then his mouth went dry with fright and he couldn't spit. For what he had touched, when he set down the bucket, was a hand, cold and unmoving. She felt his breath stop. "What's the matter?"

"We took the wrong turn."

"Are we lost?"

"No, we ain't lost. But we're in the haunted entry."

"The—"

He placed her hand over the cold thing he had touched. She screamed, and screamed again. "That's the stone—the stone they put up for him because they couldn't get him out. With the hand chiseled on it, holding a palm. And he's in there, and he keeps tamping his powder."

"I don't hear nothing," she whispered.

"You will. . . . He tamped in his powder, and lit his fuse, and started out here to wait for the shot. Then the whole room caved in. And he keeps going back there to see why it don't go off, and then he tamps in his powder again, and—"

"I still don't hear—"

But her words froze in her throat, for off in the rock somewhere began a faint *clink, clink, clink.* Then it stopped. "That's it—that's the needle. Now comes the tamping iron." The sound resumed, reached a brisk crescendo, and stopped again. "Now he's coming out! Now he's coming this way! *And we can't move; we got no light!*"

They were crouched on the floor now, locked in each other's arms, in an ecstasy of terror. Several times the sound was repeated, and they strained closer as they listened and waited. But fear is a peculiar emotion: it cannot be sustained indefinitely at the same high pitch. In spite of his horror of the ghost, he gradually became aware that there was something distinctly pleasurable about this: lying in the dark with this girl in his arms, shuddering in unison with her, mingling his breath with hers; indeed, with an almost exquisite agony he began to look forward to each repetition of the sound. He thought of her flesh again, and in a moment his hand was touching her side, patting the torn place in her dress, as though this were what the circumstances called for. She didn't seem to mind. On the contrary, his thick paw apparently soothed her; so that she relaxed slightly, and put her head on his shoulder, and sighed. He patted and patted again, and each time the sound would resume they would draw together.

Suddenly, though, she sat up, listened, and turned to him. "That ain't no miner."

"Oh, yes, it is. He—"

"That ain't no miner. That's water. I can tell by how it sounds."

"Gee, if we could only get some! But I can't even start the lamp. I'm scared so bad I can't spit."

"Give me that lamp. I can spit."

She took the lamp, and he heard it hiss from plenty of good wet spit. He struck the flint, and flame punctured the darkness. "We got to hurry. That won't last long."

"Keep still, so I can hear."

He held the light, and she crawled on her hands and knees, cocking her head now and then to listen. The flame grew smaller and smaller. Suddenly she thrust her hand under a slab of rock. "There it is."

"You sure?"

"Give me the bucket."

She took the bucket and thrust it under, and at once came the loud *clank* of water on tin. They looked at each other, and he spoke breathlessly: "That's it! That's how it sounded, only now it's in the bucket." The lamp went out, and they waited in the dark while there came a few drops, then a pause, then a few more drops, then the rapid staccato of a full trickle, then a long pause, then the separate drops again. After a long time she shook the bucket, and they heard the water slosh. "That's enough. That'll get us out."

They poured water in the lamp, struck the flint, and a fine big flame spurted out. They were off at once. They went through more dead entries, then came to where the going was better. He laughed—a high nervous giggle. "Ain't that a joke? Won't them miners feel silly when I tell them that haunt ain't nothing but water?"

"It come to me, just like that, that them was drops."

"And think of that—that was why they stopped working that coal. That's why the company had to close down them entries. Not no miner would work in there."

"Gee, that's funny."

When, still laughing at this, they popped suddenly on to the old drift mouth, it was nearly dark outside, and snowing. They said stiff good-byes; she thanked him for helping her out, and promised to protect him in his guilty secret. She started down the mountain toward the part of the camp where she lived. He watched her a moment, and then something rose in his throat, an overwhelming recollection—of a naked patch of flesh, lovely smell, and brave, hissing spit.

He called in a queer strained voice: "Yay!"

"What?"

"Come back here a minute."

She ran back and stood in front of him. He wanted to say

something; didn't know what it was; then heard himself talking, in the same queer voice, about his hope there was no hard feelings about what he had said, back there in the mine, before they started out. She didn't answer. She kept looking at him. And then, to his astonishment, she came up and put her arms around him. Then he said it. He pulled her to him, pushed his lips against hers for the first time, and the words came jerkily: "Listen. . . . The hell with going home. . . . Let's not go home. . . . Let's get married. . . . Let's . . . be together."

She stayed near him, touched his face with her fingers, then looked away. "We can't get married."

"Why not?"

"We got no money. You got no money. I got no money, nobody in a coal camp has got any money. . . . Gee, I'd love to be with you."

"My old man would take us in."

"And your old lady would throw us out."

"All right, never mind the married part. Let's not go home tonight. Let's stay up here, in one of these shacks."

"They'll be looking for us."

"Let them look."

"We'd be awful cold and hungry."

"We can build a fire, and I got two sandwiches left."

" . . . All right."

They tried to say something else, but found themselves unexpectedly embarrassed. But then he began shaking her, his eyes shining. "Who says we can't get married? Who says we got no money? Why, I'll have a job! I'll have a real job! I'll have a company job!"

"How will you get a company job?"

"The haunt! Don't you get it? *I'll* prove to them miners that haunt is nothing but water! Then they can get that coal! Boy, will they give me a company job for doing that! Will they!"

"Gee. I bet they will."

"Listen. Do you really mean it? About camping out tonight?"

"I don't want we should be separated, ever."

"Kiss me again. Maybe we can catch a rabbit. Can you cook a rabbit?"

"Yes."

Inside, an astral miner picked up an astral bucket and sadly prepared to join the great army of unemployed.

CAREER IN C MAJOR

1

All this, that I'm going to tell you, started several years ago. You may have forgotten how things were then, but I won't forget it so soon, and sometimes I think I'll never forget it. I'm a contractor, junior partner in the Craig-Borland Engineering Company, and in my business there was *nothing* going on. In your business, I think there was a little going on, anyway enough to pay the office help provided they would take a ten per cent cut and forget about the Christmas bonus. But in my business, nothing. We sat for three years with our feet on our desks reading magazines, and after the secretaries left we filled in for a while by answering the telephone. Then we didn't even do that, because the phone didn't ring any more. We just sat there, and switched from the monthlies to the weeklies, because they came out oftener.

It got so bad that when Craig, my partner, came into the office one day with a comical story about a guy that wanted a concrete chicken coop built, somewhere out in Connecticut, that we looked at each other shifty-eyed for a minute, and then without saying a word we put on our hats and walked over to Grand Central to

take the train. We wanted that coop so bad we could hardly wait
to talk to him. We built it on a cost-plus basis, and I don't think
there's another one like it in the world. It's insulated concrete, with
electric heat control, automatic sewage disposal, accommodations
for 5,000 birds, and all for $3,000, of which our share was $300,
minus expenses. But it was something to do, something to do.
After the coop was built, Craig dug in at his farm up-state, and
that left me alone. I want you to remember that, because if I made
a fool of myself, I was wide open for that, with nothing to do and
nobody to do it with. When you get a little fed up with me, just
remember those feet, with no spurs to keep them from falling off
the desk, because what we had going on wasn't a war, like now,
but a depression.

It was about four-thirty on a fall afternoon when I decided to call
it a day and go home. The office is in a remodeled loft on East
35th Street, with a two-story studio for drafting on the ground
level, the offices off from that, and the third floor for storage. We
own the whole building and owned it then. The house is on East
84th Street, and it's a house, not an apartment. I got it on a deal
that covered a couple of apartment houses and a store. It's mine,
and was mine then, with nothing owing on it. I decided to walk,
and marched along, up Park and over, and it was around five-
thirty when I got home. But I had forgotten it was Wednesday,
Doris's afternoon at home. I could hear them in there as soon as
I opened the door, and I let out a damn under my breath, but
there was nothing to do but brush my hair back and go in. It was
the usual mob: a couple of Doris's cousins, three women from the
Social Center, a woman just back from Russia, a couple of women
that have boxes at the Metropolitan Opera, and half a dozen hus-
bands and sons. They were all Social Register, all so cultured that
even their eyeballs were lavender, all rich, and all 100% nitwits.

They were the special kind of nitwits you meet in New York and nowhere else, and they might fool you if you didn't know them, but they're nitwits just the same. Me, I'm Social Register too, but I wasn't until I married Doris, and I'm a traitor to the kind that took me in. Give me somebody like Craig, that's a farmer from Reubenville, that never even heard of the Social Register, that wouldn't know culture if he met it on the street, but is an A1 engineer just the same, and has designed a couple of bridges that have plenty of beauty, if that's what they're talking about. These friends of Doris's, they've been everywhere, they've read everything, they know everybody, and I guess now and then they even do a little good, anyway when they shove money back of something that really needs help. But I don't like them, and they don't like me.

I went around, though, and shook hands, and didn't tumble that anything unusual was going on until I saw Lorentz. Lorentz had been her singing teacher before she married me, and he had been in Europe since then, and this was the first I knew he was back. And his name, for some reason, didn't seem to get mentioned much around our house. You see, Doris is opera-struck, and one of the things that began to make trouble between us within a month of the wedding was the great career she gave up to marry me. I kept telling her I didn't want her to give up her career, and that she should go on studying. She was only nineteen then, and it certainly looked like she still had her future before her. But she would come back with a lot of stuff about a woman's first duty being to her home, and when Randolph came, and after him Evelyn, I began to say she had probably been right at that. But that only made it worse. Then *I* was the one that was blocking her career, and had been all along, and every time we'd get going good, there'd be a lot of stuff about Lorentz, and the way he had raved about her voice, and if she had only listened to him instead

of to me, until I got a little sick of it. Then after a while Lorentz
wasn't mentioned any more, and that suited me fine. I had nothing against him, but he always meant trouble, and the less I heard
of him the better I liked it.

I went over and shook hands, and noticed he had got pretty
gray since I saw him last. He was five or six years older than I
was, about forty I would say, born in this country, but a mixture
of Austrian and Italian. He was light, with a little clipped moustache, and about medium height, but his shoulders went back
square, and there was something about him that said Europe, not
America. I asked him how long he had been back, he said a couple
of months, and I said swell. I asked him what he had been doing
abroad, he said coaching in the Berlin opera, and I said swell. That
seemed to be about all. Next thing I knew I was alone, watching
Doris where she was at the table pouring drinks, with her eyes big
and dark, and two bright red spots on her cheeks.

Of course the big excitement was that she was going to sing. So I
just took a back seat and made sure I had a place for my glass, so
I could put it down quick and clap when she got through. I don't
know what she sang. In those days I didn't know one song from
another. She stood facing us, with a little smile on her face and one
elbow on the piano, and looked us over as though we were a whole
concert hall full of people, and then she started to sing. But there
was one thing that made me feel kind of funny. It was the whisper-
whisper rehearsal she had with Lorentz just before she began. They
were all sitting around, holding their breaths waiting for her, and
there she was on the piano bench with Lorentz, listening to him
whisper what she was to do. Once he struck two sharp chords, and
she nodded her head. That doesn't sound like much to be upset
about, does it? She was in dead earnest, and no foolishness about
it. The whole seven years I had been married to her, I don't think I

ever got one word out of her that wasn't phoney, and yet with this guy she didn't even try to put on an act.

They left about six-thirty, and I mixed another drink so we could have one while we were dressing for a dinner we had to go to. When I got upstairs she was stretched out on the chaise longue in brassiere, pants, stockings, and high-heeled slippers, looking out of the window. That meant trouble. Doris is a Chinese kimono girl, and she always seems to be gathering it around her so you can't see what's underneath, except that you can, just a little. But when she's got the bit in her teeth, the first sign is that she begins to show everything she's got. She's got plenty, because a sculptor could cast her in bronze for a perfect thirty-four, and never have to do anything more about it at all. She's small, but not too small, with dark red hair, green eyes, and a sad, soulful face, with a sad soulful shape to go with it. It's the kind of shape that makes you want to put your arm around it, but if you do put your arm around it, anyway when she's parading it around to get you excited, that's when you made your big mistake. Then she shrinks and shudders, and gets so refined she can't bear to be touched, and you feel like a heel, and she's one up on you.

I didn't touch her. I poured two drinks, and set one beside her, and said here's how. She kept looking out the window, and in a minute or two saw the drink, and stared at it like she couldn't imagine what it was. That was another little sign, because Doris likes a drink as well as you do or I do, and in fact she's got quite a talent at it, in a quiet, refined way. " . . . Oh no. Thanks just the same."

"You better have a couple, just for foundation. They'll be plenty weak tonight, I can promise you that."

"I couldn't."

"You feel bad?"

"Oh no, it's not that."

"No use wasting it then."

I drained mine and started on hers. She watched me spear the olive, got a wan little smile on her face, and pointed at her throat. "Oh? Bad for the voice, hey?"

"Ruinous."

"I guess it would be, at that."

"You have to give up so many things."

She kept looking at me with that sad, orphan look that she always gets on her face when she's getting ready to be her bitchiest, as though I was far, far away, and she could hardly see me through the mist, and then she went back to looking out the window. "I've decided to resume my career, Leonard."

"Well gee that's great."

"It's going to mean giving up—everything. And it's going to mean work, just slaving drudgery from morning to night—I only pray that God will give me strength to do all that I'll have to do."

"I guess singing's no cinch at that."

"But—something has to be done."

"Yeah? Done about what?"

"About everything. We can't go on like this, Leonard. Don't you see? I know you do the best you can, and that you can't get work when there is no work. But something has to be done. If you can't earn a living, then I'll have to."

Now to you, maybe that sounds like a game little wife stepping up beside her husband to help him fight when the fighting was tough. It wasn't that at all. In the first place, Doris had high-hatted me ever since we had been married, on account of my family, on account of my being a low-brow that couldn't understand all this refined stuff she went in for, on account of everything she could think of. But one thing she hadn't been able to take away from me. I was the one that went out and got the dough, and plenty of it, which was what her fine family didn't seem to have so much of any more. And this meant that at last she had found a way to high-hat me, even on that. Why she was going back to singing was that she wanted to go back to singing, but she wasn't satisfied just to do that. She had to harpoon me with it, and harpoon me where it hurt. And in the second place, all we had between us and starvation was the dough I had salted away in a good bank, enough to last at least three more years, and after that the house, and after that my share of the Craig-Borland Building, and after that a couple of other pieces of property the firm had, if things got that bad, and I had never asked Doris to cut down by one cent on the household expenses, or live any different than we had always lived, or give up anything at all. I mean, it was a lot of hooey, and I began to get sore. I tried not to, but I couldn't help myself. The sight of her lying there like the dying swan, with this noble look on her face, and just working at the job of making me look like a heel, kind of got my goat.

"So. We're just starving to death, are we?"

"Well? Aren't we?"

"Just practically in the poorhouse."

"I worry about it so much that sometimes I'm afraid I'll have a breakdown or something. I don't bother you about it, and I don't ever intend to. There's no use of your knowing what I go through. But—something has to be done. If something isn't done, Leonard, what are we going to come to?"

"So you're going out and have a career, all for the husband and the kiddies, so they can eat, and have peppermint sticks on the Christmas tree, and won't have to bunk in Central Park when the big blizzard comes."

"I even think of that."

"Doris, be your age."

"I'm only trying to—"

"You're only trying to make a bum out of me, and I'm not going to buy it."

"You have to thwart me, don't you Leonard? Always."

"There it goes. I knew it. So I thwart you."

"You've thwarted me ever since I've known you, Leonard. I don't know what there is about you that has to make a woman a drudge, that seems incapable of realizing that she might have aspirations too. I suppose I ought to make allowance—"

"For the pig-sty I was raised in, is that it?"

"Well Leonard, there's *something* about you."

"How long have you had this idea?"

"I've been thinking about it quite some time."

"About two months, hey?"

"Two months? Why two months?"

"It seems funny that this egg comes back from Europe and right away you decide to resume your career;"

"How wrong you are. Oh, how wrong you are."

"And by the time he gets his forty a week, or whatever he takes, and his commission on the music you buy, and all the rest of his cuts, you'll be taken for a swell ride. There won't be much left for the husband and kiddies."

"I'm not being taken for a ride."

"No?"

"I'm not paying Lorentz anything."

" . . . What?"

"I've explained to him. About our—circumstances."

I hit the roof then. I wanted to know what business she had telling him about our circumstances or anything else. I said I wouldn't be under obligations to him, and that if she was going to have him she had to pay him. She lay there shaking her head, like the pity of it was that I couldn't understand, and never could understand. "Leonard, I couldn't pay Hugo, even if I wanted to— not now."

"Why not *now*?"

"When he knows—how hard it is for us. And it's not important."

"It's plenty important—to me."

"Hugo is that strange being that you don't seem to understand, that you even deny exists—but he exists, just the same. Hugo is an artist. He believes in my voice. That's all. The rest is irrelevant. Money, time, work, everything."

That gave me the colic so bad I had to stop, count ten, and begin all over again. " . . . Listen, Doris. To hell with all this. Nobody's opposing your career. I'm all for your career, and I don't care what it costs, and I don't care whether it ever brings in a dime. But why the big act? Why do you have to go through all this stuff that I'm thwarting you, and we're starving, and all that? Why can't you just study, and shut up about it?"

"Do we have to go back over all that?"

"And if that's how you feel about it, what the hell did you ever marry me for, anyway?"

That slipped out on me. She didn't say anything, and I took it back. Oh yes, I took it back, because down deep inside of me I knew why she had married me, and I had spent seven years with my ears stopped up, so she'd never have the chance to tell the truth about it. She had married me for the dough I brought in, and that was all she had married me for. For the rest, I just bored her, except for that streak in her that had to torture everybody that came within five feet of her. The whole thing was that I was nuts about her and she didn't give a damn about me, and don't ask me why I was nuts about her. I don't know why I was nuts about her. She was a phoney, she had the face of a saint and the soul of a snake, she treated me like a dog, and still I was nuts about her. So I took it back. I apologized for it. I backed down like I always did, and lost the fight, and wished I had whatever it would take to stand up against her, but I didn't.

"Time to dress, Leonard."

*   *   *

When we got home that night, she undressed in the dressing room, and when she came out she had on one of the Chinese kimonos, and went to the door of the nursery, where the kids had slept before they got old enough to have a room. . . . "I've decided to sleep in here for a while, Leonard. I've got exercises to do when I get up, and—all sorts of things. There's no reason why you should be disturbed."

"Any way you like."

"Or—perhaps you would be more comfortable in there."

Yes, I even did that. I slept that night in the nursery, and took up my abode there from then on. What I ought to do was go in and sock her in the jaw, I knew that. But I just looked at Peter Rabbit, where he was skipping across the wall in the moonlight, and thought to myself: "Yeah, Borland, that's you all right."

2

So for the next three months there was nothing but vocalizing all over the place, and then it turned out she was ready for a recital in Town Hall. For the month after that we got ready for the recital, and the less said about it the better. Never mind what Town Hall cost, and the advertising cost, and that part. What I hated was drumming up the crowd. I don't know if you know how a high-toned Social Registerite like Doris does when she gets ready to give a recital to show off her technique. She calls up all *her* friends, and sandbags them to buy tickets. Not just to come, you understand, on free tickets, though to me that would be bad enough. To *buy* tickets, at $2 a ticket. And not only does she call up *her* friends, but her husband calls up *his* friends, and all her sisters and her cousins and her aunts call up *their* friends, and those friends have to come through, else it's an unfriendly act. I got so I hated to go in the River Club, for fear I'd run into somebody that was on the list, and that I hadn't buttonholed, and if I let him get out of there without buttonholing him, and Doris found out about it, there'd be so much fuss that I'd buttonhole him, just to save trouble. Oh yes, culture has its practical side when you start up Park Avenue with it. It's not just that I'm a roughneck that I hate it. There are other reasons too.

I don't know when it was that I tumbled that Doris was lousy. But some time in the middle of all that excitement, it just came to me one day that she couldn't sing, that she never could sing, that it was all just a pipe dream. I tried to shake it off, to tell myself that I didn't know anything about it, because that was one thing that had always been taken for granted in our house: that she could have a career if she wanted it. And there was plenty of reason to think so, because she did have a voice, anybody could tell that. It was a high soprano, pretty big, with a liquid quality to it that made it easy for her to do the coloratura stuff she seemed to specialize in. I couldn't shake it off. I just knew she was no good, and didn't know how I knew it. So of course that made it swell. Because in the first place I had to keep on taking her nonsense, knowing all the time she was a fake, and not being able to tell her so. And in the second place, I was so in love with her that I couldn't take my eyes off her when she was around and I hated to see her out there making a fool of herself. And in the third place, there was Lorentz. If I knew she was no good then he knew she was no good, and what was he giving her free lessons for? He was up pretty often, usually just before dinner, to run over songs with her, and once or twice, while we were waiting for her to come home, I tried to get going with him, to find out what was what. I couldn't. I knew why I couldn't. It was some more of the blindfold stuff. I was afraid I'd find out something I didn't want to know. Not that I expected him to tell me. But I might find it out just the same, and I didn't want to find it out. I might lie awake half the night wondering about it, and gnaw my fingernails half off down at the office, but when it came to the showdown I didn't want to know. So we would just sit there, and have a drink, and talk about how women are always late. Then Doris would come, and start to yodel. And then I would go upstairs.

The recital was in February, at eleven o'clock of a Friday morning. About nine o'clock I was in the nursery, getting into the cutaway coat and gray striped pants that Doris said I had to wear, when the phone rang in the bedroom and I heard Doris answer. In a minute or two she came in. "Stop that for a minute, Leonard, and listen to me. It's something terribly important."

"Yeah? What is it?"

"Louise Bronson just called up. She was talking last night with Rudolph Hertz." Hertz wasn't his name, but I'll call him that. He was a critic on the Herald Tribune. "You know, he's related to her."

"And?"

"She told him he had to come and give me a review, and he promised to do it. But the fool told him it was tomorrow instead of today, and Leonard, you'll have to call him up and tell him, and be sure and tell him there'll be two tickets for him, in his name at the boxoffice—and make sure they're there."

"Why do I have to call him up?"

"Leonard, I simply haven't time to explain all that to you now. He's the most important man in town, it's just a stroke of blind luck that he promised to give me a review, and I can't lose it just because of a silly mistake over the day."

"His paper keeps track of that for him."

"Leonard, you call him up! You call him up right now! You—
stop making me scream, it's frightful for my voice. You call him
up! Do you hear me?"

"He won't be at his paper. They don't come down that early."

"Then call him up at his home!"

I went in the bedroom and picked up the phone book. He
wasn't in it. I called information. They said they would have to
have the address. Doris began screaming at me from the dressing
room. "He lives on Central Park West! In the same building as
Louise!"

I gave the address. They said they were very sorry but it was a
private number and they wouldn't be able to give it to me. Doris
was yelling at me before I even hung up. "Then you'll have to go
over there! You'll have to see him."

"I can't go over there. Not at this hour."

"You'll have to go over there. You'll have to see him! And be
sure and mention Louise, and his promise to her, and tell him
there'll be two tickets for him, in his name at the boxoffice!"

So I hustled on the rest of my clothes, and jumped in a cab,
and went over there. I found him in bathrobe and slippers, having breakfast with his wife and another lady, in an alcove just off
the living room. I mumbled about Louise Bronson, and how anxious we were to have his opinion on my wife's voice, and about
the tickets in his name at the boxoffice, and he listened to me as
though he couldn't believe his ears. Then he cut me off, and he cut
me off sharp. "My dear fellow, I can't go to every recital in Town
Hall just at an hour's notice. If notices were sent out, my paper
will send somebody over, and there was no need whatever for you
to come to me about it."

"Louise Bronson—"

"Yes, Louise said something to me about a recital, but I don't
let her run my department either."

"We were very anxious for your opinion—"

"If so, making a personal call at this hour in the morning was a very bad way to get it."

I felt my face get hot. I jumped up, said I was sorry, and got out of there as fast as I could grab my hat. The recital didn't help any. The place was packed with stooges, and they clapped like hell and it didn't mean a thing. I sat with Randolph and Evelyn, and we clapped too, and after it was over, and about a ton of flowers had gone up, and my flowers too, we went backstage with the whole mob to tell Doris how swell she was, and you would have thought it was just a happy family party. But as soon as my face wasn't red any more from thinking about the critic, it got red from something else. About a third of that audience were children. That was how they had told us to go to hell, those people we had sandbagged. They bought tickets, but they sent their children—with nursemaids.

Doris took the children home, and I went out and ate, and then went over to the office. I sat there looking at my feet, and thinking about the critic, and the children at the recital, and sleeping in the nursery, and Lorentz, and all the rest of it, and I felt just great. About two-thirty the phone rang. "Mr. Borland?"

"Speaking."

"This is Cecil Carver."

She acted like I ought to know who Cecil Carver was, but I had never heard the name before. "Yes, Miss Carver. What can I do for you?"

"Perhaps I ought to explain. I'm a singer. I happened to be visiting up in Central Park this morning when you called, and I couldn't help hearing what was said."

"I got a cool reception."

"Pay no attention to it. He's a crusty old curmudgeon until he's had his coffee, and then he's a dear. I wish you could have heard the way he was treating me."

That was all hooey, but somehow my face didn't feel red any more, and besides that, I liked the way she laughed. "You make me feel better."

"Forget it. I judged from what you said that you were anxious for a competent opinion on your wife's singing."

"Yes, I was."

"Well, I dropped in at that recital. Would you like to know what I thought?"

"I'd be delighted."

"Then why don't you come over?" She gave the name of a hotel that was about three blocks away, on Lexington Avenue.

"I don't know of any reason why not."

"Have you still got on that cutaway coat?"

"Yes, I have."

"Oh my, I'll have to make myself look pretty."

"You had better hurry up."

" . . . Why?"

"Because I'm coming right over."

3

She had a suite up on the tenth floor, with a grand piano in it and music scattered all over the place, and she let me in herself. I took her to be about thirty, but I found out later she was two years younger. Women singers usually look older than they really are. There's something about them that says woman, not girl. She was good-looking all right. She had a pale, ivory skin, but her hair was black, and so were her eyes. I think she had the biggest black eyes I ever saw. She was a little above medium height, and slim, but she was a little heavy in the chest. She had on a blue silk dress, very simple, and it came from a good shop, I could see that. But somehow it didn't look quite right, anyway to somebody that was used to the zip that Doris had in her dresses. She told me afterward she had no talent for dressing at all, that a lot of women on the stage haven't, and that she did what most of them do: go into the best place in town, buy the simplest thing they have, pay plenty for it, and take a chance it will look all right. It looked just about like that, but it didn't make any difference. You didn't think about the dress after you saw those eyes.

She had a drink ready, and asked me if I was a musician. I said no, I was a contractor, and next thing I knew I had had two drinks, and was gabbling about myself like some drummer in a Pullman. She kept smiling and nodding, like concrete railroad bridges were the most fascinating thing she had ever heard of in her life, and the big black eyes kept looking at me, and even with the drinks I knew I was making a bit of a fool of myself. I didn't care. It was the first time a woman had taken any interest in me in a blue moon, and I was having a good time, and I had still another drink, and kept right on talking.

After a while, though, I pulled up, and said well, and she switched off to Doris. "Your wife has a remarkable voice."

"Yes?"

" . . . It keeps haunting me."

"Is it that good?"

"Yes, it's that good, but that isn't why it haunts me. I keep thinking I've heard it before."

"She used to sing around quite a lot."

"Here? In New York?"

"Yes."

"That couldn't be it. I don't come from New York. I come from Oregon. And I've spent the last five years abroad. Oh well, never mind."

"Then you think she's good?"

"She has a fine voice, a remarkably fine voice, and her tone is well produced. She must have had excellent instruction. Of course . . . "

"Go on. What else?"

" . . . I would criticize her style."

"I'm listening."

"Has she been studying long?"

"She studied before we got married. Then for a while she dropped it, and she just started up again recently."

"Oh. Then that accounts for it. Good style, of course, doesn't come in a day. With more work, that ought to come around."

"Then you think she ought to go on?"

"With such looks and such a voice, certainly."

With that we dropped it. In spite of all she said, it added up to faint praise, especially the shifty way she brought up the question of style. She tried to get me going again on concrete, but somehow talking about Doris had taken all the fun out of it. After a few minutes I thanked her for all the trouble she had taken and got up to go. She sat there with a funny look on her face, staring at me. A boy came in with a note, and left, and she read it and said: "Damn."

"Something wrong?"

"I'm singing for the American Legion in Brooklyn tonight, and I promised to do a song they want, and I've forgotten to get the words of it, and the man that was to give them to me has gone out of town, and here's his note saying he'll give me a ring tomorrow—and no words."

"What song?"

"Oh, some song they sing in the Navy. Something about a destroyer. Isn't that annoying?"

"Oh, *that* song."

"You know it?"

"Sure. I had a brother that was a gob."

"Well for heaven's sake sing it."

She sat down to the piano and started to play it. She already knew the tune. I started to sing:

> *You roll and groan and toss and pitch,*
> *You swab the deck, you son-of-a——*

She got up, walked over to the sofa, and sat down, her face perfectly white. I had forgotten about that rhyme, and I began to mumble apologies for it, and explain that there was another way to sing it, so *groan* would rhyme with *moan*. But at that I couldn't see why it would make her sore. She hadn't seemed like the kind that would mind a rhyme, even if it was a little off. But she kept staring at me, and then I got a little sore myself, and said it was a pretty good rhyme, even if she didn't like it. "To hell with the rhyme."

"Oh?"

"Borland, your wife's no good."

"She's not?"

"No, she's not."

"Well—thanks."

"But *you* have a voice."

"I—what?"

"You have a voice such as hasn't been heard since—I don't know when. What a baritone! What a trumpet!"

"I think you're kidding me."

"I'm not kidding you. . . . Want some lessons?"

Her eyes weren't wide open any more. They were half closed to a couple of slits. A creepy feeling began to go up my back. It was time to go, and I knew it. I did *not* go. I went over, sat down, put my arm around her, pushed her down, touched my mouth to her lips. They were hot. We stayed that way a minute, breathing into each other's faces, looking into each other's eyes. Then she mumbled: "Damn you, you'll kiss first."

"I will like hell."

She put her arms around me, tightened. Then she kissed me, and I kissed back.

"You were slow enough."

"I was wondering what you wanted."

"I wanted you, you big gorilla. Ever since you came in there this morning with that foolish song-and-dance about getting Hertz to go to the concert. What made you do that? Didn't you know any better?"

"Yes."

"Then why did you do it?"

"I had to."

" . . . You mean she made you?"

"Something like that."

"Couldn't you say no?"

"I guess I couldn't."

She twisted her head around, where it was on my shoulder, and looked at me, and twisted my hair around her fingers. "You're crazy about her, aren't you?"

"More or less."

"I'm sorry I said she was no good. She really has a voice. She might improve, with more work. . . . Maybe I was jealous of her."

"It's all right."

"You see—"

"To hell with it. You said just what I've been thinking all along, so why apologize? She has a voice, and yet she's no good. And yet—"

"You're crazy about her."

"Yes."

She twisted my hair a while, and then started to laugh. "You could have knocked me over with a straw when I saw Hugo Lorentz coming out there to the piano."

"You know him?"

"Known him for years. I hadn't seen him since he played for me in Berlin last winter, and what a night *that* was."

"Yeah?"

"After the concert we walked around to his apartment, and he wept on my shoulder till three o'clock in the morning about some cold-blooded bitch that he's in love with, in New York, and that does nothing but torture him, and every other man she gets into her clutches for that matter. Oh, I got her whole life history. Once a year she'd send Hugo a phonograph record of herself singing some song they had worked on. He thought they were wonderful, and he kept playing them over and over again; till I got so sick of that poop's voice—" There was a one-beat pause, and then she finished off real quick: "—Well, it was a night, that's all."

"And that was where you heard my wife's voice, wasn't it?"

"What in the world are you talking about?"

"Come on, don't kid me."

" . . . I'm sorry, Leonard. I didn't mean to. From what Hugo said, I had pictured some kind of man-eating tigress, and when that dainty, wistful, perfectly beautiful creature came out there today, it never once entered my mind. It didn't anyhow, until just now."

"Then it was?"

"Yes, of course."

"I've had my suspicions about Hugo."

"You needn't have."

"I thought he was taking her for a ride."

"He's not. She's taking him."

"What about these other men she's got her clutches on?"

"For heaven's sake, can't a woman that good-looking have a little bit of a good time? What do you care? You're having a good time, aren't you? Right now? I'll sock you if you say you're not."

"Believe it or not, this is my first offense."

"—And, you've *got* her haven't you?"

"No."

"What?"

"I'm just one other man she's got her clutches on, one more sap to torture. I happen to be married to her, that's all."

"You poor dear. You are crazy about her, aren't you?"

"Come on, what about these other men?"

She thought a long time, and then she said: "Leonard, I'm not going to tell you any more of what Hugo said, except this: That no man gets any favors from her, if that's what you're worried about. And especially Hugo doesn't. She sees that they keep excited, but inside she's as cold as a slab of ice, and thinks of nothing but herself. I think you can take Hugo's word on that. He knows a lot more about women than you do, and he's not kidded about her for one second, even if he is crazy about her. Does that help?"

"Not much. You're not telling me anything I don't know, though. I've kidded myself about it for seven years, but I know. Lorentz, I think, he has the inside track on the rest, but only on account of the music."

"That's what Hugo says."

"What?"

"That she thinks of nothing but her triumphs, feminine, social, and artistic, and especially artistic. She's crazy to be a singer. And that's where he fits in."

"Her triumphs. That's it. Life in our house is nothing but a series of triumphs."

"Leonard, I have an idea."

"Shoot."

"I hate that woman."

"I spend half my time hating her and half my time insane about her. What's she got, anyway?"

"One thing she's got is a face that a man would commit suicide for. Another thing she's got is a figure that if he wasn't quite dead yet, he'd stand up and commit suicide for all over again. And another thing she's got is a healthy professional interest in the male of the species, that enjoys sticking pins into it just to see them wriggle. But if you want her, I'm determined you're going to have her. And really have her. You see, I like you pretty well."

"I like you a little, myself."

"That woman has got to be hurt."

"Oh, hurt hey? And you think you could hurt Doris? Listen, you'd be going up against something that's forgotten more about that than you'll ever know. You go and get your head lock on her and begin twisting her neck. See what happens. She'll be out in one second flat, in one minute flat she'll have you on the floor, and in five minutes she'll be pulling your toenails out with red-hot pliers. Yeah, you hurt her. I'm all sore from trying."

"You didn't hurt her where it hurt."

"And where does it hurt?"

"In that slab of ice she uses for a heart. In the triumph department, baby. You go get yourself a triumph, and see her wriggle out of that."

"I won the club championship at billiards year before last. It didn't do a bit of good."

"Wake up. Did you hear what I said about your voice?"

"Oh my God. I thought you had an idea."

"*You're* going to sing in Town Hall."

"I'm not."

"You are. And will that fix her."

"So I'm going to sing in Town Hall? Well in the first place I can't sing in Town Hall, and in the second place I don't want to sing in Town Hall, and in the third place it's just plain silly. And in addition to that, wouldn't that fix her? Just another boughten recital in Town Hall, with a lot of third-string critics dropping in for five minutes and another gang of stooges out there laughing at me. And in addition to that, I don't go out and drum up another crowd. I've had enough."

"They won't be third-string critics and it won't be a drummed-up crowd."

"I know that racket, so does she, and—"

"Not if I sing with you."

"What do you want to do, ruin me?"

"I guess that wouldn't do, at that . . . Leonard, you're right. The Town Hall idea is no good. But—Carnegie, a regular, bona fide appearance with the Philharmonic, that would be different, wouldn't it?"

"Are you crazy?"

"Leonard, if you put yourself in my hands, if you do just what I say, I'll have you singing with the Philharmonic in a year. With that voice, I guarantee it. And let her laugh that off. just let her laugh that off. Baby, do you want that woman? Do you want her eating out of your hand? Do—"

I opened my eyes to razz it some more, but all of a sudden a picture popped in front of my eyes, of how Doris would look out there, listening to me, and I started to laugh. Yes, it warmed me up.

"What's the matter?"

"It's the most cock-eyed thing I ever heard in my life. But—all right. We'll pretend that's how it's going to come out. Anyway, I'll have an excuse to see you some more."

"You don't need any excuse for that."

"Me, in soup and fish, up there in front of a big orchestra, bellowing at them."

"You'll have to work."

"I'm used to work."

"You'll have to study music, and sight-reading, and harmony, and languages, especially Italian."

"*Perche devo studiare l'italiano?*"

"You speak Italian?"

"Didn't I tell you I started out as an architect? We all take our two years in Italy, studying the old ruins. Sure, I speak Italian."

"Oh, you *darling* . . . I'll want payment."

"I've got enough money."

"Who's talking about money? I want kisses, and lots of them."

"How about a down payment now? On account?"

"M'm."

It was about six o'clock when I got home, and Ethel Gorman, a cousin of Doris', was still there, and the flowers were all around, and the kids were going from one vase to the other, smelling them, and Doris still had on the recital dress, and the phone was ringing every five minutes, and the reviews from the afternoon papers were all clipped and spread on the piano. They said she revealed an excellent voice and sang acceptably. One of the phone calls kept Doris longer than the others, and when she came back her eyes were shining. "Ethel! Guess who was there!"

"Who?"

"Cecil Carver!"

"No!"

"Alice Hornblow just called up and says she sat next to her, and would have called sooner only she had to make sure who it was from her picture in a magazine, and she was talking to her during the intermission—and Cecil Carver said I was swell!"

"Doris! You don't mean it!"

"Isn't it marvelous! It means—it means more than all those reviews put together. Think of that Ethel—Cecil Carver!"

Now who Cecil Carver was, and what the hell kind of singing she did when she wasn't entertaining contractors in the afternoon, was something we hadn't got around to yet, for some reason. I pasted a dumb look on my face, and kind of droned it out: "And who, may I ask, is Cecil Carver?"

Doris just acted annoyed. "Leonard, don't tell me you don't know who Cecil Carver is. She's the sensation of the season, that's all. She came back from abroad this fall, and after one appearance at the Hippodrome the Philharmonic engaged her, and her recital at Carnegie was the biggest thing this year and she's under contract to the Metropolitan for next season—that's who Cecil Carver is. It would seem to me that you could keep up on things, a little bit."

"Well gee that sounds swell."

She came in that night, to thank me again for the flowers, and to say good night. I thought of my date with Cecil Carver for the next afternoon. What with one thing and another, I was beginning to feel a whole lot better.

4

It's one thing to start something like that, but it's something else to go through with it. I bought a tuning fork and some exercise books, went up on the third floor of the Craig-Borland Building, locked all the doors and put the windows down, and ha-ha-ha-ed every morning, hoping nobody would hear me. Then in the afternoon I'd go down and take a lesson, and make some payments. I liked paying better than learning, and I felt plenty like a fool. But then Cecil sent me over to Juilliard for a course in sight-reading, and I went in there with a lot of girls wearing thick glasses, and boys that looked like they'd have been better off for a little fresh air. It was taught by a Frenchman named Guizot, and along with the sight-reading he gave us a little harmony. When I found out that music has structure to it, just like a bridge has, right away I began to get interested. I took Guizot on for some private lessons, and began to work. He gave me exercises to do, melodies to harmonize, and chords to unscramble, and I rented a piano, and had that moved in, so I could hear what I was doing. I couldn't play it, but I could hit the chords, and that was the main thing. Then he talked to me about symphonies, and of course I had to dig into them. I bought a little phonograph, and a flock of symphony albums, and got the scores, and began to take them apart, so I could see how they were put together. The scores you don't buy, they cost too much. But I rented them, and first I'd have one for a couple of weeks, and then I'd have another. I found out there's plenty of difference between one symphony and another symphony. Beethoven, Mozart, and Brahms were the boys I liked. All three of them, they took themes that were simple, like an architectural figure but they could get cathedrals out of them, believe me they could.

The sight-reading was tough. It's something you learn easy when you're young, but to get it at the age of thirty-three isn't so easy. Do you know what it is? You just stand up there and read it, without any piano to give you the tune, or anything else. I never heard of it until Cecil began to talk about it, didn't even know what it meant. But I took it on, just like the rest of it, and beat intervals into my head with the piano until I could hear them in my sleep. After a while I knew I was making progress, but then when I'd go down to Cecil, and try to read something off while she played the accompaniment, I'd get all mixed up and have to stop. She spotted the reason for it. "You're not watching the words. You can read the exercises because all you have to think about is the music. But songs have words too, and you have to sing them. You can't just go la-la-la. Look at the words, don't look at the notes. Your eye will half see them without your looking at them, but the main thing is the words. Get them right and the music will sing itself."

It sounded wrong to me, because what I worried about was the notes, and it seemed to me I ought to look at them. But I tried the way she said, and sure enough it came a little better. I kept on with it, doing harder exercises all the time, and then one day I knew I wouldn't have to study sight-reading any more. I could read anything I saw, without even having to stop and think about keys, or sharps, or flats, or anything else, and that was the end of it. I could do it.

The ha-ha stuff was the worst. I did what Cecil told me, and she seemed satisfied, but to me it was just a pain in the neck. But then one day something happened. It was like a hair parted in my throat, and a sound came out of it that made me jump. It was like a Caruso record, a big, round high tone that shook the room. I tried it again, and it wouldn't come. I vocalized overtime that day, trying to get it back, and was about to give up when it came again. I opened it up, and stood there listening to it swell. Then I began going still higher with it. It got an edge on it, like a tenor, but at the same time it was big and round and full. I went up with it until I was afraid to go any higher, and then I checked pitch on the piano. It was an A.

That afternoon, Cecil was so excited by it she almost forgot about payment. "It's what I've been waiting for. But I had no idea it was that good."

"Say, it sounds great. How did you know it was there?"

"It's my business to know. What a baritone!"

"To hell with it. Come here."

" . . . . . . Sing me one more song."

All right, if you think I'm a sap, falling in love with my own voice so I could hardly wait to work it out every day, and going nuts about music so I just worked at it on a regular schedule, don't say I didn't warn you. And don't be too hard on me. Remember what I told you: there was not one other thing to do, from morning till night. Not one other thing in the world to do.

I had been at it three or four months when I found out how lousy Doris really was, and maybe that wasn't a kick. She couldn't read a note, I had found that out from listening to her work with Lorentz. But the real truth about her I found out by accident. Cecil was so pleased at the way I was coming along that she decided I ought to learn a role, and put me on Germont in Traviata, partly because there wasn't much of it, and partly because it was all lyric, and I'd have to throttle down on my tendency to beef, which seemed to be my main trouble at the time. That was on a Saturday, and I thought I'd surprise her by having the whole thing learned by Monday. But when I went around to Schirmer's to get the score, they were closed. It was early summer. I went home and then I happened to remember that Doris was studying it too, so I snitched it off the piano and took it up to the nursery and hid it. Then when she went off to a show that night, I went to bed with it.

I spent that night on the second act, and was just getting it pretty well in my head when I heard Doris come in and then go down again. And what does she do but begin singing Traviata down there, right in that part I had just been going over. Get how it was: she downstairs, singing the stuff, and me upstairs, in bed, holding the book on her. Well, it was murder. In the first place, she had no rhythm. I guess that was what had bothered me before, when I knew something was wrong, and didn't know what it was. To her, the music was just a string of phrases, and that was all. When she'd get through with one, she'd just go right on to the next one, without even a stop. I tried to hum my part, under my breath, in the big duet, and it couldn't be done. Her measures wouldn't beat. I mean, I'd still have two notes to sing, to fill out the measure on my part, and she'd already be on to the next measure on her part. I did nothing but stop and start, trying to keep up. And then, even within the phrase, she didn't get the notes right. If she had a string of eighth notes, she'd sing them dotted eighths and sixteenths, so it set your teeth on edge. And every time she came to a high note, she'd hold it whether there was a hold marked over it or not, and regardless of what the other voice was supposed to be doing. I lay there and listened to it, and got sorer by the minute. By that time I had a pretty fair idea of how good you've got to be in music before you're any good at all, and who gave her the right to high-hat me on her fine artistic soul, and then sing like that? Who said she had an artistic soul, the way she butchered a score? But right then I burst out laughing. That was it. She didn't have any artistic soul. All she had was a thirst for triumphs. And I, the sap, had fallen for it.

I heard her come in the bedroom, and hid the score under my pillow. She came in after a while, and she was stark naked, except for a scarf around her neck with a spray of orchids pinned to it. I knew then that something was coming. She walked around and then went over and stood looking out the window. "You better watch yourself. Catching cold is no good for the voice."

"It's so hot. I can't bear anything on."

"Don't stand too close to that window."

" . . . Remind me to call up Hugo for my Traviata score. I wanted it just now, and couldn't find it. He must have taken it."

"Wasn't that Traviata you were singing?"

"Oh, I know it, so far as that goes. But I hate to lose things . . . I was running over a little of it for Jack Leighton. He thinks he can get me on at the Cathedral. You know he owns some stock."

Jack Leighton was the guy she had gone to the theatre with, and one of her string. I had found out who they all were by watching Lorentz at her parties. He knew her a lot better than I did, Cecil was right about that, and it gave me some kind of a reverse-English kick to check up on her by watching his face while she'd be off in a corner making a date with some guy. Lorentz squirmed, believe me he did. I wasn't the only one.

"That would be swell."

"Of course, it's only a picture house, but it would be a week's work, and they don't pay badly. It would be *something* coming in. And it wouldn't be bad showmanship for them. After all—I am prominent."

"Socialite turns pro, hey?"

"Something like that. Except that by now I hope I can consider myself already a pro."

"That was Jack you went out with?"

"Yes . . . Was it all right to wear his orchids?"

"Sure. Why not?"

She went over and sat down. I was pretty sure the orchids were my cue to get sore, but I didn't. Another night I would have, but Traviata had done something to me. I knew now I was as good as she was, and even better, in the place where she had always high-hatted me, and knew that no matter what she said about the orchids, she couldn't get my goat. I even acted interested in them, the wrong way: "How many did he send?"

"Six. Isn't it a crime?"

"Oh well. He can afford them."

Her foot began to kick. I wasn't marching up to slaughter the way I always marched. She didn't say anything for a minute, and then she did something she never did in a fight with me, because I always saved her the trouble and did it first. I mean, she lost her temper. The regular way was for me to get sore, and the sorer I got, the more angelic, and sad, and persecuted she got. But this time it was different, and I could hear it in her voice when she spoke. "—Even if we can't."

"Why sure we can."

"Oh no we can't. No more, I'm sorry to say."

"If orchids are what it takes to make you happy, we can afford all you want to wear."

"How can we afford orchids, when I've pared our budget to the bone, and—"

"We got a budget?"

"Of course we have."

"First I heard of it."

"There are a lot of things you haven't heard of. I scrimp, and save, and worry, and still I'm so frightened I can hardly sleep at night. I only hope and pray that Jack Leighton can do something for me—even if he's like every other man, and wants his price."

"What price?"

"Don't you know?"

"Well, what the hell. He's human."

"Leonard! You can say that?"

"Sure."

"Suppose he demanded his price—and I paid it?"

"He won't."

"Why not, pray?"

"Because I outweigh him by forty pounds, and can beat hell out of him, and he knows it."

"You can lie there, and look at me, wearing another man's orchids, almost on my knees to him to give me work that we so badly need—you can actually take it that casually—"

She raved on, and her voice went to a kind of shrieking wail, and I did some fast thinking. When I said what I did about outweighing Jack, it popped into my mind that there was something funny about those orchids, and that it was a funny thing for him to do, send six orchids to Doris, even if I didn't outweigh him.

"And *you* won't."

"Don't be so sure. I'm getting desperate, and—"

"In the first place, you never paid any man his price, because you're not that much on the up-and-up with them. In the second place, if you want to pay it, you just go right ahead and pay. I won't pretend I'll like it, but I'm not going down on my knees to you about it. And in the third place, they're not his orchids."

"They're—what makes you say that?"

"I just happen to remember. When Jack called me up a while ago—"

"He—?"

"Oh yeah, he called me up. During the intermission. To tell me, in case I missed my cigarette case, that he had dropped it in his pocket by mistake."

It wasn't true. Jack hadn't called me up. But I knew Doris never went out during an intermission, and that Jack can't live a half hour without a smoke, so I took a chance. I could feel things breaking my way, and I meant to make the most of it.

"—And just as he hung up, he made a gag about the swell flowers I buy my wife. I had completely forgotten it until just this second."

"Leonard, how can you be so—"

"So you went out and ordered the orchids yourself, didn't you? And rubbed them in his face all night, just to make *him* feel like a bum. And now you come home and tell me he sent them, just to make *me* feel like a bum. . . . And it turns out we *can* afford them, doesn't it?"

"He meant to send some, he told me so—"

"He didn't."

"He did, he did, he *did!* And if I just felt I had to have something to cheer me up—"

"Suppose you go in and go to bed. And shut up. See if that will cheer you up."

She had begun parading around, and now she snapped on the light. "Leonard, you have a perfectly awful look on your face!"

"Yeah, I'm bored. Just plain bored. And to you, I guess a bored man does look pretty awful."

She went out and slammed the door with a terrific bang. It was the first time I had ever taken a decision over her. I pulled out Traviata again. It fell open to the place where Alfredo throws the money in Violetta's face, after she gets him all excited by pretending to be in love with somebody else. It crossed my mind that Alfredo was a bit of a cluck.

5

It was early in October that I got the wire from Rochester. It had been a lousy summer. In August, Doris took the children up to the Adirondacks, and I wanted to go, but I hated the way she would have asked for separate rooms. So I stayed home, and learned two more roles, and played around with Cecil. I got a letter from Doris, after she had been up there a week, saying Lorentz was there too, because of course she couldn't even write a letter without putting something in it to make you feel rotten. The Lorentz part, it wasn't so good, but I gritted my teeth and hung on. She came home, and around the end of September Cecil went away. She was booked for a fall tour, and wouldn't be back until November. I was surprised how I missed her, and how the music wasn't much fun without her. Then right after that, Doris went away again. She was to sing in Wilkes-Barre. That was a phoney, of course, and all it amounted

to was that she had friends there that belonged to some kind of
a tony breakfast club, and they had got her invited to sing there.
The day after she left, I got the telegram from Cecil, dated
Rochester:

MY TENOR HAS GOT THE PIP STOP IF YOU LOVE
ME FOR GOD'S SAKE HOP ON A PLANE QUICK AND
COME UP HERE STOP BRING OLD ITALIAN ANTHOL-
OGIES ALSO OLD ENGLISH ALSO SOME OPERATIC
STUFF ESPECIALLY PAGLIACCI TRAVIATA FACTO-
TUM AND MASKED BALL ALSO CUTAWAY COAT GRAY
PANTS FULL EVENING SOUP AND FISH AND PLENTY
OF CLEAN SHIRTS STOP LOVE

CECIL

It caught me at the office about ten in the morning, and the mes-
senger waited, and as soon as I read it my heart began to pump,
not from excitement, but from fear. Because up to then it had
been just a gag, anyway on my end of it. But this brought me face
to face with it: Did I mean it enough to get up before people and
sing, or not? I stood there looking at it, and then I thought, well
what the hell? I called the Newark airport, found they had a plane
leaving around noon, and made a reservation. Then I wrote a wire
to Doris telling her I had been called out of town on business,
and another one to Cecil, telling her I'd be there. Then I grabbed
all the music I might need, went over to the bank and drew some
money, hustled up to the house and packed, and grabbed a cab.

She met me at the airport, kissed me, and bundled me into a car
she had waiting. "It was sweet of you to come. My but I'm glad
to see you."

"Me too."

"Terribly glad."

"But what happened? I didn't even know you had a tenor."

"Oh, you have to have an assistant artist, to give a little variety. Sometimes the accompanist fills in with some Liebestraum, but my man won't play solo. So I let the music bureau sell me a tenor. He was no good. He was awful in Albany, and he got the bird last night in Buffalo, so when he turned up this morning with a cold I got terribly alarmed for his precious throat and sent him home. That's all."

"What's the bird?"

"Something you'll never forget, if you ever hear it."

"Suppose they give *me* the bird?"

We had been riding along on the back seat, her hand in mine, just two people that were even gladder to see each other than they knew they were going to be, and I expected her to laugh and say something about my wonderful voice, and how they would never give *me* the bird. She didn't. She took her hand away, and we rode a little way without saying anything, and then she looked me all over, like she was measuring everything I had. "Then I'll have to get somebody else."

"Yeah?"

" . . . They *can* give you the bird."

"Hey, let's talk about something pleasant."

"It's a tough racket."

"Maybe I better go home."

"They can give you the bird, and they can give it to anybody. I think you'll win, but you've got to win, don't make any mistake about that. You've got to lam it in their teeth and make them like it."

"So."

"You can go home if you want to, and if that's how you feel about it, you'd better. But if you do, you're licked for good."

"I'm here. I'll give it a fall."

"Look at me now."

"I'm looking."

"Don't let that applause fool you, when you come on. They're a pack of hyenas, they're always a pack of hyenas, just waiting to tear in and pull out your vitals, and the only way you can keep them back is to lick them. It's a battle, and you've got to win.

"When is the concert?"

"Tonight."

"Ouch."

"Did you hear me?"

"I heard you."

When we got to the hotel I took a room and sent up my stuff, and then we went up to her suite. A guy was there, reading a newspaper. "Mr. Wilkins, who plays our accompaniments. Mr. Borland, Ray. Our baritone."

We shook hands, and he fished some papers out of his pocket. "The printer's proofs of the program. It came while you were out, Cecil. He's got to have it back, with corrections, by five o'clock. I don't see anything, but you better take a look at it."

She passed one over to me. It gave me a funny feeling, just to look at it. I've still got that proof, and here it is, in case you're interested, [see below]:

JOHN FREDERICK JEVONS

PRESENTS

Miss Cecil Carver

SOPRANO

In a Song Recital

AT

THE EASTMAN THEATRE

Thursday Evening, October 5, at 8:30
Leonard Borland, Baritone
Ray Wilkins, Accompanist

Cavatina

ROSSINI

Fac Ut Portern Christi Mortem,
from the Stabat Mater
Miss Carver

Three Songs from the 17th Century

CARISSIMI   *Vittoria, Mio Core*

SCARLATTI,
A.   *O Cessate Di Piagarmi*

CALDARA   *Come Raggio Di Sol*

Mr. Borland

Songs
Brahms

Der Schmied
Von Eviger Liebe
An Die Nachtigall

Miss Carver

Songs
SCHUBERT   *Halt*
Auf Dem Flusse
Der Wetterfahne
Gretchen Am Spinnrade
Miss Carver

Intermission

Aria
MOZART   *Batti, Batti*
                    From Don Giovanni
                    Miss Carver
Aria
VERDI   *Eri Tu*
                    From Un Ballo In Maschera (Preceded
                    by the Recitative, *Alzati! La Tuo Figlio)*

                    Mr. Borland

Songs from the British Isles
CAREY   *Sally in Our Alley*
MOORE   *Oft in the Stilly Night*
BAYLY   *Gaily the Troubadour*
MARZIALS   *The Twickenham Ferry*

                    Miss Carver

Songs of the Southwest
                    Billy the Kid
                    Green Grow the Lilacs
                    The Trail to Mexico
                    Lay Down, Dogies
                    Strawberry Roan
                    I'd Like to Be in Texas
                    Miss Carver
                    The piano is a Steinway

"It's all right, pretty nifty. Except that Leonard Borland is gradually on purpose going to turn into Logan Bennett."

"Oh, yes. I meant to ask you about that. Yes, I think that's better. Will you change it, Ray? On the proof that goes to the printer. And make sure it's changed on all his groups."

"I only sing twice?"

"That's all. Did you bring the music I said?"

"Right here in the briefcase."

"Give it to Ray, so he can go over it. He always plays from memory. He never brings music on stage."

"I see."

"You'll attend to the program, Ray?"

"I'm taking it over myself."

Wilkins left, she had me ha-ha for ten minutes, then said my voice was up and stopped me. Some sandwiches and milk came up. "They fed us on the plane. I'm not hungry."

"You better eat. You don't get any dinner."

" . . . No dinner?"

"You always sing on an empty stomach. We'll have some supper later."

I tried to eat, and couldn't get much down. Seeing that program made me nervous. When I had eaten what I could, she told me to go in and sleep. "A fat chance I could sleep."

"Lie down, then. Be quiet. No walking around, no vocalizing. That's one thing you can learn. Don't leave your concert in the hotel room."

I went in my room, took off my clothes, and lay down. Somewhere downstairs I could hear Wilkins at the piano, going over the Italian songs. It made me sick to my stomach. None of it was turning out the way I thought it was going to. I had expected a kind of a cock-eyed time, with both of us laughing over what a joke it was that I should be up here, singing with her. Instead of that she was as cold as a woman selling potatoes, and over something I didn't really care about. There didn't seem to be any fun in it.

I must have slept, though, because I had put a call in for seven o'clock, and when it came it woke me up. I went in the bathroom, took a quick shower, and started to dress. My fingers trembled so bad I could hardly get the buttons in my shirt. About a quarter to eight I rang her. She seemed friendly, more like her usual self, and told me to come in.

A hotel maid let me in. Cecil was just finishing dressing, and in a minute or two she came out of the bedroom. She had on a chiffon velvet dress, orange-colored, with salmon-colored belt and salmon-colored shoes. It had a kind of Spanish look to it, and was probably what she had always been told she ought to wear with her eyes, hair, and complexion, and yet it was heavy and stuffy, and made her look exactly like an opera singer all dressed up to give a concert. It startled me, because I had been married for so long to a woman that knew all there was to know about dressing that I had forgotten what frumps they can make of themselves when they really try. She saw my look and glanced in the mirror. "What's the matter?"

"Nothing."

"Don't I look right?"

"Sure."

She told the maid to go, and then she kept looking at herself in the mirror, and then at me again, but when she lit a cigarette and sat down she wasn't friendly any more. " . . . All right, we'll check over what you're to do."

"I'm listening."

"First, when you come on."

"Yeah, I've been wondering about that. What do I do?"

"At all recitals, the singer comes on from the right, that is, stage right. Left, to the audience. Walk straight out from the wings, past the piano to the center of the stage. Be quick and brisk about it. Be aware of them, but don't look at them till you get there. By that time they'll start to applaud."

"Suppose they don't?"

"If you come on right, they will. That's part of it. I told you, it's a battle, and it starts the moment you show your face. You've got to make them applaud, and that means you've got to come on right. You go right to the center of the stage, stop, face them, and bow. Bow once, from the hips, as though you meant it."

"O. K., what then?"

"You bow once, but no more. If it's a friendly house, they may applaud quite a little, but not enough for more than one bow. Besides, it's only a welcome. You haven't done anything yet to warrant more than one bow, and if you begin grinning around, you'll look silly, like some movie star being gracious to his public."

"All right, I got that. What next?"

"Then you start to sing."

"Do I give Wilkins a sign or something?"

"I'll come to that, but I'm not done yet about how you come on. Look pleasant, but don't paste any death house smile on your face, don't look sheepish, as though you thought it was a big joke, don't try to look more confident than you really are. Above all, look as though you meant business. They came to hear you sing, and as long as you act as though that's what you're there for, you'll be all right, and you don't have to kid them with some kind of phoney act. If you look nervous, that's all right, you're supposed to be nervous. Have you got that? *Mean* it."

"All right, I got it."

"When you finish your song, stop. If the piano has the actual finish, hold everything until the last note has been played, no

matter whether they break in with applause or not. Hold everything, then relax. Don't do any more than that, just in your own
mind relax. If you've done anything with the song at all, they
ought to applaud. When they do, bow. Bow straight to the center.
Then take a quarter turn on your feet, and bow to the left. Then
turn again, and bow to the right. Then walk off. As quickly as you
can get to the wings without actually running, walk off."

"The way I came on?"

"Right back the way you came on."

"All right, what then?"

"Are you sure you've got that all straight?"

"Wait a minute. Do I do that after every song, or—"

"No, no, no! Not after every song. At the end of your group.
You don't leave the stage after every song. There won't be much
applause at the end of your first two songs, they only applaud the
group. Bow once after the first song, and when the applause has
died down, start the second, and then on with the third."

"All right, I got it now."

"If the applause continues, go out, exactly as you went out the
first time, and bow three times, first center, then left, then right,
then come off."

"Go ahead. What else?"

"Now about the accompanist. Most singers turn and nod to
the accompanist when they are ready, but to my mind it's just
one more thing that slows it up, that adds to the chill that hangs
over a recital anyway. That's why I have Wilkins. He can feel that
audience as well as the singer can, and he knows exactly when
it's time to start. Another thing about him is that he plays from
memory, has no music to fool with, and so he can watch you the
whole time you sing. That gives you better support, and it helps
you in another way. They don't really notice him, but they feel
him there, and when he can't take his eyes off you, they think

you must be pretty good. You wait for him. While you're waiting, look them over. Use those five seconds to get acquainted.
Look them over in a friendly way, but don't smirk at them. Be
sure you look up at the balcony, and all over the house, so they
all feel you're singing to them, and not to just a few. Use that
time to get the feel of the house, to project yourself out there,
even if it's just a little bit."

"Must be a swell five seconds."

"I'm trying to get it through your head that it's a battle, that it's
a tough spot at best, and that you have to use every means to win."

"All right. I hear what you say."

"Now go in the bedroom, and come out and do it. I want to
see you go through it all. The center of the stage is over by the
window, and I'm the audience."

I went in the bedroom, then came out and did like she said.
"You came on too slow, and your bow is all wrong. Shake the lead
out of your feet. And bow from the hips, bow low, as though you
meant it. Don't just stand there jerking your head up and down."

I went in and did it over again. "That's better, but you're still much
too perfunctory about it. You're not a business man, getting up to give
a little talk at the Engineers' Club. You're a singer, getting ready to put
on a show, and there's got to be some formality about it."

"Can't I just act natural?"

"If you act natural, you'll look just like what you are, a contractor that thinks he looks like a fool. Can't you understand what I
mean? This is a concert, not a meeting to open bids."

I did it all over again, and felt like some kind of a tin soldier
on hinges, but she seemed satisfied. "It's a little stiff, but anyway
it's how it's done. Now do it three or four more times, so you get
used to it."

I did it about ten times, and then she stopped me. "And now one
more thing. That first number, *Vittoria, Mio Core*, I picked out for

you to begin with because it's a good lively tune and you can race through with it without having to worry about fine effects. After that you ought to be all right. But don't forget that it has no introduction. He'll give you one chord, for pitch, and then you start."

"Sure, I know."

"You know, but be ready. One chord. One chord, and as soon as you have the pitch clear in your head, start. Don't let it catch you by surprise."

"I won't."

We had another cigarette, and didn't say much. I looked at the palms of my hands. They were wet. Wilkins came in. "Taxi's waiting."

We put on our coats, went down, got in the cab. There was a little drizzle of rain. "The Eastman Theatre. Stage entrance."

The stage was all set for the recital, with a big piano out there, and a drop back of it. There was a hole in the drop, so we could look out. First she would look, and then I would look. Wilkins found a chair, and read the afternoon paper. She kept looking up. "Balcony's filling. It's a sell-out."

But I wasn't looking at the balcony. All I could see was those white shirts, marching down into the orchestra. Rochester is a musical town, and formal, and a lot of those white shirts, they had those dreamy faces over top of them, with curly moustaches, that meant musician. They meant musician, and they meant tony musician, and they scared me to death. I don't know what I expected. Anybody that lives in New York gets to thinking that any town north of the Harlem River is out in the sticks, and I must have been looking for a flock of country club boys and their wives, or something, but not this. My mouth began to feel dry. I went over to the cooler and had a drink, but I kept swallowing.

At 8:25 a stagehand went out and closed the top of the piano. He came back and another herd of white shirts came down the aisle. They were hurrying now. Wilkins took out his watch, held it up to Cecil. "Ready?"

"All right."

We all three went to the wings, stage right. He raised his hand. "One—two"—then lifted his foot and gave her a little kick in the tail. She swept out there like she owned the place and the whole block it was built on. There was a big hand. She bowed once, the way she had told me to do, and then stood there, looking up, down, and around, a little friendly smile coming on her face every time she warmed up a new bunch, while he was playing the introduction to the Rossini. Then she started to sing. It was the first time I had heard her in public. Well, I didn't need any critic to tell me she was good. She stood there, smiling around, and then, as the introduction stopped, she turned grave, and seemed to get taller, and the first of it came out, low and soft. It was Latin, and she made it sound dramatic. And she made every syllable so distinct that I could even understand what it meant, though it was all of fifteen years since I had had my college Plautus. Then she got to the part where there are a lot of sustained notes, and her voice began to swell and throb so it did things to you. Up to then I hadn't thought she had any knockout of a voice, but I had never heard it when it was really working. Then she came to the fireworks at the end, and you knew there really was a big leaguer in town. She finished, and there was a big hand. Wilkins came off, wiped his hands on his handkerchief. She bowed center, left, and right, and came off. She listened. The applause kept up. She went out and bowed three times again. She came off, stood there and listened, then shook her head. The applause stopped, and she looked at me. "All right, baby. Here's your kick for luck."

She kicked me the way Wilkins had kicked her. He put the handkerchief in his pocket, raised his hand. "One—two—"

I aimed for the center of the stage, got there, and bowed, the way I had practiced. They gave me a hand. Then I looked up, and tried to do what she had told me to do, look them over, top, bottom, and around. But all I could see was faces, faces, faces, all staring at me, all trying to swim down my throat. Then I began to think about that first number, and the one chord I would get, and how I had to be ready. I stood there, and it seemed so long I got a panicky feeling he had forgotten to come out, and that there wouldn't be any opening chord. Then I heard it, and right away started to sing:

> *Vittoria, vittoria,*
> *Vittoria, vittoria, mio core;*
> *Non lagrimar più, non lagrìmar più,*
> *E sciolta d'amore la vil servitù!*

My voice sounded so big it startled me, and I tried to throttle it down, and couldn't. There's no piano interludes in that song. It goes straight through, for three verses, at a hell of a clip, and the more I tried to pull in, and get myself under some kind of control, the louder it got, and the faster I kept going, until at the finish Wilkins had a hard time keeping up with me. They gave me a little bit of a hand, and I didn't want to bow, I wanted to apologize, and explain that that wasn't the way it was supposed to go. But I bowed, some kind of way.

Then came the *O Cessate*. It's short, and ought to start soft, lead up to a crescendo in the middle, and die away at the end. I was so rung up by then I couldn't sing soft if I tried. I started it, and my voice bellowed all over the place, and it was terrible. There was a bare ripple after that, and Wilkins went into the opening of the *Come Raggio*. That's another that opens soft, and I sang it soft for about two measures, and then I exploded like some radio when you turn it up too quick. After that it was a hog-calling contest. Wilkins saw it was hopeless, and came down on the loud pedal so it would maybe sound as though that was the way it was supposed to go, and a fat chance we could fool that audience. I finished, and on the pianissimo at the end it sounded like a locomotive whistling for a curve. When it was over there was a little scattering of applause, and I bowed. I bowed center, and took the quarter turn to bow to the side. The applause stopped. I kept right on turning and walked off stage.

She was there in the wings, a murderous look on her face. "You've flopped!"

"All right, I've flopped."

"Damn it, you've—"

But Wilkins grabbed her by the arm. "Do you want to lose them for good? Get out there, get out there, get out there!"

She stopped in the middle of a cussword and went on, smiling like nothing had happened at all.

I tried to explain to her in the intermission what had ailed me, but she kept walking away from me, there behind the drop. It wasn't until I saw her blotting her eyes with a handkerchief, to keep the mascara from running down her cheeks, that I knew she was crying. "Well—I'm sorry I ruined your concert."

" . . . Oh well. It's a turkey anyhow."

"I didn't do it any good."

"They're as cold as dead fish. There's nothing to do about it. You didn't ruin it."

"Was that the bird?"

"Oh no. You don't know the half of it yet."

"Oh."

"Did you have to blast them out of their seats?"

"I've been telling you. I was nervous."

"After all I've told you about not bellowing. And then you have to—what did you think you were doing, announcing trains?"

"Maybe I'd better go home."

"Maybe you'd better."

"Shall I do this other number?"

"As you like."

She did the Mozart, and took an encore, and came off. Wilkins had heard us rowing, and looked at me, and motioned me on. She went off to her dressing room without looking at me. I went out there. There were one or two handclaps, and I made my bow, and then paid no more attention to them at all. I felt sick and disgusted. He struck the opening chord and I started the recitative. There's a lot of it, and I sang it just mechanically. After two or three phrases I heard a murmur go over the house, and if that was the bird I didn't care. I got to the end of the recitative, and then stepped back a little while he played the introduction to the aria. I heard him mumble, so I could just hear him above the triplets: "You got 'em. Just look noble now, and it's in the bag."

It hit me funny. It relaxed me, and it was just what I needed. I tried to look noble, and I don't know if I did or not, but all the time my voice was coming nice and easy. We got to the end of the first strain, and he really began to go places with the lead into the next. It was the first time all night the piano had really had much to do, and it came over me all of a sudden that the guy was one hell of an accompanist, and that it was a pleasure to sing with him. I went into the next strain, and really made it drip. There was a little break, and I heard him say, "Swell, keep it up." I was nearly to the high G. I took the little leading phrase nice and light, and hit it right on the nose. It felt good, and I began to let it swell. Then I remembered about not yelling, and throttled it back, and finished the phrase under nice control. There wasn't much more, and when I hit the high F at the end, it was just right.

For a second or so after he struck the last chord it was as still as

death. Then some guy in the balcony yelled. My heart skipped a
beat, but then others began to yell, and what they were yelling was
bravo. The applause broke out in a roar then, and I remembered
to bow. I bowed center, right, and left, and then I walked off.
She was there, and kissed me. Wilkins whipped out his handkerchief, wiped the lipstick off my mouth, and shoved me out there
again. I bowed three times again, and hated to leave. When I came
back she nodded, told Wilkins to go out with me this time for an
encore. "Yeah, but what the hell is his encore?"

"Let him do Traviata."

"O. K."

I went out, and he started Traviata. Now *Di Provenza Il Mar* I
guess is the worst sung aria you ever hear, because the boys always
think about tone and forget about the music, and that ruins it. I
mean they don't sing it smooth, with all the notes even, and that
makes it jerky, and takes all the sadness out of it. But it's a cake-
walk for me, because I think I told you about all that work I did
on music, and it seemed to me that I kind of knew what old man
Verdi was trying to do with it when he wrote it. Wilkins started it,
and he played it slower than Cecil had been playing it, and I no
sooner heard it than I knew that was right too. I took it just the
way he had cued me. I just rocked it along, and kept every note
even, and didn't beef at all. When I got to the G flat, I held it, then
let it swell a little, but only enough to come in right on the forte
that follows it, and then on the finish I loaded it with all the tears
of the world. You ought to have heard the bravos that time. I went
out and took more bows, and it was no trouble to look them in
the eye that time. They seemed like the nicest people in the world.

At the end, after she had finished a flock of encores, Cecil took
me out for a bow with her, and then my flowers came up, and she
pinned one on me, and they clapped some more, and she had me

do a duet with her, "*Crudel, Perché, Finora,*" from the Marriage of Figaro. It went so well they wanted more, but she rang down and the three of us went out to eat. Wilkins and I were pretty excited, but she didn't have much to say. When she went out to powder her nose, he started to laugh. "They're all alike, aren't they?"

"How do you mean, all alike?"

"I thought she was a little different, at first. Letting you take that encore, and singing a duet with you, that looked kind of decent. And then I got the idea, somehow, that she liked you. I mean for your sex appeal, or whatever it is that they go for. But you see how she's acting, don't you? They're all alike. Opera singers are the dumbest, pettiest, vainest, cruelest, egotisticalest, jealousest breed of woman you can find on this man's earth, or any man's earth. You did too good, that's all. Two bits that tomorrow morning you're on your way back."

"I think you're wrong."

"I'm not wrong. First the tenor stinks and then the baritone don't stink enough."

"Not Cecil."

"Just Cecil, the ravishing Cecil."

"Something's eating on her, but I don't think it's that."

"You'll see."

"All right, I'll match your two bits."

We got back to the hotel, Wilkins went to his room, and I went up with her for a goodnight cigarette. She snapped on the lights, then went over to the mirror and stood looking at herself. "What's the matter with the dress?"

"Nothing."

"There's something."

" . . . It's all wrong."

"I paid enough for it. It came from one of the best shops in New York."

"I guess one of the best shops in New York wouldn't have some lousy Paris copy they would wish off on a singer that didn't know any better. . . . It makes you look like a gold plush sofa. It makes that bozoom look like some dairy, full of Grade A milk for the kiddies. It makes you look about ten years older. It makes you look like an opera singer, all dressed up to screech."

"Isn't the bozoom all right?"

"The bozoom, considered simply as a bozoom, is curviform, exciting, and even distinguished. But for God's sake never dress for anything like that, even if you're secretly stuck on it, which I think you are. That's what a telephone operator does, when she puts on a yoo-hoo blouse. Or a chorus girl, wearing a short skirt to show her legs. Dress the woman, not the shape."

"Did you learn that from her?"

"Anyway I learned it."

She sat down, and kept on looking at the velvet, and fingering it. "All right, I'm a hick."

I went over and sat down beside her and took her hand. "You're not a hick, and you're not to feel that way about it. You asked me, didn't you? You wanted to know. Just to sit there, and keep on saying the dress was all right, when you knew I didn't think so—that wouldn't have been friendly, would it? And what is it? You haven't been yourself tonight."

"I'm a hick. I know I'm a hick, and I don't try to make anybody think any different. You or anybody. . . . I haven't had time to learn how to dress. I've spent my life in studios and hotels and theatres and concert halls and railroad trains, and I've spent most of it broke—until here recently—and all of it working. If you think that teaches you the fine points of dressing, you're mistaken. It doesn't teach you anything, except how tough everything is. And she, she's done nothing all her life but look at herself in a mirror, and—"

"What's she got to do with it?"

"—And study herself, and take all the time she needs to find the exact thing that goes with her, and make some man pay for it, and—all right, she can dress. I know she can dress. I don't have to be told. No woman would have to be told. And—all right, you wanted to know what she's got, I'll tell you what she's got. She's got class, so when she says hop, you—*jump!* And I haven't got it. All right, I know I haven't got it. But was that any reason for you to look at me that way?"

"Is that why you fought with me?"

"Wasn't it enough? As though I was some poor thing that you felt sorry for. That you felt—*ashamed of!* You've never felt ashamed of her, have you?"

"Nor of you."

"Oh, yes. You were ashamed tonight. I could see it in your eye. Why did you have to look at me that way?"

"I wasn't ashamed of you, I was proud of you. Even when you were quarreling with me, back there during the intermission, the back of my head was proud of you. Because it was your work, and there was no fooling around about it, even with me. Because you were a pro at your trade, and were out there to win, no matter whose feelings got hurt. And now you try to tell me I was ashamed of you."

She dropped her head on my shoulder and started to cry. "Oh Leonard, I feel like hell."

"What about? All this is completely imaginary."

"Oh no it isn't. . . . The tenor was all right. He wasn't much good, but I could have done with him, once he got over his cold. I wanted you up here, don't you see? I was so glad to see you, and then I didn't want you to see it, for fear you wouldn't want me to be that glad. And I tried to be businesslike, and I was doing fine—and then you looked at me that way. And then I swallowed that down, because I knew I didn't care how you looked at me, so long as you were here. And then—you flopped. And I knew you weren't just a tenor that would put up with anything for a job. I knew you'd go back, and I was terrified, and furious at you. And then you sang the way *I* wanted you to sing, and I loved you so much I wanted to go out there and hold on to you while you sang the other one. And now you know. Oh no, it's not just imaginary. What have *you* got?"

I held her tight, and patted her cheek, and tried to think of something to say. There wasn't anything to say, not about what she was talking about. I had got so fond of her that I loved every minute I spent with her, and yet there was only one woman that meant to me what she wanted to mean to me, and that was Doris. She could torture me all she wanted to, she could be a phoney and make a fool of me all over town with other men, and yet Cecil had hit it: when she said hop, I jumped.

"*I* know what you've got. You've got big hard shoulders, and shaggy hair, and you're a man, and you build bridges, and to you this is just some kind of foolish tiddle-de-winks game that you play until it's time to go to work. And that's just what it is to me! I don't want to be a singer. I want to be a woman!"

"If I'm a man, you made me one."

"Oh yes, that's the hell of it. It's mostly tiddle-de-winks, but it's partly building yourself up to her level, so you're not afraid of her any more. And that's what I'm helping you at. Making a man out of you, so she can have you. . . . I feel like hell. I could go right out that window."

I held her a long time, then, and she stopped crying, and began to play with my hair. "All right, Leonard. I've been rotten, and a poor sport to say anything about it at all, because this isn't how it was supposed to come out—and now I'll stop. I'll be good, and not talk any more about it, and try to give you a pleasant trip. It's a little fun, isn't it, out here playing tiddle-de-winks?"

"It is with you."

"Wouldn't they be surprised, all your friends at the Engineers' Club, if they could see you?"

I wanted to cry, but she wanted me to laugh, so I did, and held her close, and kissed her. "You sang like an angel, and I'm terribly proud of you, and—that's right. Hold me close."

I held her close a long time, and then she started to laugh. It was a real cackle, over something that had struck her funny, I could see that. " . . . What is it?"

"You."

"Tonight? At the hall?"

"Yes."

"?"

But she just kept right on laughing, and didn't tell me what it was about. Later on, though, I found out.

6

We sang Syracuse, Cincinnati, and Columbus after that, the same program, and I did all right. She paid my hotel bills, and offered me $50 a night on top of that, but I wouldn't take anything. I was surprised at the reviews I got. Most of them wrote her up, and let me out with a line, but a few of them called me "the surprise of the evening," said I had a voice of "rare power and beauty," and spoke of the "sweep and authority" of my singing. I didn't exactly know what they meant, and it was the first time I knew there was anything like that about me, but I liked them all right and saved them all.

The Columbus concert was on a Thursday, and after we closed with the duet again, and took our bows, and went off, a little wop in gray spats followed her into her dressing room and stayed there quite a while. Then he left and we went out to eat. I was pretty hungry, and I hadn't liked waiting. "Who was your pretty boy friend?"

"That was Mr. Rossi."

"And who is Mr. Rossi?"

"General secretary, business agent, attorney, master of the hounds, bodyguard, scout, and chief cook-and-bottle-washer to Cesare Pagano."

"And who is Cesare Pagano?"

"He's the American Scala Opera Company, the only impresario in the whole history of opera that ever made money out of it."

"And?"

"I'm under contract to them, you know. For four weeks, beginning Monday. After that I go back to New York to get ready for the Metropolitan."

"No, I didn't know."

"I didn't say anything about it."

"Then after tonight I'm fired. Is that it?"

"No. I didn't say anything about it, because I thought I might have a surprise for you. I've been wiring Pagano about you, and wiring him and wiring him—and tonight he sent Rossi over. Rossi thinks you'll do."

"*What?* Me sing in grand opera?"

"Well what did you think you were learning those roles for?"

"I don't know. Just for something to do. Just so I could come down and see you. Just—to see if I could do it. Hell, I never *been* to a grand opera."

"Anyway, I closed with him."

It turned out I was to get $125 a week, which was upped $25 from what he had offered, and that was what they were arguing about. I was to get transportation, pay my own hotel bills, and have a four-week contract, provided I did all right on my first appearance. It sounded so crazy to me I didn't know what to say, and then something else popped in my head. "What about this grand opera, anyway? Do they—dress up or something?"

"Why of course. There's costumes, and scenery—just like any other show."

"*Me*—put on funny clothes and get out there and—do I have to paint up my face?"

"You use make-up, of course."

"It's out."

But then when I asked her what she got, and she said $400 a night, and that she had taken a cut from $500, I knew perfectly well that that was part of what they had been arguing about too, that she had taken that cut to get me in, so I could be with her, and that kind of got me. I thought it was the screwiest thing I had ever heard of, but I finally said yes.

If you think a concert is tough, don't ever try grand opera. I hear it's harder to go out there all alone, with only a piano to play your accompaniments and no scenery to help you out, and I guess it is, when you figure the fine points. But if you've never even heard of the fine points yet, and you're not sure you can even do it at all, you stick to something simple. Remember what I'm telling you: lay off grand opera.

We hit Chicago the next day, just the two of us, because Wilkins went back to New York after the Columbus concert. The first thing we did, after we got hotel rooms, was go around to the costumer's. That's a swell place. There's every kind of costume you ever heard of, hanging on hooks, like people that have just been lynched, from white flannel tenor suits with brass buttons up the front, to suits of armor, to naval uniforms, to cowboy clothes, to evening clothes and silk hats. It's all dark, and dusty, and shabby, and about as romantic as a waxworks.

They were opening in Bohème Monday night, and we were both in it, and that meant the first thing we had to get was the Marcel stuff. She already had her costumes, you understand. This was all on account of me. Marcel was the character I was to sing in the opera, the baritone role. There wasn't any trouble about him. I mean, they didn't have to make any stuff to order, because a pair of plaid pants, a velvet smoking jacket of a coat, and a muffler and floppy hat for the outdoor stuff, were all I had to have. They had that stuff, and I tried it on, and it was all right, and they set it aside. But when it came to the Rigoletto stuff, and they opened a book and showed me a picture of what I would have to have, I almost broke for the station right there. I knew he was supposed to be some kind of a hump-backed jester, but that I would have to come out in a foolish-looking red suit, and actually wear cap and bells, that never once entered my mind.

"I really got to wear that outfit?"

"Why of course."

"My God."

She paid hardly any attention to me, and went on talking with the costumer. "He has to sing it Wednesday, and he'll have no chance for a fitting Monday. Can you fit Tuesday and deliver Wednesday?"

"Absolutely, Miss. We guarantee it."

"Remember to fit over the hump."

"We'll even measure over the hump. I think he'd better put a hump on right now. By the way, has he got a hump?"

"No, he'll have to get one."

"We have two types of hump. One that goes on with straps, the other with elastic fabric fastenings, adjustable. I recommend the elastic fabric, myself. It's more comfortable, stays in place better, doesn't interfere with breathing—"

"I think that's better."

So I put on a hump, and got measured for the monkey suit. Then it turned out that for two of the acts I would have to have dark stuff, and a cape, and another floppy hat. They argued whether the Bohème hat wouldn't do, and finally decided it would. Then we tried on capes. The one that seemed to be elected hiked up in back, on account of the hump, but the costumer thought I ought to take it, just the same. "We could make you a special one, to hang even all around, but if you take my advice, you'll have this one. That little break in the line won't make much difference, and then, if you have a cape that really fits *you*, without that hump I mean, you can use it in other operas—Lucia, Trovatore, Don Giovanni, you know what I mean? A nice operatic cape comes in handy any time, and—"

"O. K. I'll take that one."

Then it turned out I would have to have a red wig, and we tried wigs on. When we got around to the Traviata stuff I didn't even have the heart to look, and ordered blind. Anything short of a hula skirt, I thought, would be swell. Then it seemed I had to have a trunk, a special kind, and we got that. I'd hate to tell you what all that stuff cost. We came out of there with the Marcel stuff, the wig, the hump, the cape, and a make-up kit done up in two big boxes, the other stuff to come. When we got back to the hotel we went up and I dumped the stuff down on the floor. "What's the matter, Marcellino? Don't you feel well?"

"I feel lousy."

There's no rehearsals for principals in the American Scala. You know your stuff or you don't get hired. But I was a special case, and Pagano wasn't taking any chances on me. He posted a call for the whole Boheme cast to take me through it Sunday afternoon, and maybe you think that wasn't one sore bunch of singers that showed up at two o'clock. The men were all Italians, and they wanted to go to a pro football game that was being played that afternoon. The only other woman in the cast, the one that sang Musetta, was an American, and she was sore because she was supposed to give a lecture in a Christian Science temple, and had to cancel it. They couldn't get the theatre, for some reason, so we did it downstairs in the new cocktail lounge of the hotel, that they didn't use on Sundays. Rossi put chairs around to show doors, windows, and other stuff in the set, took the piano, and started off. The rest of them paid no attention to him at all, or to me. They knew Bohème frontwards, backwards, and sidewise, and they sat around with their hats on the back of their heads, working crossword puzzles in the Sunday paper. When it came time for them to come in they came in without even looking up. Cecil acted just like the others. She didn't work puzzles, but she read a book. Every now and then a tall, disgusted-looking Italian would walk through and walk out again. I asked who he was, and they told me Mario, the conductor. He looked like if he had to listen to me much longer he would get an acute case of the colic. It was all as cheerful as cold gravy with grease caked on the top.

Rossi rehearsed me until I swear blood was running out of my nose, throat, and eyeballs. I never got enough pep in it to suit him. I had always thought grand opera was a slow, solemn, kind of dignified show, but the way he went about it it was a race between some sprinter and a mechanical rabbit. I was surprised how bad the others sounded. It didn't seem to me any of them had enough voice to crush a grape.

Monday I tried to keep quiet and not think about it, but it was one long round of costumes, phone calls, and press releases. I was still singing under the name of Bennett, and when they called me down to give them some stuff about myself to go out to the papers, I was stumped. I wasn't going to say who I really was. I gave them the biography of an uncle that came from Missouri, and went abroad to study medicine. Instead of the medical stuff in Germany, I made it musical stuff in Italy, and it seemed to get by all right. Around six-thirty, when I had just laid down, and thought I could relax a few minutes and get myself a little bit in hand, the phone rang and Cecil said it was time to go. We had to go early, because she had to make me up.

When we went in the stage door of the Auditorium Theatre that night, and I got my first look at that stage, I almost fainted. What I had felt in Rochester was nothing compared to this. In the first place, I had never had any idea that a stage could be that big, and still be a stage and not a blimp hangar. You only see about half of it from out front. The rest of it stretches out through the wings, and back, and up overhead, until you'd think there wasn't any end of it. In the second place, it was all full of men, and monkey wrenches, and scenery going up on pulleys, and noise, so you'd think nobody could possibly sing on it, and be heard more than three feet. And in the third place, there was something about it that felt like big stuff about to happen. I guess that was the worst. Maybe an army headquarters, the night before a drive, or a convention hall, just before a big political meeting, would affect you that way too, but if you really want to get that feeling, so you really feel it, and it scares you to death, you go in a big opera house about an hour and a half before curtain time.

Cecil didn't waste any time on it. She went right up to No. 7 dressing room, where I was, and I followed her up. She was in No. 1 dressing room, on the other side of the stage. When we got up there, there was nothing in there at all but a long table against the wall, a mirror above that, a couple of chairs, and my trunk, that had been sent around earlier in the day. I opened it, and she took out the make-up kit, and spread it out on the table. "Always watch that you have plenty of cloths and towels. You need them to get the make-up off after you get through."

"All right, I'll watch it."

"Now get out your costume, check every item that goes with it, and hang it on hooks. When you have more than one costume in an opera, hang each one on a separate hook, in the order you'll need them."

"O. K. What else?"

"Now we'll make you up."

She showed me how to put the foundation on, how to apply the color, how to put on the whiskers with gum arabic, and trim them up with a scissors so they looked right. They come in braids, and you ravel them out. She showed me about darkening under the eyes, and made me put on the last touches myself, so I could feel I looked right for the part. Then she had me put on the costume, and inspected me. I looked at myself in the mirror, and thought I looked like the silliest zany that ever came down the pike, but she seemed satisfied, so I shut up about it. "These whiskers tickle."

"They will until the gum dries."

"And they feel like they're falling off."

"Leave them alone. For heaven's sake, get that straight right now. Don't be one of those idiots that go around all night asking everybody if their make-up is in place. Put it on when you dress, and if you put it on right, it'll stay there. Then forget it."

"Don't worry. I'm trying to forget it."

"Around eight o'clock you'll get your first call. Take the hat and muffler with you, and be sure you put them in their proper place on the set. They go on the table near the door, and you put them on for your first exit."

"I know."

"When you've done that, read the curtain calls."

"To hell with curtain calls. If I ever—"

"*Read your curtain calls!* You're in some and not in others, and God help you if you come bobbing out there on a call that belongs to somebody else."

"Oh."

"Keep quiet. You can vocalize a little, but not much. When you feel your voice is up, stop."

"All right."

"Now I leave you. Good-bye and good luck."

I lit a cigarette, walked around. Then I remembered about the vocalizing. I tried a ha-ha, and it sounded terrible. It was dull, heavy, and lifeless, like a horn in a fog. I looked at my watch. It was twenty to eight. I got panicky that I had only a few minutes, and maybe couldn't get my voice up in time. I began to ha-ha, m'm-m'm, ee-ee, and everything I knew to get a little life into it. There was a knock on the door, and somebody said something in Italian. I took the hat and muffler, and went down.

They were all there, Cecil and the rest, all dressed, all walking around, vocalizing under their breaths. Cecil was in black, with a little shawl, and looked pretty. Just as I got down, the chorus came swarming in from somewhere, in soldier suits, plaid pants like mine, ruffled dresses, and everything you could think of. They weren't in the first act, but Rossi lined them up, and began checking them over. I went on the set and put the hat and muffler where she told me. The tenor came and put his hat beside mine. The basses came and moved both hats, to make more room on the table. There had to be places for their stuff when they came on, later. I went to the bulletin board and read the calls. We were all in the first two of the first act, Cecil, the tenor, the two basses, the comic, and myself, then for the other calls it was only Cecil and the tenor. On the calls for the other acts I was in most of them, but I did what she said, read them over carefully and remembered how they went.

"Places!"

I hurried out on the set and sat down behind the easel. I had already checked that the paint brush was in place. The tenor came on and took his place by the window. His name was Parma. He vocalized a little run, with his mouth closed. I tried to do the same, but nothing happened. I swallowed and tried again. This time it came, but it sounded queer. From the other side of the curtain there came a big burst of handclapping. Parma nodded. "Mario's in. Sound like nice 'ouse."

From where you sat out front, I suppose that twenty seconds between the time Mario got to his stand, and made his bow, and waited till a late couple got down the aisle, and the time he brought down his stick on his strings, was just twenty seconds, and nothing more. To me it was the longest wait I ever had in my life. I looked at the easel, and swallowed, and listened to Parma vocalizing his runs under his breath, and swallowed some more, and I thought nothing would ever happen. And then, all of a sudden, all hell broke loose.

Were you ever birdshooting? If you were, on your first time out, you know what I'm talking about. You were out there, in your new hunting suit, and the dogs were out there, and your friends were out there, and you were all ready for business when the first thing that hit you was the drumming of those wings. Then they were up, and going away from you, and it was time to shoot. But if you could hit anything with that thunder in your ears, you were a better man than I think you are. It was like that with me, when that orchestra sounded off. It was terrific, the most frightening thing I ever heard in my life. And it no sooner started than the curtain went up, except that I never saw it go up. All I saw was that blaze of the footlights in my eyes, so I was so rattled I didn't even know where I was. Cecil had warned me about it a hundred times, but you can't warn anybody about a thing like that. Light was hitting me from everywhere, and then I saw Mario out there, but he looked about a mile away, and my heart just stopped beating.

My heart stopped, but that orchestra didn't. It ripped through that introduction a mile a minute, and I knew then what Rossi had been trying to get through my head about speed. There's a page and a half of it in the score, and that looks like plenty of music, doesn't it? They ate it up in nothing flat, and next thing I knew they were through with it, and it was time for me to sing. Oh yes, I was the lad that had to open the opera. Me, the lousy four-flusher that was so scared he couldn't even breathe.

But they thought about that. Mario found me up there, and that stick came down on me, and it meant get going. I began to sing the phrase that begins *Questo Mar Rosso*, but I swear I had no more to do with it than a rabbit looking at a snake. That stick told my mouth what to do, and it did it, that was all. Oh yes, an operatic conductor knows buck fever when he sees it, and he knows what to do about it.

There was some more stuff in the orchestra, and I sang the next two phrases, where he says that to get even with the picture for looking so cold, he'll drown a Pharaoh. The picture is supposed to be the passage of the Red Sea. But I was to take the brush and actually drown one, and it was a second or two before I remembered about it. When I actually did it, I must have looked funny, because there was a big laugh. I was so rattled I looked around to see what they were laughing at, and in that second I took my eye off Mario. It was the place where I was supposed to shoot a *Che fai?* at the tenor. And while I was off picking daisies, did that conductor wait? He did not. Next thing I knew the orchestra was roaring again, and I had missed the boat. Parma sang the first part of his *Nel cielo bigi* at the window, then as he finished it he crossed in front of me, and it was murderous the way he shot it at me as he went by: "Watch da conductor!"

I watched da conductor. I glued my eyes on him from then on, and didn't miss any more cues, and by the help of hypnotism, prayer, and the rest of them shoving me around, we got through it somehow. What I never got caught up with was the speed. You see, when you learn those roles, and then coach them with a piano, you always think of them as a series of little separate scenes, and you take a little rest after each one, and smoke, and relax. But it's not like that at a performance. It goes right through, and it's cruel the way it sweeps you along.

I remembered the hat and muffler, and when I came off she was back there, smoking a cigarette, ready to go on. "You're doing all right. Sing to them, not to Mario."

She rapped at the door, sang a note or two, put her heel on the cigarette, and went on.

We had a little off-stage stuff coming, I and the two basses, and we stood in the wings listening to them out there, doing their stuff. I found out something about an operatic tenor. He doesn't shoot it in rehearsals, and he doesn't shoot it in the preliminary stuff either. He saves it for the place where it counts. Parma, who at the rehearsal hadn't shown enough even to make me look at him, uncorked a voice that was a beauty. He uncorked a voice, and he uncorked a style that even I knew was good. He took his aria, the *Che Gelida Manina*, slow and easy at first, he just drifted along with it, he made them wait until he was ready to give it to them. But when he did give it to them he had it. That high C near the end was a beauty, and well they knew it. Cecil sang better than I had ever heard her sing. I began to see what they were all talking about, why they paid her the dough.

I went out on the first two calls, like the bulletin said, but when we came in from the second Parma whispered at me: "You hide, you. You hear me, guy? You keep out a way dat Mario!"

I didn't argue. I got behind some flats out there in the wings and stayed there. Cecil had heard him, and after a few minutes she found me there. "What happened?"

"I missed a cue."

"Well what's he talking about? He missed three."

"I wasn't watching the conductor."

"Oh."

"Is that bad?"

"It's the cardinal sin, the only unforgivable sin, in all grand opera. Always watch him. Sing to them, try not to let them see you watch him. But—never let him out of your sight. He's the performance, the captain of the ship, the one on whom everything depends. Always watch him."

"I got it now."

The next act was better. I was getting used to it now. I got a couple of laughs in the first part, and then when it came time for me to take up the waltz song he threw the stick on me and I gave her the gun. It got a hand, but he played through it to the end of the act. The Musetta and I did the carry-off we had practiced, and it went all right. The regular way is for Marcel to pick her up and run off with her, but she was small and I'm big, so instead of that, I threw her up on my shoulder and she kicked and waved, and the curtain came down to cheers. The third act I was all right, and we had another nice curtain. The four of us, Parma, I, Cecil, and the Musetta were in all the calls, and after we took the last one Parma followed me to the hole where I did my hiding. "O. K., boy, now on a duet."

"Yeah?"

"Make'm *dolce*. Mak'm nice, a sweet, no loud at all. No big dramatic. Nice, a sweet, a sad. Yeah?"

"I'll do my best."

"You do like I say, we knock hell out of'm. You watch."

So we went out there, and got through the gingerbread, and he threw down his pen and I threw down my paint brush, and we got out the props, and the orchestra played the introduction to the duet. Then he started to sing, and I woke up. I mean, I got it through my head that when that bird said *dolce* he meant *dolce*. He sang like that bonnet of Mimi's was some little bird he had in his hand, so it made a catch come in your throat to listen to him. When he hit the A he lifted his eyes, with the side of his face to the audience, and held it a little, and then melted off it almost with a sigh. When he did that he looked at me and winked. It was that wink that told me what I had to do. I had to put *dolce* in it. I came in on my beat and tried to do it like he did it. When it came to my little solo, I put tears in it. Maybe they were just imitation tears, but they were tears just the same. When I came to my high F sharp I swelled it a little, then pulled it in and melted off it just like he had melted off the A. When I got through the orchestra had a few bars, and he sat there shaking his head over the bonnet, and out of the side of his mouth he said: "You old son-bitch-bast."

We went into the finish, and laid it right on the end of Mario's stick, and slopped out the tears in buckets. Buckets, hell, we turned the fire hose on them. It stopped the show. They didn't only clap, they cheered, so we had to repeat it. That's dead against the rules, and Mario tried to go on, but they wouldn't let him. We got through the act, and Parma flopped on the bed for the last two "*Mimi's*," and the curtain came down to a terrific hand. We took our first two bows, the whole gang that were in the act, and when we came back from the second one, Mario was back there. Cecil yelled in my ear, "Take him out, take him out!" So I took him out.

I grabbed him by one hand, she by the other, and we led him out on the next bow, and they gave him a big hand, too. That seemed to fix it up about that missed cue.

It was a half hour before I could start to dress. I went to my dressing room, and had just about got my whiskers pulled off when about fifty people shoved in from outside, wanting me to autograph their programs. It was a new one on me, but it's a regular thing at every performance of grand opera, those people, mostly women, they come back and tell you how beautifully you sang, and would you please sign their program for them. So I obliged, and signed "Logan Bennett." Then I got washed up and met Cecil and we got a cab and went off to eat. "You hungry, Leonard?"

"As a mule."

"Let's go somewhere."

"All right."

We went to a night club. It had a dance floor, and tables around that, and booths around the wall. We took a booth. We ordered a steak for two, and then she ordered some red burgundy to go with it, and sherry to start. That was unusual with her. She's like most singers. She'll give you a drink, but she doesn't take much herself. She saw me look at her. "I want something. I—want to celebrate."

"O. K. with me. Plenty all right."

"Did you enjoy yourself?"

"I enjoyed the final curtain."

"Didn't you enjoy the applause after the *O Mimi* duet? It brought down the house."

"It was all right."

"Is that all you have to say about it?"

"I liked it fine."

"You mean you really liked it?"

"Yeah, I hate to admit it, but I *really* liked it. That was the prettiest music I heard all night."

The sherry came and we raised our glasses, clinked, and had a sip. "Leonard, I love it."

"You're better at it than in concert."

"You're telling me? I hate concerts. But opera—I just love it, and if you ever hear me saying again that I don't want to be a singer, you'll know I'm temporarily insane. I love it, I love everything about it, the smell, the fights, the high notes, the low notes, the applause, the curtain calls—everything."

"You must feel good tonight."

"I do. Do you?"

"I feel all right."

"Is it—the way you thought it would be?"

"I never thought."

"Not even—just a little bit?"

"You mean, that it's nice, and silly, and cock-eyed, that I should be here with you, and that I should be an opera singer, when all God intended me for was a dumb contractor, and that it's a big joke that came off just the way you hoped it would, and I never believed it would, and—something like that?"

"Yes, that's what I mean."

"Then yes."

"Let's dance."

We danced, and I held her close, and smelled her hair, and she nestled it up against my face. "It's gay, isn't it?"

"Yes."

"I'm almost happy, Leonard."

"Me too."

"Let's go back to our little booth. I want to be kissed."

So we went back to the booth, and she got kissed, and we laughed about the way I had hid from Mario, and drank the wine, and ate steak. I had to cut the steak left-handed, so I wouldn't joggle her head, where it seemed to be parked on my right shoulder.

We stayed a second week in Chicago, and I did my three operas over again, and then we played a week in the Music Hall in Cleveland, and then another week in Murat's Theatre, Indianapolis. Then Cecil's contract was up, and it was time for her to go back and get ready for the Metropolitan.

The Saturday matinee in Indianapolis was Faust. I met Cecil in the main dining room that morning, around ten o'clock, for breakfast, and while we were eating Rossi came over and sat down. He didn't have much to say. He kept asking the waiter if any call had come for him, and bit his fingernails, and pretty soon it came out that the guy that was to sing Wagner that afternoon couldn't come to the theatre, on account of unfortunately being in jail on a traffic charge, and that Rossi was waiting to find out if some singer in Chicago could come down and do it. His call came through, and when he came back he said his man was tied up. That meant somebody from the chorus would have to do it, and that wasn't so good. And then Cecil popped out: "Well what are we talking about, with *him* sitting here. Here, baby. Here's my key, there's a score up in my room; you can just hike yourself up there and learn it."

"*What?* Learn it in one morning and then sing it?"

"There's only a few pages of it. Now. Go."

"Faust is in French, isn't it?"

"Oh damn. He doesn't sing French."

But Rossi fixed that part up. He had a score in Italian, and I was to learn it in that and sing it in that, with the rest of them singing French. So the next thing I knew I was up there in my room with a score, and by one o'clock I had it learned, and by two o'clock Rossi had given me the business, and by three o'clock

I was in a costume they dug up, out there doing it. That made more impression on them than anything I had done yet. You see, they don't pay much attention to a guy that knows three roles, all coached up by heart. They know all about them. But a guy that can get a role up quick, and go out there and do it, even if he makes a few mistakes, that guy can really be some use around an opera company. Rossi came to my dressing room after I finished Traviata that night and offered me a contract for the rest of the season. He said Mr. Mario was very pleased with me, especially the way I had gone on in Wagner, and was willing to work with me so I could get up more leading roles and thought I would fit in all right with their plans. He offered me $150 a week, $25 more than I had been getting. I thanked him, thanked Mr. Mario for the interest he had taken in me, thanked all the others for a pleasant association with them, and said no. He came up to $175. I still said no. He came up to $200. I still said no and asked him not to bid any higher, as it wasn't a question of money. He couldn't figure it out, but after a while we shook hands and that was that.

That night she and I ate in a quiet little place we had found, and at midnight we were practically the only customers. After we ordered she said: "Did Rossi speak to you?"

"Yes, he did."

"Did he offer $150? He said he would."

"He came up to $200, as a matter of fact."

"What did you say?"

"I said no."

" . . . Why?"

"What the hell? I'm no singer. What would I be trailing around with this outfit for after you're gone?"

"They play Baltimore, Philadelphia, Boston, and Pittsburgh before they swing West. I could visit you week-ends, maybe oftener than that. I—I might even make a flying trip out to the Coast."

"I'm not the type."

"Who is the type? Leonard, let me ask you something. Is it just because his $200 a week looks like chicken-feed to you? Is it because a big contractor makes a lot more than that?"

"Sometimes he does. Right now he doesn't make a dime."

"If that's what it is, you're making a mistake, no matter what a big contractor makes. Leonard, everything has come out the way I said it would, hasn't it? Now listen to me. With that voice, you can make money that a big contractor never even heard of. After just one season with the American Scala Opera Company, the Metropolitan will grab you sure. It isn't everybody that can sing with the American Scala. Their standards are terribly high, and very well the Metropolitan knows it, and they've raided plenty of Scala singers already. Once you're in the Metropolitan, there's the radio, the phonograph, concert, moving pictures. Leonard, you can be rich. You—you can't help it."

"Contracting's my trade."

"All this—doesn't it mean anything to you?"

"Yeah, for a gag. But not what you mean."

"And in addition to the money, there's fame—"

"Don't want it."

She sat there, and I saw her eyes begin to look wet. "Oh, why don't we both tell the truth? You want to get back to New York—for what's waiting for you in New York. And I—I don't want you ever to go there again."

"No, that's not it."

"Yes it is. I'm doing just exactly the opposite of what I thought I was doing when we started all this. I thought I would be the good fairy, and bring you and her together again. And now, what am I doing? I'm trying to take you away from her. Something I'd hate any other woman for, and now—I might as well tell the truth. I'm just a—home-wrecker."

She looked comic as she said it, and I laughed and she laughed. Then she started to cry. I hadn't heard one word from Doris since I left New York. I had wired her every hotel I had stopped at, and you would think she might have sent me a postcard. There wasn't even that. I sat there, watching Cecil, and trying to let her be a home-wrecker, as she called it. I knew she was swell, I respected everything about her, I didn't have to be told she'd go through hell for me. I tried to feel I was in love with her, so I could say to hell with New York, let's both stay with this outfit and let the rest go hang. I couldn't. And then the next thing I knew I was crying too.

7

We hit New York Monday morning, but there was a freight wreck ahead of us, so we were late, and didn't get into Grand Central until ten o'clock. She and I didn't go up the ramp together. I had wired Doris, so I went on ahead, but a fat chance there would be anybody there, so when nobody showed I put Cecil in a cab. We acted like I was just putting her in a cab. I said I'd call her up, she said yes, please do, we waved goodbye, and that was all. I went back and sent the trunk down to the office, then got in a cab with my bag and went on up. On the way, I kept thinking what I was going to say. I had been away six weeks, and what had kept me that long? On the Rochester part, I had it down pat. There had been stuff in the papers about grade-crossing elimination up there, and I went up to see if we could bid on the concrete. But what was I doing in those other places? The best I could think of was that I had taken a swing around to look at "conditions," whatever they were, and it sounded fishy, but I didn't know anything else.

When I got home I let myself in, carried my grip, and called to Doris. There was no answer. I went out in the kitchen, and there was nobody there. I took my grip upstairs, called to Doris again, knocked on the door of the bedroom. Still there was no answer. I went in. The bed was all made up, the room was in order, and no Doris. The room being in order, though, that didn't prove anything, even at that time of day. Her room was always in order. I took the bag in the nursery, set it down, went out in the hall again, let out a couple more hallo's. Still nothing happened.

I went downstairs, began to get nervous. I wondered if she had walked out on me for good, and taken the children with her, but the house didn't smell like it had been locked up or anything like that. About eleven o'clock Nils came home. He was the houseman. He had been out taking the children to school, he said, and buying some stuff at a market. He said he was glad to see me back, and I shook hands with him, and asked for Christine. Christine is his wife, and does the cooking, and in between acts as maid to Doris and nurse to the children. He said Christine had gone with Mrs. Borland. He acted like I must know all about it, and I hated to show I didn't, so I said oh, of course, and he went on back to the kitchen.

About a quarter to twelve the phone rang. It was Lorentz. "Borland, you'd better come down and get your wife."

" . . . What's the matter?"

"I'll tell you."

"Where is she?"

"The Cathedral Theatre. Come to the stage door. I'm at the theatre now. I'll meet you and take you to her."

I had a glimmer, then, of what was going on. I went out, grabbed a cab, and hustled down there. He met me outside, took me in, and showed me a dressing room. I rapped on the door and went in. She was on a couch, and a theatre nurse was with her, and Christine. She was in an awful state. She had on some kind of theatrical looking dress with shiny things on it, and her face was all twisted, and her hands were clenching and unclenching, and I didn't need anybody to tell me she was giving everything she had to fight back hysteria. When she saw me it broke. She cried, and stiffened on the couch, and then kept doubling up in convulsive jerks, where she was fighting for control, and turning away, so I couldn't see her face. The nurse took me by the arm. "It'll be better if you wait outside. Give me a few more minutes with her, and I'll have her in shape to be moved."

I went out in the corridor with Lorentz. "What's this about?"

"She got the bird."

"Oh."

There it was again, this thing that Cecil had said if I ever heard I'd never forget. I still didn't know what it was, but that wasn't what I was thinking about. "She sang here, then?"

"It didn't get that far. She went out there to sing. Then they let her have it. It was murder."

"Just didn't like her, hey?"

"She got too much of a build-up. In the papers."

"I haven't seen the papers. I've been away."

"Yeah, I know. Socialite embraces stage career, that kind of stuff. It was all wrong, and they were ready for her. Just one of those nice morning crowds in a big four-a-day picture house. They didn't even let her open her mouth. By the time I got to the piano the stage manager had to ring down. The curtain dropped in front of her, the orchestra played, and they started the newsreel. I never saw anything like it."

He stood there and smoked, I stood there and smoked, and then I began to get sore. "It would seem to me you would have had more sense than to put her on here."

"I didn't."

"Oh, you did your part."

"I pleaded with her not to do it. Listen, Borland, I'm not

kidded about Doris, and I don't think you are either. She can't sing for buttons. She can't even get on the set before they've got her number. I tried my best to head her off. I told her she wasn't ready for it, that she ought to wait, that it wasn't her kind of a show. I even went to Leighton. I scared him, but not enough. You try to stop Doris when she gets set on something."

"Couldn't you tell her the truth?"

"Could you?"

That stopped me, but I was still sore. "Maybe not. But you started this, just the same. If you knew all this, what did you egg her on for? You're the one that's been giving her lessons, from 'way back, and telling her how good she is, and—"

"All right, Borland, granted. And I think you know all about that too. I'm in love with your wife. And if egging her on is what makes her like me, I'm human. Yeah, I trade on her weakness."

"I've socked guys for less than that."

"Go ahead, if it does you any good. I've about got to the point where a sock, that would be just one more thing. If you think being chief lackey to Doris is a little bit of heaven, you try it—or maybe you have tried it. This finishes me with her, if that interests you. Not because I started it. Not because I egged her on. No—but I *saw* it. I was there, and *saw* them nail her to the cross, and rip her clothes off, and throw rotten eggs at her, and ask her how the vinegar tasted, and all the rest of it. That she'll never forgive me for. But why sock? You're married to her, aren't you? What more do you want?"

He walked off and left me. I found a pay phone, put in a call for a private ambulance. When it came I went in the dressing room again. Doris was up, and Christine was helping her into her fur coat. She was over the hysteria, but she looked like something broken and shrunken. I carried her to the ambulance, put her in it, made her lie down. Christine got in. We started off.

I carried her upstairs and undressed her, and put her to bed, and called a doctor. Undressing Doris is like pulling the petals off a flower, and a catch kept coming in my throat over how soft she was, and how beautiful she was, and how she wilted into the bed. When the doctor came he said she had to be absolutely quiet, and gave her some pills to make her sleep. He left, and I closed the door, and sat down beside the bed. She put her hand in mine. "Leonard."

"Yes?"

"I'm no good."

"How do you know? From what Lorentz said, they didn't even give you a chance to find out."

"I'm no good."

"A morning show in a picture house—"

"A picture house, a vaudeville house, an opera house, Carnegie Hall—it's all the same. They're out there, and it's up to you. I'm just a punk that's been a headache to everybody she knows, and that's got wise to herself at last. I've got voice, figure, looks—everything but what it takes. Isn't that funny? Everything but what it takes."

"For me, you've got everything it takes."

"You knew, didn't you?"

"How would I know?"

"You knew. You knew all the time. I've been just rotten to you, Leonard. All because you opposed my so-called career."

"I didn't oppose it."

"No, but you didn't believe in it. That was what made me so furious. You were willing to let me do whatever I wanted to do, but you wouldn't believe I could sing. I hated you for it."

"Only for that?"

"Only for that. Oh, you mean Hugo, and Leighton, and all my other official hand-kissers? Don't be silly. I had to tease you a little, didn't I? But that only showed I cared whether you cared."

"Then you do care?"

"What do you think?"

She took my head in her hands, and kissed my eyes, and my brow, and my cheeks, like I was something too holy for her to be worthy to touch, and I was so happy I couldn't even talk. I sat there a long time, my head against hers, while she held my hand against her cheek, and now and then kissed it. " . . . The pills are working."

"You want to sleep?"

"No, I don't want to. I could stay this way forever. But I'm going to. I can't help it."

"I'll leave you."

"Kiss me."

I kissed her, and she put her arms around me, and sighed a sleepy little sigh. Then she smiled, and I tip-toed out, and I think she was asleep before I got to the door.

I had a bite to eat, went down to the office, checked on the trunk, had a look at what mail there was, and raised the windows to let a little air in the place. Then I sat down at the desk, hooked my heels on the top, and tried to keep my head from swimming till it would be time to go back to Doris. I was so excited I wanted to laugh all the time, but a cold feeling began to creep up my back, and pretty soon I couldn't fight it off any more. It was about Cecil. I had to see her, I knew that. I had to put it on the line, how I felt about Doris, and how she felt about me, and there couldn't be but one answer to that. Cecil and I, we would have to break. I tried to tell myself she wouldn't expect to see me for a day or so, that it would be better to let her get started on her new work, that if I just let things go along, she would make the move anyway. It was no good. I had to see her, and I couldn't stall. I walked around to her hotel. I went past it once, turned around and walked past it again. Then I came back and went in.

* * *

She had the same suite, the same piano, the same piles of music
lying around. She had left the door open when they announced
me from the lobby, and when I went in she was lying on the sofa,
staring at the wall, and didn't even say hello. I sat down and asked
her how she felt after the trip. She said all right. I asked her when
her rehearsals started. She said tomorrow. I said that was swell,
that she'd really be with an outfit where she could do herself justice. " . . . What is it, Leonard?"

Her voice sounded dry, and mine was shaky when I answered.
"Something happened."

"Yes, I heard."

"It—broke her up."

"It generally does."

"It's—made her feel different—about a lot of things. About—
quite a few things."

"Go on, Leonard. What did you come here to tell me? Say it. I
want you to get it over with."

"She wants me back."

"And you?"

"I want her back too."

"All right."

She closed her eyes. There was no more to say and I knew it. I
ought to have walked out of there then. I couldn't do it. I at least
wanted her to know how I felt about her, how much she meant to
me. I went over, sat down beside her, took her hand. " . . . Cecil,
there's a lot of things I'd like to say."

"Yes, I know."

"About how swell you've been, about how much I—"

"Good-bye, Leonard."

" . . . I wanted to tell you—"

"There's only one thing a man ever has to tell a woman. You can't tell me that. I know you can't tell me that, we've been all over it—don't offer me consolation prizes."

"All right, then. Good-bye."

I bent over and kissed her. She didn't open her eyes, didn't move. "There's only one thing I ask, Leonard."

"The answer is yes, whatever it is."

"Don't come back."

" . . . What?"

"Don't come back. You're going now. You're going with all my best wishes, and there's no bitterness. I give you my word on that. You've been decent to me, and I've no complaint. You haven't lied to me, and if it hasn't turned out as I thought it would, that's my fault, not yours. But—don't come back. When you go out of that door, you go out of my life. You'll be a memory, nothing more. A sweet, lovely, terrible memory, perhaps—but I'll do my own grieving. Only—don't come back."

"I had sort of hoped—"

"Ah!"

" . . . What's the matter?"

"You had sort of hoped that after this little honeymoon blows up, say in another week, you could give me a ring, and come on over, and start up again just as if nothing had happened."

"No. I hoped we could be friends."

"That's what you think you hoped. You know in your heart it was something else. All right, you're going back to her. She's had a bad morning, and been hurt, and you feel sorry for her, and she's whistled at you, and you're running back. But remember what I say, Leonard: you're going back on her terms, not yours. You're still her little whimpering lapdog, and if you think she's not going to dump you down on the floor, or sell you to the gypsies, or put you out in the yard in your little house, or do anything else to you that enters her head, just as soon as this blows over, you're mistaken. That woman is not licked until you've licked her, and if you think this is licking her, it's more than I do, and more than she does."

"No. You're wrong. Doris has had her lesson."

"All right, I'm wrong. For your sake, I hope so. But—don't come back. Don't come running to me again. I'll not be a hot towel—for you or anybody."

"Then friendship's out?"

"It is. I'm sorry."

"All right."

"Come here."

She pulled me down, and kissed me, and turned away quick, and motioned me out. I was on the street before I remembered I had left my coat up there. I went in and sent a bellboy up for it. When he came down I was hoping he would have some kind of a message from her. He didn't. He handed me my coat, I handed him a quarter, and I went out.

When I got back to the house, the kids were home, and came running downstairs, and said did I know we were all going that night to hear Mamma sing. I said there had been a little change in the plans on that, and they were a little down in the mouth, but I said I had brought presents for them, and that fixed it all up, and we went running up to get them. I went in the nursery for my bag. It wasn't there. Then I heard Doris call, and we went in there.

"Were you looking for something?"

"Yes. Are you awake?"

"Been awake. . . . You *might* find it in there."

She gave a funny little smile and pointed to the dressing room. I went in there, and there it was. The kids began jumping up and down when I gave them the candy, and Doris kept smiling and talking over their heads. "I would have had Nils take your things out, but I didn't want him poking around."

"I'll do it."

"Where did you go?"

"Just down to the office to look at my mail."

"No, but I mean—"

"Oh—Rochester, Chicago, Indianapolis, and around. Thought it was about time to look things over."

"Did you have a nice trip?"

"Only fair."

"You certainly took plenty of glad rags."

"Just in case. Didn't really need them, as it turned out."

Christine called the kids, and they went out. I went over to her and took her in my arms. "Why didn't you want Nils poking around?"

"Well—do *you* want him?"

"No."

We both laughed, and she put her head against mine, and let her hair fall over my face, and made a little opening in front of my mouth, and kissed me through that. Oh, don't think Doris couldn't be a sweet armful when she wanted to be. "You glad to be back, Leonard? From Chicago—and the nursery?"

"Yes. Are you?"

"So glad, Leonard, I could—cry."

8

I kept letting her hair fall over my face, and holding her a little tighter, and then all of a sudden she jumped up. "Oh my God, the cocktail party!"

"What cocktail party?"

"Gwenny Blair's cocktail party. Her lousy annual stinkaroo

that nobody wants to go to and everybody does. I said I'd drop in before the supper show, and I had completely forgotten it. The supper show, think of that. Wasn't I the darling little trouper then? My that seems a long time ago. And it was only this morning."

"Oh, let's skip it."

"What! And have them think I'm dying of grief? I should say not. We're going. And we're going quick, so we can leave before the whole mob gets there. Hurry up. Get dressed."

The last thing I wanted to do was go to Gwenny Blair's cocktail party. I wanted to stay where I was, and inhale hair. There was nothing to it, though, but to get dressed. I began changing my clothes, and she began pulling things out and muttering: " . . . No, not that. . . . It's black, and looks like mourning. . . . And not that. It makes me look too pale. . . . Leonard, I'm going to wear a suit."

"Well, why not?"

"A suit, that's it. Casual, been out all day, just dropped in, got to run in a few minutes, lovely party—it will be, like hell. That's it, a suit."

I always loved Doris when she dropped the act and came out as the calculating little wench that she really was. She heard me laugh, and laughed too. "Right?"

"Quite right."

She was dressed in five minutes flat, and for once she had to wait on me. The suit was dark gray, almost black, and cut so she looked slim as a boy. The blouse was light green, but with a copper tone in it, so it was perfect for her hair. Trust Doris not to put on anything that was just green. When I got downstairs she was pinning on a white camellia that had come on the run from the florist. Another woman would have had a gardenia, but not Doris. She knew the effect of those two shiny green leaves lying flat on the lapel.

"How do I look?"

How she looked was like some nineteen-year-old flapper that spent her first day at the races, cashed $27.50 on a $2 ticket, and was feeling just swell. But she didn't want hooey, she wanted the low-down, so I just nodded, and we started out.

It was only four or five blocks away, in a big penthouse on top of one of those apartment buildings on Park Avenue, so we walked. On the way, she kept damning Gwenny, and all of Gwenny's friends, under her breath, and saying she'd rather take a horsewhipping than go in and face them. But when we got there, she was all smiles. Only twenty or thirty people had shown up by then, and most of them hadn't heard of it. That was the funny thing. I had bought some papers on my way up from Cecil's, and two or three of them had nothing about it at all, and the others let it out with a line. In the theatrical business, bad news is no news. It's only the hits that cause excitement.

So they were all crowding around her with their congratulations, and wanted to know what it felt like to be a big headliner. Of course, that made it swell. But Doris leveled it out without batting an eye. "But I flopped! I'm not a headliner! I'm an *ex*-headliner!"

"You—! Come on, stop being funny!"

"I flopped. I'm out. They gave me my notice."

"*How* could you flop?"

"Oh please, please, don't ask me—it just breaks my heart. And now I can't go to Bermuda! Honestly, it's not the principle of the thing, it's the money! Think of all those lovely, lovely dollars that I'm not going to get!"

She didn't lie about it, or pretend that she had done better than she had done, or pretty it up in any way. She had too much sense for that. But in twenty seconds she had them switched off from the horrible part, and had managed to work it in that she must have been getting a terrific price to go on at all, and had it going her way. Leighton came in while she was ₃alking, and said the publicity was all wrong, and he was going to raise hell about it. They all agreed that was it, and in five minutes they were talking about the Yale game Saturday.

She drifted over to me. "Thank God *that's* over. Was it all right?"

"Perfect."

"Damn them."

"Just a few minutes, and we'll blow. We've still got my bag to unpack."

She nodded, and looked at me, and let her lashes droop over her eyes. It was Eve looking at the apple, and my heart began to pound, and the room swam in front of me.

Lorentz came in. He didn't come over. He waved, and smiled, and Doris waved back, but looked away quick. "I'm a little out of humor with Hugo. He must have known. You did, didn't you? He could have given me some little hint."

I thought of what he had said, but I didn't say anything. I didn't care. I was still groggy from that look.

We got separated then, but pretty soon she had me by the arm, pulling me into a corner. "We've got to go. Make it quick with Gwenny, and then—*out!*"

"Why sure. But what's the matter?"

"The fool."

"Who?"

"Gwenny. I could kill her. She knows how crazy I've been about that woman, and how I've wanted to meet her, and now, today of all days she had to pick out—she's invited her! And she's coming!"

"What woman?"

"Cecil Carver! Haven't you heard me speak of her a hundred times? And now—I can't meet her today. I can't have her—pitying me! . . . Can I?"

"No. We'll blow."

"I'll meet you at the elevator—Oh my, there she is!"

I looked around, and Cecil was just coming in the room. I turned back to Doris, and she wasn't there.

She was with Wilkins, Cecil I mean. That meant she was going to sing. There wasn't much talk while Gwenny was taking her around. They piped down, and waited. They all had money, and position from 'way-back, but all they ever saw was each other. When a real celebrity showed up, they were as excited as a bunch of high school kids meeting some big-league ball player. I was still in the corner, and she didn't see me until Gwenny called me out. She caught her breath. Gwenny introduced me, and I said "How do you do, Miss Carver," and she said "How do you do, Mr. Borland," and went on. But in a minute she came back. "Why didn't you tell me you were coming here?"

"I didn't know it."

"Is she here?"

"Didn't Gwenny tell you?"

"No."

"It was on her account she asked you."

"*Her* account?"

"She's wanted to meet you. So I just found out."

"Gwenny didn't say anything. She called an hour ago and said come on up—and I wanted to go somewhere. I *had* to go somewhere. Why has she wanted to meet me?"

"Admires you. From afar."

"Only that?"

"Yes."

"Where is she?"

"Back there somewhere. In one of the bedrooms, would be the best bet. Hiding."

"From what?"

"You, I think."

"Leonard, what is this? She wants to meet me, she's hiding from me—what are you getting at? She's not a child, to duck behind curtains when teacher comes."

"I should say not."

"Then what is this nonsense?"

"It's no nonsense. Gwenny asked you, as a big favor to her. But Gwenny hadn't heard about the flop. And on account of the flop, she'd rather not. Just—prefers some other time."

"And that's all?"

"Yeah, but it was an awful flop."

"You're sure you haven't told her about me? Gone and got all full of contrition, and made a clean breast of it, and wiped the slate clean, so you can start all over again—have you? *Have* you?"

"No, not a word."

She stood twisting a handkerchief and thinking, and then she turned and headed back toward the bedrooms. "Cecil—!"

"She had a flop, didn't she? Then I guess I'm the one she wants to talk to."

She went on back. I went over and had a drink. I needed one.

I was on my third when she came back, and I went over to her. "What happened?"

"Nothing."

"What did you say?"

"Told her to forget it. Told her it could happen to anybody— which it can, baby, and don't you forget it."

"What did she say?"

"Asked if it had ever happened to me. I told her it had, and then we talked about Hugo."

"He's here, by the way."

"Is he? She's not bad. I halfway liked her."

She still didn't look at me, but I had the same old feeling about her, of how swell she was, and thought I'd die if I couldn't let her know, anyway a little. "Cecil, can I say something?"

"Leonard, I cut my heart out after you left. I cut it out, and put it in the electric icebox, to freeze into—whatever a heart is made of. Jelly, I guess. Anyway my heart. So if you've got anything to say, you'd better go down there and see if it can still hear you. Me, I've got other things to do. I've got to be gay, and sing tra-la-la-la, and get my talons into the first man that—"

She saw Lorentz then, and went running over to him, and put her arms around him, and kissed him. It was gay, maybe, but it didn't make me feel any better.

Doris came out then, and I hurried to her. I didn't want to let on about Cecil, so I began right where we left off, and asked if she was ready to go. "Oh—the tooth's out now. I think she's going to sing. Let's stay."

"Oh—you saw her then?"

"She came back to powder. I didn't start it. She spoke to me. She remembered me. She came to my recital, you may recall."

"Oh yes, so she did."

"Don't ever meet your gods face to face, and especially not your goddesses. It's a most disillusioning experience. They have clay feet. My, what an awful woman."

"You didn't like her?"

"She knew about it. And she couldn't wait to make me feel better. She was just so tactful and sweet—and mean—that I just hated her. And did she love it. Did she enjoy purring over me."

"Maybe not. Maybe she meant it."

"Of course she meant it—her way."

"And what way is that?"

"Don't be so dense. Perhaps a man doesn't see through those things, but a woman does. Oh yes, she meant it. She meant every word of it—the cat. She was having the time of her life."

I could feel myself getting hot under the collar, and all my romantic humor was gone. After what Cecil had done, and what it had cost her to do it, this kind of talk went against my grain. "And what a frump. Did you ever see such a dress?"

"What's the matter with it?"

"Well—never mind. She did say one thing, though. To forget it. That it can happen to anybody, that it has even happened to her. 'All in a day's work, a thing you expect now and then, so what? Forget it and go on.' Leonard, are you listening?"

"I'm listening."

"That's it. Nothing has happened. How silly I was, to feel that way about it. I don't have to quit. I just go on. Why certainly. Even she had sense enough to know that."

I could hardly believe my eyes, and certainly not my ears. Here it had only been that morning when she was broken on the wheel, when she heard the gong ring for her if ever anybody did. And now, after just a few words from Cecil, she was standing there with her eyes open wide, telling herself that nothing had happened, that it was all just a dream. And all of a sudden, I knew that nothing *had* happened, and that it *was* all just a dream. She was the same old Doris, and it would be about one more day before we'd be right back where we always had been, with me having the fool career rubbed into me morning, noon and night, and everything else just as it was, only worse. I wondered if the way she was acting was what they call pluck. To me, it was not having sense enough to know when you've been hit with a brick.

*   *   *

A whole mob was there by then, and pretty soon Gwenny began to stamp her foot, and got them quiet, and she said Cecil was going to sing. But when Cecil stood up, it wasn't Wilkins that took the piano, it was Lorentz. She made a little speech, and told how he had played for her in Berlin, and how she would do one of the things they had done that night, and how she hoped it would go better this time, and he wouldn't have to yell the words at her from the piano, the way he had then. They all laughed, and she waited till they had found seats and got still, and then she sang the Titania song from Mignon.

She had made her little speech with her arm around Lorentz, and Doris looked like murder, and during the little wait she began to whisper. "That's nice."

"What's nice?"

"She brought her own accompanist, but oh no. She had to have Hugo."

"Well what of it?"

"Don't you see through it?"

"No. They seem to be old friends."

"Oh, *that's* not it."

"And what *is* it?"

"She knows he's my accompanist, and that he's been attentive to me—"

"And how would she know that?"

"She must know it, from what I said. The first thing she asked me about was Hugo, and—"

"I thought Hugo was out."

"Maybe he is, but *she* doesn't know it. And these people don't know it. My goodness, but you're stupid about some things. Oh no, this I'll not forgive. The other, I pass over. But this is a public matter, and I'll get even with her for it, if I—"

The music started then. About the third bar Doris leaned over to me. "She's flatting."

I wanted to get out of there. I could smell trouble, especially after that crack about getting even. I said something about going, but there was as much chance of getting Doris out of there with that singing going on as there would have been of getting a rat away from a piece of cheese. All I could do was sit there.

After the Mignon, Cecil sang a little cradle song that's been written on Kreisler's Caprice Viennois, and then she came over to Doris. "How was I?"

"Marvelous! I never heard you better."

"I thought I was a little off myself, but they seem to like it, so I guess it was all right. Do a duet with me?"

Now I ask you, was that being nice to Doris, or wasn't it? Because that was letting her right into the big league park, it was treating her as an equal, and in front of all her friends. Doris looked scared, and stammered something about how she'd love to, if only there was something they could get together on, and Cecil said: "How about *La Dove Prende?*"

"Why—that would be all right, but of course I only know the first part, and—"

"Fine. I'll do the second."

"If you really think I can—"

"Come on, come on, it'll do you good. You've got to ride the horse that threw you, haven't you? We'll knock 'em for a loop, and then good-bye to all that business this morning, and you'll feel fine."

"Well—"

Cecil went back to the piano and Doris put down her hand-bag. Her face was savage with jealousy, rage, and venom. She whispered to me: "Show me up, hey? We'll see about that!"

Wilkins took the piano, and they started. It was terrible. Mozart has to be sung to beat, and I think I told you Doris' ideas on rhythm. I saw Wilkins look up, but Cecil dead-panned, and they went on with her. She could have sung it backwards and that pair would have carried her through, so it got a hand. They had a little whisper, and then they sang the Barcarolle from the Tales of Hoffman. That was a little more Doris' speed, and a little more that mob's speed too, so they got a big hand on it, and started over to me.

As they left the piano, Doris put her arm around Cecil's waist, and I had a cold feeling that something was about to pop. They got to me, and I started to talk fast, about how fine they had sounded, anything I could think of. They laughed, and Cecil turned to Doris. "Well—how was the support?"

"Oh fine—even if you do try to steal my men."

Doris laughed as she said it, and it wasn't supposed to be such a hell of a dirty crack. It was just a preliminary. I could give you the rest of the talk, almost word for word, the way she intended it to go. First Cecil was supposed to look surprised, and then Doris would apologize, and laugh some more, and say it was only intended as a joke. Then it would come out about Lorentz, and Doris would say please, please, he didn't mean a thing to her— really. And then would come the real dirty crack, something that would mean Lorentz wasn't really worth having, and if Cecil was interested in him she could have him, and welcome.

That was how it was supposed to go, I can guarantee you, knowing Doris. But it never got that far. Cecil winced like she had been hit with a whip. Then she looked me straight in the eye, the first time she had, all day. "Leonard, why did you lie to me?"

"I didn't."

"You did. You let me go to her, and you swore you hadn't told a word—"

She tried to bite it back. It wasn't what I said. It was the look on Doris' face that stopped her. She knew, then, what Doris had really meant, but it was too late. We all three stood there, and Doris looked first at Cecil, and then at me. Then she gave a little rasping laugh, and her eyes were as hard as glass. " . . . Ah—so that was what you were doing in Rochester, and Syracuse, and Columbus, and Chicago, and—"

"I—"

"Don't give me that foolish story again, about looking things over. I've followed her. I've followed her whole career since— I know everything she's done! She sang in all those places, and you—! The fool that I was! I never once thought of it!"

Cecil licked her lips. "Mrs. Borland, I'm sure I've never meant a thing to your husband—"

"Miss Carver, I don't believe you."

Cecil closed her eyes, opened them again, grabbed for the one last thing she could say. "We saw quite a lot of each other, that's true. We could hardly help that. We were singing together. We were singing in the same opera company, and—"

Doris gave a shrieking laugh, and half the room stopped talking and turned around. Gwenny came up, Doris put her head on her shoulder and kept on with that laugh. Then she turned to them all. "Oh my—isn't that funny? If they took a trip together— I don't mind. It means nothing to me—let them enjoy life while they're young. But darlings! Singing together! In the same—I can't stand it! Imagine Leonard—singing—ha-ha-ha-ha-ha-ha!"

Gwenny decided to play it funny. She laughed too. A few others laughed. Then she decided to get witty. "Perhaps he'll sing us something!—From Pagliacci!"

If that was what she said, I think I could have stood it. But that wasn't it. That was only what she thought she said. What she really said was, "From Polly-achy," and at the dumb, ignorant way she pronounced that word, something in me cracked. All the rotten, phoney, mean, cruel stuff I had taken off Doris, and all the stuff I had taken off Gwenny and her kind, came swelling up in my throat, and I knew I was going to kick over the apples or bust. I turned to Gwenny. "Since you ask me, I think I will."

I went in the dining room and found Wilkins. He hadn't heard any of it. "Feeling like playing for me?"

"Sure. What'll it be?"

"How about the Prologue from Pagliacci?"

"The Prologue it is."

We went in and there was a laugh, and they all started to whisper. He started the introduction, and they looked at each other, and looked at me, and looked at Doris. They were her friends, remember, not mine. Cecil came over. "I wouldn't, baby. It was awful, but—I wouldn't. You'll regret it."

"Maybe."

She went away, and I started to sing. At the first *Si può* Doris sank into a chair. She didn't turn white. She turned gray. I went on. Maybe Tibbett can do it better than I did it that day, but I doubt it. He couldn't take the interest in it, you might say, that I took. I rolled it out and my head felt light and dizzy, because I could see every note of it going like a knife into her heart. When I got to the andante I gave it the gun, and when I reached the high A flat I stepped into it with a smile on my face, and held it, and swelled it, until the room began to shake, then I pulled it in, and cut. I closed it out solemn as I knew, as though a real performance was about to start, and I wanted them to get it all straight.

Wilkins played the finish, and waited. Nothing happened. They sat there like they were frozen, and then they began to talk, as if I wasn't there. He looked up at me, like he was in a madhouse or something. I smiled at him, and bowed three times, the way I was taught, center, left and right. Then I went over and poured myself a drink. When I turned around, Doris was leaving the room. She walked like she had just gone blind.

9

I don't know how I got out of there. But pretty soon I was down on the twelfth floor, where you change from the private elevator that runs up to the penthouse, to the main cars. Cecil was there, with Wilkins. She was leaning against the wall talking, with her head back against it, and her eyes closed, and he was standing close, listening to her like he thought somebody must be crazy. When they saw me they stopped. We went down, and when we got on the street a cab came up. He offered us a lift, but he had a dinner date uptown instead of down, so I told him to take the cab and I sent the doorman after another one. He went off, and I stood there looking Cecil up and down, and decided she was what I wanted in the way of a woman, and that I was going to hook up with her for the rest of my life. Maybe the love part wouldn't be so hot, anyway on my part, but I had had all I wanted of that. She was decent and you could stick to her, and not feel you had a viper on your chest every time you put your arms around her. I hooked my arm in hers, and pressed it, and tried to get over what I felt.

The doorman came, riding the running board of the cab, and I put her in. I fished in my pocket to tip him, but when I tried to get in, the cab was moving away, and all I could see was a gloved hand waving at me from the window. In another second it was gone.

I started down the street. Then I wondered where I was going. Here I had just made a decision that was to change my whole life, and now it seemed to have evaporated into thin air. I crossed Park, and headed for home. My legs felt queer, and I couldn't seem to walk straight. I remembered I had had four drinks. Then I heard myself laugh. It was like hell the four drinks.

I let myself in, and the hall was dark, and upstairs I could hear Evelyn crying. I opened my mouth to call, and nothing came out of it. I groped for the switch. Then I heard a rustle behind me. I half turned, and felt something horrible coming at me. It hit me. She was panting like an animal, and got my face with both hands at once, I went down, and those claws raked me. I must have let out some kind of a yell, because one hand grabbed my mouth, and the other hand raked me again. I tried to throw her off, and couldn't. She held me, and pounded my head against the floor. Then I felt myself being beaten with something. The marks afterward showed it was the heel of her shoe. And all the time she was talking to me, not loud, but in a terrible whisper: " . . . You would do that to me . . . You beast . . . You swine . . . You can have her . . . What do I care who you have . . . But that . . . But *that* . . . Get out of here . . . Get out of here! *Get out of here! . . .* "

Her voice rose to a scream at that, and upstairs both children began to wail, and I threw her off, and got the door open, and staggered down the steps to the street.

Next thing I knew, I was in Central Park, on a bench. I still had the light topcoat on, that I had worn to the party, but I didn't have my hat. The coat sleeve was down over my hand. I felt the shoulder. It was torn. Something tickled my mouth. I brushed it off, and it was blood. Then I saw blood on the coat. I took out my handkerchief, and my whole face was running blood. I wiped it, and wiped it again, until the whole handkerchief was nothing but a red rag, and it kept on bleeding. I tried to think where I was going to go. I couldn't go to a good hotel. I remembered a dump on Twenty-third Street, where I had once made a speech to a banquet of equipment manufacturers, flagged a cab, and went down there.

I pushed through the revolving door, and hated to cross the lobby. The clerk looked up, with his plastered-on smile, and it stayed plastered on, when he saw me, like in one of those movies where they stop the camera a second, to get a laugh. He swung his turntable around, but slow, like he hated to do it. I registered:

Leonard Borland   *City*

While I was writing, his hand wandered to the key rack, and then it wandered to a button, and pressed it. In a second a big gimlet-eyed guy was standing beside me, and everything about him said house detective. They looked at each other. The clerk swung the turntable around again, read my card, and spoke mechanically, while he was blotting it, like an announcement on an old-time phonograph record: "Single room, Mr. Borland? We have them at a dollar-and-a-half, two and two-and-a-half. With bath, three, four and five."

"I want a bedroom, bath and sitting room."

I needed a sitting room about as much as an ourang-outang does, but I had to say something to take them off guard. I was in terror they'd give me the bum's rush across the lobby. If they tried that, I didn't know what I would do. I might take the joint apart, and I might do nothing, and just land in the gutter, and that was what I dreaded most of all.

They looked at each other again. "We have a very nice suite on the tenth floor, outside—bedroom, bath, sitting room, and small kitchenette with ice box—seven dollars."

"That'll be all right."

"Ah—have you luggage, Mr. Borland?"

"No."

I took out my bill-fold. I still had a hunk of cash that I'd brought back from the trip, and I laid down a $50 bill. They relaxed, and so did I, and began to talk like myself. "Have you a house doctor?"

"No, but we have one on call."

"Will you get him, and send him up to me as quick as you can? I've—been in an accident."

"Yes, sir. Right away, Mr. Borland."

The house dick took charge of me then. He put his arm around me like I could hardly walk, and called a boy, and took me up to my room, and talked like I had been in a taxi accident, and said it was a crime the way those guys drove. If anybody could get a face like mine in a taxi accident, it would be a miracle, but it was his way of saying everything was O. K., that there would be no questions asked, that he'd take care of me. "You haven't had dinner yet, Mr. Borland?"

"No, I haven't."

"I'll send the waiter up right away."

"Fine."

"Or maybe you'd rather wait till you've seen the doctor? Tell you what I'll do. I'll send the waiter up now, and after the doc gets through, you ring room service and tell them you're ready. I recommend the turkey, sir. They've got nice roast turkey on the bill tonight, fine, young, Vermont turkey, from our farm up there—and the chef has a way with it. He really has, sir."

"Turkey sounds all right."

They sent the coat out to be cleaned and fixed up, and had a boy go down and buy me pajamas on Fourteenth Street, and the doctor came and plastered me up, and I had the turkey and a bottle of wine with it. I kept the waiter while I ate, and we talked and we got along fine. But then he took the table down, and I was alone, and I went in and had a hot bath, and by then it was about half past nine, and there wasn't anything to do but go to bed. I took off my clothes, and put on the Fourteenth Street pajamas, and got in bed, and pulled up their sleazy cotton blankets, and lay there looking at the paper, where it was beginning to peel off the walls. I tried to think what there was funny about that paper. Then I remembered that paper hadn't been used on hotel walls for fifteen years. Only the old ones have paper.

I turned out the light and tried to sleep. I didn't seem to be thinking about anything at all. But every time I'd drop off I'd wake up, dreaming I was standing there, bellowing at the top of my lungs, and nobody would even turn around and look at me. Then one time this horrible thing was coming at me in the dark, and I woke up moaning. I tried to get to sleep again, and couldn't. I told myself it was just a dream, to forget it, but it wasn't just a dream. I must have dropped off, though, because here it was, coming at me again, and this time I wasn't moaning. I was sobbing. I quit kidding myself then. I knew I'd give anything to have it back, what I had pulled at the party that afternoon. It wasn't brave, it wasn't big, it was just plain silly. I had made a jackass of myself, and put something terrible between me and Doris. I began thinking of her, then, and knew it didn't make any difference what she had done to me, or anything else. I wanted her so bad it was just a terrible ache, wanted her worse than ever. And here I was, I had no wife, I had no home, I had no kids, I had no work, I didn't even have Cecil. I was in this lousy dump, and had just made a mess of my life. I think I hit an all-time low that night. I never felt worse. I couldn't feel worse.

10

Three days later, when I could leave, I went up and took a suite at a hotel in the fifties. I took it by the month. I didn't hear anything from Doris. I began reading the society pages after a couple of days, and she was in. Every time I saw her name I saw Leighton's. On the singing, I never opened my trap. One day a guy showed up at the office by the name of Horn. He sat down, and kept looking around kind of puzzled at the drafting room, and in a minute I asked him pretty sharp what he wanted.

"You're Mr. Borland? Mr. Leonard Borland?"

"Yes, I'm Leonard Borland."

"Well—I got the address out of the phone book, but it certainly doesn't look like the right place, and you don't look like the right guy. What are you, in the construction business?"

"That's right."

"I'm looking for the Leonard Borland that sang with the American Scala Opera Company under the name of Logan Bennett. Anyway, I hear he did."

"Where did you hear that?"

"I was in Pittsburgh last week. I heard it from a friend of mine. Giuseppe Rossi."

" . . . Well? What of it?"

He knew then he had the right guy, and kept looking me over. "I tell you what of it. I'm connected with this outfit that's giving opera over at the Hippodrome, and—"

"Not interested."

"Rossi said you were pretty good."

"Nice guy, Rossi. Remember me to him if you see him."

"I need a baritone."

"Still not interested."

"If you're as good as he says you are, I could make you a pretty nice proposition. You understand, a singer's no draw until he gets known, but I could offer you $125 a night, say, with three appearances a week guaranteed. That's a little more than Rossi was paying you, isn't it?"

"Yeah, quite a little."

"Well—will you think it over?"

"No, I won't think it over."

"Listen, I need a baritone."

"So I judge."

"I got a couple of good tenors, and another one coming. I got a couple of sopranos I think are comers. But in opera, you've got to have one good baritone before you've got a show."

"You certainly have."

"All right then, I'll come up a little. How about a hundred and fifty?"

"Maybe you didn't understand what I said when you came in here. I appreciate what you say, I'm grateful to Rossi,—but I'm just not interested."

The idea of singing made me sick. He went and I put on my hat and engaged in my favorite outdoor sport, about that time. That was walking around the Metropolitan Opera House hoping I'd see Cecil. A couple of days after that I did see her. I raced back to the office as fast as I could get there, and put in a call for her at her hotel. They said she wasn't in. I knew she wouldn't be. That was why I had been watching. I left word that Mr. Borland called. Then for a week I stuck at my desk from nine to six, hoping she would call back. She never did.

All that, what I've just been telling you, was in the last part of November. When the first of December came, it crossed my mind it was funny no bills had been forwarded to me. On the third I found out why. When I came downstairs in the morning and crossed the lobby, the clerk called me and he had my check in his hand, the one I had given him for my next month's room rent. It had bounced. I blinked at it, and I knew then why there hadn't been any bills. Doris was paying her own bills. The money was in a joint account, in her name and mine, and she had drawn every cent of it out, started an account somewhere else, and there I was.

I don't know why it never occurred to me that she would do it. It never entered my head.

I said there must be some mistake, and I would see him that afternoon. I went out, and hustled over to Newark, and borrowed $300 from a manufacturer of power shovels we had done some business with. I got back just in time to get in the bank, so I could cover that check before they closed, then went back and told the clerk it was all right, I had drawn on the wrong account, and he could put it through. I went up to my suite and counted my money. I had $75 over what I had deposited in the bank, and $7 over that. My expenses, over the $170 a month I was paying for the suite, were about $50 a week, not counting club dues and other things I couldn't stave off very long. I was just about a week and a half from the boneyard, and I began to feel it again, that thick rage against Doris and the way she treated me. It would suit her fine, I knew, to have me coming on my knees to her, begging for money, and then give me a song and dance about how she had the children to think of, and send me out with the $12 she could spare from the crumbs she was saving for the household. I didn't have to be told how that would go. I walked around the suite, and after a while something in me clicked. I knew I'd never go to her if I starved first. I began to think about Horn and his $150 a night.

Next day he called up. "Mr. Borland?"

"Yes?"

"This is Bert Horn again. Remember?"

"Oh yeah. How are you?"

"All right. Listen, my other tenor got to town last night. Fact of the matter, I stole him off Rossi and that was what I was doing in Pittsburgh. Guy by the name of Parma. You know him?"

"Yeah, I sang with him. Tell him I said hello."

"I will, and he said to tell you hello. Listen, if you're as good

as *he* says you are, I might raise that offer. I might up the ante to
$200."

"Well now you're talking. Come on over."

He came, and looked me over again, and the place over again,
and then he laughed and shook his head. "Well, if you're a singer
you're the funniest-looking thing in the way of a singer that I ever
saw. No offense, but I swear to God you don't look it.".

"You play?"

"Some kind of way, yes."

"Come on up."

I took him up on the third floor, where the piano was, and
opened the windows, and shoved the Traviata aria in front of him.
He played it and I sang it. When I got through he nodded. "I
guess they weren't kidding me."

We went down again, and he got down to cases. "All right, how
many roles do you know?"

"Three."

" . . . Just three."

"Marcel, Germont, and Rigoletto. I sang one other role, but it
was a pinch-hitting job, and I wouldn't know it now if I heard it."

"What role was it?"

"Wagner in Faust. I don't sing French, but they let me do it in
Italian. They shoved it at me in the morning, I sang it that afternoon, and I had forgotten it by night."

That made the same impression on him it had on the others.
An opera impresario, he's a little like a baseball manager. He knows
all about smoke. He gets that every day. But a guy that can come
out of the bull-pen and finish a ball game, that's different. When
he heard that, he quit worrying, and began to lay it out what I'd
have to do. The hitch came over the guarantee. With just those
three operas, he couldn't make it three times a week, because they
weren't giving Traviata on a weekly schedule. He wanted me to

get up Trovatore, Lucia, and Aida, and then later Don Giovanni, and they would revive it if they thought I was right for it. I said I couldn't get up that many roles by the end of the winter if I had to sing three times a week too. So then he had a different idea. "All right, we'll say Lucia and Trovatore, but get Pagliacci up by next week, and then we can put you on three times. You see, ham-and-eggs is once a week too, and—"

" . . . What is?"

"Ham and eggs. Cavalleria Rusticana and Pagliacci, the double bill. Pagliacci you can get up quick. After the prologue, which I suppose you know, you have almost nothing to do, just two real scenes, not over ten minutes of actual singing altogether. Then we can—"

"Oh. All right then."

"You'll need a coach. I recommend Lorentz. Hugo Lorentz, I'll give you his address, a good man, works with us, and—"

"You know anybody else?"

" . . . Well, there's Siegal. He's more of a voice teacher, but he knows the routines, and—"

"Fine, I'll take him. When do we start?"

"Next week. Get Pagliacci up by then, and then later we can work you in on the others. But we want to bring you out in Rigoletto. That makes you important."

"Nothing I like so well as to be important."

So by that afternoon I had connected with Siegal, and was back in the same old groove. I found out then how much Cecil had been giving me for nothing. Do you know what that bird took? He charged me $25 an hour, and I had to have him every day. I had to borrow $200 more in Newark, and it was an awful crimp in my $600 a week. But at that, $450 was nothing to be sneezed at.

I asked for a rehearsal on Rigoletto, with three or four of the

choristers. In the scene before the courtiers there was some stuff I
wanted to do, and I had to make them slam me down so I really
hit the deck, so when I came crawling back to them I would really
be on my knees. They told me to come over to the theatre. I went
up to the third floor and put on an old suit of corduroys I always
wore around concrete work, and walked over. That was so I could
practice the stage falls. I hadn't remembered about the Hippodrome, while Horn was talking. I mean, it just sounded like a
theatre on Sixth Avenue, and nothing more. So when I went in the
stage door and through, the stage caught me by surprise. I don't
know if you were ever back there to see that stage. It would have
done pretty good for a railroad station if they laid tracks and put
train sheds in, except there would be an awful lot of waste space
up top. But did it feaze me? It did not. I was a pro now. I walked
to the middle of it, let out a couple of big ones, and it felt pretty
good. I stuck out my chest. I thought how I was putting it over on
Doris, and how like hell I would come begging her for anything.

The conductor, Gustav Schultz, was at the piano, and we went
through it. I think he wanted to look me over. I showed them
how I wanted them to heave me, and after a while they got it so it
suited me. When we quit, I saw Parma in the wings, and went over
and shook hands. "Hello boy, hello, how's a old kid?"

"Fine. How's yourself?"

"O. K. Say, is swell, how you do this scene. What da hell? A
goddam baritones, run for a bedroom, make little try, audience all
a time wonder why he don't get in. Look like he must be weak.
Ought to fight like hell, just like you do'm now, and then *pow!*—
down he go, just like this!"

He threw his shoulder under my belly, and I went head over
heels on to the floor. It was one stage fall I didn't expect. Then he
laughed like hell. Singers, they're a funny breed. They've got what
you might call a rudimentary sense of humor, in the first place,

and they're awful proud of their muscles, in the second place. They spend half their time telling the conductor they're going to knock him back into the customers' laps if he doesn't quit his cussedness, and I'll say for them they could do it if they tried. People think they're a flock of fairies. They're more like wrestlers. Well, singing doesn't come from the spirit. It comes from the belly, and it takes plenty of belly and chest to do it right.

I got up, and laughed, and he and Schultz and I went out and had a drink. He took red wine with seltzer. They don't drink much, but a wop tenor likes red ink.

The afternoon of the performance I put off lunch till three o'clock, then went out and had a good one. I came back to the office and vocalized my voice. It came up quick, and felt good. I was beginning to get nervous. They all get nervous, but this was different from what I had felt before. It had a little tingle to it. I felt I was good. I walked up to the hotel and it was about half past four. I lay down and got a little sleep.

It seemed funny to be putting the make-up on without Cecil bobbing in to give me the double O, but I got it in place, and put on the funny clothes, and tried my voice. It was still up, and was all right. Horn came in, looked me over, and nodded. "The contracts are ready."

"You got them with you?"

"My secretary's bringing them over. I'll be in with them after the show. How do you feel?"

"I feel all right."

There came a knock on the door, and a little wop in a derby hat came in and stood beside me where I was at the table and began to talk about how some of my admirers wanted to hear me sing, but their tickets would cost them a lot, and more stuff like that, and I didn't know what the hell he was talking about, except it seemed to be some kind of a touch. Horn was behind him. He nodded and held up ten fingers. I got my pocketbook, passed out $10 and the guy left. "What was that?"

"The claque."

"What's the claque?"

"A bunch of self-elected noise-makers, that you pay to clap when you sing, and whether they do or not nobody knows. If you don't pay, they're supposed to take some terrible revenge, like blowing whistles at you or something like that. Whether they do or not, nobody knows. I generally go along with them, and so do the singers. They're harmless, just one of those things that opera has like a dog has fleas."

"There was nothing like that in the American Scala."

"Maybe they took care of it for you."

He went, and I wished everything that came up didn't remind me of Cecil. I knew who had taken care of it all right, without being told. And I knew why. Knowing the applause was paid, or any part of it was paid, would have taken all the fun out of it for me. So it was taken care of. I tried my voice again, then remembered she had told me when it was right to leave it alone. There didn't seem to be any help for it. Everywhere I turned, she was standing there beside me.

I went down, then walked over and had a look at the calls. Then my heart skipped a beat. On the first two calls at the end of the second act, we were all in it, me, Parma, the Gilda, and the people in the small parts. Then on the next two it was just the Gilda and me. And then it said:

Mr. Borland (If)

I walked out on the stage to get the feel of the set, and the tingle was clear down to my feet. I made up my mind there wasn't going to be any *if* about it. I was going to get that call or split my throat.

Parma was right in the *Questa o Quella*, so Act I got off to a swell start, and they ripped right along with it. I got a hand when I came on, whether it was the claque or the publicity I don't know, but I don't think it could have all been claque. There had been a lot of stuff in the papers about me. I was singing under my own name now, and it seemed to strike them as a good story that a big contractor should turn into a singer, but anyway it made me feel good, and I hit it right in the scene with the second baritone, and we got a fine curtain. Hippodrome opera wasn't like Metropolitan opera. It was 99-cent opera, and that audience acted the way it felt. The second scene of the act went even better. The bass was a pretty good comic, and I fed to him all I could, so we got away with the duet in swell shape. The Gilda was all right in the *Caro Nome*, not like Cecil, but plenty good. The duets went well, and we got another good curtain, and were on our way.

When it came to the scene before the courtiers, the one I had rehearsed with the choristers, I did it a little different than I had been doing it. I got a break at the start. The Ceprano had one of these small, throaty baritones, and when it came to the place where I was to mock him on *Ch'hai di nuovo, buffon*, I shot it back to him just the way he had given it to me, and it got a big laugh. I had them then, and I chucked tone quality out the window. The first part of the scene I shouted, talked, and whispered, till I got to the place where they slammed me back on my hunkers. Then I remembered Bohème. I came crawling back, and plucked the hem of Marullo's doublet, and gave them tears. I sang it *dolce*, and then some. I opened every spigot there was, and at the end of it I was flat on the floor, hanging on to the high F like my heart would break, and finishing off like I could just barely make myself do it. There wasn't any pause then. The first "bravo" came like a pistol shot before I even got through, and then they came from all over the house, and the applause in a swelling roar. I lay there, the heart bowed down, for quite a time. There were thousands of them, and it took them longer to quiet down than in other places. The Gilda came running on, then, and we did the duet, and the curtain came down.

Did I get that call? I'm telling you I did. I took the Gilda out twice, and then Parma aimed a kick at me, and then there I was, in front of them all alone, trying to remember how to bow. There's nothing like it.

I went to my dressing room, walked around, and was so excited I couldn't even sit down. I wanted to go out there and do it all over again. It didn't seem two minutes before they called me, and I went down for the last act.

The Gilda and I did the stuff that starts it, and then went off, and Parma had it to himself for the *La Donna è Mobile*. I think I've given you the idea by now that that dumb wop is a pretty good tenor. He knocked them over with it, and by the time the Maddalena came on, and the Gilda and I went out again for the quartet, we were in the homestretch of one of those performances you read about. So the quartet started. Well, you've heard the Rigoletto quartet a thousand times, but don't let anybody tell you it's a pushover. The first part goes a mile a minute, the second part slower than hell, and if there's one thing harder to sing than a fast allegro it's a slow andante, and three times out of five something happens, and many times as you've heard it you haven't often heard it right. But we were right. Parma started it like a breeze, and the Maddalena was right on top of him, and the Gilda and I were right on top of her, and we closed out the allegro with all our cylinders clicking and the show doing seventy. Parma laid it down nice on the andante, and we were right with him, and we brought it home just right. We were right on the end of the stick. Well, that stopped the show too. They clapped, and cheered, and clapped some more, and Schultz threw the stick on me to go on, and a fat chance I could. We had to give them some more. So after about a minute, Schultz played the cue for the andante, and Parma started again.

He started, and the Maddalena came in, and the Gilda came in, and I came in. It seemed to me we got in there with it awful quick, but I was so excited by that time I hardly knew where I was, and I didn't pay much attention to it. And then all of a sudden I had this awful feeling that something was wrong.

I want you to get it straight now, what happened. The andante is the same old tune, *Bella figliav dell'amore*, that you've heard all your life and could whistle in your sleep. The tenor sings it through once, then he goes up to a high B flat, holds it, comes down again, and sings it over again. The second time he sings it, the contralto comes in, then the soprano, then the baritone, and they're off into the real quartet. Well, our contralto, the Maddalena, was an old-time operatic hack that had sung it a thousand times, but something got into her, and instead of waiting for Parma to finish that strain once, she came in like she would on the repeat. And she pulled the Gilda in. And the Gilda pulled me in. You remember what I told you about speed? Up there you've got no time to think. You hear your cue, and you come in, and God help you if you miss the boat. So there was Parma and there was the orchestra, in one place in the score, and there were the Maddalena, the Gilda, and me, in another place in the score, and there was Schultz, trying like a wild man to straighten it out. Not a whisper from the audience, you understand. So long as you keep going, and do your best, they'll give you a break, and even if you crack up and have to start over they'll give you a break—so long as you do your best. They all want to laugh, but they won't—so long as you keep your head down and sock.

But I didn't know then what was wrong. All I knew was that it was getting sourer by the second, and I started looking around for help. That was all they needed. That one little flash of the white feather, and they let out a roar.

You can think of a lot of things in one beat of music. It flashed through my head I had heard the bird at last. It flashed through my head, in some kind of dumb way, why I had heard it. I turned around and faced them. I must have looked sore. They roared again.

That whole big theatre then was spinning around for me like a cage with a squirrel in it, and me the squirrel. I had to know where I was at. I looked over, and tried to see Parma. And then, brother, and then once more, I committed the cardinal sin of all grand opera. I forgot to watch the conductor. I didn't know that he had killed his orchestra, killed his singers, brought the whole thing to a stop, and was wigwagging Parma to start it over. And here I came, bellowing out with my part:

Taci e mia saràla cura, la vendetta d'affrettar!

They howled. They let out a shriek you could hear in Harlem. Some egg yelled "Bravo!" A hundred of them yelled "Bravo!" A million of them yelled "Bravo," and applauded like hell.

I ran.

Next thing I knew, I was by a stairway, holding on to the iron railing, almost twisting it out by the roots trying to keep myself from flying into a million pieces. The Gilda was beside me, yelling at me at the top of her lungs, and don't think a coloratura soprano can't put on a nice job of plain and fancy cussing when she gets sore. The stagehands were standing around, looking at me as though I was some leper that they didn't dare touch. Outside, Schultz was playing the introduction to the stuff between the contralto and the bass. He had had to skip five whole pages. I just stood there, twisting at those iron bars.

Somewhere off, I heard the fire door slam, and next thing I knew, Cecil was there, her eyes big as saucers with horror. She grabbed hold of me. "You go out there and finish this show, or I'll—"

"I can't!"

"You've got to! You've simply got to. You went yellow! You went yellow out there, and you've got to go back and lick them! You've got to!"

"Let me alone!"

"But what are they going to do? You can't let them down like that!"

"I don't *care* what they do!"

"Leonard, listen to me. They're out there. They're all out there, she, and your two kids, and you've got to finish it. You've just got to do it!"

"I won't! I'll *never* go out there—"

They were playing my cue. She took hold of me, tried to pull me away from the stairs, tried to throw me on stage by main force. I hung on. I hung on to that iron like it was a life raft. The bass started singing my part. She looked at me and bit her lip. I saw two tears jump out of her eyes and run down her face. She turned around and left me.

I got to my dressing room, locked the door, and then I cracked. No iron bars there to hold on to. I clenched my teeth, my fists, my toes, and it was no good. Here they came, those awful, hysterical sobs I had heard coming out of Doris that day, and the more I fought them back, the worse they got. I knew the truth then, knew why Cecil had laughed at me that night in Rochester, why Horn had been so doubtful about me, and all the rest of it. I was no trouper, and they knew it. I had smoke, and nothing else. But you can't lick that racket with smoke. You've got to care about it, you can't get by on a little voice and a little music. You've got to dig up the heart to take it when it's tough, and the only way you can find the heart is to love it. I was just another Doris. I had everything but what it takes. Down on the stage, the bass was doubling for me. He carried the Gilda in, put her on the rock, then picked up a cape, turned around, and did my part. They gave him an ovation. After Parma had taken Schultz out, and they had all taken their bows, they shoved him out there alone, and the audience stood up and gave him a rising vote, in silence, before they started to clap. His name was Woods. Remember it, Woods: the man that had what it takes. But Rigoletto didn't know anything about that, yet. He was up there in his dressing room, blubbering like some kid that saw the boogey man, and looking at himself and his cap and bells. Maybe you think he didn't look sick.

11

Back in 1921, when Dempsey fought Carpentier in Jersey, some newspaper hired a lady novelist, I think it was Alice Duer Miller, to do a piece on it. She decided that what she wanted to write up was the loser's dressing room after it was all over. She had been reading all her life about the winner, and thought she would like to know for once what happened to the loser. She found out. What happened to him was nothing. Carpentier was there, and a couple of rubbers were there, working on him, and his manager was there, and that was all. Nobody came in to tell him he had put up a good fight, or that it was a hell of a wallop he hit Dempsey in the second round, or even to borrow a quarter. Outside you could hear them still yelling for Dempsey, but not one in all that crowd had a minute for Gorgeous Georges, the Orchid Man.

That's how it was with me. There were no autograph hunters that night. There were feet, running past the door and voices saying "I'll meet you outside," and tenors showing their friends they knew "*La Donna è Mobile*," and the whistle brigade, but none of them stopped, none of them had a word for me. It got quiet after a while, and the noise outside died away, and I lit a cigarette and sat there. After a long time there was a tap on the door. I never moved. It came again and still again, and then I heard my first name called. It sounded like Doris, and I went to the door and opened it. She was there, in a little green suit, and a brown felt hat, and brown shoes. She came in without looking at me. "What happened?"

"Weren't you there?"

"I had to take the children home after the second act. I heard some people talking, on my way backstage."

I remembered Lorentz and his real crime at the Cathedral Theatre that day. I was glad there was one person in the world that hadn't seen it. Three, because that meant she had taken the kids out before it happened. " . . . I got the bird."

"Damn them."

She walked around, saying what she thought of them. Cecil never talked like that. She might tell you they were a pack of hyenas, but she never got sore at them, never regarded them as anything but so many people to be licked. But Doris had felt their teeth, and besides she had a gift for polishing them off, you might say, on account of her cobra blood. The cobra strain was what I wanted then. She snarled it out, and I wanted all she could give. Down in my heart, I knew Cecil was right, that it's never anybody's fault but your own. But I was still bleeding. What Doris had to say, it hit the spot.

But it wasn't any consolation scene. That wasn't what she came in there for, I could see that. She seemed to be under some kind of a strain, and kept talking without looking at me. When I started to take the make-up off, she got busy with the towel, and when I was ready for my clothes, she helped me into them. That was funny. Nothing like that had ever happened before. We went out, and got a cab, and I called out the name of my hotel. She didn't say anything. On the way up I kept thinking there was something I had forgotten, something I had intended to do. Then I remembered. I was to sign the contracts. I sat back and watched the El posts go back. That was one thing I didn't have to worry about.

When we got into the lobby, I could see something glaring at me from a chair near the elevators, and I didn't tumble at first to what it was. There had been so many glares coming my way lately that one more didn't make much impression. But then I came out of the fog. It was Craig, my partner, that I hadn't seen since we built the gag chicken coop up in Connecticut, and he had dug in at his place up-state. I blinked, and looked at Doris, and thought maybe that was why she had come around, or anyway had something to do with it. But she seemed as surprised as I was. He still sat there, glaring at us, and then he got up and came over. He didn't shake hands. He started in high, and he was plenty sore. "Where've you been?"

"Why—right here."

"And why here? What's the idea of hiding out in this goddam dump? I've been looking for you all night, and it was just by accident that I found you. Just by accident."

Doris cut in, meeker than I ever heard her. "Why—one of the children was threatened with measles, and Leonard came down here so he wouldn't be quarantined."

"Couldn't he let somebody know?"

"He—it was only to be for a few days."

That seemed to cool him off a little, and I tried to be friendly.

"When did you get to town? I thought you were up there milking cows."

"Never mind when I got to town, and never mind the cows. And cut the comedy. Get this."

"I'm listening."

"You've got just forty minutes to make a train, and you pay attention to what I'm telling you."

"Shoot."

"Alabama. You've heard of it?"

"Sounds familiar."

"There's a big government-aid railroad bridge going up down there, and we build bridges, this here Craig-Borland Company that we've got, even if you seem to have forgotten it. You get down there, and you get that contract."

"Where is this bridge?"

"I got no time for that. It's all in here, in this briefcase, the whole thing, and you can read it going down. Here's your tickets for the two of you, and remember, you got thirty-nine minutes. When you get there, I'll wire you our bid. I'll put the whole thing on the wire, it's being figured up now. The main thing now is—get there."

"O. K. Chief."

He turned to Doris. "And you—"

"Yes sir."

"Listen to what I'm telling you. This is a bunch of well-bo'n South'ners dat dey grandaddy had slaves befo' de wa', lo's'n lo's o' slaves, and they've got to be impressed. You hear that? You take a whole floor in that hotel, and you roll out the liquor, and you step on it. You do all the things that your bum, sassiety, high-toned, good-for-nothing upbringing has taught you how to do, and then you do it twice."

"Booh. I know you."

"For once in your life, maybe you can be of some use."

"Just once?"

"If you don't put it across, you needn't come back."

"We'll put it across."

So we put it across. They've got a bird in my business too, that rides the trusses while the scows are taking them out, and flies around and flaps its wings and crows whenever one of them falls in the river. But his wings didn't get much exercise on that job, and neither did his voice. It was my trade. The river got pretty tough once or twice, and we had some close squeaks. But not one of those trusses took a dive.

But I'm ahead of my story. Craig had a paper stuck in his pocket, and after he had laid the law down he began to get sore again and remembered it. He tapped it with his finger. "And you keep in touch with me. If it hadn't been for this, seeing your name in this paper just by accident, I wouldn't have known *where* to look for you."

He took it out and opened it, and pointed to a great big picture of me in the whiskers, and wig and cap, and bells, on the theatrical page. "Is that you?"

Doris let out a cackle that made everybody in the lobby look up. It was just a silvery peal that came from the heart, and did you good to hear it. She wasn't laughing at me. She was laughing at Craig, and when I looked at him I had to laugh too. I had to laugh so hard I folded into one of the lobby chairs, and so did she. The look on that old hard-rock man's face, holding up that picture, was the funniest thing I ever saw in my life, or ever hope to see.

I scrambled up and threw my stuff into a bag, and was so excited over getting back in harness that I kept singing all the time and didn't even feel bad about it, and down in the lobby Doris called the house and we made the train. We had the drawing room, but

I was out of cigarettes, and I went in the club car to get some. I would have sent the porter, but he was still making up berths, and I didn't want to bother him. When I got back she was already tucked in, in the upper berth, and all you could see was a tousle of red hair. I undressed, got into the lower. I waited, and she didn't say anything. I turned out my light, and still nothing from her. All you could hear was the wheels, going clickety click: They kind of beat time, and I started to sing the opening of a duet:

> *Là ci darem la mano!*
> *Là mi dirai di sì*
> *Vedi non è lontano*
> *Partiam ben mio da qui*

It was time for her to come in, and I waited. Then: "Did you sing that with her?"

"No, I never did."

"Are you sure?"

"They were going to have me do Don Giovanni. This last outfit, I mean. So I got the score, and found it in there. I had heard you humming it around, so—I learned it."

She came tumbling down the ladder, all floppy in a suit of my pajamas. She slipped in beside me, put her arms around me. "Leonard."

"Yes?"

"I'm glad you flopped. Because I flopped, and—if you could do this one thing I've always wanted to do, and can't—I couldn't stand it. And—"

"Go on. And what?"

"It'll be all mine, now, this that you have in your throat. That's why I came back there. Leonard, when you sang that day it almost killed me. I think you wanted it to. Oh, I've been a terrible wife to you, Leonard. I'm jealous, and spiteful, and mean and nothing will ever change me. But when I get too terrible, just sing to me, and I'll be your slave. I'll come crawling to you, just the way you came crawling to them, in the second act tonight. That woman has given us something that was never there before, and I'm going to thank her, and win her, and make her my friend. Oh, I can, I don't care what has gone before, I can win anybody when I really want them. . . . Now I'll say it. Something you've never heard me say before. I've fallen in love. With my own husband."

I held her tight. She put her mouth against my throat, and began kissing it. "Now sing, and I'll sing."

Là ci darem la mano!
Là mi dirai di sì
Vedi non è lontano
Partiam ben mio da qui.
Vorrei e non vorrei
Mi trema un poco il cor
Felice è ver sarei
Ma può burlarmi ancor . . . . .

We sang it together, and it was terrible, and it was the sweetest duet I ever heard. That's all.

DEATH ON THE BEACH

His name was Diego, and he was bound for Playa Washington, a beach in Northern Mexico, partly for a Sunday's outing, partly to drum up business for the "taxi" he was driving. He was a good-looking Mexican in his late twenties, a bit taller than average, and of the *café con leche* color, lightly flushed with cinnamon, that bespeaks the *mestizo*, or mixture of Spanish and Indian. He wore khaki shorts, sport shirt, two-toned shoes, and brown cloth hat with eyelets. He whistled Cielito Lindo and glanced occasionally at the tremendous afternoon sky, but his attention was on his gauges, especially the speedometer, for the road, through improved, was rough, and tended, at too fast a clip, to heat tires and explode them. His car was a sedan, and though he operated it for hire around Matamoras, a little city on the Rio Grande, there was nothing about it that was different from any family bus.

After 22 miles from Matamoras the road ended, and he pulled off to a field, parking with other cars and leaving the road clear for the special buses that are a feature of fiestas in Mexico, and often run on rough-and-ready principles. To the boys who swarmed over him, he amiably passed out coppers, Mexican coins the size of half dollars, and to a character in snuffy cottons, who professed to be in charge, twenty-five cents American. Then, after locking up, he headed for the dunes which give this coast its special character. They are 8-10-12 feet high, of sand so bright it blazes under the sun and sends up shimmering refractions of light. The result is, the land is screened from the sea, the sea from the land, so Diego didn't see the beach until he popped through a break in the dunes, and was in the middle of it. It was well worth the smile it brought to his face. It was a riot of color, from rugs, robes, rubber animals, and gaudy beach umbrellas; and thousands of people lolled, joked, flirted, and snoozed on it. Also, many swam, especially girls in infra-Bikini suits, with the eager zest for water that is the immemorial heritage of these people. When they went out too far, so far the porpoises offshore took an interest, the nearest Gendarme blew his whistle, calling them in. they came, but not meekly. Volubly they expressed their opinion, and volubly he answered them back. Lately, proper lifeguards have been provided for Playa Washington, with pulmotors and fancy equipment, but at this time the Gendarmes were the only supervision it had, and if they overworked their whistles, the danger, as we shall see, was real.

Diego brushed off some mariachi singers, and made his way through comestible vendors to the soft-drink stand, a tiny thatched thing on pilings, the only actual, nailed-together structure that Playa Washington had. He bought a Bimbo. As he stood swigging it from the bottle, his eye fell on a boy in red trunks who dashed through the crowd, yanking women by their shoulder straps, men by their pant-legs, boys by their ears, and girls by their hair, interspersing these pranks with challenges to wrestle. Through no more than four, such was his strength that several bigger boys got dumped on their backs in a minute or two. After each such triumph, he ran to a girl, who was seated at the foot of a dune and who seemed to be his mother. When she gave him admiration, he ran out to find more victims. "That boy," said another customer at the stand, "is a pest. He needs treatment on his backside. He needs it tanned up good with a belt."

"Oh," said Diego, "he's little."

"So's a goat. But I don't like him."

"He has his points. Sure."

"Name me one. Name me a point."

"Hey," Diego called to the boy. "Hey, you."

The boy, running over, chose a Jippo, and when Diego bought it for him, grabbed it, stuck out his tongue, and ran off. "Gil!" cried the girl on the dune. "You must thank the gentleman. Say gracias."

"You win, she's a point. O.K."

The other customer surveyed her enviously as Diego strolled over lifting his hat, and she got up to smooth her skirt. She was tiny, with something doll-like about her figure, though it didn't lack for voluptuousness. She was the color of dark red mahogany, and her features were delicate, showing little of the flat, massive moulding that goes with the Indian. Her eyes were a mischievous, flirty black, matching her hair, and her teeth, against the mulberry of her lips, looked blue. Her dress was pizen purple, but considering the form it covered, no dress could really look bad. Her shoes were red, as her bag was. At her throat were big red wooden beads. She was possibly 20 years old.

"Fine boy," said Diego. "Quite a lad."

"He must thank you," she said. "—Gil!"

But Gil paid no attention, and Diego told her: "It's nothing, let him be . . . . He's yours?"

"But of course."

"And his—Papa? You're married?"

" . . . Not now."

"Perhaps you'll have a Jippo?"

"Please, for me, Orange Crush."

He got her Orange Crush, and they sat on the dune together. She confessed she had seen him parked, in front of the cafe where she worked, in Matamoras. He expressed surprise he hadn't seen her, as he was in the cafe quite often. She said she didn't serve in the dining room, but worked in the kitchen. "I am only a poor galopina," she added, but in a flirty, provocative way. He then told her his name, and she said hers was Maria.

"You live in Matamoras?" he asked her.

"In a little jacal, by the river."

"You and your boy?"

"I and Gil. My little Hercules."

They had considerable talk about Gil, his exuberance, his strength, his skill at swimming, acquired in the river, which he swam several times daily, " . . . across to Fort Brown and back." It was clear that if Gil was a pest to others, to her he was wonderful. However, after Diego prodded with inquiries, she admitted that if Diego would buy the boy his supper, perhaps a snack from the vendors, she had neighbors who would keep an eye on him, so they could tuck him away in the jacal, and have the evening to themselves. He mentioned he might have passengers going up, but she said that was all right, "as I can ride front with you, and hold Gil in my lap."

"Wouldn't mind holding you in *my* lap."

"Ah-ha-ha."

With various such sallies from him, and suitable parries from her, the discussion took a while, during which Gil outdid himself, presently arousing a gang which meant to thump him, and running into her arms. Then he darted for the sea, waited for a wave to smash, waded in, and was out, swimming, before the next one rolled in. When the Gendarme screeched his whistle, he waved derisively and kept on. The Gendarme screeched again, and Maria ran out like a little hornet to tell him off. She said Gil swam better than anyone, and it was up to stupid Gendarmes to let him alone. The Gendarme said regardless of who he swam better than, she could get him in or she'd spend the night in the carcel. Diego called "Jippo, Jippo, Jippo," and this had the desired effect. Gill came in on a comber, ducked past the Gendarme, and ran to the stand for his Jippo. Diego led Maria back to the dune.

Things might have eased off then, but Gil had the Gendarme to settle with. Tossing the bottle away, he ran over, stuck out his tongue, made a noise. The Gendarme paid no heed. He did it again, and still the Gendarme, who was big, handsome, and cold, didn't look, simply standing there, his hand on his pistol butt, his eye roving the beach. Gil made one more pass, then plunged into the sea as before and swam out as before. However, he went much further this time, and Maria ran down, commanding the Gendarme to whistle. Couldn't he see that the boy was out too far? What kind of policing was this, to let a child get into danger and then do nothing about it?

"It is a beautiful day," said the Gendarme.

"But Gil, my little Gil!"

"He swims so well, who am I to interfere?"

Maria now called to Gil but he paid no attention. Diego, joining her, repeated his previous ruse, calling "Jippo, Jippo, Jippo," and anything else he could think of, but this time unsuccessfully. Gil simply swam on, until he was 200-300-400 yards out, and quite a few people, gathering back of the Gendarme, were beginning to take an interest. And then suddenly disaster struck. The porpoises cavorted over, obviously bent on a play, but Gil's cry told of his terror. Then he wasn't there, and a murmur went through the crowd. Maria started to scream. Diego put his arms around her and tried to calm her, but she broke away, and called "Gil" at the top of her lungs.

During this, which took just a few seconds, the Gendarme stared out to sea, then spoke to a boy. The boy ran down to where some girls had a raft in the sea, an inflated rubber thing they were paddling. After a shouted exchange, they wrestle it through the surf, hiked it to the boys' shoulders, and as he ran to the Gendarme with it, followed with the paddles. The Gendarme hadn't moved, and didn't, during the choosing of volunteers, the relaunching of the raft, and its trip out through the swells. He stayed right where he was, his boot-heel marking the spot where Gil had gone out, so he could indicate, with wigwags, the spot where he had gone down. When the raft got there, a boy slipped over the side, but in a second or two came up, to be pulled in by a companion. Cupping his hands, he reported: The porpoises were all around, especially under the surface. One of them had bumped him, and he was sure they were fighting him off. He was afraid to go over again, and asked permission to call the search off. "Come in," called the Gendarme. "We don't endanger more lives for the sake of one which is lost."

No voice was raised in protest, though many by now were watching. But as the raft started in, Maria ran at the surf, to be scooped up by the Gendarme. He held her, talked to her, threatened her. "Anyone know this girl?" he presently asked.

"I do, she's a friend," said Diego.

"Get her out of here," said the Gendarme.

"I'll do what I can."

"Soon as I'm done with her, take her home. When the body washes in she'll be notified. Keep her away from the water. Because if this goes on, and people have to risk their lives to save her, I'll have to act. I won't have any more of it."

"My poor, poor little Gil," sobbed Maria.

"You might have controlled him, Senora."

"Who could control one so strong?"

"For lack of control he has drowned."

"No! I will not believe it!"

"The *cuerpo* perhaps will convince you."

Diego half carried her to the dune, whispered to her, patted her, and got her a little quieter. The Gendarme commandeered an *escriban public*, who came over, set up his table in front of Maria, and asked names, ages, place of residence, etc., for the official *relato*. It had a Doomsday sound, and upset her horribly, but at last he was done, the Gendarme signed, and he went. Maria, it appeared, could now go.

However, she didn't, remaining where she was, a huddled heap of purple at the foot of the dune, Diego sitting beside her. The sun dropped low, and people lined up for busses. Men approached Diego to engage his car, preferring the expense to a wait, but he said he wasn't libre. Twilight came, and quite suddenly, dark, bringing a chill to the air. It wasn't this, however, that emptied the beach of its revelers, but the food situation, for the Playa had no facilities, and people have to eat. Soon no one was there but the soft-drink lady, the Gendarmes, taking a last look around, and the lonely pair on the dune. A vendor offered tamales, and when Diego waved him off, his boy tried to be helpful. Why wait? he wanted to know. The sharks, which come in at night, would eat the body anyhow, so what point was there in hanging around?

"Out!" screamed Maria. "No!"

"Such talk!" said the soft-drink lady. "And to a mother! About sharks!"

"It's a well-know fact," said the boy.

"It's horrible!"

"Why? He's dead, isn't he?"

Baffled at such irrationality, he went with his father, and the soft-drink lady had a try. Maria made no response, only staring at the sea, which had changed from its day-time color, of deep indigo, to a nighttime black shot with streaks of iridescent blue, and topped at the surf by bright white feathers rushing in. the Gendarme appeared from up the beach, and clumped on down, his eyes shooting around, possibly looking for drunks buried in the sand. At last Diego took her hand. "Maria," he said, "it is time. You do Gil no good. You only do yourself harm."

"And you harm, is that it?"

"I don't complain, but it is time."

"Then, I'll come."

"You're a good girl," said the soft-drink lady.

"I'll take you home," said Diego.

"Whatever you say."

"We'll have dinner somewhere first."

She got up, dusted the sand off her hips, got a comb from her bag and began running it through her hair.

As she stood, refastening her silver barette, a wail came from the sea. " . . . What was that?" she asked sharply. "Did you hear something?"

"No," said the soft-drink lady.

"Perhaps a gull," said Diego.

"At night, a gull?" said Maria.

The wail repeated, so no one could fail to hear it, or pretend it was only a bird. It quavered, and with an unmistakable insistence, as though intended for those on the beach.

"It is Gil!" screamed Maria. "He is there! He is calling me! . . . Gil! I'm coming! *Gil!*"

She dashed once more at the sea, and this time it was Diego who caught her, bringing her back by main force. The soft-drink lady talked to her, but uselessly. The Gendarme came from down the beach, took in the situation, and told Maria if she didn't stop her nonsense, he was putting her in his car, taking her to Matamoras, and locking her up for disorderly conduct. But as he started to say it all over again, to impress it on her mind, the wail came again, so even he was jolted, and stood irresolute, not knowing what to make of it.

Maria was beside herself, and as the wail kept up, seeming to come closer all the time, it was all Diego could do to hold her. Finally, motioning the Gendarme to take charge, he walked to one side, sad down, and took off his two-toned shoes. Then, stuffing his stockings into them and laying his hat on top of them, he marched down to the surf. "What are you doing?" asked the Gendarme.

"What do you think?" said Diego.

"You're crazy."

"If this keeps up," Diego told him "we'll *all* be crazy and that girl will be dead. She's going after that boy, and something's got to be done. I don't know who that is, but if you'll kindly hand on to *her*, I mean to find out."

"Suppose it's not a who?"

"All right then, it's a what."

"You may find out more than you expect."

"At least, we'll know."

He faced the sea, closed his eyes in prayer, and went in. He took a comber sidewise, then straightened out and started to swim. He confessed later to a horrible fear, as it seemed to him the wail was from the other world and suggested death. He reached the spot where it seemed to come from, then was started to hear it behind him. With a sense of being cut off, he pulled his feet up, reversed direction, and started back. Then, in horror, he saw a fin and remembered the sharks. He panicked, digging for shore. Then red trucks flashed at his eyes, and Gil rose in front of him. He rose clear out of the sea, moaning as Diego insisted later, and landed plop in his arms. In utter terror by now, afraid to hold on, for fear the shark would close in, ashamed to let go, he did nothing but thresh with his feet and beat around with one free arm. But the roll of the waves was with him, and in a few moments he made it, Gill still on his shoulder. As he staggered out on the sand, Maria grabbed the boy, the soft-drink woman grabbed her, and the Gendarme grabbed Diego, thumping him on the back for his bravery, and blowing his whistle for help.

Exhausted, Diego collapsed, but revived and yelled to them all: "Work on him—give him artificial respiration! He's alive! He spoke to me! He spoke and leaped out of the sea!"

"He's dead," said the soft-drink lady.

"He's cold, so cold," said Maria.

"Thus the tale," said my friend, the pilot at the Brazos Santiago station, a few miles north of Playa Washington, "as I heard it around Matamoras."

"I admit it's spooky," I said, "and as a feat of derring-do, quite romantic. Only trouble is, I don't believe it."

"I do," he said. "That's the difference."

"Captain, you surprise me."

"Maybe, but I think it's true."

"Shark and all?"

"Wasn't a shark, but sharks figure in it."

"What was it, then?"

"Porpoise."

"And the wail, what about that?"

"That was a porpoise too."

"Bringing the boy in to Mamma?"

"That's just about it."

He said, looking at the thing from the point of view of the porpoises, they were probably delighted when Gil swam out where they were, as "they love to play and love little boys. That statue they put in the picture, of a boy riding a dolphin, was not far-fetched. It has happened in the aquariums, as those things aren't fish. They're animals. And when Gil began to sink, their idea was, get him up to the surface again, get him breathing. So they handled him just like one of their own pups. They began bumping him up to the surface, and when the boy on the raft said they were fighting him off, he probably was telling the truth. But of course it didn't work, and then night came on and changed the whole picture."

"In what way, Captain?"

"The sharks."

"Then they *do* come in at night?"

"Or, like most fish, they begin to bite at night."

"So they're more dangerous."

"As anyone who knows them will tell you."

"And what then?

"The porpoises began bringing him in."

"Bumping him with their noses?"

"Exactly that."

"To Maria?"

"I wouldn't put it past them."

He said the interest animals take in people is more than is commonly realized. "And in the case of porpoises," he went on, "they talk. I've heard them many a time, standing watch on deck, as they swim along with the ship, especially at night. But I'm telling you, I don't know as we sit here if they talk to themselves, each other, or me. Maybe they're just breathing, but maybe it's something more, and they were calling Maria that night, bringing her little boy in, saving him from the sharks. They can handle a shark—they bump him too, and hard, right in the gills, and as they bump they bite, tearing his gill feathers out. But they can't handle all sharks all night. So they did what they could in their way. But she interested me more than they did."

"Maria? In what way, Captain?"

"As the eternal *soldadera*."

"The soldier's girl?"

"A *muchacha* who must have a hero."

"First little Gil—?"

"And then big Diego. Kind of nice."

He told me the rest of the story, how the Gendarme, with the *cuerpo* recovered all the difficult questions settled, outdid himself to make things easy for her. He paced the way, in the patrol car, up to Matamoras, while she followed with Diego holding the little cold body to her warm one. He routed the undertaker out, made all the arrangements for the inquest next day, the services, and burial. He had everything fixed up in a few minutes, so when she walked out, the band was just ending its concert, in the Plaza de Hidalgo, for the same people as had been at the beach, now all dressed up for the evening.

As she sat on a bench with Diego, she felt his clothes, which were wet, clucking with concern. But he motioned toward the band. It was playing Estrellita, and suddenly she started to weep. "For you," he said, taking her hand and drawing it through his arm. "The play to your Little Star."

"Yes, my little Gil."

"If I had only gone sooner!" Diego exclaimed.

"You did your best. You are now . . . "

She caught herself, then half defiantly, as he waited, went on:
" . . . my Big Star. My brave one."

"You want me, then?"

"Diego, I do . . . "

"And so," said the pilot, "she lost someone, and gained someone. They're married now, and as I hear, quite happy. Neither of them, probably, have any idea of the true explanation of what happened, but neither of them are wrong as to the amount of bravery involved. Because, my friend, would you have answered that call, in that sea, on that night? I wouldn't, but he did."

DEAD MAN

I

He felt the train check, knew what it meant. In a moment, from up toward the engine, came the chant of the railroad detective: "Rise and shine, boys, rise and shine." The hoboes began dropping off. He could hear them out there in the dark, cursing as the train went by. That was what they always did on these freights: let the hoboes climb on in the yards, making no effort to dislodge them there; for that would have meant a foolish game of hide-and-seek between two or three detectives and two or three hundred hoboes, with the hoboes swarming on as fast as the detectives put them off. What they did was let the hoboes alone until the train was several miles under way; then they pulled down to a speed slow enough for men to drop off, but too fast for them to climb back on. Then the detective went down the line, brushing them off, like caterpillars from a twig. In two minutes they would all be ditched, a crowd of bitter men in a lonely spot; but they always cursed, always seemed surprised.

He crouched in the coal gondola and waited. He hadn't boarded a flat or a refrigerator with the others, back in the Los

Angeles yards, tempting though this comfort was. He wasn't long on the road, and he still didn't like to mix with the other hoboes, admit he was one of them. Also, he couldn't shake off a notion that he was sharper than they were, that playing a lone hand he might think of some magnificent trick that would defeat the detective, and thus, even at this ignoble trade, give him a sense of accomplishment, of being good at it. He had slipped into the gond not in spite of its harshness, but because of it; it was black, and would give him a chance to hide, and the detective, not expecting him there, might pass him by. He was nineteen years old, and was proud of the nickname they had given him in the poolroom back home. They called him Lucky.

"Rise and shine, boys, rise and shine."

Three dropped off the tank car ahead, and the detective climbed into the gond. The flashlight shot around, and Lucky held his breath. He had curled into one of the three chutes for unloading coal. The trick worked. These chutes were dangerous, for if you stepped into one and the bottom dropped, it would dump you under the train. The detective took no chances. He first shot the flash, then held on to the side while he climbed over the chutes. When he came to the last one, where Lucky lay, he shot the flash, but carelessly, and not squarely into the hole, so that he saw nothing. Stepping over, he went on, climbed to the boxcar behind, and resumed his chant: there were more curses, more feet sliding on ballast on the roadbed outside. Soon the train picked up speed. That meant the detective had reached the caboose, that all the hoboes were cleared.

Lucky stood up, looked around. There was nothing to see, except hot-dog stands along the highway, but it was pleasant to poke your head up, let the wind whip your hair, and reflect how you had outwitted the detective. When the click of the rails slowed and station lights showed ahead, he squatted down again, dropped his feet into the chute. As soon as lights flashed along-side, he braced against the opposite side of the chute: that was one thing he had learned, the crazy way they shot the brakes on these freights. When the train jerked to a shrieking stop, he was ready, and didn't get slammed. The bell tolled, the engine pulled away, there was an interval of silence. That meant they had cut the train, and would be picking up more cars. Soon they would be going on.

"Ah-ha! Hiding out on me, hey?"

The flashlight shot down from the boxcar. Lucky jumped, seized the side of the gond, scrambled up, vaulted. When he hit the roadbed, his ankles stung from the impact, and he staggered for footing. The detective was on him, grappling. He broke away, ran down the track, past the caboose, into the dark. The detective followed, but he was a big man and began to lose ground. Lucky was clear, when all of a sudden his foot drove against a switch bar and he went flat on his face, panting from the hysteria of shock.

The detective didn't grapple this time. He let go with a barrage of kicks.

"Hide out on me, will you? Treat you right, give you a break, and you hide out on me. I'll learn you to hide out on me."

Lucky tried to get up, couldn't. He was jerked to his feet, rushed up the track on the run. He pulled back, but couldn't get set. He sat down, dug in with his sliding heels. The detective kicked and jerked, in fury. Lucky clawed for something to hold on to, his hand caught the rail. The detective stamped on it. He pulled it back in pain, clawed again. This time his fingers closed on a spike, sticking an inch or two out of the tie. The detective jerked, the spike pulled out of the hole, and Lucky resumed his unwilling run.

"Lemme go! Why don't you lemme go?"

"Come on! Hide out on me, will you? I'll learn you to hide out on Larry Nott!"

"Lemme go! Lemme—"

Lucky pulled back, braced with his heels, got himself stopped. Then his whole body coiled like a spring and let go in one convulsive, passionate lunge. The spike, still in his hand, came down on the detective's head, and he felt it crush. He stood there, looking down at something dark and formless, lying across the rails.

II

Hurrying down the track, he became aware of the spike, gave it a toss, heard it splash in the ditch. Soon he realized that his steps on the ties were being telegraphed by the listening rail, and he plunged across the ditch to the highway. There he resumed his rapid walk, trying not to run. But every time a car overtook him his heels lifted queerly, and his breath first stopped, then came in gasps as he listened for the car to stop. He came to a crossroads, turned quickly to his right. He let himself run here, for the road wasn't lighted as the main highway was, and there weren't many cars. The running tired him, but it eased the sick feeling in his stomach. He came to a sign that told him Los Angeles was seventeen miles, and to his left. He turned, walked, ran, stooped down sometimes, panting, to rest. After a while it came to him why he had to get to Los Angeles, and so soon. The soup kitchen opened at seven o'clock. He had to be there, in that same soup kitchen where he had had supper, so it would look as though he had never been away.

When the lights went off, and it came broad daylight with the suddenness of Southern California, he was in the city, and a clock told him it was ten minutes after five. He thought he had time. He pressed on, exhausted, but never relaxing his rapid, half-shuffling walk.

It was ten minutes to seven when he got to the soup kitchen, and he quickly walked past it. He wanted to be clear at the end of the line, so he could have a word with Shorty, the man who dished out the soup, without impatient shoves from behind, and growls to keep moving.

Shorty remembered him. "Still here, hey?"

"Still here."

"Three in a row for you. Holy smoke, they ought to be collecting for you by the month."

"Thought you'd be off."

"Who, me?"

"Sunday, ain't it?"

"Sunday? Wake up. This is Saturday."

"Saturday? You're kidding."

"Kidding my eye, this is Saturday, and a big day in this town, too."

"One day looks like another to me."

"Not this one. Parade."

"Yeah?"

"Shriners. You get that free."

"Well, that's my name, Lucky."

"My name's Shorty, but I'm over six feet."

"Nothing like that with me. I really got luck."

"You sure?"

"Like, for instance, getting a hunk of meat."

"I didn't give you no meat."

"Ain't you going to?"

"Shove your plate over quick. Don't let nobody see you."

"Thanks."

"Okay, Lucky. Don't miss the parade."

"I won't."

He sat at the rough table with the others, dipped his bread in the soup, tried to eat, but his throat kept contracting from excitement and he made slow work of it. He had what he wanted from Shorty. He had fixed the day, and not only the day but the date, for it would be the same date as the big Shriners' parade. He had fixed his name, with a little gag. Shorty wouldn't forget him. His throat relaxed, and he wolfed the piece of meat.

Near the soup kitchen he saw signs: LINCOLN PARK PHARMACY, LINCOLN PARK CAFETERIA.

"Which way is the park, buddy?" If it was a big park, he might find a thicket where he could lie down, rest his aching legs.

"Straight down, you'll see it."

There was a fence around it, but he found a gate, opened it, slipped in. Ahead of him was a thicket, but the ground was wet from a stream that ran through it. He crossed a small bridge, followed a path. He came to a stable, peeped in. It was empty, but the floor was thickly covered with new hay. He went in, made for a dark corner, burrowed under the hay, closed his eyes. For a few moments everything slipped away, except warmth, relaxation, ease. But then something began to drill into the back of his mind: Where did he spend last night? Where would he tell them he spent last night? He tried to think, but nothing would come to him. He would have said that he spent it where he spent the night before, but he hadn't spent it in Los Angeles. He had spent it in Santa Barbara, and come down in the morning on a truck. He had never spent a night in Los Angeles. He didn't know the places. He had no answers to the questions that were now pounding at him like sledge hammers:

"What's that? Where you say you was?"

"In a flophouse."

"Which flophouse?"

"I didn't pay no attention which flophouse. It was just a flophouse."

"Where was this flophouse at?"

"I don't know where it was at. I never been to Los Angeles before. I don't know the names of no streets."

"What this flophouse look like?"

"Looked like a flophouse."

"Come on, don't give us no gags. What this flophouse look like? Ain't you got eyes, can't you say what this here place looked like? What's the matter, can't you talk?"

Something gripped his arm, and he felt himself being lifted. Something of terrible strength had hold of him, and he was going straight up in the air. He squirmed to get loose, then was plopped on his feet and released. He turned, terrified.

An elephant was standing there, exploring his clothes with its trunk. He knew then that he had been asleep. But when he backed away, he bumped into another elephant. He slipped between the two elephants, slithered past a third to the door, which was open about a foot. Out in the sunlight, he made his way back across the little bridge, saw what he hadn't noticed before: pens with deer in them, and ostriches, and mountain sheep, that told him he had stumbled into a zoo. It was after four o'clock, so he must have slept a long time in the hay. Back on the street, he felt a sobbing laugh rise in his throat. *That* was where he had spent the night. "In the elephant house at Lincoln Park."

"*What?*"

"That's right. In the elephant house."

"What you giving us? A stall?"

"It ain't no stall. I was in the elephant house."

"With them elephants?"

"That's right."

"How you get in there?"

"Just went in. The door was open."

"Just went in there, seen the elephants, and bedded down with them?"

"I thought they was horses."

"You thought them elephants was horses?"

"It was dark. I dug in under the hay. I never knowed they was elephants till morning."

"How come you went in this place?"

"I left the soup kitchen, and in a couple of minutes I came to the park. I went in there, looking for some grass to lie down on. Then I come to this here place, looked to me like a stable. I peeped in, seen the hay, and hit it."

"And you wasn't scared of them elephants?"

"It was dark, I tell you, and I could hear them eating the hay, but I thought they was horses. I was tired, and I wanted someplace to sleep."

"Then what?"

"Then when it got light, and I seen they was elephants, I run out of there, and beat it."

"Couldn't you tell them elephants by the smell?"

"I never noticed no smell."

"How many elephants was there?"

"Three."

III

He brushed wisps of hay off his denims. They had been fairly new, but now they were black with the grime of the coal gond. Suddenly his heart stopped, a suffocating feeling swept over him. The questions started again, hammered at him, beat into his brain.

"Where that coal dust come from?"

"I don't know. The freights, I guess."

"Don't you know it ain't no coal ever shipped into this part of the state? Don't you know that here all they burn is gas? Don't you know it ain't only been but one coal car shipped in here in six months, and that come in by a misread train order? Don't you know that car was part of that train this here detective was riding that got killed? *Don't you know that?* Come on, out with it. WHERE THAT COAL DUST COME FROM?"

Getting rid of the denims instantly became an obsession. He felt that people were looking at him on the street, spying the coal dust, waiting till he got by, then running into drugstores to phone the police that he had just passed by. It was like those dreams he sometimes had, where he was walking through crowds naked, except that this was no dream, and he wasn't naked, he was wearing these denims, these telltale denims with coal dust all over them. He clenched his hands, had a moment of terrible concentration, headed into a filling station.

"Hello."

"Hello."

"What's the chances on a job?"

"No chances."

"Why not?"

"Don't need anybody."

"That's not the only reason."

"There's about forty-two other reasons, one of them is I can't even make a living myself, but it's all the reason that concerns you. Here's a dime, kid. Better luck somewhere else."

"I don't want your dime. I want a job. If the clothes were better, that might help, mightn't it?"

"If the clothes were good enough for Clark Gable in the swell gambling-house scene, that wouldn't help a bit. Not a bit. I just don't need anybody, that's all."

"Suppose I got better clothes. Would you talk to me?"

"Talk to you any time, but I don't need anybody."

"I'll be back when I get the clothes."

"Just taking a walk for nothing."

"What's your name?"

"Hook's my name. Oscar Hook."

"Thanks, Mr. Hook. But I'm coming back. I just got a idea I can talk myself into a job. I'm some talker."

"You're all that, kid. But don't waste your time. I don't need anybody."

"Okay. Just the same, I'll be back."

He headed for the center of town, asked the way to the cheap clothing stores. At Los Angeles and Temple, after an hour's trudge, he came to a succession of small stores in a Mexican quarter that were what he wanted. He went into one. The storekeeper was a Mexican, and two or three other Mexicans were standing around smoking.

"Mister, will you trust me for a pair of white pants and a shirt?"

"No trust. Hey, scram."

"Look. I can have a job Monday morning if I can show up in that outfit. White pants and a white shirt. That's all."

"No trust. What you think this is, anyway?"

"Well, I got to get that outfit somewhere. If I get that, they'll let me go to work Monday. I'll pay you soon as I get paid off Saturday night."

"No trust. Sell for cash."

He stood there. The Mexicans stood there, smoked, looked out at the street. Presently one of them looked at him. "What kind of job, hey? What you mean, got to have white pants a white shirt a hold a job?"

"Filling station. They got a rule you got to have white clothes before you can work there."

"Oh. Sure. Filling station."

After a while the storekeeper spoke. "Ha! Is a joke. Job in filling station, must have a white pants, white shirt. Ha! Is a joke,"

"What else would I want them for? Holy smoke, these are better for the road, ain't they? Say, a guy don't want white pants to ride freights, does he?"

"What filling station? Tell me that."

"Guy name of Hook, Oscar Hook, got a Acme station. Main near Twentieth. You don't believe me, call him up."

"You go to work there, hey?"

"I'm *supposed* to go to work. I *told* him I'd get the white pants and white shirt, somehow. Well—if I don't get them, I don't go to work."

"Why you come to me, hey?"

"Where else would I go? If it's not you, it's another guy down the street. No place else I can dig up the stuff over Sunday, is there?"

"Oh."

He stood around. They all stood around. Then once again the storekeeper looked up. "What size you wear, hey?"

He had a wash at a tap in the backyard, then changed there, between piled-up boxes and crates. The storekeeper gave him a white shirt, white pants, necktie, a suit of thick underwear, and a pair of shoes to replace his badly worn brogans. "Is pretty cold, nighttime, now. A thick underwear feel better."

"Okay. Much obliged."

"Can roll this other stuff up."

"I don't want it. Can you throw it away for me?"

"Is pretty dirty."

"Plenty dirty."

"You no want?"

"No."

His heart leaped as the storekeeper dropped the whole pile into a rubbish brazier and touched a match to some papers at the bottom of it. In a few minutes, the denims and everything else he had worn were ashes.

He followed the storekeeper inside. "Okay, here is a bill, I put all a stuff on a bill, no charge you more than anybody else. Is six dollar ninety-eight cents, then is a service charge one dollar."

All of them laughed. He took the "service charge" to be a gyp overcharge to cover the trust. He nodded. "Okay on the service charge."

The storekeeper hesitated. "Well, six ninety-eight. We no make a service charge."

"Thanks."

"See you keep a white pants clean till Monday morning."

"I'll do that. See you Saturday night."

"*Adios.*"

Out in the street, he stuck his hand in his pocket, felt something, pulled it out. It was a $1 bill. Then he understood about the "service charge," and why the Mexicans had laughed. He went back, kissed the $1 bill, waved a cheery salute into the store. They all waved back.

He rode a streetcar down to Mr. Hook's, got turned down for the job, rode a streetcar back. In his mind, he tried to check over everything. He had an alibi, fantastic and plausible. So far as he could recall, nobody on the train had seen him, not even the other hoboes, for he had stood apart from them in the yards, and had done nothing to attract the attention of any of them. The denims were burned, and he had a story to account for the whites. It even looked pretty good, this thing with Mr. Hook, for anybody who had committed a murder would be most unlikely to make a serious effort to land a job.

But the questions lurked there, ready to spring at him, check and recheck as he would. He saw a sign, 5-COURSE DINNER, 35 CENTS. He still had ninety cents, and went in, ordered steak and fried potatoes, the hungry man's dream of heaven. He ate, put a ten-cent tip under the plate. He ordered cigarettes, lit one, inhaled. He got up to go. A newspaper was lying on the table.

He froze as he saw the headline:

L. R. NOTT, R. R. MAN, KILLED.

IV

On the street, he bought a paper, tried to open it under a street light, couldn't, tucked it under his arm. He found Highway 101, caught a hay truck bound for San Francisco. Going out Sunset Boulevard, it unexpectedly pulled over to the curb and stopped. He looked warily around. Down a side street, about a block away, were the two red lights of a police station. He was tightening to jump and run, but the driver wasn't looking at the lights. "I told them bums that air hose was leaking. They set you nuts. Supposed to keep the stuff in shape and all they ever do is sit around and play blackjack."

The driver fished a roll of black tape from his pocket and got out. Lucky sat where he was a few minutes, then climbed down, walked to the glare of the headlights, opened his paper. There it was:

L. R. NOTT, R. R. MAN, KILLED. The decapitated body of L. R. Nott, 1327 De Soto Street, a detective assigned to a northbound freight, was found early this morning on the track near San Fernando station. It is believed he lost his balance while the train was shunting cars at the San Fernando siding and fell beneath the wheels. Funeral services will be held tomorrow from the De Soto Street Methodist Church.

Mr. Nott is survived by a widow, formerly Miss Elsie Snowden of Mannerheim, and a son, L. R. Nott, Jr., 5.

He stared at it, refolded the paper, tucked it under his arm, walked back to where the driver was taping the air hose. He was clear, and he knew it. "Boy, do they call you Lucky? Is your name Lucky? I'll say it is."

He leaned against the trailer, let his eye wander down the street. He saw the two red lights of the police station-glowing. He looked away quickly. A queer feeling began to stir inside him. He wished the driver would hurry up.

Presently he went back to the headlights again, found the notice, re-read it. He recognized that feeling now; it was the old Sunday-night feeling that he used to have back home, when the bells would ring and he would have to stop playing bide in the twilight, go to church, and hear about the necessity for being saved. It shot through his mind, the time he had played hookey from church, and hid in the livery stable; and how lonely he had felt, because there was nobody to play hide with; and how he had sneaked into church, and stood in the rear to listen to the necessity for being saved.

His eyes twitched back to the red lights, and slowly, shakily, but unswervingly he found himself walking toward them.

"I want to give myself up."

"Yeah, I know, you're wanted for grand larceny in Hackensack, New Jersey."

"No, I—"

"We quit giving them rides when the New Deal come in. Beat it."

"I killed a man."

"You—? . . . When was it you done this?"

"Last night."

"Where?"

"Near here. San Fernando. It was like this—"

"Hey, wait till I get a card. . . . Okay, what's your name?

"Ben Fuller."

"No middle name?"

"They call me Lucky."

"Lucky like in good luck?"

"Yes, sir. . . . Lucky like in good luck."

THE GIRL IN THE STORM

He woke up suddenly, feeling that ice had touched him, but it was an interval before his mind caught up with what he saw. Through the open door of the boxcar it was pouring rain: that much was as he remembered it from the night before. But on the floor was a spreading puddle. It was the puddle, indeed, which had touched his ribs and awakened him; he was edging away from it, even while he was blinking his eyes. When he scrambled to his feet and looked out, the breath left his body in a wailing moan. For as far as he could see no land was visible, nothing but brown, swirling water full of trees, bushes, and what might have been houses, moving in the direction of the bridge, off to his right. It was already lapping at the door of the boxcar; it was what was causing the rapidly deepening puddle.

He stood staring out at it, and became fascinated by a pile of ties across from the car. One by one the flood lifted them, as though some invisible elephant were riding it, and carried them spinning into the current, to bang against the boxcar at his feet, then go swiftly on to the bridge. He watched several go by, then turned his back to them and caught the roof of the car with his hands. He chinned himself, in an effort to climb to the roof, but there was no support for his feet, and he dropped back.

When the next tie came by, he stooped down and caught it. Hugging it to his stomach, he dragged it into the car. Then he jammed it across the door slantwise, one end at the bottom, the other halfway up. He caught the roof of the car again and, clambering up the slanting tie, pushed up high enough to get his chin over the edge. Then he managed to reach the catwalk on the roof of the car, and pulled himself toward it. Wriggling on his belly, he was safely on the walk in a few moments, and stood up.

All around him was the flood, and behind him he could hear it thunder under the bridge. About a quarter of a mile ahead of him was a loading platform, and beyond that the station. No locomotive was in sight; he had been shunted with a string of empties onto a siding and left there. Beyond the station, on higher ground, was what appeared to be a village, and he could see trucks backed up there, evidently evacuating whole families. He wondered if he could get a place on a truck. But it took him ten minutes, clambering down from boxcars to flatcars, and then over boxcars again, to reach the loading platform, and when he ran around it to yell at them, they were gone.

He stood looking at the station, read the name of the place: Hildalgo, California. For the moment he was sheltered from the rain; but his respite was short. The loading platform was only a few inches higher than the floor of the cars, and even while he was standing there another puddle appeared and he was retreating from it. He found himself facing the county road. It was higher than the platform, and although water was running over it in a sheet, and back toward the bridge it dipped into the flood, between this point and the village it was not inundated. To reach it he would have to go through water at least waist-deep, and he eyed it dismally. Then he squatted down, held his breath, and plunged in.

When he scrambled up on the concrete he was so wet he could feel the weight of his denim pants hanging off his hips. He started up the road at a half trot, the storm driving him from behind. He didn't know where he was going, except that he had to find shelter. And who would shelter him he had no idea, for he knew from bitter experience that nineteen-year-old hoboes are seldom welcome guests, whether rain-soaked or not.

He passed a stalled car, with nobody in it. He passed several houses, in front of which he had seen the trucks. They were obviously empty, but they were below road level and surrounded by yellow ponds pocked with rain. He came to a sidewalk, but between him and the curbs was a torrent, and he stayed in the center of the road. He came to a filling station, but it was deserted and six inches deep in water. Next to the filling station was a store, a chain grocery store. He headed for it, going in up to his knees in the torrent. The force of it almost upset him and forced him several paces below his goal. When he gained the sidewalk he ran at the door, wrenching at the knob and driving against it with one motion.

It was locked. As his face smashed against the glass, he remembered it was Sunday.

He stood there, furiously rattling the door. Facing him, inside, he could see the clock: ten minutes to three. But nothing answered his rattling except the rain. He kicked the door, dashed away, and in a second was under cover. Next to the store was a half-finished house, and his dive for the porch was automatic. He turned in anger at the rain, stood stamping the water off his legs, then went inside. The floor was laid, but the walls were only half finished and there was a damp smell of plaster. Off to one side were piled lumber, tar paper, and sawbucks. But the doors and windows were not in place yet, and the air felt even colder than the air outside.

He stood shivering in his soaking denims; started to take off the coat. As the air met his wet chest, he pulled it around him again. At the touch of the clammy cloth he gritted his teeth and took it off. He took off his shoes and his pants. He wore no socks or undershirt. He was left in a pair of tattered shorts, and while he was draping the denims over a sawbuck he collapsed on the tar paper, shaking with chill. But soon he was quiet, and he could think of but one thing: that he had to get warm. He thought of fire, and looked around.

On one side of the room was a fireplace, the mortar in it still damp. The tar paper would do to start it, all right, and there were bricks outside he could use to build it on. The lumber would burn, if there were any pieces short enough to go in the fireplace. He spied a kit of carpenter's tools in one corner, went over to examine it, wincing as the crumbs of plaster hurt his feet.

The main tool in the kit was a saw. Quickly he set up two sawbucks, laid a joist between them and cut it up with the saw. The exercise made him feel better. When he had a pile of wood, he got two bricks and began to build the fire. He tore up tar paper and laid it on the bricks, found the carpenter's trimming knife and whittled kindling, laid the big pieces he had sawed on top. But when he went to his coat and fished the matches out of the pocket, the tips were nothing but smelly wet smears.

He cursed, screamed, and pounded his fist against the wall. He went all through the house, searching every place he could think of, trying to find a match. He began to shake from chill again, and ran to the front door to shake his fist at the rain.

Down the road, creeping slowly, came a car, its lights on. It was a small sedan, and it went cautiously past him. Bitterly he wondered where the driver thought he was going, for the lake of floodwaters down by the station would make further progress impossible. About this time the driver seemed to see the flood too, for a little beyond the grocery store the car came to a stop. Then,

as though it were part of a slow movie, it began to slide. It slid into
the torrent, lurched against the curb, stopped. Almost at once the
taillight went out. That, he decided, was because the water had
shorted the ignition. This car, like the other one, was there to stay
awhile.

He watched, wondered if the guy would have a match. Then
the door opened, the left-hand door, next to the road, and a foot
appeared, then a leg. It wasn't a man's leg; it was a woman's. A girl
got out, and staggered as the storm hit her. She was a smallish girl,
in a raincoat. She slammed the door shut and started toward him,
around the back of the car, heading for the curb. He opened his
mouth to yell at her, but he was too late. The water staggered her
and she went down. She tried to get up; the current tumbled her
under the wheels of the car.

He leaped from the porch, went scampering to her in his
shorts. Taking her by the hand, he jerked her to her feet, put his
arms around her, ran her to the house. As he pulled her into the
cold interior, her teeth chattered. He grabbed her dripping hand-
bag, clawed it open. "You got a match? We'll freeze if we don't get
a match!"

"There's some in the car."

He dashed out again, ran down to the car, jerked the door
open, jumped inside. In the dashboard compartment he found a
package of paper matches, wiped his hand dry on the seat before
he touched them. He looked around for something to wrap them
in, to keep the rain off them. On the back seat he saw robes. He
grabbed them, wrapped them around the matches.

When he got back to the house he waited only to open the
robes and dry his hands again, pawing with them on the wool,
Then he struck a match, and it lit. He touched the tar paper
with it. A blue flame appeared, hesitated, spread out, and licked
the wood. The fire crackled. It turned yellow and light filled the

room. He felt warmth. He crowded so close he was almost in the fireplace.

"Come on, kid, you better get warm."

"I'm already here."

She picked up one of the robes, held it in front of the fire to warm it, put it around him. Then she warmed the other one, pulled it around herself, squatted down beside him. He sat down on the robe, tucked it around his feet. The fire burned up, scorched his face. He didn't move. The heat reached him through the robe. His shivering stopped, he relaxed with a long, quavering sigh. She looked at him.

"My, you must have been cold."

"You don't know the half of it."

"I almost died, myself. If you hadn't come, I don't know what I would have done. I went clear down, in that water."

"I yelled at you, but you was already in it."

"I don't know what's going to happen to the car,"

"It'll be all right soon as it dries out."

"You think so?"

"Just got water in it, that's all."

"I hope that's all."

"Some rain!"

"It's awful, and it's going to get worse. I had the radio on in the car. They're warning people. Over in Hildalgo they took everybody out. Half the town's washed away."

"Yeah, I seen them."

"You were in Hildalgo?"

"Yeah . . . .What you talking about? This *is* Hildalgo."

"This is Hildalgo?"

"That's what it says on the sign at the station."

"Oh, my! I thought Hildalgo was on the other road."

"Well? So it's Hildalgo."

"But there's nobody here. They took them all away."

"O.K. Then it's us."

"Suppose this washes away?"

"Till it does, we got a fire."

She got up, holding the robe tightly around her, and pulled a sawbuck over to the fire. On it, he noticed for the first time, were her sweater, stockings, and skirt. She must have taken them off while he was down in the car. She looked around.

"Are those your things over there? Don't you want me to move them closer to the fire, so they'll dry?"

"I'll do it."

The sight of her absurdly small things had made him suddenly aware of her as a person, and he was afraid to let her move his denims to the fire for fear that in the heat they would stink. He got up, pulled the pile of tar paper to the fire for her to sit on. Then he took the denims off the sawbuck and went back with them to the kitchen. The fixtures were in, though caked with grit, and on his previous tour of the place he had seen a bucket and some soap. He dumped the denims on the floor, filled the bucket with water, carried it to where she was. By poking with a piece of flooring he made a place for it on the fire, and while it was heating, studied her.

She wasn't a pretty girl exactly. She was small, with sandy hair, and freckles on her nose. But she had a friendly smile, and she wasn't bawling at her plight. Indeed, she seemed to take it more philosophically than he did. He took her to be about his own age.

"What's your name?"

"Flora. Flora Hilton. . . . It's really Dora, but they all began calling me Dumb Dora, so I changed it."

"Yes, I guess that was bad."

"What's yours?"

"Jack. Jack Schwab."

"You come from California?"

"Pennsylvania. I—kind of travel around."

"Hitchhike?"

"Sometimes. Other times I ride the freights."

"I didn't think you talked like California."

"What you doing out in this storm?"

"I went over to my uncle's. I went over there last night, to stay till Monday. But when it started to rain I thought I better get back. It wasn't so bad over where he lives, and I didn't know it was going to be like this. They've got no radio or anything. But then, when I turned the car radio on, I found out. I still thought I could make it, though. I thought I was on the main road. I didn't know I was coming through Hildalgo."

"Well, they'll be coming for you. The cops, or somebody. We'll see them when they find the car."

"I don't know if they'll be coming for me."

"Oh, they will."

"My father, he don't even know I started out, and my uncle, he probably thinks I'm home by now."

"Then we got it to ourselves."

"Sure looks like it."

The water was steaming by now. He wrapped the hot bucket handle in tar paper, lifted it off the fire, and went back to the kitchen with it. First washing out the sink, then using a piece of tar paper as a stopper, he soaped the denims and washed them. The water turned so black he felt a sense of shame. He put them through two or three waters, wrung them dry. The last of the hot water he saved for the shorts he had on. With a quick glance toward the front of the house, he stepped out of them, washed them, wrung them out. Then he spread them, to step back into them. They were no wetter than when he took them off, but he hated the idea of having them touch him. However, they were hot from the water, and felt unexpectedly pleasant when he buttoned them up.

Back at the fire, he draped the denims on the sawbuck, beside her things, to dry.

"Well, Flora, nice climate you got."

"Sunny California! It can rain harder here than any place on earth. Well, you know what they say. We only have two kinds of weather in California, magnificent and unusual."

"I'll say it's unusual."

"Just listen to that rain come down."

"What do you do with yourself, Flora?"

"Me? Oh, I work. I got a job in a drive-in."

"Slinging hot dogs, hey?"

"I wish you'd talk about something else."

"A hot dog sure would go good now, wouldn't it?"

"I was the one that played dumb this morning. They wanted me to wait for breakfast, but I was in such a hurry to get away I wouldn't listen to them. I haven't had anything to eat all day."

"Breakfast? Say, that's a laugh."

"Haven't you had anything to eat either?"

"I haven't et a breakfast in so long I've forgot what it tastes like. By the time they get around to me it's always dinnertime, and even then, when they get to me, sometimes they close the window in my face."

"I guess it's hard, hitchhiking and—"

"Flora! Are we the couple of dopes!"

"What's the matter, Jack?"

"Talking about hot dogs and breakfast. That store! There's enough grub in there to feed an army!"

"You mean—just take it?"

"You think it's going to walk over here and ask us to eat it? Come on! Here's where we eat!"

When he seized the largest of the carpenter's chisels and the hammer, she still sat there, watching him, and didn't follow when he went outside. He splashed around to the rear of the store, drove the chisel into the crack of the door, pulled. Something snapped, and he pushed the door open. He waited a moment, the rain pouring on him from the roof, for the sound of the burglar alarm, but he heard nothing. He groped for the light switch, found it, snapped it, but nothing happened. If all wires were down in the storm, that might explain the silent burglar alarm. He began to grope his way toward the shelves. Suddenly he felt her beside him, there in the murk.

"If you've got the nerve, I have."

She was looking square into his eyes, and he felt a throb of excitement.

"The worst they can do is put us in jail. Well—I been there before, haven't I? Plenty of times—but I'm still here."

He turned to the shelves again, didn't see her look at him queerly, hesitate, and start to leave before deciding to follow him. His hand touched something and he gave an exclamation.

"What is it, Jack?"

"Matches! Now we're coming."

Lighting matches, poking and peering, they located the canned goods section.

"Here's soup. My, Jack, that'll be good!"

"O.K. on soup."

"What kind do you like?

"Any kind. So it's got meat in it."

"Mulligatawny?"

"Take two. Small size, so they'll heat quick."

"Peas?"

"O.K."

She set the cans on the counter, but he continued searching, and presently yelled:

"Got it, Flora, got it! I knew it had to be there!"

"What is it, Jack?"

"Chicken! Canned chicken! Just look at it!"

He found currant jelly, found instant coffee, condensed milk, a package of lump sugar, found cigarettes.

"O.K., Flora. Anything else you want?"

"I can't think of anything else, Jack."

"Let's go."

When they got back to the house again, it was dark. He put more wood on the fire, went back to the kitchen, filled the bucket again. When he returned, to put it on the fire, he noticed she had put on her stockings, sweater, and skirt. He felt his own denims. They were dry. He put them on. But when he went to put on his shoes his feet recoiled from their cold dampness. He let them lie, sat down, and pulled the robe over his feet. She started to laugh.

"Wonder what we're going to eat off of?"

"We'll soon fix that."

He found the saw, found a piece of smooth board, sawed off two squares. "How's that?"

"Fine. Just like plates."

"Here's a couple of chisels for forks."

"We sure do help ourselves."

"If you don't help yourself, nobody'll do it for you."

When the water began to steam, they dropped the cans in— the big can of chicken shaped like a flatiron first, the others on top of it. They sat side by side and watched. After a while they fished out the soup, and he took a chisel and hammer and neatly excised the tops. "Take it easy, Flora. Watch you don't cut your lip."

They put the cans to their mouths, drank. "Oh, is that good! Is that good!" Her voice throbbed as she spoke.

Panting, they gulped the soup, tilting the cans to let the meat and vegetables slip down their throats.

They fished out the other cans then, and he opened them, the chicken last. She took it by a leg and quickly lifted it to one of their plates.

"Don't spill the juice. We'll drink that out of the can."

"I haven't spilled a drop, Flora. Wait a minute. There's a knife here, I'll cut it in half."

He jumped up, looked for the carpenter's trimming knife he had used to whittle the kindling. He couldn't find it.

"Damn it, there was a knife here. What did I do with it?"

She said nothing.

He cut the chicken in half with the hammer and chisel. They ate like a pair of animals, sometimes stopping to gasp for breath. Presently nothing was left but wet spots on the board plates. He got fresh water and set it on the fire. It heated quickly. He went to the kitchen, washed out the soup cans, came back, made the coffee in them. He opened the milk and sugar, gave each can a judicious dose.

"There you are, Flora. You can stir it with a chisel."

"That's just what I was wishing for all the time—that I could have a good cup of coffee, and then it would be perfect."

"Is it O.K.?"

"Grand."

He offered her a cigarette, but she said she didn't smoke. He lit up, inhaled, lay back on the couch of tar paper. He was warm, full, and content. He watched her when she got up and cleared away the cans and bucket. She found a rag in the tool kit, dipped it in the last of the hot water.

"Don't you want me to wipe the grease off your hands?"

He held out his hands, and she wiped them. She wiped her own hands, put the rag with the other stuff, sat down beside him. He held out his hand, open. She hesitated, looked at him a moment as she had looked at him in the store, put her hand in his.

"We ain't got it so bad, Flora."

"I'll say we haven't. Not to what we might have. We could have been drowned."

He put his arm around her, drew her to him. She let her head fall on his shoulder. He could smell her hair, and his throat contracted, as though he were going to cry. For the first time in his short battered life he was happy. His grip on her tightened, he pushed his cheek against hers. She buried her face in his neck. He kept nuzzling her, felt his lips nearing her mouth. Then he pulled her to him hard, felt her yield, turn her head for his kiss.

Convulsively he winced. There was a sharp pain in the pit of his stomach. He looked down, saw something rough and putty-stained about the neck of her sweater. Instantly he knew what it was, what it was there for. He jumped up.

"So—that's where the knife was. I pull you out of the gutter, feed you, take you in my arms, and all the time you're getting ready to stick me in the back with that thing."

She started to cry. "I never saw you before. You said you'd been in jail, and I didn't know what you were fixing to do to me!"

He lit a cigarette, walked around the room. Once more he felt cold, forlorn, and bitter, the way he felt on the road. He looked out. The rain was slackening. He threw away the cigarette, sat down on the floor, drove his feet into the cold clammy shoes. Savagely he knotted the stiff laces. Then, without a word to her, he went slogging out into the night.

JOY RIDE TO GLORY

I was assigned to the kitchen, dipping grub for the guards, not the cons like the radio said I was. I had been in the laundry, but my fingers and toes all swelled up and I got a ringing in the ears from the liquid soap, so they switched me to the kitchen. My name is Red Conley. If you don't quite recollect who Red Conley is, go down to the public library and look him up in the Los Angeles newspapers. You'll find out a funny thing about him. According to them write-ups, Red Conley is dead.

It had been raining all morning, and around eleven the meat truck drives up. They let it right in the yard, and Cookie yells for me and Bugs Calenso to unload it. Bugs, he's got three concurrents and two consecutives running against him, and some of it's violation of parole, so they don't bother to figure it up any more. Along about 2042, with good behavior and friends on the outside, he's eligible. Me, I'm in for rolling six tires down the hill from Mullins's Garage, which seemed to be a good idea at the time, but I was doing a one-to-five before we even got the papers off them. Still, I had served a year, and was up for parole, and it looked O.K., and if I'd let it ride I'd have been out in a month.

So me and Bugs, we split it up with me handling the meat,

account I'm younger, and him handling the hooks, account he knows how. I'd pull out a quarter of beef, then brace under it, then come up. Then I'd tote it to the cold storage room, and Bugs would catch it with the hook that swiveled to the overhead trolley. Then he'd throw the switch and I'd shove the stuff in place, the forequarters on one rail, the hindquarters on another. There was four steers on the truck, two of them for someplace down the line, two of them for the prison. That meant eight quarters of meat, and I guess I took ten minutes, because beef is not feathers, and I needed a rest in between. But then it was all moved, and Bugs give a yelp for the driver, who was not outside, where he generally waited, but inside, account of the rain. So he yelped back, from inside the corridors someplace, and then we hollered some more and said what was he doing, stalling around so he could get a free meal off the taxpayers of the state of California, and why don't he take away his truck? So Cookie joins in, and quite a few joins in, and some very good gags was made, and it was against the rules but it felt good to holler.

So Bugs was grinning at me, standing there in the door, but then all of a sudden he wasn't grinning any more and he was looking at me hard. Then overhead I hear the planes. You understand how this was? The kitchen door is out back, and there's a guard on that part of the wall. But he's a spotter, see? He's a spotter for the army, and just to make sure, he spots everything, and there he is now, with his rifle over one arm and his head thrown back, to see what's coming. Three fast ones break out of a cloud, the split-tail jobs with two motors, but Bugs, he don't wait. He motions to me and we take two steps. Then he checks front and I check rear. Then he vaults in the truck and I follow him. Then we lay down, in between quarters of beef.

We were hardly flat when the driver came out, still yelling gags at the guys in the kitchen. He climbs in, starts, rolls a little way, and stops, and we hear him say something to the guards at the gate. Then he gets going again, and starts down the hill on the motor, so it begins to backfire. He goes so fast I have to lock my throat to keep the wind from being shook out of me, ha-ha-ha-ha like that. Bugs, he seems to be having the same kind of trouble, but we both hang on and choke it back, whatever the driver might hear. He's a little fat guy, and he sings the "Prisoner's Song" pretty lousy, but he slows down for the boulevard stop at the bottom of the hill. That was when Bugs grabs my neck for a handhold and stands up. He stands right over me, so I can see his face, where it's all twisted with this maniac look, and his hands, where they were hooked to come in on the driver's neck.

Then I woke up for the first time to the spot I was in. Here, with one month to go only, I had got myself in the same truck with this killer, and made myself just as guilty of whatever was done as he was. I yelled at the driver then, as loud as I could scream. He hit the brake and turned around, but he was too late. That jerk threw Bugs right on top of him, and them hooks came together so his tongue popped out of his mouth. I grabbed at Bugs and begged him to quit, but then I woke up to what was going on outside. The truck was still rolling, and if something wasn't done in about two seconds it was going over in the ditch. I reached over and grabbed the wheel, then I slid over the seat on my belly till I was on the right-hand side beside the driver, so with my left foot I could shove down the brake.

All during that time the driver was being pulled over backwards, so he arched up till his knees touched the wheel. Then something cracked, and I felt sick to my stomach. Then it wasn't the driver back of the wheel, it was Bugs. He was panting like some kind of an animal, but he threw it in gear and we started off. Pretty soon he says: "Get back there, go through his pockets, and find his cigarettes."

"Get back there yourself."

"Oh, just a passenger, hey?"

"Just a fall guy, maybe."

"O.K., fall guy, suppose you keep an eye out behind, see if they're following us. Because if they're not, maybe we still got a little time, before it's a general alarm."

"Haven't you got a mirror?"

"Oh, just a passenger after all, hey?"

"What you kill that guy for?"

"What you think I killed him for? So he cooperates, and he's doing it. Like he is now, he don't give no trouble."

"We could have tied him up, or dropped him off, or knocked him out. We could have handled him somehow, so they wouldn't have this on us."

"You done all you could."

"You bet I did."

"I hope he appreciates it."

"Shut up and drive."

"Says who?"

I hauled off and let him have it, right in the mouth. His foot came off the gas, and we slowed, and I stamped on the brake, and we stopped. I let him have it again, so the blood spurted out of his lip. Then I grabbed him, jerked him out from behind the wheel, and drove my fist in till my arm was numb and his face looked like something the butcher would pitch in the bucket. Then I kicked him into my seat, took the wheel myself, and went on. It didn't do any good. We were in the same old truck, with the rain pouring down in front, a dead man in behind, and headed nowhere. But it made me feel better.

On the dashboard was a button at the top of what looked like a grill, and I give it a twist. Plenty of drivers have shortwave, so they can pick up the police calls, and I figured I could find out what was being done about us. But 'stead of a grill it was a panel, and it opened up on a compartment full of cigarettes, chewing gum, maps, apples, and what looked to me like a flashlight. I took the cigarettes and lit up, and had me a deep inhale, and all the time he was looking at me, and I was wondering whether to give him one, just because he couldn't help being like he was, and anyway I'd done all I wanted to do to him, and maybe more than I really wanted to do. I began sliding one out of the pack, when he moved. When I looked up I knew that flashlight wasn't a flashlight at all, it was a automatic. Because I was looking straight into it.

"Rat, you listening what I say?"

"I hear every word, Bugs."

"Drive."

"I'm driving."

"Drive like I tell you to drive."

"Just say it, Bugs."

He told me, and we began a zigzag course, part on the main highways, part on the crossroads, but as near as I could tell we were zigzagging for Los Angeles, and getting there. Then we had to stop for a freight that was crossing. Ahead of us was a green sedan, and for a while Bugs sat there looking at it and bearing down on some chocolate bars he found in with the apple. Then he sits up and says: "Bump him! *Bump him!*"

"What do you mean, bump him?"

"Bump him so he has to get out!"

I came up slow, then stepped on it so I smacked right into the rear bumper of the sedan. I no sooner untangled than Bugs jumped out and ran around front, shoving the gun in his pants as he went. Sure enough, the guy gets out, and Bugs began yelling and pointing at the truck. But the guy can't make any sense out of it because he's looking at Bugs's face, where it's still running blood, and he can't connect all that grief with the little bump he felt. Bugs just keeps on talking. All that time the freight is going by, and he can't take a chance the train crew might hop off to help some guy out. But soon as the bell stops he whips out the gun and tells the guy to peel off his clothes and hand over his dough. I hop out then, and run around the right-hand side and jump in the sedan and slide over behind the wheel. But Bugs thought of that. By the time I was set he had the guy out front, blocking me off. The guy's taking orders now, and each piece of his clothes he peels, Bugs lays it on the hood and covers it with the guy's raincoat. When the guy's stripped naked, so his teeth are chattering and he's begging Bugs not to keep him out there in the rain any more, Bugs plugs him. It was like something in a movie. First I could see them in front, on the other side of this pile of clothes on the hood, then comes the shot, and I can see Bugs and I can't see him. Then Bugs has scooped up the clothes under his arm and is jumping in the back door of the sedan, telling me to drive. I start up, and I cut the wheel hard left. But the right side of the car goes up, then bumps down, as we go over something soft.

When Bugs climbed up in the front seat, maybe a half hour later, he was all dressed up in the guy's clothes and his face was wiped off a little. He didn't really look good, but he wasn't in prison denims, like I was, and he could take out some money and count it. There was quite a little money, and he took quite a while. Then he says: "I guess you wonder why you killed *him* too?"

"You're running it, Bugs."

"Nekkid like he is, they may be quite a while identifying him, see? Without any driver's license, or Elks' pin, or tailor's label, or that stuff they generally go on, they might be some little time. Well, all that time we're moving, you get it, stupid? We're on our way, and they don't know what car we got, or the number of it, or anything at all, except we're not no longer hauling meat. Pretty, isn't it?"

"Oh, it's clever. I can see that."

"I killed him so he can't talk to the cops and tell them what they might want to know. Of course, we all know *you* killed him."

"Yeah, that's right."

"What do you mean, 'that's right'?"

"I mean if you say I killed him."

"Quit cracking smart."

"O.K."

"And quit chattering them teeth."

Changing cars I had got wet, and he hadn't give me any chocolate bars, and I was cold and hungry and weak, and my teeth were chattering all right. I bit down on them, and they stopped. It was four or five in the afternoon by then, and we were in Los Angeles already, and I began wondering why he didn't kill me. He had everything he wanted, a car, a suit, a raincoat, and dough. He didn't need me any more. Then I got this awful sensation in the pit of my stomach, when I saw he *was* going to kill me, and it was just a question of when. He sat there staring at me, the gun in his lap, and I figured it would be at the next stop. So when we come to it I went right through. He snarled like a mad dog. "What's the big idea, going through that light?"

"I didn't see it."

"I told you quit cracking smart."

"I swear I didn't see it."

"You want some cops stopping us?"

"If you don't see it, why would you stop?"

"You stop at the next one, though."

"Oh, sure."

The next one, I went through at seventy, and he began to scream. He'd have plugged me right there, but at that speed he was afraid. But I had the mirror and he didn't, and back of us I see a light, just a single. Then behind that there's another one, and then still another. I hold on seventy, but they begin closing in. The next light, I come off the gas, like I'm going to do like I'm told, and stop. I feel him tighten, and aim the gun. When we dropped to forty I hit the brake and cut the wheel. We spun around like something crazy. Inside, it's like we've exploded, because he's thrown on the floor but he shoots just the same. Whether I'm hit I don't know, but I throw open the door and jump. Inside there's more shots, and outside the motorcycles deploy, all three guns barking. I start to run, then I go down. But I don't lay there. Because it was the torrent in the gutter that threw me, and it rushed me along like I was a hunk of rubble. I try to get up and can't. Then all of a sudden it's pitch dark and I'm falling. Then I crash down, so I think my back is broken. Then the water is rushing me along again, and I tumble where I am.

I'm in a storm drain.

They have them all over the city, some little, made out of terracotta pipe, some big, made out of concrete sections. They run under streets, and every so often there's a manhole, so they can clean them out, and off under the sidewalks are intakes, to tap the flow in the gutter. In the intakes, they got handholds and bars, just in case somebody did fall in, and if I'd been quick I might have saved myself, but I was too crossed up. How big the pipe was that I was in I don't know, but at a guess I would say three feet, maybe. In that was running about a foot of water, and I was bumping along with it, feet first. I kept trying to stop, but I couldn't. Over my face all the time the water kept pouring, and I kept gasping for air, and every time I'd gasp I'd swallow a gallon and then start over again.

How long that went on I don't know. It seemed like an hour, but figuring it up now, I'd say about a minute. Then I see some gray light, and almost before I knew it, I was shooting past another intake pipe. I caught it, and four or five feet away, I could see bars. I reached and tried to grab one, but the water was pulling me back. I slipped off and went helloing down the black pipe again, still trying to breathe, still strangling from the water that was pouring over me. But my mind began to work, anyway a little bit. I knew there'd be another intake further on, and I set myself to watch for it and grab for a handhold. But I was watching on the right-hand side, where the other one had come in, and I shot right by one on the left. Then a couple more went by and I began to scream. It came to me, somehow, what a no-account life I'd led, and here I was, winding it up like a rat in a sewer, and even with the water in my mouth I began to scream like a maniac.

I saw light again, and got ready, but it wasn't an intake this time. It was a grating over a big square drain that my pipe spilled me into, and then I really began to move, and for just that long I could breathe better and my back didn't bump any more, because it was deeper. I put my head up, and there must have been two feet of clearance above me. But then I noticed there wasn't that much, and pretty soon I knew why. Every so often pipes came roaring in, and each one filled the big drain fuller, and pretty soon it would be running full with no air, like a water pipe. I wasn't screaming any more. I had just give up. I was going along, but I didn't care any more.

Pretty soon something clipped my nose, and I put up my hands. I almost died then, because the top was only six inches from my face. There was a roar, and I figured another pipe was coming in. I knew I was up tight, and drew the biggest breath I could. When the top bumped my face I pushed down under to keep it away. Then I rolled over. I could feel the top bumping my back, and I kept telling myself I mustn't breathe. I had that many seconds to live till I breathed, and I clamped down on my throat like I had in the truck, when we were bumping down the hill. Then something bumped my belly, and I breathed. But what I

breathed was air. I opened my eyes and it was almost dark, and
street lights were on, and I was washed up on a slab of concrete
in the middle of water that was boiling all around me. About
twenty feet away I could see the square mouth of a drain, and
I figured it was what I come out of. It was at least five minutes,
I guess, before I doped it out I was in the middle of the Los
Angeles River.

I won't tell you much about how I got out of there, about the
guy that seen me, and stopped his car, and found a length of rubber hose, and threw me one end of it, and then ran me home, and
wrapped me in blankets, and opened up a can of hot soup, and
then give me hot coffee and hot milk mixed, and then put me to
bed. If I told you too much, maybe you could figure out who he is,
and he'd be in more trouble than I'm worth. And anyway, what I
want to tell about, what I been leading up to all this time, was next
morning, when he come in the little room he had put me in, and
sat down beside the bed, and it was just him and me. He kind of
mentioned that his wife and little boy were visiting her folks over
the weekend, and I got the idea that was what he was trying to tell
me, that it was just him and me, that nobody else knew anything.
After a while he says: "What's your name?"

" . . . Bud O'Brien's my name."

"Funny. I thought it was Conley."

"What made you think that?"

"There was a convict named Conley that made his escape yesterday. From the stencil marks on those denims you were wearing,
I figured you came from a prison yourself."

"In that case, you might be right."

"Want to read about it, Conley?"

"Yeah, I'd kind of like to."

He went out and came back with the papers, and it was all
plastered over the front pages how me and Bugs had slipped out

in the meat truck, killed the driver, then killed another guy and taken his car, then been shot by the cops, with Bugs wounding a cop before they got him, and my body washing down the storm drain. Identification was certain, though, it said, because a cop recognized me before I went down. So I read all that stuff, and then I started to talk, and I told the guy what I've just told you, and 'specially I tried to make him believe I never killed anybody, which I didn't. He listened, and sat there a long time, and then he said: "I figured it might be something like that. 'Specially when I read that item that covered Calenso's record and your record. . . . All right, let's say it's true, the way you tell it. Well—O.K. I guess I really believe it. You didn't kill anybody, and you're dead. So far as the cops are concerned, they know they got you, and that means that today, this Sunday morning, you can, if I say the word, begin a new life. Suppose I do say the word, what then? What are you going to do with this life?"

Well, what was I going to say? The last I did any thinking about my life, I was ten feet under the street, in a drain pipe that was drowning me so fast I couldn't see myself sink, and I wasn't ready to talk. I began mumbling about I hope I would die if I ever pulled any crooked stuff again, and how I sure was going to get a job and go to work, and he listened, and then cut me off short. "That's not good enough, Conley."

"It's all I know to do."

"How old are you?"

"Twenty-three."

"There's just one place for a guy your age, these days, with your country in a war. Just one place, and you haven't once mentioned it."

"Well, I'm all registered up."

"You sure of that?"

"You bet I'm registered up. O.K., so it's the army, but don't you think I'd have been in it long ago if it hadn't been for that rap I was doing?"

"Which is your draft board?"

We talked for a minute about that, and then we both seen that wouldn't do, because even if I give a new name to the draft board, the fingerprints would trip me, and then all of a sudden I said: "O.K., mister, I got it. This man's army, the one we got, it can't take me, because before it does, it's got to turn me over to the state of California to die for what Bugs Calenso done. But that's not the only army. There's other armies—"

He looked up and come over and shook hands. So that's where I am now, on my way to another army, that's fighting for the same thing and that needs guys just as much as our army does. And I'm writing this on the deck of a freighter headed west, and the agreement is I mail it to him, to prove I did like I promised. If it all goes O.K., he keeps this locked up, and that's that. If something goes wrong, and the ship gets it, or maybe my number goes up and I check in over there, why then maybe he hands it to some guy, to be printed if somebody wants to read it. So—

Say, that's a funny one. Them reporters, they generally get it right, don't they? Because now, if you happen to read this, why then Red Conley, he is dead!

PASTORALE

I

Well, it looks like Burbie is going to get hung. And if he does, what he can lay it on is, he always figured he was so damn smart.

You see, Burbie, he left town when he was about sixteen year old. He run away with one of them travelling shows, "East Lynne" I think it was, and he stayed away about ten years. And when he come back he thought he knowed a lot. Burbie, he's got them watery blue eyes what kind of stick out from his face, and how he killed the time was to sit around and listen to the boys talk down at the poolroom or over at the barber shop or a couple other places where he hung out, and then wink at you like they was all making a fool of theirself or something and nobody didn't know it but him.

But when you come right down to what Burbie had in his head, why it wasn't much. 'Course, he generally always had a job, painting around or maybe helping out on a new house, like of that, but what he used to do was to play baseball with the high school team. And they had a big fight over it, 'cause Burbie was so old nobody wouldn't believe he went to the school, and them other teams was all the time putting up a squawk. So then he couldn't play no more. And another thing he liked to do was sing at the entertainments. I reckon he liked that most of all, 'cause he claimed that a whole lot of the time he was away he was on the stage, and I reckon maybe he was at that, 'cause he was pretty good, 'specially when he dressed hisself up like a old-time Rube and come out and spoke a piece what he knowed.

Well, when he come back to town he seen Lida and it was a natural. 'Cause Lida, she was just about the same kind of a thing for a woman as Burbie was for a man. She used to work in the store, selling dry goods to the men, and kind of making hats on the side. 'Cepting only she didn't stay on the dry goods side no more'n she had to. She was generally over where the boys was drinking Coca-Cola, and all the time carrying on about did they like it with ammonia or lemon, and could she have a swallow outen their glass. And what she had her mind on was the clothes she had on, and was she dated up for Sunday night. Them clothes was pretty snappy, and she made them herself. And I heard some of them say she wasn't hard to date up, and after you done kept your date why maybe you wasn't going to be disappointed. And why Lida married the old man I don't know, lessen she got tired working at the store and tooken a look at the big farm where he lived at, about two mile from town.

By the time Burbie got back she'd been married about a year and she was about due. So her and him commence meeting each other, out in the orchard back of the old man's house. The old man would go to bed right after supper and then she'd sneak out and meet Burbie. And nobody wasn't supposed to know nothing about it. Only everybody did, 'cause Burbie, after he'd get back to town about eleven o'clock at night, he'd kind of slide into the poolroom and set down easy like. And then somebody'd say, "Yay, Burbie, where you been?" And Burbie, he'd kind of look around, and then he'd pick out somebody and wink at him, and that was how Burbie give it some good advertising.

So the way Burbie tells it, and he tells it plenty since he done got religion down to the jailhouse, it wasn't long before him and Lida thought it would be a good idea to kill the old man. They figured he didn't have long to live nohow, so he might as well go now as wait a couple of years. And another thing, the old man had kind of got hep that something was going on, and they figured if he throwed Lida out it wouldn't be no easy job to get his money even if he died regular. And another thing, by that time the Klux was kind of talking around, so Burbie figured it would be better if him and Lida was to get married, else maybe he'd have to leave town again.

So that was how come he got Hutch in it. You see, he was afeared to kill the old man hisself and he wanted some help. And then he figured it would be pretty good if Lida wasn't nowheres around and it would look like robbery. If it would of been me, I would of left Hutch out of it. 'Cause Hutch, he was mean. He'd been away for a while too, but him going away, that wasn't the same as Burbie going away. Hutch was sent. He was sent for ripping a mail sack while he was driving the mail wagon up from the station, and before he come back he done two years down to Atlanta.

But what I mean, he wasn't only crooked, he was mean. He had a ugly look to him, like when he'd order hisself a couple of fried eggs over to the restaurant, and then set and eat them with his head humped down low and his arm curled around his plate like he thought somebody was going to steal if off him, and handle his knife with his thumb down near the tip, kind of like a nigger does a razor. Nobody didn't have much to say to Hutch, and I reckon that's why he ain't heard nothing about Burbie and Lida, and et it all up what Burbie told him about the old man having a pot of money hid in the fireplace in the back room.

So one night early in March, Burbie and Hutch went out and done the job. Burbie he'd already got Lida out of the way. She'd let on she had to go to the city to buy some things, and she went away on No. 6, so everybody knowed she was gone. Hutch, he seen her go, and come running to Burbie saying now was a good time, which was just what Burbie wanted. 'Cause her and Burbie had already put the money in the pot, so Hutch wouldn't think it was no put-up job. Well, anyway, they put $23 in the pot, all changed into pennies and nickels and dimes so it would look like a big pile, and that was all the money Burbie had. It was kind of like you might say the savings of a lifetime.

And then Burbie and Hutch got in the horse and wagon what Hutch had, 'cause Hutch was in the hauling business again, and they went out to the old man's place. Only they went around the back way, and tied the horse back of the house so nobody couldn't see it from the road, and knocked on the back door and made out like they was just coming through the place on their way back to town and had stopped by to get warmed up, 'cause it was cold as hell. So the old man let them in and give them a drink of some hard cider what he had, and they got canned up a little more. They was already pretty canned, 'cause they both of them had a pint of corn on their hip for to give them some nerve.

And then Hutch he got back of the old man and crowned him with a wrench what he had hid in his coat.

II

Well, next off hutch gets sore as hell at Burbie 'cause there ain't no more'n $23 in the pot. He didn't do nothing. He just set there, first looking at the money, what he had piled up on a table, and then looking at Burbie.

And then Burbie commences soft-soaping him. He says hope my die he thought there was a thousand dollars anyway in the pot, on account the old man being like he was. And he says hope my die it sure was a big surprise to him how little there was there. And he says hope my die it sure does make him feel bad, on account he's the one had the idea first. And he says hope my die it's all his fault and he's going to let Hutch keep all the money, damn if he ain't. He ain't going to take none of it for hisself at all, on account of how bad he feels. And Hutch, he don't say nothing at all, only look at Burbie and look at the money.

And right in the middle of while Burbie was talking, they heard a whole lot of hollering out in front of the house and somebody blowing a automobile horn. And Hutch jumps up and scoops the money and the wrench off the table in his pockets, and hides the pot back in the fireplace. And then he grabs the old man and him and Burbie carries him out the back door, hists him in the wagon, and drives off. And how they was to drive off without them people seeing them was because they come in the back way and that was the way they went. And them people in the automobile, they was a bunch of old folks from the Methodist church what knowed Lida was away and didn't think so much of Lida nohow and come out to say hello. And when they come in and didn't see nothing, they figured the old man had went in to town and so they went back.

Well, Hutch and Burbie was in a hell of a fix all right. 'Cause there they was, driving along somewhere with the old man in the wagon and they didn't have no more idea than a bald-headed coot where they was going or what they was going to do with him. So Burbie, he commence to whimper. But Hutch kept a-setting there, driving the horse, and he don't say nothing.

So pretty soon they come to a place where they was building a piece of county road, and it was all tore up and a whole lot of tool-boxes laying out on the side. So Hutch gets out and twists the lock off one of them with the wrench, and takes out a pick and a shovel and throws them in the wagon. And then he got in again and drove on for a while till he come to the Whooping Nannie woods, what some of them says has got a ghost in it on dark nights, and it's about three miles from the old man's farm. And Hutch turns in there and pretty soon he come to a kind of a clear place and he stopped. And then, first thing he's said to Burbie, he says,

"Dig that grave!"

So Burbie dug the grave. He dug for two hours, until he got so damn tired he couldn't hardly stand up. But he ain't hardly made no hole at all. 'Cause the ground is froze and even with the pick he couldn't hardly make a dent in it scarcely. But anyhow Hutch stopped him and they throwed the old man in and covered him up. But after they got him covered up his head was sticking out. So Hutch beat the head down good as he could and piled the dirt up around it and they got in and drove off.

After they'd went a little ways, Hutch commence to cuss Burbie. Then he said Burbie'd been lying to him. But Burbie, he swears he ain't been lying. And then Hutch says he *was* lying and with that he hit Burbie. And after he knocked Burbie down in the bottom of the wagon he kicked him and then pretty soon Burbie up and told him about Lida. And when Burbie got done telling him about Lida, Hutch turned the horse around. Burbie asked then what they was going back for and Hutch says they're going back for to git a present for Lida. So they come back to the grave and Hutch made Burbie cut off the old man's head with the shovel. It made Burbie sick, but Hutch made him stick at it, and after a while Burbie had it off. So Hutch throwed it in the wagon and they get in and start back to town once more.

Well, they wasn't no more'n out of the woods before Hutch takes hisself a slug of corn and commence to holler. He kind of raved to hisself, all about how he was going to make Burbie put the head in a box and tie it up with a string and take it out to Lida for a present, so she'd get a nice surprise when she opened it. Soon as Lida comes back he says Burbie has got to do it, and then he's going to kill Burbie. "I'll kill you!" he says. "I'll kill you, damn you! I'll kill you!" And he says it kind of singsongy, over and over again.

And then he takes hisself another slug of corn and stands up and whoops. Then he beat on the horse with the whip and the horse commence to run. What I mean, he commence to gallop. And then Hutch hit him some more. And then he commence to screech as loud as he could. "Ride him, cowboy!" he hollers. "Going East! Here come old broadcuff down the road! Whe-e-e-e!" And sure enough, here they come down the road, the horse a-running hell to split, and Hutch a-hollering, and Burbie a-shivering, and the head a-rolling around in the bottom of the wagon, and bouncing up in the air when they hit a bump, and Burbie damn near dying every time it hit his feet.

III

After a while the horse got tired so it wouldn't run no more, and they had to let him walk and Hutch set down and commence to grunt. So Burbie, he tries to figure out what the hell he's going to do with the head. And pretty soon he remembers a creek what they got to cross, what they ain't crossed on the way out 'cause they come the back way. So he figures he'll throw the head overboard when Hutch ain't looking. So he done it. They come to the creek, and on the way down to the bridge there's a little hill, and when the wagon tilted going down the hill the head rolled up between Burbie's feet, and he held it there, and when they got in the middle of the bridge he reached down and heaved it overboard.

Next off, Hutch give a yell and drop down in the bottom of the wagon. 'Cause what it sounded like was a pistol shot. You see, Burbie done forgot that it was a cold night and the creek done froze over. Not much, just a thin skim about a inch thick, but enough that when that head hit it it cracked pretty loud in different directions. And that was what scared Hutch. So when he got up and seen the head setting out there on the ice in the moonlight, and got it straight what Burbie done, he let on he was going to kill Burbie right there. And he reached for the pick. And Burbie jumped out and run, and he didn't never stop till he got home at the place where he lived at, and locked the door, and climbed in bed and pulled the covers over his head.

Well, the next morning a fellow come running into town and says there's hell to pay down at the bridge. So we all went down there and first thing we seen was that head laying out there on the ice, kind of rolled over on one ear. And next thing we seen was Hutch's horse and wagon tied to the bridge rail, and the horse damn near froze to death. And the next thing we seen was the hole in the ice where Hutch fell through. And the next thing we seen down on the bottom next to one of the bridge pilings, was Hutch.

So the first thing we went to work and done was to get the head. And believe me a head laying out on thin ice is a pretty damn hard thing to get, and what we had to do was to lasso it. And the next thing we done was to get Hutch. And after we fished him out he had the wrench and the $23 in his pockets and the pint of corn on his hip and he was stiff as a board. And near as I can figure out, what happened to him was that after Burbie run away he climbed down on the bridge piling and tried to reach the head and fell in.

But we didn't know nothing about it then, and after we done got the head and the old man was gone and a couple of boys that afternoon found the body and not the head on it, and the pot was found, and them old people from the Methodist church done told their story and one thing and another, we figured out that Hutch done it, 'specially on account he must of been drunk and he done time in the pen and all like of that, and nobody ain't thought nothing about Burbie at all. They had the funeral and Lida cried like hell and everybody tried to figure out what Hutch wanted with the head and things went along thataway for three weeks.

Then one night down to the poolroom they was having it some more about the head, and one says one thing and one says another, and Benny Heath, what's a kind of a constable around town, he started a long bum argument about how Hutch must of figured if they couldn't find the head to the body they couldn't prove no murder. So right in the middle of it Burbie kind of looked around like he always done and then he winked. And Benny Heath, he kept on a-talking, and after he got done Burbie kind of leaned over and commence to talk to him. And in a couple of minutes you couldn't of heard a man catch his breath in that place, accounten they was all listening at Burbie.

I already told you Burbie was pretty good when it comes to giving a spiel at a entertainment. Well, this here was a kind of a spiel too. Burbie act like he had it all learned by heart. His voice trimmled and ever couple of minutes he'd kind of cry and wipe his eyes and make out like he can't say no more, and then he'd go on.

And the big idea was what a whole lot of hell he done raised in his life. Burbie said it was drink and women what done ruined him. He told about all the women what he knowed, and all the saloons he's been in, and some of it was a lie 'cause if all the saloons was as swell as he said they was they'd of throwed him out. And then he told about how sorry he was about the life he done led, and how hope my die he come home to his old home town just to get out the devilment and settle down. And he told about Lida, and how she wouldn't let him cut it out. And then he told how she done led him on till he got the idea to kill the old man. And then he told about how him and Hutch done it, and all about the money and the head and all the rest of it.

And what it sounded like was a piece what he knowed called "The Face on the Floor," what was about a bum what drawed a picture on the barroom floor of the woman what done ruined him. Only the funny part was that Burbie wasn't ashamed of hisself like he made out he was. You could see he was proud of hisself. He was proud of all them women and all the liquor he'd drunk and he was proud about Lida and he was proud about the old man and the head and being slick enough not to fall in the creek with Hutch. And after he got done he give a yelp and flopped down on the floor and I reckon maybe he thought he was going to die on the spot like the bum what drawed the face on the barroom floor, only he didn't. He kind of lain there a couple of minutes till Benny got him up and put him in the car and tooken him off to jail.

So that's where he's at now, and he's went to work and got religion down there, and all the people what comes to see him, why he sings hymns to them and then he speaks them his piece. And I hear tell he knows it pretty good by now and has got the crying down pat. And Lida, they got her down there too, only she won't say nothing 'cepting she done it same as Hutch and Burbie. So Burbie, he's going to get hung, sure as hell. And if he hadn't felt so smart, he would of been a free man yet.

Only I reckon he done been holding it all so long he just had to spill it.

MOMMY'S A BARFLY

On the bar, in the space between the fat man's Tom Collins and the sailor's beer, a girl was dancing. She wore a white muslin blouse, a red print dress with shoulder straps, black shoes, and white socklets; she was an uncommonly pretty girl, she was known as Pokey, and she was four years old. As she danced, she smiled at the pianist, who thumped a tiny instrument that had been tucked under the bar, and held out her skirts. When the tune ended, she did a pirouette, bowed, and received a crackling hand. Then, from a booth, a woman came over, kissed her, and listed her down. She was a woman of medium height and undeniably arresting-looking. She was dark, and there was something slightly gaunt about her figure and haggard about her face. She would have touched tragic beauty if there hadn't been something bummy about her.

When Pokey had run over to the soldier with whom the woman was sitting and climbed in his lap, the pianist clapped loudly and called for an encore. The bartender, who was also the owner of the place, said: "It's OK, Fred. She taps nice and she's sweet. But when she's using the bar for a dance floor I can't use it for a bar, and it's as a bar that it pays."

"Says who?"

"The register."

"So?"

"Sing me a song, Fred. Not no 'Rosie.' Not no 'Daisy.' And specially not no 'Annie.' Something nice. Sing me a song about Paris."

"Jake, have you become refined?"

"Them hop waltzes, they're beer music. But a nice song about Paris, that puts people in mind to drink B&B and other imported stock that shows a profit when you move it, it's OK."

"Then that clears it up."

But before Fred could sing about Paris, Pokey was back. When the fat man lifter her up, she said: "Mommy says if you want me to, I can dance once encore. And Fred, play 'Little Glow-Worm."

Pokey got a terrific hand that time. When she had returned to the booth, Jake made a beautiful drink of lemonade, sliced orange, cherries, and sugared mint, and carried it to Pokey. When he came back he said to Fred: "Mommy's no good if you ask me."

"Nobody was asking you."

"She's still no good."

"She's good-*looking*, though, if you ask *me*."

"*If* you like a good-looking barfly."

"Aren't barflies OK? You knowing our clientele?"

"Why not?"

In response to a blonde girl's request, Fred sang "Night and Day," then said reflectively: "I don't say a lot of them wouldn't look good on a rock pile, but they're the only clientele we got, so it's up to us to be broad-minded."

"Why ain't that kid home in bed?"

"Maybe she's not sleepy."

"At ten o'clock at night she's not sleepy and she's only four years old? You know when they get tucked in at her age? She ought to been in bed with all the prayers said and doll-baby's night diaper put on and the light put out three hours ago."

"I give up. What's the answer?"

"Mommy."

"Well, she likes booze. Don't we all?"

"And that's not all she likes."

"Quiz Kid, what is it now?"

"Fred, it's the twentieth century and there's a war going on and, like you say, with this here clientele we got to be broad-minded, *but*—a married woman out with a soldier cuts up the same any time, any place, and any war, and when a little kid gets mixed up in it it's not pretty."

"You got this woman all wrong."

"No, I haven't"

"You thinking about Willie?"

"I don't think much of Willie either, so far as that goes. Every night they come in here with Pokey, and OK, you say he don't know better. Well if not, why not? Even them rats out back don't bring little Sissie Rat in here. Speaking of her, when she's in here with a soldier the first night Willie don't show, that's all I want to know."

"You're doing great, except for one thing."

"*What?*"

"Kind of changes things around."

Jake stared at the man who now held Pokey in his lap, then said incredulously to Fred: "You mean that good-looking sergeant is the one she's married to and that other pie-faced runt is her . . . *sweetie?*"

"Talk louder, so they can all hear."

"I'm asking you."

"Why me? She's the one."

After Fred had sung "Lady Be Good," the soldier came over. He was a big, smiling man, with jet-black curly hair and a face burned the color of dark mahogany. He said to Fred: "You like my daughter, I notice."

"Your daughter is my one and only."

"Do me a favor?"

"Shoot."

"Take care of her a little while, will you?

At Fred's puzzled look, he made a sheepish face. "So I can see my wife. Since I went away she only keeps a small apartment and—"

"I got it. It's OK."

The soldier had been holding his hat in his hand. From it a little trickle of sand ran out on the bar. He laughed, said: "No trouble to see where I've been. I bumped into them on their way to the beach, so of course we couldn't disappoint Pokey. But, being as you're taking her for a little while, it's kind of a nice wife I've got, so—"

Smiling, he went back to the booth. Jake, who had been nearby, said: "That's what *he* thinks."

"Look: He says she's nice and he don't think. He *knows*."

"He's kidding hisself. You see what I see?"

"I don't see a thing."

"Neither does he, but I do. Fred, a wife that's wig-wagging for more Scotch in the last two hours of twenty-four-hour leave, and he hasn't even been home yet—she's not nice."

Jake served the Scotch, went back to his station beside the piano. The soldier looked at the drink in surprise. Then his face darkened. Then he started to say something, but looked at the child in his arms and checked himself. Then he got up, came over with Pokey, kissed her, nodded to Fred, and set her on the bar. Then he went back to the booth, started somewhat grimly to talk.

Pokey, her face pasty by now, her stance uncertain, her brown eyes yellow from lack of sleep, blinked uncertainly, then spread her skirts as though to dance. Fred struck a chord, but Jake lifter her down, said: "Fred, get me that cushion."

"That—?"

"Cushion. From the booth. On the end."

The cushion, when Fred came back with it, was leather, but stuffed full and soft. Jake put it under the bar, first clearing out several cases of bottles. Then he went out the door with "his" and "her" pictures on it and came back with his street coat. Then he beckoned Pokey, who was watching him, as was everybody except the couple in the booth. Fred said: "You going to put her *there?*"

"I am."

"One awful place."

"You know a better one?"

"What's the matter with the back room?"

"Was you ever put in a back room?"

"Anyway it's quiet."

"Quiet she don't have to have. Love, she does. Listen, she ain't no rag doll. She's a little thing four years old that gets scared and feels lonesome and wants to cry and so would you if you wasn't no bigger than she is that noise you et paid for, she'll sleep right through it, so keep right on and don't feel no embarrassment on *her* account if that's what's bothering you."

"Don't she get a pillow?"

"Pillows is out of date."

"Just asking."

"Now you know."

Jake stooped down, put his arm around Pokey, loosened her dress, took the ribbon from around her hair, tied it to a shoulder strap so it wouldn't get lost. Then he picker her up, put her on the little bed, spread his coat over her. It just covered her feet. Behind him, a light over the register glared down in her eyes. He turned it off. Pokey stared sleepily at Fred, said: "Play 'Little Glow-Worm.'"

Fred played it softly and a woman at the end of the bar, who could see Pokey from where she sat, sang it. But before the little glow-worm had given its first glimmer, Pokey was asleep. The soldier in the booth stared into his glass and occasionally said something in a short, jerky way, but the woman made no move to go.

For the next hour, the place was a blue twilight, with Fred's voice hovering over it in songs that didn't seem to end but rather to trail off into pure sadness. Then the spell was broken by the jangle of the phone. Jake answered, but the woman in the booth was there almost as soon as he was and took the receiver from him with eager hands and spoke in low, indistinguishable tones. The soldier came over, had a look at Pokey when Fred pointed her out, said: "Gee, that's sweet of you. I guess she'll be all right there till my bus leaves. We didn't go home. My wife's been expecting this call. From the USO. Sometimes they need her on the late shift and she gave them this number. She had to stand by."

"We all have to do our share."

"That's it."

The woman returned to the booth and the soldier joined her. It was some time before Jake, who did a little visiting with is customers, returned to the piano. Then he said: "This is murder, plain murder. Every person in this room know what's going on except two people. One's that sergeant, because he's stuck on her. The other is this kid under the bar, because she's asleep."

"Was that Willie? That called?"

"What do you think? That couple up there the ones drinking rye and soda, even made a bet that it was him, and they're sore because I won't tell them. It's so raw it burns my stomach. First give the husband a runaround at the beach all day, then have the sweetie call in to find out when the bus leaves, then at one minute after twelve meet him outside, and then her and him put Pokey to bed. I wouldn't ask much to kick her out."

"Oh you couldn't do that."

"Why not?"

"All God's chillun, you know. Maybe she came for a good time too."

"Be a funny kind of heaven with her flying around in it. If she's got wings, why hasn't she got a heart?"

"For Willie, maybe she has."

"I wish he didn't look quite so much like a dignified weasel."

"I wish that damned bus would *go*."

Fred began to sing again and little by little the blue twilight came back. The couple in the booth were friendlier now and the soldier, who had been drinking beer, ordered double Scotch. Then abruptly Fred broke off in the middle of a song, looked at his watch. With a look of alarm, he pointed his finger at the soldier, said: "Hey!"

"Yeah?"

"It's five minutes to twelve."

The soldier got up, came over to the bar, picked up his hooker of Scotch, downed it in a series of gulps. After a second in which he seemed to be strangling, he said: "So what?"

"Your bus is coming."

"Whose bus?"

"Did you forget you're standing reveille?"

"Me and who else?"

"Listen sergeant, you like those three stripes?"

"Not to the point of being silly about them."

"You like that extra dough they bring in though, don't you ? For the little woman overt there? And the little woman under here? Pokey? So she can have a nice warm coat for school, with a little fur collar on it? And peppermint for Christmas? And—"

"Shut up."

"I won't shut up."

"You will or I'm socking you."

"OK then, I clam."

Weaving a little, the soldier went back to the booth. The woman stared at him, looked at her watch. Then she came over to the bar. "What did he say?"

Fred made no answer. Jake swabbed a section of bar, then looked her straight in the eye and spoke slowly, quietly, deliberately; "He said he's going AWOL so he can be with a woman that's been two-timing him for a month, that didn't think enough of him even to bring him home when he came all the way up here to see her, and that needn't come back in this bar after tonight, if she don't mind."

How much of this after "AWOL" she actually heard, it would be hard to say. Her great black eyes opened in horror, and even after Jake had finished she stared at him. Then, breathlessly, she said: "I'll be back in a minute," and hurried out to the street.

Jake said: "It's so raw it stinks."

In a few minutes she was back, but instead of going to the booth, she flitted through the door with the pictures on it. The soldier ordered another double hooker of Scotch. Jake served a single, with soda. The soldier asked: "What time is it?"

"Little after twelve."

"I was supposed to catch a bus."

"It left. I seen it go by."

"OK."

Jake returned to the bar and Fred sang several songs. Then a woman came out of the door with the pictures on it, walked quickly around to where Jake was, leaned over, and said quietly to him: "You better get back there."

"Back where?"

"Ladies' room."

"What for?"

"There's trouble."

Conversation stopped and the row of people perched on stools looked at each other, then looked at Jake as he walked to the door, opened it, and disappeared. The soldier wig-wagged for Scotch. Fred took a bottle to the booth, poured a drink, came back to the piano. After some minutes, Jake reappeared, went to the phone, made a call. When he came back to the bar, he said loudly: "OK, folks, one on the house—what'll it be?"

Two or three ordered refills and the rest took the hint and began to talk. Two men paid their checks and left. When Jake got back to the piano, Fred said: "Where's Mommy?"

"Flying around."

"*Where?*"

"Heaven. Or will be soon."

" . . . Why?"

"She's going to be dead."

"Jake, what the hell are you talking about?"

"She's took six of the blue ones. She dissolved them all before she put them down and she won't take anything I fix for her ad it's too late now for anything to be done and this time tomorrow night she's going to die. That's what the hell I'm talking about."

"Holy Smoke."

"That's right, only hit it harder."

"Aren't you sending her to a hospital?"

"I already called."

"Aren't you—staying with her?"

"She don't want me. And—" with a jerk of a thumb toward the soldier—"She don't want *him*. And *I'll not call Willie.*"

"This boy has to be told."

"Then tell him."

Another hush had fallen over the bar. Then suddenly it was cut by a whisper: "Play 'Little Glow-Worm.'"

Jake said: "Yes, play it. God, play something!"

When he played a few bars, Fred said: "And *she's* got to be told."

"No she hasn't"

"How do you figure that out?"

"She's coming with me. She's coming with my wife and our two kids, and take the place of the one that died. Anyway till this guy is free and maybe for good. She's going to get up with the sun and go to bed with the sun and drink milk and chase butterflies. And she's *not going to be told.* Mommy just gave her to us, that's all."

The soldier called for "Smoke Gets In Your Eyes." Jake said: "Get over there now and tell him. About how it was, tell him what's good for him to know, and not nothing about Willie. About how it's going to be, you give him the works. And get the name of his outfit. So I can get his captain on the line and explain why he's not standing reveille."

From the street came the sound of an ambulance siren, and soon an interne and two orderlies entered the bar. Fred stopped playing, got up, and started his dreadful walk toward the soldier in the booth.

THE TAKING OF MONTFAUCON

I

I been asked did I get a DSC in the late war, and the answer is no, but I might of got one if I had not run into some tough luck. And how that was is pretty mixed up, so I guess I better start at the beginning, so you can get it all straight and I will not have to do no backtracking. On the 26th of September, 1918, when the old 79th Division hopped off with the rest of the AEF on the big drive that started that morning, the big job ahead of us was to take a town named Montfaucon, and it was the same town where the Crown Prince of Germany has his PC [Post of Command] in 1916, when them Dutch was hammering on Verdun and he was watching his boys fight by looking up at them through a periscope. And our doughboys was in two brigades, the 157th and 158th, with two regiments in each, and the 157th Brigade was in front. But they ain't took the town because it was up on a high hill, and on the side of the hill was a whole lot of pillboxes and barbed wire what made it a tough job. Only I ain't seen none of that, because I spent the whole day on the water wagon, along with another guy name of Armbruster, and we was driving it up from

the Division PC what we left to the Division PC where we was
going. And that there weren't so good, because neither him, me,
nor the horse hadn't had no sleep, account of the barrage shooting
off all night, and every time we come to one of them sixteen-inch
guns going through the woods and a Frog would squat down and
pull the cord, why the horse would pretty near die and so would
we. But sometime we seen a little of what was going on, like when
a Jerry aviator come over and shot down four of our balloons and
then flew over the road where we was and everybody tooken a
shot at him, only I didn't because I happen to look at my gun after
I pulled the bolt and it was all caked up with mud and I kind of
changed my mind about taking a shot.

So after a while we come to a place in a trench and they said it
was the new Division PC, and Ryan, who was the stable sergeant,
come along and took the horse, and we got something to eat and
there was still plenty shelling going on, but not bad like it was,
and we figured we could get some sleep. So then it was about
six o'clock in the evening. But pretty soon Captain Madeira, he
come to me and says I was to go on duty. And what I was to do
was to go with another guy, name of Shepler, to find the PC of
the 157th Brigade, what was supposed to be one thousand yards
west of where we was, and then report back. And why we was
to do that was so we could find the Brigade PC in the night and
carry messages to it. Because us in the Headquarters Troops, what
we done in the fighting was act as couriers and all like of that, and
what we done in between the fighting was curry horse belly. So
me and Shepler started out. And as the Brigade PC was supposed
to be one thousand yards west, and where we was was in a trench,
and the trench run east and west, it looked like all we had to do
was to follow the trench right into where the sun was setting and
it wouldn't be no hard job to find what we was looking for.

And it weren't. In about ten minutes we come to the Brigade

PC and there was General Nicholson [Brigadier General William J. Nicholson, commanding 157th Infantry Brigade] and his aides, and a bunch of guys what was in Brigade Headquarters, all setting around in the trench. But they was moving. They was all set to go forwards somewheres, and had their packs with them.

"Well," says Shep, "we ain't got nothing to do with that. Let's go back."

"Right," I says. But then I got to thinking. "What the hell good is it," I says, "for us to go back and tell them we found this PC when in a couple of minutes there ain't going to be nobody in it?"

"What the hell good is the war?" says Shep. "We was told to find this PC and we've found it. Now we go back and let them figure out what the hell good it is."

"This PC," I says, "soon as the General clears out, is same as a last year's bird nest."

"That's jake with me," says Shep. "In this man's army you do what you're told to do, and we've done it. We ain't got nothing to do with what kind of a bird's nest it is."

"No," I says, "we ain't done it. We was told to find a PC. And soon as Nick gets out this ain't going to be no PC, but only a dug-out. We got to go with him. We got to find where his new PC is at, and then we go back."

"Well, if we ain't done it," says Shep, "that's different."

So in a couple of minutes Nick started off, and we went with him, and a hell of a fine thing we done for ourself that we ain't went back in the first place, like Shep wanted to do. Because where we went, it weren't over no road and it weren't through no trench. It was straight up toward the front line over No Man's Land, and a worse walk after supper nobody ever took this side of Hell. How we went was single file, first Nick, and then them aides, and then them headquarters guys, and then us. About every fifty yards, a runner would pick us up, and point the way, and then fall back and let us pass. And what we was walking over was all shell holes and barbed wire, and you was always slipping down and busting your shin, and then all them dead horses and things was laying around, and you didn't never see one till you had your foot in it, and then it made you sick. And dead men. The first one we seen was in a trench, kind of laying up against the side, what was on a slant. And he was sighting down his gun just like he was getting ready to pull the trigger, and when you come to him you opened your mouth to beg his pardon for bothering him. And then you didn't.

Well, we went along that way for a hell of a while. And pretty soon it seemed like we wasn't nowheres at all, but was slugging along through some kind of black dream what didn't have no end, and them goddam runners look like ghosts what was standing there to point, only we wasn't never going to get where they was pointing nor nowheres else.

But after a while we come to a road and on the side of the road was a piece of corrugated iron. And Nick, soon as he come to that, wishing his musette bag and sat down on it. And then all them other guys sat down too. So me and Shep, we figured on that awhile, because at first we thought they was just taking a rest, but then Shep let on it looked like to him they was expecting to stay awhile. So then we went up to Nick.

"Sir," I says, "is this the new Brigade PC?"

"Who are you?" he says.

"We're from Division Headquarters," I says. "We was ordered to find the Brigade PC and report back."

"This is the new PC," he says.

"This piece of iron?" I says.

"Yes," says he.

"Thank you, sir," I says, and me and Shep saluted and left him.

"A hell of a looking PC," says Shep, soon as we got where he couldn't hear us.

"A hell of a looking PC all right," I says, "but it's pretty looking alongside of that trip we got going back."

"I been thinking about that," he says.

So then we sat down by the road a couple of minutes.

"Listen," he says. "I ain't saying I like that trip none. But what I'm thinking about is suppose we get lost. I don't mind telling you I can't find my way back over them shell holes."

"I got a idea," I says.

"Shoot," he says.

"This here road we're setting on," I says, "must go somewheres."

"They generally do," he says.

"If we can find someplace what's on one end of it," I says, "I can take you back if you don't mind a little walking. Because I know all these roads around here like a book." And how that was, was because I had been on observation post before the drive started, and had to study them maps, and even if I hadn't never been on the roads I knowed how they run.

"I'll walk with you to sunup," he says, "if it's on a road and we know where we're going. But I ain't going to try to get back over that No Man's Land, boy, I'll tell you that. Because I just as well try to fly."

So we asked a whole lot of guys did they know where the road run, and not none of them knowed nothing about it. But pretty soon we found a guy in the engineers, what was fixing the road, and he said he thought the road run back to Avocourt.

"Let's go," I says to Shep. "I know where we're at now."

So we started out, and sure enough after a while we come to Avocourt. And I knowed there was a road run east from Avocourt over the ridge to Esnes, if we could only figure out which the hell way was east. So the moon was coming up about then, and we remembered the moon come up in the east, and we headed for it, and hit the road. And a bunch of rats come outen a trench and began going up the road in front of us, hopping along in a pretty good line, and Shep said they was trench camels, and that give us a laugh, and we felt better. And pretty soon, sure enough we come to Esnes, and turned left, and in a couple minutes we was right back in the Division PC what we had left after supper, and it weren't much to look at, but it sure did feel like home.

II

Well, we weren't no sooner there than a bunch of guys begun to holler out to Captain Madeira that here we was, and he came a-running, and if we had of been a letter from home he couldn't of been more excited about us.

"Thank God, you've come," he says.

"Sure we've come," says Shep; "you wasn't really worried about us, was you?"

But I seen it was more than us the Captain was worrying about, so I says:

"What's the matter?"

"General Nicholson has broken liaison," he says, "and we've got not a way on earth to reach him unless you fellows can do it."

"Well, I guess we can, hey kid?" I says to Shep.

But Shep shook his head. "Maybe you can," he says, "but I ain't got no more idea where we been than a blind man. I'll keep you company, though, if you want."

"Company hell," says the Captain. "Here," he says to me, "you come in and see the General."

So he brung me into the dugout what was the PC to see General Kuhn [Major General Joseph E. Kuhn, commanding general,

79th Division]. And most of the time, the General was a pretty snappy-looking soldier. He was about medium size, and he had a cut to his jaw and a swing to his back what look like them pictures you see in books. But he weren't no snappy-looking soldier that night. He hadn't had no shave, and his eyes was all sunk in, and no wonder. Because when the Division ain't took Montfaucon that day, like they was supposed to, it balled everything up like hell. It put a pocket in the American advance, a kind of a dent, what was holding up the works all along the line. And the General was getting hell from Corps, and he had lost a lot of men, and that was why he was looking like he was.

"Do you know where General Nicholson is?" he says to me, soon as Captain Madeira had told him who I was.

"Yes, sir," I says, "but I don't think *he* does."

Now what the General said to that I ain't sure, but he mumbled something to hisself what sound like he be damned if he did either.

"I want you to take a message to him," he says.

"Yes, sir," I says.

So he commenced to write the message. And while I was standing there I was so sleepy everything look like it was turning around, like them things you see in a dream. It was a couple of aides in there, and maybe an orderly, and Captain Madeira, and it was in behind a lot of blankets, what they wet and hang over the door of a dugout to keep out gas. And in the middle of it was General Kuhn, writing on a pad in lead pencil, and I remember thinking how old he looked setting there, and then that would blank out and I couldn't see nothing but his whiskers, and then that would blank out and I would be thinking it was pretty tough on him, and I would do my best to help him out. It weren't no more than a minute, mind. Why I was thinking all them things jumbled up together was because I hadn't had no sleep.

"All right," he says to me; "listen now while I read it to you."

And why they read it to you is so if you lose it you can tell them what was in it and you ain't no worse off. And he hadn't no sooner started to read it then I snapped out of that dream pretty quick. Because it was short and sweet. It said that Nick was to attack right away soon as he got it. And I knowed a little about this Montfaucon stuff from hearing them brigade guys talk while we was going over No Man's Land, so I knowed I weren't carrying no message what just said good morning.

"Is that clear to you?" he says.

"Yes, sir," I says.

"Captain, give this man a horse. As good a horse as you've got."

"Yes, sir," says the Captain.

"You better ride pretty lively. And report back to me here."

"Yes, sir."

"No, wait a minute. I'm moving my PC to Malancourt in the next hour. Do you know where Malancourt is?"

"Yes, sir."

"Hunh," he says, like he meant thank God there was somebody in the outfit what knowed right from left and I was glad I had studied them maps good like I had and could be some use to him.

"Then report to me in Malancourt." And me and the Captain saluted and went out.

So the Captain took me to Ryan, and Ryan saddled me a horse, and while he was doing it Shep came up and begun to talk about the argument we had about whether we was going with Nick or not, and he handed it to me for figuring out the right thing to do, and the Captain said he was goddam proud of us both for carrying out orders with some sense when everybody else act like they had went off their nut and things was all shot to hell, and I felt pretty good. So pretty soon Ryan come with the horse, and I started out, and after I had went about a couple of miles it was commencing to get light, so I dug my heels in, because I knowed I didn't have much time.

III

Well, in another five minutes I come to Avocourt. And soon as I rode around the bend I got a funny feeling in my stomach. Because I seen something I had forgot when me and Shep was there, and that was that there was two roads what run from Avocourt up to the front line, one of them running north and the other running northeast, and they kind of forked off from each other in such a way that when you was coming down one of them like we done you wouldn't notice the other one at all. And I knowed as soon as I looked at them that I didn't have no idea which one we had come over and it weren't no way to find out.

So I pulled in and figured. And I closed my eyes and tried to remember how that road had looked when we was coming back down it into Avocourt with the moon rising on our left before we hit the road to Esnes, and that was damn hard, because I was so blotto from not having no sleep that soon as I closed my eyes all I got was a bellering in my ears. But I squinted them up good, and pretty soon it jumped in front of me, how that road looked, and right near Avocourt was a bunch of holes in the middle of it, what look like a tank had got stuck there and dug them up trying to get out. So I opened my eyes and was all set to hit for them holes. But then I knowed I was in for it good. Because in between while we had been over the road, them engineers had surfaced it, and it weren't no holes, because they was all covered up with stone.

But it weren't doing no good setting on top of the horse figuring, so I picked the right-hand road and started up it. I figured I would go about as far as me and Shep had come, and then maybe I would run into Nick, or somebody that could tell me where he was at, or what the right road was to take, and that the main thing was to get a move on. But that there sounds easier than it was. Because once you start out somewheres, and get to wondering are you headed right or not, you're bad off, and you might just as well be standing still for all you're going to get there.

I kept pushing the horse on, and every step he took I would look around to see if I could see something that me and Shep had seen, and about all I seen was tanks and engineers forking stone, what was what we had saw the night before, but it didn't prove nothing because you could see tanks and engineers on any road. And them engineers wasn't no help, because engineers is dumb as hell and then they ain't got nothing to do with fighting outfits and 157th Brigade sounds just the same to them as any other brigade, and a hell of a wonder me and Shep had found one the night before that could even tell us which way the road run.

Well, after I had went a ways, about as far as I thought me and Shep had come, and ain't seen a thing that I could say for certain we had saw the night before, and no sign of Nick or his piece of corrugated iron, what might be covered up with stone too for all I knowed, I figured I was on the wrong road sure as hell, and I got a awful feeling that I would have to go back to Avocourt and start over again. Because that order in my pocket, it weren't getting no cooler, I'm here to tell you. It was damn near burning a hole in my leg, and a funny hiccuppy noise would come up out of my neck every time I thought of it.

But I went a little bit further, just to make sure, and then I come to something that I thought straightened me all out. It was kind of a crossroads, bearing off to the left. And I couldn't remember that we had passed it the night before, so I figured I must of gone wrong, when I tooken the right-hand fork at Avocourt. But this road, I thought, will put me right, because it leads right acrost to the other one and I won't have to lose all that time going back to Avocourt. So I helloed down it, and for the first time since I left Avocourt I felt I was going right. And sure enough, pretty soon I come to the other road, and it weren't no new stone on it at that place, so I turned right, toward the front, and started up it. And I worked on the horse a little bit, because without no loose stone under his foot he could go better, and kind of patted him on the neck and talked to him, because he hadn't had no sleep neither and he was tired as hell by this time, and then I lifted him along so he went in a good run. And it weren't quite light yet, and I thought thank God I'll be in time.

IV

So pretty soon I come to some soldiers what wasn't engineers. So I pulled up and hollered out:

"What way to the Hundred and fifty-seventh Brigade PC?"

"The what?" they says.

"The Hundred and fifty-seventh Brigade PC," I says. "General Nicholson's PC."

"Never hear tell of it," they says.

"The hell you say," I says. "And you're a hell of a goddam comical outfit, ain't you?"

Because that was one of them gags they had in the army. They would ask a guy what his outfit was, and then when he told them they would say they never hear tell of it.

So I rode a little further and come to another bunch. "Which way is the Hundred and fifty-seventh Brigade PC?" I says. "General Nicholson's PC?"

But they never said nothing at all. Because they was doughboys going up in the lines, and when you hear somebody talk about doughboys singing when they're going to fight, you can tell him he's a damn liar and say I said so. Doughboys when they're going up in the lines they look straight in front of them and they swaller every third step and they don't say nothing.

So pretty soon I come to another bunch what wasn't doughboys and I asked them. "Search me, buddy," they says, and I went on. And I done that a couple of times, and I ain't found out nothing. So then I figured it weren't no use asking for the Brigade PC no more, because a lot of them guys they wouldn't never of hear tell of the Hundred and fifty-seventh Brigade even if they was in it, so I figured I would find out what outfit they was in and then I could figure out from that about where I was at. So that's what I done.

"What outfit, buddy?" I says to the next bunch I come to. But all they done was look dumb, so I didn't waste no more time on them, but went on till I come to another bunch, and I asked them.

"AEF," a guy sings out.

"What the hell," I says. "You think I'm asking for fun?"

"YMCA," says another, and I went on. And then all of a sudden I knowed why them guys was acting like that, and why it was was this: Ever since they come to France, they had been told if somebody up in the front lines asks you what your outfit is, don't you tell him because maybe he's a German spy trying to find out something. Because of course they wasn't really worried none that I was a German spy. What they was worried about was that maybe I was a MP or something what was going around finding out how they was minding the rule, and they wasn't taking no chances. Later on, when a whole hell of a lot of couriers had got lost and the American Army didn't know was it coming or going, they changed that rule. They marked all the PC's good so you could see them, and had arrows pointing to them a couple miles away so you couldn't get lost. But the rule hadn't been changed that morning, and that was why them guys wouldn't say nothing.

Well, was you ever in a lunatic asylum? That was what it was like for me from that time on. I would ask and ask, and all I ever got was "YMCA," or "Company B," or something like that, and it getting later all the time, and me with that order in my pocket. And after a while I thought well I got to pretend to he an officer and scare somebody into telling me where I'm at. So the first ones I come to was a captain and a lieutenant setting by the side of the road, and they was wearing bars. But me not having no bars didn't make no difference, because up at the front some officers wore bars but most of them didn't, and if you take the bars off, one guy without a shave looks pretty much like another. So I went up to them and saluted and spoke sharp, like I had been bawling out orders all my life.

"Which way is General Nicholson's PC?" I says, and the captain jumped up and saluted.

"General Nicholson?" he says. "Not around here, I'm pretty sure, sir," he says.

"Hundred and fifty-seventh Brigade?" I says, pretty short, like he must be asleep or something if he didn't know where that was.

"Oh, no," he says. "That wouldn't be in this Division. This is all Thirty-seventh."

So then I knowed I was sunk. The 37th Division, it was on our left, and that meant I had been on the right road all the time when I left Avocourt, as I seen many a time since by checking it up on the maps, and had went wrong by wondering about that fork. And it weren't nothing to do but cut across again, and hope I might bump into General Nicholson somehow, and if I didn't to keep on beating to Malancourt, so I could report to General Kuhn like I had been told to do. And what I done from then on I ain't never figured out, even from them maps, because I was thinking about that order all the time, and how it ought to been delivered already if it was going to do any good, and I got a little wild. I put the horse over the ditch and went through the woods, and never went back to the crossroads at all. And them woods was all full of shell holes, so you couldn't go straight, and the day was still cloudy, so you couldn't tell by the sun which way you was headed, and it weren't long before I didn't know which the hell way I was going. One time I must of been right up with the fighting, because a guy got up out of a shell hole and yelled at me for Christ sake not go over the top of that hill with the horse, because there was a sniper a little ways away, and I would get knocked off sure as hell. But by that time a sniper, if he only knowed where the hell he was sniping from, would of looked like a brother, so I went over. But it weren't no sniper, because I didn't get knocked off.

And another time I come to the rim of a shell hole what was so big you could of dropped a two-story house in it, and right new, but it weren't no dirt around it and you couldn't see no place the dirt had went. And right then the horse he wheeled and begun to cut back toward where he had come from. Because he was so tired by then he was stumbling every step and didn't want to go on. So I had to fight him. And then I got off and begun to beat him. And then I begun to blubber. And then I begun to blubber some more on account of how I was treating the horse, because he ain't done nothing and it was up to me to make him go.

And while I was standing there blubbering, near as I can figure out, the 313th, what was part of the 157th Brigade, was taking Montfaucon. Because General Kuhn he ain't sat back and waited for me. Soon as I left him he got on a horse and rode up to the front line hisself, there in the dark, and passed the word over they was to advance, and then relieved a general what didn't seem to be showing no signs of life, and put a colonel in command at that end of the line, and pretty soon things were moving. So Nick, he got the order that way and went on, and the boys, if they had Nick in command, they would take the town. So they took it.

V

It must of been after eleven o'clock when I got in to Malancourt. And there by the side of the road was General Kuhn, all smeared up with mud and looking like hell. And I went up to him and saluted.

"Did you deliver that message?" he says.

"No, sir," I says.

"What!" he says. "Then what are you doing coming in here at this hour?"

"I got lost," I says.

He never said nothing. He just looked at me, starting in from my eyes and going clear down to my feet, and that there was the saddest look I ever seen one man turn on another. And it weren't nothing to do but stand there and hold on to the reins of the goddam horse, and wish to hell the sniper had got me.

But just then he looked away quick, because somebody was saluting in front of him and commencing to talk. And it was Nick. And what he was talking about was that Montfaucon had been took. But he didn't no more than get started before General Kuhn started up hisself.

"What do you mean!" he says, "by breaking liaison with me? And where have you been anyway?"

"Where have I been?" says Nick. "I've been taking that position, that's where I've been. And I did not break liaison with you!"

So come to find out, them runners what had showed us the way over No Man's Land was supposed to keep liaison, only it was their first day of fighting, same as it was everybody else's, and what they done was keep liaison with that last year's bird nest what Nick had left, and didn't get it straight they was supposed to space out a little bit till they reached to the Division PC.

"And, anyway," says Nick, "there was a couple of your own runners that knew where I was. Why didn't you use them?"

So of course that made me feel great.

So they began to cuss at each other, and the generals can out-cuss the privates, I'll say that for them. So I kind of saluted and went off, and then Captain Madeira, he come to me.

"What's the matter?" he says.

"Nothing much," I says.

"You didn't make it, hey?"

"No. Didn't make it."

"Don't worry about it. You did the best you could."

"Yeah, I done the best I could."

"You're not the only one. It's been a hell of a night and a hell of a day."

"Yeah, it sure has."

"Well—don't worry about it."

"Thanks."

So that is how I come not to get no DSC in the late war. If I had of done what I was sent to do, maybe they would of give me one, because Shep, he got cited, and they sure needed me bad. But I never done it, and it ain't no use blubbering over how things might be if only they was a little different.

CIGARETTE GIRL

Bullets weren't in Cameron's line, but he couldn't back out. He couldn't' leave the girl alone again.

I'd never so much as laid eyes on her before going in this place, the *Here's How*, a night-club on Route 1, a few miles north of Washington, on business that was 99% silly, but that I had to keep to myself. It was around 8 at night, with hardly anyone there, and I'd just taken a table, ordered a drink, and started to unwrap a cigar, when a whiff of perfume hit me, and she swept by with cigarettes. As to what she looked like, I had only a rear view, but the taffeta skirt, crepe blouse, and silver earrings were quiet, and the chassis was choice, call it fancy, a little smaller than medium. So far, a cigarette girl, nothing to rate any cheers, but not bad either, for a guy unattached who'd like an excuse to linger.

But then she made a pitch, or what I took for a pitch. Her middle-aged customer was trying to tell her some joke, and taking so long about it the proprietor got in the act. He was a big, blond, blocky guy, with kind of a decent face, but he went and whispered to her as though to hustle her up, for some reason apparently, I couldn't quite figure it out. She didn't much seem to like it, until her eye caught mine. She gave a little pout, a little shrug, a little wink, and then just stood there, smiling.

Now I know this pitch and it's nice, because of course I smiled back, and with that I was on the hook. A smile is nature's freeway: it has lanes, and you can go any speed you like, except you can't go back. Not that I wanted to, as I suddenly changed my mind about the cigar I had in my hand, stuck it back in my pocket, and wigwagged for cigarettes. She nodded, and when she came over said: "You stop laughing at me."

"Who's laughing? Looking."

"Oh, of course. That's different."

I picked out a pack, put down my buck, and got the surprise of my life: she gave me change. As she started to leave, I said: "You forgot something, maybe?"

"That's not necessary."

"For all this I get, I should pay."

"All what, sir, for instance?"

"I told you: the beauty that fills my eye."

"The best things in life are free."

"On that basis, fair lady, some of them, here, are tops. Would you care to sit down?"

"Can't."

"Why not?"

"Not allowed. We got rules."

With that she went out toward the read somewhere, and I noticed the proprietor again, just a short distance away, and realized he'd been edging in. I called him over and said: "What's the big idea? I was talking to her."

"Mister, she's paid to work."

"Yeah, she mentioned about rules, but now they got other things too. Four Freedoms, all kinds of stuff. Didn't anyone ever tell you?"

"I heard of it, yes."

"You're Mr. *Here's How?*"

"Jack Connor, to my friends."

I took a V from my wallet, folded it, creased it, pushed it toward him. I said: "Jack, little note of introduction I generally carry around. I'd like you to ease these rules. She's cute, and I crave to buy her a drink."

He didn't see any money, and stood for a minute thinking. Then: "Mister, you're off on the wrong foot. In the first place, she's not a cigarette girl. Tonight, yes, when the other girl is off. But not regular, no. in the second place, she's not any chiselly-wink, that orders rye, drinks tea, takes the four bits you slip her, the four I charge for the drink—and is open to propositions. She's class. she's used to class—out West, with people that have it, and that brought her East when they came. In the third place she's a friend, and before I eased any rules I'd have to know more about you, a whole lot more, than this note tells me."

"My name's Cameron."

"Pleased to meet you and all that, but as to who you are, Mr. Cameron, and what you are, I still don't know—"

"I'm a musician."

"Yeah? What instrument?"

"Any of them. Guitar, mainly."

Which brings me to what I was doing there. I do play the guitar, play it all day long, for the help I get from it, as it gives me certain chords, the big ones that people go for, and heads me off from some others, the fancy ones on the piano, that other musicians go for. I'm an arranger, based in Baltimore, and had driven down on a little tune detecting. The guy who takes most of my work, Art Lomak, the band leader, writes a few tunes himself, and had gone clean off his rocker about one he said had been stolen, or thefted as they call it. It was one he'd been playing a little, to try it and work out bugs, with lyric and title to come, soon as the idea hit him. And then he rang me, with screams. It had already gone on the air, as 20 people had told him, from this same little honky-tonk, as part of a 10 o'clock spot on the Washington FM pick-up. He begged me to be here tonight, when the trio started their broadcast, pick up such dope as I could, and tomorrow give him the low-down.

That much was right on the beam, stuff that goes on every day, a routine I knew by heart. But his tune had angles, all of them slightly peculiar. One was, it had already been written, though it was never a hit and was almost forgotten, in the days when states were hot, under the title *Nevada*. Another was, it had been written even before that, by a gent named Giuseppe Verdi, as part of the *Sicilian Vespers*, under the title *O Tu Palermo*. Still another was, Art was really burned, and seemed to have no idea where the thing had come from. They just can't get it, those big schmalzburgers like him, that what leaks out of their head might, just once, have leaked in. But the twist, the reason I had to come, and couldn't just play it for laughs, was: Art could have been right. Maybe the lift *was* from him, not from the original opera, or from the first theft, *Nevada*. It's a natural for a ¾ beat, and that's how Art had been playing it. So if that's how they were doing it here, instead of with Nevada's 4/4, which followed the Verdi signature, there might still be plenty of work for the lawyers Art had put on it, with screams, same like to me.

Silly, almost.

Spooky.

But maybe, just possibly, moola.

So Jack, this boss character, by now had smelled something fishy, and suddenly took a powder, to the stand where the fiddles were parked, as of course the boys weren't there yet, and came back with a Spanish guitar. I took it, thanked him, and tuned. To kind

of work it around, in the direction of Art's little problem, and at
the same time make like there was nothing at all to conceal, I said
I'd come on account of his band, to catch it during the broadcast,
as I'd heard it was pretty good. He didn't react, which left me
nowhere, but I thought it well to get going.

I played him *Night and Day*, no Segovia job, but plenty good,
for free. On "Day and Night," where it really opens up, I knew
things to do, and talk suddenly stopped among the scattering of
people that were in there. When I finished there was some little
clapping, but still he didn't react, and I gave thought to mayhem.
But then a buzzer sounded, and he took another powder, out
toward the rear this time, where she had disappeared. I began
a little beguine, but he was back. He bowed, picked up his V,
bowed again: "Mr. Cameron, the guitar did it. She heard you,
and you're in."

"Will you set me up for two?"

"Hold on, there's a catch."

He said until midnight, when one of his men would take over,
she was checking his orders. "That means she handles the money,
and if she's not there, I could just as well close down. You're invited
back with her, but she can't come out with you."

"Oh. Fine."

"Sir, you asked for it."

I wasn't quite the way I'd have picked to do it, but the main
thing was the girl, and I followed him through the OUT door, the
one his waiters were using, still with my Spanish guitar. But then,
all of a sudden, I loved it, and felt even nearer to her.

This was the works of the joint, with a little office at one side,
service bar on the other, range rear and center, the crew in white
all around, getting the late stuff ready. But high on a stool, off by
herself, on a little railed-in platform where waiters would have
to pass, she was waving at me, treating it all as a joke. She called

down: "Isn't this a balcony scene for you? You have to play me some music!"

I whapped into it quick, and when I told her it was *Romeo and Juliet*, she said it was just what she'd wanted. By then Jack had a stool he put next to hers, so I could sit beside her, back of her little desk. He introduced us, and it turned out her name was Stark. I climbed up and there we were, out in the middle of the air, and yet in a way private, as the crew played it funny, to the extent they played it at all, but mostly were too busy even to look. I put the guitar on the desk and kept on with the music. By the time I'd done some Showboat she was calling me Bill and to me she was Lydia. I remarked on her eyes, which were green, and showed up bright against her creamy skin and ashy blond hair. She remarked on mine, which are light, watery blue, and I wished I was something besides tall, thin, and red-haired. But it was kind of cute when she gave a little pinch and nipped one of my freckles, on my hand back of the thumb.

Then Jack was back, with champagne iced in a bucket, which I hadn't ordered. When I remembered my drink, the one I *had* ordered, he said Scotch was no good, and this would be on him. I thanked him, but after he'd opened and poured, and I'd leaned the guitar in a corner and raised my glass to her, I said: "What's made him so friendly?"

"Oh, Jack's always friendly."

"Not to me. Oh, no."

"He may have thought I had it coming. Some little thing to cheer me. My last night in the place."

"You going away?"

"M'm-h'm."

"When?"

"Tonight."

"That why you're off at 12?"

"Jack tell you that?"

"He told me quite a lot."

"Plane leaves at 1. Bag's gone already. It's at the airport, all check and ready to be weighed."

She clinked her glass to mine, took a little sip, and drew a deep, trembly breath. As for me, I felt downright sick, just why I couldn't say, as it had to all be strictly allegro, with nobody taking it serious. It struck in my throat a little when I said: "Well—happy landings. It is permitted to ask which way that plane is taking you?"

"Home."

"And where's that?"

"It's—not important."

"The West, I know that much."

"What else did Jack tell you?"

I took it, improvised, and made up a little stuff, about her high-toned friends, her being a society brat, spoiled as all get-out, and the heavy dough she was used to—a light rib, as I thought. But it hadn't gone very far when I saw it was missing bad. When I cut it off, she took it. She said: "Some of that's true, in a way. I was—fortunate, we'll call it. But—you still have no idea, have you, Bill, what I really am?"

"I've been playing by ear."

"I wonder if you want to know?"

"If you don't want to, I'd rather you didn't say."

None of it was turning out quite as I wanted, and I guess maybe I showed it. She studied me a little and asked: "The silver I wear, that didn't tell you anything? Or my giving you change for your dollars? It didn't mean anything to you, that a girl would run a straight game?"

"She's not human."

"*It means she's a gambler.*"

And then: "Bill does that shock you?"

"No, not at all."

"I'm not ashamed of it. Out home, it's legal. You know where that is now?"

"Oh! *Oh!*"

"Why oh? And *oh?*"

"Nothing. It's—Nevada, isn't it?"

"Something wrong with Nevada?"

"No! I just woke up, that's all."

I guess that's what I said, but whatever it was, she could hardly miss the upbeat in my voice. Because, of course, that wrapped it all up pretty, not only the tunes, which the band would naturally play for her, but her too, and who she was. Society dame, to tell the truth, hadn't pleased me much, and maybe that was one reason my rib was slightly off key. But gambler I could go for, a little cold, a little dangerous, a little brave. When she was sure I had really brought it, we were close again, and after a nip on the freckle her fingers slid over my hand. She said play her *Smoke*—the smoke she had in her eyes. But I didn't, and we just sat there some little time.

And then, a little bit at a time, she began to spill it: "Bill, it was just plain cock-eyed. I worked in a club, the Paddock, in Reno, a regular institution. Tony Rocco—Rock—owned it, and was the squarest bookie ever—why he was a Senator, and civic, and everything. And I worked from him, running his wires practically being his manager, with a beautiful salary, a bonus Christmas, and everything. And then wham, it struck. This federal thing. This 10% tax on gross. And we were out of business. It just didn't make sense. Everything else was exempted. Wheels and boards and slots, whatever you could think of, but us. Us and the numbers racket, in Harlem and Florida and Washington."

"Take it easy."

"That's right, Bill. Thanks."

"Have some wine."

" . . . Rock, of course, was fixed. He had property, and for the building, where the Paddock was, he got $250,000—or so I heard. But then came the tip on Maryland."

That crossed me up, and instead of switching her off, I asked her what she meant. She said: "That Maryland would legalize wheels."

"What do you smoke in Nevada?"

"Oh, I didn't believe it. And Rock didn't. But Mrs. Rock went nuts about it. Oh well, she had reason."

"Dark, handsome reason?"

"I don't want to talk about it, but that reason took the Rocks for a ride, for every cent they got for the place, and tried to take me too, for other things beside money. When they went off to Italy, they thought they had it fixed, he was to keep me at my salary, in case Maryland *would* legalize, and if not, to send me home, with severance pay, as it's called. And instead of that—"

"I'm listening."

"I've said too much."

"What's this guy to you?"

"Nothing! I never even saw him until the three of us stepped off the plane—with our hopes. In a way it seemed reasonable. Maryland had tracks, and they help with the taxes. Why not wheels?

"And *who* is this guy?"

"I'd be ashamed to say, but I'll say this much: I won't e a kept floozy. I don't care who he thinks he is, or—"

She bit her lip, started to cry, and really shut up then. To switch off, I asked why she was working for Jack, and she said: "Why not? You can't go home in a barrel. But he's been swell to me."

Saying people were swell seemed to be what she like, and she calmed down, letting her hand stay when I pressed it in both of mine. Then we were really close, close enough that I'd be warranted in laying it on the line, she should let that plane fly away, and not go to Nevada at all. But while I was working on that, business was picking up, with waiters stopping by to let her look at their trays, and I hadn't much chance to say it, whatever I wanted to say. Then, through the IN door, a waiter came through with a tray that had a wine bottle on it. A guy followed him in, a little noisy guy, who said the bottle was full and grabbed it off the tray. He had hardly gone out, when Jack was in the door, watching him as he staggered back to the table. The waiter swore the bottle was empty, but all Jack did was nod.

Then Jack came over to her, took another little peep through the window in the OUT door, which was just under her balcony, and said: "Lydiay, what did you make of him?"

"Why—he's drunk, that's all."

"You notice him, Mr. Cameron?"

"No—except it crossed my mind he wasn't as tight as the act he was putting on."

"Just what crossed *my* mind! How could he get that drunk on a split of Napa red? What did he want back here?"

by now, the waiter had gone out on the floor and come back, saying the guy wanted his check. But as he started to shuffle it out of the bunch he had tucked in his best, Jack stopped him and said: "He don't get any check—not till I give the word. Tell Joe I said stand by and see he don't get out. *Move!*"

The waiter had looked kind of blank, but hustled out as told, and then Jack looked at her. He said: "Lady, I'll be back. I'm taking a look around."

He went, and she drew another of her long, trembly breaths. I cut my eye around, but no one had noticed a thing, and yet it seemed kind of funny they'd all be slicing bread, wiping glass, of fixing cocktails set-ups, with Jack mumbling it low out of the side of his mouth. I had a creepy feeling of things going on, and my mind took it a little, fitting it together, what she had said about the bag checked at the airport, the guy trying to make her, and most of all, the way Jack had acted, the second she showed with her cigarettes, shooing her off the floor, getting her out of sight. She kept staring through the window, at the drunk where he sat with his bottle, and seemed to ease when a captain I took to be Joe planted himself pretty solid in a spot that would block off a run-out.

Then Jack was back, marching around, snapping his fingers, giving orders for the night. But as he passed the back door, I noticed his hand touched the lock, as though putting the catch on. He started back to the floor, but stopped as he passed her desk, and shot it quick in a whisper: "He's out there, Lydia, parked in back. This drunk, like I thought, is a finger he sent in to spot you, but he won't be getting out till you're gone. You're leaving for the airport, right now."

"Will you call me a cab, Jack?"

"Cab? I'm taking you."

He stepped near me and whispered: "Mr. Cameron, I'm sorry, this little lady has to leave, for—"

"I know about that."

"She's in danger—"

"I've also caught on to that."

"From a no-good imitation goon that's been trying to get to her here, which is why I'm shipping her out. I hate to break this up, but if you'll ride with us, Mr. Cameron—"

"I'll follow you down."

"That's right, you have your car. It's Friendship Airport, just down the road."

He told her to get ready, while he was having his car brought up, and the boy who would take her place on the desk was changing his clothes. Step on it, he said, but wait until he came back. He went out on the floor and marched past the drunk without even turning his head. But she sat watching me. She said: "You're not coming, are you?"

"Friendship's a little cold."

"But not mine, Bill, no."

She got off her stool, stood near me and touched my hair. She said: "Ships that pass in the night pass so close, so close." And then: "I'm ashamed, Bill, I'd have to go for this reason. I wonder, for the first time, if gamblings's really much good." She pulled the chain of the light, so we were half in the dark. Then she kissed me. She said: "God bless and keep you, Bill."

"And you, Lydia."

I felt her tears on my cheek, and then she pulled away and stepped to the little office, where she began putting a coat on and tying a scarf on her head. She looked so pretty it came to me I still hadn't given her the one little bouquet I'd been saving for the last. I picked up the guitar and started *Nevada*.

She wheeled, but what stared at me were eyes as hard as glass. I was so startled I stopped, but she kept right on staring. Outside a car door slammed, and she listened at the window beside her. Then a last she looked away, to peep through the Venetian blind. Jack popped in, wearing his coat and hat, and motioned her to hurry. But he caught something and said, low yet so I could hear him: "Lydia! What's the matter?"

She stalked over to me, with him following along, pointed her finger, and then didn't say it, but spat it: "He's the finger—that's what's the matter, that's all. He played *Nevada*, as though we hadn't had enough trouble wit it already. And Vanny heard it. He hopped out of his car and he's under the window right now."

"Then O.K., let's go."

I was a little too burned to make with the explanations, and took my time, parking the guitar, sliding off, and climbing down, to give them a chance to blow. But she still had something to say, and to me, not to him. She pushed her face up to mine, and mocking how I had spoken, yipped: "Oh! . . . *Oh!* OH!" Then she went, with Jack. Then I went, clumping after.

Then it broke wide open.

The drunk, who was supposed to sit there, conveniently boxed in, while she went slipping out, turned out more of a hog-calling type, and instead of playing his part, jumped up and yelled: "Vanny! *Vanny!* Here she comes! She's leaving! VANNY"

He kept I up, while women creamed all over, then pulled a gun from his pocket, and let go at the ceiling, so it sounded like the field artillery, as shots always do when fired inside a room. Jack jumped for him and hit the deck, as his feet shot from under him on the slippery wood of the dance floor. Joe swung, missed, swung again, and landed, so Mr. Drunk went down. But when Joe scrambled for the gun, there came this voice through the smoke: "Hold it! As you were—and leave that gun alone."

Then hulking in came this short-necked, thick-shouldered thing, in Homburg hat, double-breasted coat, and white muffler, one hand in his pocket, the other giving an imitation of a movie gangster. He said keep still and nobody would get hurt, but "I won't stand for tricks." He helped Jack up, asked how he'd been. Jack said: "Young man, let me tell you something—"

"How you been? I asked."

"Fine, Mr. Rocco."

"Any telling, Jack—I'll do it."

Then, to her: "Lydia, how've *you* been?"

"That doesn't concern you."

Then she burst out about what he had done to his mother, the gyp he'd handed his father, and his propositions to her, and I got it, at last, who this idiot was. He listened, but right in the middle of it, he waved his hand toward me and asked: "Who's this guy?"

"Vanny, I think you know."

"Guy, are you the boy friend?"

"If so I don't tell you."

I sounded tough, but my belly didn't feel that way. They had it some more, and he connected me with the tune, and seemed to enjoy it a lot, that it had told him where to find her, on the broadcast as here now tonight. But he kept creeping closer, to where we were all lined up, with the drunk stretched on the floor, the gun under his hand, and I suddenly felt the prickle, that Vanny was really nuts, and in a minute meant to kill her. It also crossed my mind, that a guy who plays the guitar has a left hand made of steel, from squeezing down on the strings, and is a dead sure judge of distance, to the last eighth of an inch. I prayed I could forget it, told myself I owed her nothing at all, that she'd turned on me cold, with no good reason. I concentrated, to dismiss the thought entirely.

No soap.

I grabbed for my chord and got it.

I choked down on his hand, the one he held in his pocket, while hell broke loose in the place, with women screaming, men running, and fists trying to help, I had the gun hand all right, but when I reached for the other he twisted, butted, and bit, and for that long I thought he'd get loose, and that I was a gone pigeon. The gun barked, and a piledriver hit my leg. I went down. Another gun spoke and he went down beside me. Then here was Jack, the drunk's gun in his hand, stepping in close, and firing again to make sure.

I blacked out.

I came to, and then she was there, a knife in her hand, ripping the cloth away from the outside of my leg, grabbing napkins, stanching blood, while somewhere ten miles off I could hear Jack's voice, as he yelled into a phone. On the floor right beside me was something under a tablecloth.

That went on for some time, with Joe calming things down and some people sliding out. The band came in, and I heard a boy ask for his guitar. Somebody brought it to him. And then, at last, came the screech of sirens, and she whispered some thanks to God.

Then, while the cops were catching up, with me, with Jack, and what was under the cloth, we both went kind of haywire, me laughing, she crying, and both in each others' arms. I said: "Lydia, Lydia, you're not taking that plane. They legalize things in Maryland, one thing specially, except that instead of wheels, they generally use a ring."

Still holding my leg with one hand she pulled me close with the other, kissed me and kept on kissing me, and couldn't speak at all. All legalized now, is what I started to tell about—with Jack as best man, naturally.

THE ROBBERY

"Good evening."

"Good evening."

"I guess we've seen each other a couple of times before, haven't we? Me and my wife, we live downstairs."

"Yeah, I know who you are. What do you want?"

"Just want to talk to you about something."

"Well—come in."

"No. Just close that door behind you and we'll sit on the steps."

"All right. That suits me. Now what's the big idea?"

"Today we was robbed. Somebody come in the apartment, turned the whole place inside out, and got away with some money, and my wife's jewelry. Three rings and a couple of wrist watches. It's got her broke up pretty bad. I got her in bed now, but she's crying and carrying on all the time. I feel right down sorry for her."

"Well, that's tough. But what you coming to me about it for?"

"Nothing special. But of course I'm trying to find out who done it, so I thought I would come around and see you. Just to see if you got any idea about it."

"Yeah?"

"That's it."

"Well, I haven't got no idea."

"You haven't? That's funny."

"What's funny about it?"

"Seems like most everybody on the block has an idea about it. I ain't got in the house yet before about seven people stopped me and told me about it, and all of them had an idea about who done it. Of course, some of them ideas wasn't much good, but still they was ideas. So you haven't got no idea?"

"No. I haven't got no idea. And what's more, you're too late."

"How you mean, too late?"

"I mean them detectives has been up here already. I mean that fine wife of yours sent them up here, and what I had to say about this I told them, and I ain't got time to say it over again for you. And let me tell you something: You tell any more detectives I was the one robbed your place, and that's right where the trouble starts. They got laws in this country. They got laws against people that goes around telling lies about their neighbors, and don't you think for a minute you're going to get by with that stuff no more. You get me?"

"I'll be doggone. Them cops been up here already? Them boys sure do work fast, don't they?"

"Yeah, they work fast when some fool woman that has lost a couple of rings calls up the station house and fills them full of lies. They work fast, but they don't always work so good. They ain't got nothing on me at all, see? So you're wasting your time, just like they did!"

"What did you tell them, if you don't mind my asking?"

"I told them just what I'm telling you: that I don't know a thing about you or your wife, or your flat, or who robbed you, or what goes on down there, 'cepting I wish to hell you would turn off that radio at night once, so I can get some sleep. That's what I told them, and if you don't like it you know what you can do."

"Well, now, old man, I tell you. Fact of the matter, my wife didn't send them cops up here at all. When she come home, and found out we was robbed, why it got her all excited. So she rung up the station house, and told the cops what she found, and then she went to bed. And that's where she's at now. She ain't seen no detectives. She's to see them tomorrow. So it looks like them detectives thought up that little visit all by theirself, don't it?"

"What do you mean?"

"I mean maybe even them detectives could figure out that this here job was done by somebody that knowed all about me and my wife, when we was home, when we was out, and all like of that. And 'specially, that it was done by somebody that knowed we had the money in the house to pay the last installment on the furniture."

"How would I know that?"

"Well, you might know by remembering what time the man came around to get the money last month and figuring he would come around the same day this month, and that we would have the money here waiting for him. That would be one way, wouldn't it?"

"Let me tell you something, fellow: I don't know a thing about this, or your furniture, or the collector, or nothing. And there ain't nothing to show what I know. So you ain't got nothing on me, see? So shag on. Go on down where you come from. So shut up. So that's all. So good-bye."

"Now, not so fast,"

"What now? I ain't going to stay but here all night."

"I'm just thinking about something. First off, we ain't got nothing on you. That sure is a fact. We ain't got nothing on you at all. Next off, them detectives ain't got nothing on you. They called me up a little while ago and told me so. Said they couldn't prove nothing."

"It's about time you was getting wise to yourself."

"Just the same, you are the one that done it."

"Huh?"

"I say you are the one that done it."

"All right. All right. I'm the one that done it. Now go ahead and prove it."

"Ain't going to try to prove it. That's a funny thing, ain't it? Them detectives, when they start out on a thing like this, they always got to prove something, haven't they? But me, I don't have to prove nothing."

"Come on. What you getting at?"

"Just this: Come on with that money, and come on with them jewels, or I sock you. And make it quick."

"Now wait a minute . . . . Wait a minute."

"Sure. I ain't in no hurry."

"Maybe if I was to go in and look around. . . . Maybe some of my kids done that, just for a joke—"

"Just what I told my wife, old man, now you mention it. I says to her, I says, 'Them detectives is all wrong on that idea. Them kids upstairs done it,' I says, 'just for a joke.'"

"I'll go in and take a look—"

"No. You and me, we set out here till I get them things in my hand. You just holler inside and tell the kids to bring them."

"I'll ring the bell and get one of them to the door—"

"That sure is nice of you, old man. I bet there's a whole slew of them robberies done by kids just for a joke, don't you? I always did think so."

MONEY AND THE WOMAN
(THE EMBEZZLER)

I

I first met her when she came over to the house one night, after calling me on the telephone and asking if she could see me on a matter of business. I had no idea what she wanted, but supposed it was something about the bank. At the time, I was acting cashier of our little Anita Avenue branch, the smallest of the three we've got in Glendale, and the smallest branch we've got, for that matter. In the home office, in Los Angeles, I rate as vice president, but I'd been sent out there to check up on the branch, not on what was wrong with it, but what was right with it. Their ratio of savings deposits to commercial deposits was over twice what we had in any other branch, and the Old Man figured it was time somebody went out there and found out what the trick was, in case they'd invented something the rest of the banking world hadn't heard of.

I found out what the trick was soon enough. It was her husband, a guy named Brent that rated head teller and had charge of the savings department. He'd elected himself little White Father to all those workmen that banked in the branch, and kept after them and made them save until half of them were buying their homes

and there wasn't one of them that didn't have a good pile of dough
in the bank. It was good for us, and still better for those workmen,
but in spite of that I didn't like Brent and I didn't like his way of
doing business. I asked him to lunch one day, but he was too busy,
and couldn't come. I had to wait till we closed, and then we went
to a drugstore while he had a glass of milk, and I tried to get out
of him something about how he got those deposits every week,
and whether he thought any of his methods could be used by the
whole organization. But we got off on the wrong foot, because he
thought I really meant to criticize, and it took me half an hour
to smooth him down. He was a funny guy, so touchy you could
hardly talk to him at all, and with a hymn-book-salesman look to
him that made you understand why he regarded his work as a kind
of a missionary job among these people that carried their accounts
with him. I would say he was around thirty, but he looked older.
He was tall and thin, and beginning to get bald, but he walked
with a stoop and his face had a gray color that you don't see on a
well man. After he drank his milk and ate the two crackers that
came with it, he took a little tablet out of an envelope he carried
in his pocket, dissolved it in his water, and drank it.

But even when he got it through his head I wasn't sharpening
an axe for him, he wasn't much help. He kept saying that savings
deposits have to be worked up on a personal basis, that the man at
the window has to make the depositor feel that he takes an interest
in seeing the figures mount up, and more of the same. Once he
got a holy look in his eyes, when he said that you can't make the
depositor feel that way unless you really feel that way yourself, and
for a few seconds he was a little excited, but that died off. It looks
all right, as I write it, but it didn't sound good. Of course, a big
corporation doesn't like to put things on a personal basis, if it can
help it. Institutionalize the bank, but not the man, for the good
reason that the man may get an offer somewhere else, and then

when he quits he takes all his trade with him. But that wasn't the only reason it didn't sound good. There was something about the guy himself that I just didn't like, and what it was I didn't know, and didn't even have enough interest to find out.

So when his wife called up a couple of weeks later, and asked if she could see me that night, at my home, not at the bank, I guess I wasn't any sweeter about it than I had to be. In the first place, it looked funny she would want to come to my house, instead of the bank, and in the second place, it didn't sound like good news, and in the third place, if she stayed late, it was going to cut me out of the fights down at the Legion Stadium, and I kind of look forward to them. Still, there wasn't much I could say except I would see her, so I did. Sam, my Filipino houseboy, was going out, so I fixed a highball tray for myself, and figured if she was as pious as he was, that would shock her enough that she would leave early.

It didn't shock her a bit. She was quite a lot younger than he was, I would say around twenty-five, with blue eyes, brown hair, and a shape you couldn't take your eyes off of. She was about medium size, but put together so pretty she looked small. Whether she was really good-looking in the face I don't know, but if she wasn't good-looking, there was something about the way she looked at you that had that thing. Her teeth were big and white, and her lips were just the least little bit thick. They gave her a kind of a heavy, sullen look, but one eyebrow had a kind of twitch to it, so she'd say something and no part of her face would move but that, and yet it meant more than most women could put across with everything they had.

All that kind of hit me in the face at once, because it was the last thing I was expecting. I took her coat, and followed her into the living room. She sat down in front of the fire, picked up a cigarette and tapped it on her nail, and began looking around. When her eye lit on the highball tray she was already lighting her cigarette, but she nodded with the smoke curling up in one eye, "Yes, I think I will."

I laughed, and poured her a drink. It was all that had been said, and yet it got us better acquainted than an hour of talk could have done. She asked me a few questions about myself, mainly if I wasn't the same Dave Bennett that used to play halfback for U.S.C., and when I told her I was, she figured out my age. She said she was twelve years old at the time she saw me go down for a touchdown on an intercepted pass, which put her around twenty-five, what I took her for. She sipped her drink. I put a log of wood on the fire. I wasn't quite so hot about the Legion fights.

When she'd finished her drink she put the glass down, motioned me away when I started to fix her another, and said: "Well."

"Yeah, that awful word."

"I'm afraid I have bad news."

"Which is?"

"Charles is sick."

"He certainly doesn't look well."

"He needs an operation."

"What's the matter with him—if it's mentionable?"

"It's mentionable, even if it's pretty annoying. He has a duodenal ulcer, and he's abused himself so much, or at least his stomach, with this intense way he goes about his work, and refusing to go out to lunch, and everything else that he shouldn't do, that it's got to that point. I mean, it's serious. If he had taken better care of himself, it's something that needn't have amounted to much at all. But he's let it go, and now I'm afraid if something isn't done—well, it's going to be very serious. I might as well say it. I got the report today, on the examination he had. It says if he's not operated on at once, he's going to be dead within a month. He's—verging on a perforation."

"And?"

"This part isn't so easy."

" . . . How much?"

"Oh, it isn't a question of money. That's all taken care of. He has a policy, one of these clinical hook-ups that entitles him to everything. It's Charles."

"I don't quite follow you."

"I can't seem to get it through his head that this has to be done. I suppose I could, if I showed him what I've just got from the doctors, but I don't want to frighten him any more than I can help. But he's so wrapped up in his work, he's such a fanatic about it, that he positively refuses to leave it. He has some idea that these people, these workers, are all going to ruin if he isn't there to boss them around, and make them save their money, and pay up their installments on their houses, and I don't know what all. I guess it sounds silly to you. It does to me. But—he won't quit."

"You want me to talk to him?"

"Yes, but that's not quite all. I think, if Charles knew that his work was being done the way he wants it done, and that his job would be there waiting for him when he came out of the hospital, that he'd submit without a great deal of fuss. This is what I've been trying to get around to. Will you let me come in and do Charles's work while he's gone?"

" . . . Well—it's pretty complicated work."

"Oh no, it's not. At least not to me. You see, I know every detail of it, as well as he does. I not only know the people, from going around with him while he badgered them into being thrifty, but I used to work in the bank. That's where I met him. And—I'll do it beautifully, really. That is, if you don't object to making it a kind of family affair."

I thought it over a few minutes, or tried to. I went over in my mind the reasons against it, and didn't see any that amounted to anything. In fact, it suited me just as well to have her come in, if

Brent really had to go to the hospital, because it would peg the job while he was gone, and I wouldn't have to have a general shake-up, with the other three in the branch moving up a notch, and getting all excited about promotions that probably wouldn't last very long anyway. But I may as well tell the truth. All that went through my mind, but another thing that went through my mind was her. It wasn't going to be a bit unpleasant to have her around for the next few weeks. I liked this dame from the start, and for me anyway, she was plenty easy to look at.

"Why—I think that's all right."

"You mean I get the job?"

"Yeah—sure."

"What a relief. I hate to ask for jobs."

"How about another drink?"

"No, thanks. Well—just a little one."

I fixed her another drink, and we talked about her husband a little more, and I told her how his work had attracted the attention of the home office, and it seemed to please her. But then all of a sudden I popped out: "Who are you, anyway?"

"Why—I thought I told you."

"Yeah, but I want to know more."

"Oh, I'm nobody at all, I'm sorry to say. Let's see, who am I? Born, Princeton, New Jersey, and not named for a while on account of an argument among relatives. Then when they thought my hair was going to be red they named me Sheila, because it had an Irish sound to it. Then—at the age of ten, taken to California. My father got appointed to the history department of U.C.L.A."

"And who is your father?"

"Henry W. Rollinson—"

"Oh, yes, I've heard of him."

"Ph.D. to you, just Hank to me. And—let's see. High school, valedictorian of the class, tagged for college, wouldn't go. Went

out and got myself a job instead. In our little bank. Answered
an ad in the paper. Said I was eighteen when I was only sixteen,
worked there three years, got a one-dollar raise every year. Then—
Charles got interested, and I married him."

"And, would you kindly explain *that?*"

"It happens, doesn't it?"

"Well, it's none of my business. Skip it."

"You mean we're oddly assorted?"

"Slightly."

"It seems so long ago. Did I mention I was nineteen? At that
age you're very susceptible to—what would you call it? Idealism?"

" . . . Are you still?"

I didn't know I was going to say that, and my voice sounded
shady. She drained her glass and got up.

"Then, let's see. What else is there in my little biography? I
have two children, one five, the other three, both girls, and both
beautiful. And—I sing alto in the Eurydice Women's Chorus. . . .
That's all, and now I have to be going."

"Where'd you put your car?"

"I don't drive. I came by bus."

"Then—may I drive you home?"

"I'd certainly be grateful if you would. . . . By the way, Charles
would kill me if he knew I'd come to you. About him, I mean. I'm
supposed to be at a picture show. So tomorrow, don't get absent-
minded and give me away."

"It's between you and me,"

"It sounds underhanded, but he's very peculiar."

I live on Franklin Avenue in Hollywood, and she lived on
Mountain Drive, in Glendale. It's about twenty minutes, but
when we got in front of her house, instead of stopping, I drove
on. "I just happened to think; it's awful early for a picture show
to let out."

"So it is, isn't it?"

We drove up in the hills. Up to then we had been plenty gabby, but for the rest of the drive we both felt self-conscious and didn't have much to say. When I swung down through Glendale again the Alexander Theatre was just letting out. I set her down on the corner, a little way from her house. She shook hands. "Thanks ever so much."

"Just sell him the idea, and the job's all set."

" . . . I feel terribly guilty, but—"

"Yes?"

"I've had a grand time."

II

She sold me the idea, but she couldn't sell Brent, not that easy, that is. He squawked, and refused to go to the hospital, or do anything about his ailment at all, except take pills for it. She called me up three or four times about it, and those calls seemed to get longer every night. But one day, when he toppled over at the window, and I had to send him home in a private ambulance, there didn't seem to be much more he could say. They hauled him off to the hospital, and she came in next day to take his place, and things went along just about the way she said they would, with her doing the work fine and the depositors plunking down their money just like they had before.

The first night he was in the hospital I went down there with a basket of fruit, more as an official gift from the bank than on my own account, and she was there, and of course after we left him I offered to take her home. So I took her. It turned out she had arranged that the maid should spend her nights at the house, on account of the children, while he was in the hospital, so we took a ride. Next night I took her down, and waited for her outside, and we took another ride. After they got through taking X-rays they operated, and it went off all right, and by that time she and I had got the habit. I found a newsreel right near the hospital, and while she was with him, I'd go in and look at the sports, and then we'd go for a little ride.

I didn't make any passes, she didn't tell me I was different from other guys she'd known, there was nothing like that. We talked about her kids, and the books we'd read, and sometimes she'd remember about my old football days, and some of the things she'd seen me do out there. But mostly we'd just ride along and say nothing, and I couldn't help feeling glad when she'd say the doctors wanted Brent to stay there until he was all healed up. He could have stayed there till Christmas, and I wouldn't have been sore.

The Anita Avenue branch, I think I told you, is the smallest one we've got, just a little bank building on a corner, with an alley running alongside and a drugstore across the street. It employs six people, the cashier, the head teller, two other tellers, a girl book-keeper, and a guard. George Mason had been cashier, but they transferred him and sent me out there, so I was acting cashier. Sheila was taking Brent's place as head teller. Snelling and Helm were the other two tellers, Miss Church was the bookkeeper, and Adler the guard. Miss Church went in for a lot of apple-polishing with me, or anyway what I took to be apple-polishing. They had to stagger their lunch hours, and she was always insisting that I go out for a full hour at lunch, that she could relieve at any of the windows, that there was no need to hurry back, and more of the same. But I wanted to pull my oar with the rest, so I took a half hour like the rest of them took, and relieved at whatever window needed me, and for a couple of hours I wasn't at my desk at all.

One day Sheila was out, and the others got back a little early, so I went out. They all ate in a little cafe down the street, so I ate there too, and when I got there she was alone at a table. I would have sat down with her, but she didn't look up, and I took a seat a couple of tables away. She was looking out the window, smoking, and pretty soon she doused her cigarette and came over where I was. "You're a little standoffish today, Mrs. Brent."

"I've been doing a little quiet listening."

"Oh—the two guys in the corner?"

"Do you know who the fat one is?"

"No, I don't."

"That's Bunny Kaiser, the leading furniture man of Glendale. 'She Buys 'Er Stuff from Kaiser.'"

"Isn't he putting up a building or something? Seems to me we had a deal on, to handle his bonds."

"He wouldn't sell bonds. It's his building, with his own name chiseled over the door, and he wanted to swing the whole thing himself. But he can't quite make it. The building is up to the first floor now, and he has to make a payment to the contractor. He needs a hundred thousand bucks. Suppose a bright girl got that business for you, would she get a raise?"

"And how would *she* get that business?"

"Sex appeal! Do you think I haven't got it?"

"I didn't say you haven't got it."

"You'd better not."

"Then that's settled."

"And—?"

"When's this payment on the first floor due?"

"Tomorrow."

"Ouch! That doesn't give us much time to work."

"You let *me* work it, and *I'll* put it over."

"All right, you land that loan, it's a two-dollar raise."

"Two-fifty."

"O.K.—two-fifty."

"I'll be late. At the bank, I mean."

"I'll take your window."

So I went back and took her window. About two o'clock a truck driver came in, cashed a pay check with Helm, then came over to me to make a $10 deposit on savings. I took his book, entered the amount, set the $10 so she could put it with her cash when she came in. You understand: They all have cash boxes, and lock them when they go out, and that cash is checked once a month. But when I took out the card in our own file, the total it showed was $150 less than the amount showing in the passbook.

In a bank, you never let the depositor notice anything. You've got that smile on your face, and everything's jake, and that's fair enough, from his end of it, because the bank is responsible, and what his book shows is what he's got, so he can't lose no matter how you play it. Just the same, under that pasted grin, my lips felt a little cold. I picked up his book again, like there was something else I had to do to it, and blobbed a big smear of ink over it. "Well, that's nice, isn't it."

"You sure decorated it."

"I tell you what, I'm a little busy just now—will you leave that with me? Next time you come in, I'll have a new one ready for you."

"Anything you say, Cap."

"This one's kind of shopworn, anyway."

"Yeah, getting greasy."

By that time I had a receipt ready for the book, and copied the amount down in his presence, and passed it out to him. He went and I set the book aside. It had taken a little time, and three more depositors were in line behind him. The first two books corresponded with the cards, but the last one showed a $200 difference, more on his book than we had on our card. I hated to do what he had seen me do with the other guy, but I had to have that book. I started to enter the deposit, and once more a big blob of ink went on that page.

"Say, what you need is a new pen."

"What they need is a new teller. To tell you the truth, I'm a little green on this job, just filling in till Mrs. Brent gets back, and I'm hurrying it. If you'll just leave me this book, now—"

"Sure, that's all right."

I wrote the receipt, and signed it, and he went, and I put that book aside. By that time I had a little breathing spell, with nobody at the window, and I checked those books against the cards. Both accounts, on our records, showed withdrawals, running from $25 to $50, that didn't show on the passbooks. Well, brother, it had to show on the passbooks. If a depositor wants to withdraw, he can't do it without his book, because that book's his contract, and we're bound by it, and he can't draw any dough unless we write it right down there, what he took out. I began to feel a little sick at my stomach. I began to think of the shifty way Brent had talked when he explained about working the departments up on a personal basis. I began to think about how he refused to go to the hospital, when any sane man would have been begging for the chance. I began to think of that night call Sheila made on me, and all that talk about Brent's taking things so seriously, and that application she made, to take things over while he was gone.

All that went through my head, but I was still thumbing the cards. My head must have been swimming a little when I first checked them over, but the second time I ran my eye over those two cards I noticed little light pencil checks beside each one of those withdrawals. It flashed through my mind that maybe that was his code. He had to have a code, if he was trying to get away with anything. If a depositor didn't have his book, and asked for his balance, he had to be able to tell him. I flipped all the cards over. There were light pencil checks on at least half of them, every one against a withdrawal, none of them against a deposit. I wanted to run those checked amounts off on the adding machine, but I didn't. I was afraid Miss Church would start her apple-polishing again, and offer to do it for me. I flipped the cards over one at a time, slow, and added the amounts in my head. If I was accurate I didn't know. I've got an adding machine mind, and I can do some of those vaudeville stunts without much trouble, but I was too excited to be sure. That didn't matter, that day. I wouldn't be far off. And those little pencil checks, by the time I had turned every card, added up to a little more than $8,500.

Just before closing time, around three o'clock, Sheila came in with the fat guy, Bunny Kaiser. I found out why sex appeal had worked, where all our contact men, trying to make a deal for bonds a few months before, had flopped. It was the first time he had ever borrowed a dollar in his life, and he not only hated it, he was so ashamed of it he couldn't even look at me. Her way of making him feel better was not to argue about it at all, but to pat him on the hand, and it was pathetic the way he ate it up. After a while she gave me the sign to beat it, so I went back and got the vault closed, and chased the rest of them out of there as fast as I could. Then we fixed the thing up, I called the main office for O.K.'s, and around four-thirty he left. She stuck out her hand, pretty excited, and I took it. She began trucking around the floor, snapping her fingers and singing some tune while she danced. All of a sudden she stopped, and made motions like she was brushing herself off.

"Well—is there something *on* me?"

" . . . No. Why?"

"You've been *looking* at me—for an *hour!*"

"I was—looking at the dress."

"Is there anything the *matter* with it?"

"It's different from what girls generally wear around a bank. It—doesn't look like an office dress."

"I made it myself."

"Then that accounts for it."

III

Brother, if you want to find out how much you think of a woman, just get the idea she's been playing you for a sucker. I was trembling when I got home, and still trembling when I went up to my room and lay down. I had a mess on my hands, and I knew I had to do something about it. But all I could think of was the way she had taken me for a ride, or I thought she had anyway, and how I had fallen for it, and what a sap I was. My face would feel hot when I thought of those automobile rides, and how I had been too gentlemanly to start anything. Then I would think how she must be laughing at me, and dig my face into the pillow. After a while I got to thinking about tonight. I had a date to take her to the hospital, like I had for the past week, and wondered what I was going to do about that. What I wanted to do was give her a stand-up and never set eyes on her again, but I couldn't. After what she had said at the bank, about me looking at her, she might tumble I was wise if I didn't show up. I wasn't ready for that yet. Whatever I had to do, I wanted my hands free till I had time to think.

So I was waiting, down the street from her house, where we'd been meeting on account of what the neighbors might think if I kept coming to the door, and in a few minutes here she came, and I gave the little tap on the horn and she got in. She didn't say anything about me looking at her, or what had been said. She kept talking about Kaiser, and how we had put over a fine deal, and how there was plenty more business of the same kind that could be had if I'd only let her go out after it. I went along with it, and for the first time since I'd known her, she got just the least little bit flirty. Nothing that meant much, just some stuff about what a team we could make if we really put our minds to it. But it brought me back to what my face had been red about in the afternoon, and when she went in the hospital I was trembling again.

I didn't go to the newsreel that night. I sat in the car for the whole hour she was in there, paying her visit to him, and the longer I sat the sorer I got. I hated that woman when she came out of the hospital, and then, while she was climbing in beside me, an idea hit me between the eyes. If that was her game, how far would she go with me? I watched her light a cigarette, and then felt my mouth go dry and hot. I'd soon find out. Instead of heading for the hills, or the ocean, or any of the places we'd been driving, I headed home.

We went in, and I lit the fire without turning on the living-room light. I mumbled something about a drink, and went out in the kitchen. What I really wanted was to see if Sam was in. He wasn't, and that meant he wouldn't be in till one or two o'clock, so that was all right. I fixed the highball tray, and went in the living room with it. She had taken off her hat, and was sitting in front of the fire, or to one side of it. There are two sofas in my living room, both of them half facing the fire, and she was on one of them swinging her foot at the flames. I made two highballs, put them on the low table between the sofas, and sat down beside her. She looked up, took her drink, and began to sip it. I made a crack about how black her eyes looked in the firelight, she said they were blue, but it sounded like she wouldn't mind hearing more. I put my arm around her.

Well, a whole book could be written about how a woman

blocks passes when she doesn't mean to play. If she slaps your face, she's just a fool, and you might as well go home. If she hands you a lot of stuff that makes *you* feel like a fool, she doesn't know her stuff yet, and you better leave her alone. But if she plays it so you're stopped, and yet nothing much has happened, and you don't feel like a fool, she knows her stuff, and she's all right, and you can stick around and take it as it comes, and you won't wake up next morning wishing that you hadn't. That was what she did. She didn't pull away, she didn't act surprised, she didn't get off any bum gags. But she didn't come to me either, and in a minute or two she leaned forward to pick up her glass, and when she leaned back she wasn't inside of my arm.

I was too sick in my mind though, and too sure I had her sized up right for a trollop, to pay any attention to that, or even figure out what it meant. It went through my mind, just once, that whatever I had to do, down at the bank, I was putting myself in an awful spot, and playing right into her hands, to start something I couldn't stop. But that only made my mouth feel drier and hotter.

I put my arm around her again, and pulled her to me. She didn't do anything about it at all, one way or the other. I put my cheek against hers, and began to nose around to her mouth. She didn't do anything about that either, but her mouth seemed kind of hard to reach. I put my hand on her cheek, and then deliberately let it slide down to her neck, and unbuttoned the top button of her dress. She took my hand away, buttoned her dress, and reached for her drink again, so when she sat back I didn't have her.

That sip took a long time, and I just sat there, looking at her. When she put the glass down I had my arm around her before she could even lean back. With my other hand I made a swipe, and brushed her dress up clear to where her garters met her girdle. What she did then I don't know, because something happened that I didn't expect. Those legs were so beautiful, and so soft, and warm, that something caught me in the throat, and for about one second I had no idea what was going on. Next thing I knew she was standing in front of the fireplace, looking down at me with a drawn face. "Will you kindly tell me what's got into you tonight?"

"Why—nothing particular."

"Please, I want to know."

"Why, I find you exciting, that's all."

"Is it something I've done?"

"I didn't notice you doing anything."

"Something's come over you, and I don't know what. Ever since I came in the bank today, with Bunny Kaiser, you've been looking at me in a way that's cold, and hard, and ugly. What is it? Is it what I said at lunch, about my having sex appeal?"

"Well, you've got it. We agreed on that."

"Do you know what I think?"

"No, but I'd like to."

"I think that remark of mine, or something, has suddenly wakened you up to the fact that I'm a married woman, that I've been seeing quite a little of you, and that you think it's now up to you to be loyal to the ancient masculine tradition, and try to make me."

"Anyway, I'm trying."

She reached for her drink, changed her mind, lit a cigarette instead. She stood there for a minute, looking into the fire, inhaling the smoke. Then:

" . . . I don't say it couldn't be done. After all, my home life hasn't been such a waltz dream for the last year or so. It's not so pleasant to sit by your husband while he's coming out of ether, and then have him begin mumbling another woman's name, instead of your own. I guess that's why I've taken rides with you every night. They've been a little breath of something pleasant. Something more than that. Something romantic, and if I pretended they haven't meant a lot to me, I wouldn't be telling the truth. They've

been—little moments under the moon. And then today, when I
landed Kaiser, and was bringing him in, I was all excited about
it, not so much for the business it meant to the bank, which I
don't give a damn about, or the two-dollar-and-a-half raise, which
I don't give a damn about either, but because it was something
you and I had done together, something we'd talk about tonight,
and it would be—another moment under the moon, a very bright
moon. And then, before I'd been in the bank more than a minute
or two, I saw that look in your eye. And tonight, you've been—
perfectly horrible. It could have been done, I think. I'm afraid I'm
only too human. But not this way. And not any more. Could I
borrow your telephone?"

I thought maybe she really wanted the bath, so I took her to
the extension in my bedroom. I sat down by the fire quite a while,
and waited. It was all swimming around in my head, and it hadn't
come out at all like I expected. Down somewhere inside of me,
it began to gnaw at me that I had to tell her, I had to come out
with the whole thing, when all of a sudden the bell rang. When I
opened the door a taxi driver was standing there.

"You called for a cab?"

"No, nobody called."

He fished out a piece of paper and peered at it, when she came
downstairs. "I guess that's my cab."

"Oh, you ordered it?"

"Yes. Thanks ever so much. It's been so pleasant."

She was as cold as a dead man's foot, and she was down the
walk and gone before I could think of anything to say. I watched
her get in the cab, watched it drive off, then closed the door and
went back in the living room. When I sat down on the sofa I could
still smell her perfume, and her glass was only half drunk. That
catch came in my throat again, and I began to curse at myself out
loud, even while I was pouring myself a drink.

I had started to find out what she was up to, but all I had found out was that I was nuts about her. I went over and over it till I was dizzy, and nothing she had done, and nothing she had said, proved anything. She might be on the up-and-up, and she might be playing me for a still worse sucker than I had thought she was, a sucker that was going to play her game for her, and not even get anything for it. In the bank, she treated me just like she treated the others, pleasant, polite, and pretty. I didn't take her to the hospital any more, and that was how we went along for three or four days.

Then came the day for the monthly check on cash, and I tried to kid myself that was what I had been waiting for, before I did anything about the shortage. So I went around with Helm, and checked them all. They opened their boxes, and Helm counted them up, and I counted his count. She stood there while I was counting hers, with a dead pan that could mean anything, and of course it checked to the cent. Down in my heart I knew it would. Those false entries had all been made to balance the cash, and as they went back for a couple of years, there wasn't a chance that it would show anything in just one month.

That afternoon when I went home I had it out with myself, and woke up that I wasn't going to do anything about that short-age, that I couldn't do anything about it, until at least I had spoken to her, anyway acted like a white man.

So that night I drove over to Glendale, and parked right on Mountain Drive where I had always parked. I went early, in case she started sooner when she went by bus, and I waited a long time. I waited so long I almost gave up, but then along about half past seven, here she came out of the house, and walking fast. I waited till she was about a hundred feet away, and then I gave that same little tap on the horn I had given before. She started to run, and I had this sick feeling that she was going by without even speaking, so I didn't look. I wouldn't give her that much satisfaction. But before I knew it the door opened and slammed, and there she was on the seat beside me, and she was squeezing my hand, and half whispering:

"I'm so glad you came. So glad."

We didn't say much going in. I went to the newsreel, but what came out on the screen I couldn't tell you. I was going over and over in my mind what I was going to say to her, or at least trying to. But every time when I'd get talking about it, I'd find myself starting off about her home life, and trying to find out if Brent really had taken up with another woman, and more of the same that only meant one thing. It meant I wanted her for myself. And it meant I was trying to make myself believe that she didn't know anything about the shortage, that she had been on the up-and-up all the time, that she really liked me. I went back to the car, and got in, and pretty soon she came out of the hospital, and ran down the steps. Then she stopped, and stood there like she was thinking. Then she started for the car again, but she wasn't running now. She was walking slow. When she got in she leaned back and closed her eyes.

"Dave?"

It was the first time she had ever called me by my first name. I felt my heart jump. "Yes, Sheila?"

"Could we have a fire tonight?"

"I'd love it."

"I've—I've got to talk to you."

So I drove to my house. Sam let us in, but I chased him out. We went in the living room, and once more I didn't turn on the light. She helped me light the fire, and I started into the kitchen to fix something to drink, but she stopped me.

"I don't want anything to drink. Unless you do."

"No. I don't drink much."

"Let's sit down."

She sat on the sofa, where she had been before, and I sat beside her. I didn't try any passes. She looked in the fire a long time, and then she took my arm and pulled it around her. "Am I terrible?"

"No."

"I want it there."

I started to kiss her, but she raised her hand, covered my lips with her fingers, then pushed my face away. She dropped her head on my shoulder, closed her eyes, and didn't speak for a long time. Then: "Dave, there's something I've got to tell you."

"What is it?"

"It's pretty tragic, and it involves the bank, and if you don't want to hear it from me, this way, just say so and I'll go home."

" . . . All right. Shoot."

"Charles is short in his accounts."

"How much?"

"A little over nine thousand dollars. Nine one one three point two six, if you want the exact amount. I've been suspecting it. I noticed one or two things. He kept saying I must have made mistakes in my bookkeeping, but tonight I made him admit it."

"Well. That's not so good."

"How bad is it?"

"It's pretty bad."

"Dave, tell me the truth about it. I've got to know. What will they do to him? Will they put him in prison?"

"I'm afraid they will."

"What, actually, does happen?"

"A good bit of what happens is up to the bonding company. If they get tough, he needn't expect much mercy. It's dead open-and-shut. They put him under arrest, have him indicted, and the rest of it's a question of how hard they bear down, and how it hits the court. Sometimes, of course, there are extenuating circumstances—"

"There aren't any. He didn't spend that money on me, or on the children, or on his home. I've kept all expenses within his salary, and I've even managed to save a little for him, every week."

"Yeah, I noticed your account."

"He spent it on another woman."

"I see."

"Does it make any difference if restitution is made?"

"All the difference in the world."

"If so, would he get off completely free?"

"There again, it all depends on the bonding company, and the deal that could be made with them. They might figure they'd make any kind of a deal, to get the money back, but as a rule they're not lenient. They can't be. The way they look at it, every guy that gets away with it means ten guys next year that'll try to get away with it."

"Suppose they never knew it?"

"I don't get you."

"Suppose I could find a way to put the money back, I mean suppose I could get the money, and then found a way to make the records conform, so nobody ever knew there was anything wrong."

"It couldn't be done."

"Oh yes, it could."

"The passbooks would give it away. Sooner or later."

"Not the way I'd do it."

"That—I would have to think about."

"You know what this means to me, don't you?"

"I think so."

"It's not on account of me. Or Charles. I try not to wish ill to anybody, but if he had to pay, it might be what he deserves. It's on account of my two children. Dave, I can't have them spend the rest of their lives knowing their father was a convict, that he'd been in prison. Do you, can you, understand what that means, Dave?"

For the first time since she had begun to talk, I looked at her then. She was still in my arms, but she was turned to me in a strained, tense kind of way, and her eyes looked haunted. I patted her head, and tried to think. But I knew there was one thing I had to do. I had to clear up my end of it. She had come clean with me, and for a while, anyway, I believed in her. I had to come clean with her.

"Sheila?"

"Yes?"

"I've got to tell *you* something."

" . . . What is it, Dave?"

"I've known this all along. For at least a week."

"Is that why you were looking at me that day?"

"Yes. It's why I acted that way, that night. I thought you knew it. I thought you had known it, even when you came to me that night, to ask for the job. I thought you were playing me for a sucker, and I wanted to find out how far you'd go, to get me where you wanted me. Well—that clears *that* up."

She was sitting up now, looking at me hard.

"Dave, I *didn't* know it."

"I know you didn't—now, I know it."

"I knew about *her*—this woman he's been—going around with. I wondered sometimes where he got the money. But this, I had no idea. Until two or three days ago. Until I began to notice discrepancies in the passbooks."

"Yeah, that's what I noticed."

"And that's why you turned seducer?"

"Yeah. It's not very natural to me, I guess. I didn't fool you any. What I'm trying to say is I don't feel that way about you. I want you every way there is to want somebody, but—I mean it. Do you know what I'm getting at, if anything?"

She nodded, and all of a sudden we were in each other's arms, and I was kissing her, and she was kissing back, and her lips were warm and soft, and once more I had that feeling in my throat, that catch like I wanted to cry or something. We sat there a long time, not saying anything, just holding each other close. We were halfway to her house before we remembered about the shortage and what we were going to do about it. She begged me once more to give her a chance to save her children from the disgrace. I told her I'd have to think it over, but I knew in my heart I was going to do anything she asked me to.

IV

"Where are you going to get this money?"

"There's only one place I can possibly get it."

"Which is?"

"My father."

"Has he got that much dough?"

"I don't know. . . . He owns his house. Out in Westwood. He could get something on that. He has a little money. I don't know how much. But for the last few years his only daughter hasn't been any expense. I guess he can get it."

"How's he going to feel about it?"

"He's going to hate it. And if he lets me have it, it won't be on account of Charles. He bears no goodwill to Charles, I can tell you that. And it won't be on account of me. He was pretty bitter when I even considered marrying Charles, and when I actually went and did it—well, we won't go into that. But for his grandchildren's sake, he might. Oh, what a mess. What an awful thing."

It was the next night, and we were sitting in the car, where I had parked on one of the terraces overlooking the ocean. I suppose it was around eight-thirty, as she hadn't stayed at the hospital very long. She sat looking out at the surf, and then suddenly I said I might as well drive her over to her father's. I did, and she didn't have much to say. I parked near the house, and she went in, and she stayed a long time. It must have been eleven o'clock when she came out. She got in the car, and then she broke down and cried, and there wasn't much I could do. When she got a little bit under control, I asked, "Well, what luck?"

"Oh, he'll do it, but it was awful."

"If he got sore, you can't blame him much."

"He didn't get sore. He just sat there, and shook his head, and there was no question about whether he'd let me have the money or not. But—Dave, an old man, he's been paying on that house for fifteen years, and last year he got it clear. If he wants to, he can spend his summers in Canada, he and Mamma both. And now— it's all gone, he'll have to start paying all over again, all because of this. And he never said a word."

"What did your mother say?"

"I didn't tell her. I suppose he will, but I couldn't, I waited till she went to bed. That's what kept me so long. Fifteen years, pay- ing regularly every month, and now it's to go, all because Charles fell for a simpleton that isn't worth the powder and shot to blow her to hell."

I didn't sleep very well that night. I kept thinking of the old his- tory professor, and his house, and Sheila, and Brent lying down there in the hospital with a tube in his belly. Up to then I hadn't thought much about him. I didn't like him, and he was washed up with Sheila, and I had just conveniently not thought of him at all. I thought of him now, though, and wondered who the simpleton was that he had fallen for, and whether he was as nuts about her as I was about Sheila. Then I got to wondering whether

I thought enough of her to embezzle for her, and that brought me sitting up in bed, staring out the window at the night. I could say I wouldn't, that I had never stolen from anybody, and never would, but here I was already mixed up in it some kind of way. It was a week since I uncovered that shortage, and I hadn't said a word about it to the home office, and I was getting ready to help her cover up.

Something popped in me then, about Brent, I mean, and I quit kidding myself. I did some hard figuring in bed there, and I didn't like it a bit, but I knew what I had to do. Next night, instead of heading for the ocean, I headed for my house again, and pretty soon we were back in front of the fire. I had mixed a drink this time, because at least I felt at peace with myself, and I held her in my arms quite a while before I got to it. Then: "Sheila?"

"Yes?"

"I've had it out with myself."

"Dave, you're not going to turn him in?"

"No, but I've decided that there's only one person that can take that rap."

"Who do you mean?"

"Me."

"I don't understand you."

"All right, I drove you over to see your father last night, and he took it pretty hard. Fifteen years, paying on that house, and now it's all got to go, and he don't get anything out of it at all. Why should he pay? I got a house, too, and I do get something out of it."

"What do *you* get out of it?"

"You."

"What are you talking about?"

"I mean I got to cough up that nine thousand bucks."

"You *will* not!"

"Look, let's quit kidding ourselves. All right, Brent stole the dough, he spent it on a cutie, he treated you lousy. He's father of two children that happen also to be your father's grandchildren, and that means your father's got to pay. Well, ain't that great. Here's the only thing that matters about this: Brent's down and out. He's in the shadow of the penitentiary, he's in the hospital recovering from one of the worst operations there is, he's in one hell of a spot. But me—I'm in love with his wife. While he's down, I'm getting ready to take her away from him, the one thing he's got left. O.K., that's not so pretty, but that's how I feel about it. But the least I can do is kick in with that dough. So, I'm doing it. So, quit bothering your old man. So, that's all."

"I can't let you do it."

"Why not?"

"If you paid that money, then I'd be bought."

She got up and began to walk around the room. "You've practically said so yourself. You're getting ready to take a man's wife away from him, and you're going to salve your conscience by replacing the money he stole. That's all very well for him, since he doesn't seem to want his wife anyway. But can't you see where it puts me? What can I say to you now? Or what could I say, if I let you put up that money? I can't pay you back. Not in ten years could I make enough to pay you nine thousand dollars. I'm just your—creature."

I watched her as she moved around, touching the furniture with her hands, not looking at me, and then all of a sudden a hot, wild feeling went through me, and the blood began to pound in my head. I went over and jerked her around, so she was facing me. "Listen, there's not many guys that feel for a woman nine thousand dollars' worth. What's the matter with that? Don't you want to be bought?"

I took her in my arms, and shoved my lips against hers. "Is that so tough?"

She opened her mouth, so our teeth were clicking, and just breathed it: "It's grand, just grand."

She kissed me then, hard. "So it was just a lot of hooey you were handing me?"

"Just hooey, nothing but hooey. Oh, it's so good to be bought. I feel like something in a veil, and a harem skirt—and I just love it."

"Now—we'll put that money back."

"Yes, together."

"We'll start tomorrow."

"Isn't that funny. I'm completely in your power. I'm your slave, and I feel so safe, and know that nothing's going to happen to me, ever."

"That's right. It's a life sentence for you."

"Dave, I've fallen in love."

"Me, too."

V

If you think it's hard to steal money from a bank, you're right. But it's nothing like as hard as it is to put the money back. Maybe I haven't made it quite clear yet what that bird was doing. In the first place, when there's a shortage in a bank, it's always in the savings, because no statements are rendered on them. The commercial depositor, the guy with a checking account, I mean, gets a statement every month. But no statements are rendered to savings depositors. They show up with their passbooks, and plunk their money down, and the deposit is entered in their books, and their books are their statements. They never see the bank's cards, so naturally the thing can go on a long time before it's found out, and when it's found out, it's most likely to be by accident, like this was, because Brent didn't figure on his trip to the hospital.

Well, what Brent had done was fix up a cover for himself with all this stuff about putting it on a personal basis, so no savings depositor that came in the bank would ever deal with anybody but him. That ought to have made George Mason suspicious, but Brent was getting the business in, and you don't quarrel with a guy that's doing good. When he got that part the way he wanted it, with him the only one that ever touched the savings file, and the depositors dealing only with him, he went about it exactly the way they all go about it. He picked accounts where he knew he wouldn't be likely to run into trouble, and he'd make out a false withdrawal slip, generally for somewhere around fifty bucks. He'd sign the depositor's name to it, just forge it, but he didn't have to be very good at that part, because nobody passed on those signatures but himself. Then he'd put fifty bucks in his pocket, and of course the false withdrawal slip would balance his cash. Our card had to balance too, of course, so he'd enter the withdrawal on that, but beside each false entry he'd make that little light pencil check that I had caught, and that would tell him what the right balance ought to be, in case the depositor made some inquiry.

Well, how were you going to get that money put back, so the daily cash would balance, so the cards would balance, and so the passbooks would balance, and at the same time leave it so nothing would show later, when the auditors came around? It had me stumped, and I don't mind telling you for a while I began to get cold feet. What I wanted to do was report it, as was, let Sheila fork up the dough, without saying where she got it, and let Brent get fired and go look himself up a job. It didn't look like they would do much to him, if the money was put back. But she wouldn't hear of that. She was afraid they might send him up anyway, and then I would be putting up the money all for nothing, her children would have to grow up under the disgrace, and where we would be was nowhere. There wasn't much I could say to that. I figured they would probably let him off, but I couldn't be sure.

It was Sheila that figured out the way. We were riding along one night, just one or two nights after I told her I was going to put up the dough myself, when she began to talk. "The cards, the cash, and the passbooks, is that it?"

"That's all."

"The cards and the cash are easy."

"Oh yeah?"

"That money goes back the same way it came out. Only instead of false withdrawals, I make out false deposits. The cash balances, the posting balances, and the card balances."

"And the passbooks don't balance. Listen. If there's only one passbook—just one—that can tell on us after you're out of there, and I'm out, we're sunk. The only chance we've got is that the thing is never suspected at all—that no question is ever raised. And, what's more, we don't dare make a move till we see every one of the passbooks on those phoney accounts. We think we've got his code, how he ticked his false withdrawals, but we can't be sure, and maybe he didn't tick them all. Unless we can make a clean job of this, I don't touch it. Him going to jail is one thing. All three of us going, and me losing my job and nine thousand bucks—oh no."

"All right then, the passbooks."

"That's it—the passbooks."

"Now when a passbook gets filled up, or there's some mistake on it, what do we do?"

"Give him a new one, don't we?"

"Containing how many entries?"

"One, I suppose. His total as of that date."

"That's right. And that one entry tells no tales. It checks with the card, and there's not one figure to check against all those back entries—withdrawals and deposits and so on, running back for years. All right, then; so far, perfect. Now what do we do with his old book? Regularly, I mean."

"Well—what *do* we do with it?"

"We put it under a punch, the punch that goes through every page and marks it void, and give it back to him."

"And then he's got it—any time an auditor calls for it. Gee, that's a big help."

"But if he doesn't want it?"

"What are you getting at?"

"If he doesn't want it, we destroy it. It's no good to us, is it? And it's not ours, it's his. But he doesn't want it."

"Are you *sure* we destroy it?"

"I've torn up a thousand of them. . . . And that's just what we're going to do now. Between now and the next check on my cash, we're going to get all those books in. First we check totals, to know exactly where we're at. Then the depositor gets a new book that tells no tales."

"Why does he get a new book?"

"He didn't notice it when he brought the old one in, but the stitching is awfully strained, and it's almost falling apart. Or I've accidentally smeared lipstick on it. Or I just think it's time he got one of our nice new books, for luck. So he gets a new book with one entry in it—just his total, that's all. Then I say: 'You don't want this, do you?' And the way I'll say it, that old book seems positively *contaminated.* And then right in front of his eyes, as though it's the way we do it every day, I'll tear it up, and drop it in the wastebasket."

"Suppose he *does* want it?"

"Then I'll put it under the punch, and give it to him. But somehow that punch is going to make its neat little holes in the exact place where the footings are, and it's going to be impossible for him, or an auditor, or anybody else, to read those figures. I'll punch five or six times, you know, and his book will be like Swiss cheese, more holes than anything else."

"And all the time you're getting those holes in exactly the right place, he's going to be on the other side of the window looking at you, wondering what all the hocus-pocus is about."

"Oh no—it won't take more than a second or two. You see, I've been practicing. I can do it in a jiffy. . . . But he won't want that book back. Trust me. I know how to do it."

There was just a little note of pleading on that, as she said it. I had to think it over. I did think it over, for quite a while, and I began to have the feeling that on her end of it, if that was all, she could put it over all right. But then something else began to bother me. "How many of these doctored accounts are there?"

"Forty-seven."

"And how are you going to get those passbooks in?"

"Well, interest is due on them. I thought I could send out little printed slips—signed 'per Sheila Brent,' in ink, so they'd be sure to come to me about it—asking them to bring in their books for interest credits. I never saw anybody that wouldn't bring in his book if it meant a dollar and twenty-two cents. And a printed slip looks perfectly open and aboveboard, doesn't it?"

"Yeah, a printed slip is about the most harmless, open, and aboveboard thing there is. But this is what I'm thinking: You send out your printed slips, and within a couple of days all those books come in, and you can't hold them forever. You've got to hand them back—or the new ones they're going to get—or somebody's going to get suspicious. That means the money's got to be put back all at once. That's going to make one awful bulge in your cash. Everybody in the bank is going to wonder at the reason for it, because it's going to show in the posting."

"I've thought of that. I don't have to send out all those slips at

once. I can send out four or five a day. And then, even if they do
come in bunches—the passbooks I mean—I can issue the new
books, right away as the old ones are presented, but make the
adjustments on the cards and in my cash little by little—three or
four hundred dollars a day. That's not much."

"No, but while that's going on, we're completely defenseless.
We've got our chins hanging out and no way in the world of putting up a guard. I mean, while you're holding out those adjust-
ment entries, so you can edge them in gradually, your cash doesn't
balance the books. If then something happened—so I had to call
for a cash audit on the spot, or if I got called away to the home
office for a couple of days, or something happened to you, so you
couldn't come to work—then watch that ship go out of water. You
may get away with it. But it'll have to be done, everything squared
up, before the next check on your cash. That's twenty-one days
from now. And at that, a three- or four-hundred-dollar bulge in
your cash every day is going to look mighty funny. In the bank, I
mean."

"I could gag it off. I could say I'm keeping after them, to keep
their deposits up, the way Charles always did. I don't think there's
any danger. The cash will be there."

So that was how we did it. She had the slips printed, and began
mailing them out, three or four at a time. For the first few days'
replacement, the cash replacement I mean, I had enough in my
own checking account. For the rest, I had to go out and plaster
my house. For that I went to the Federal people. It took about
a week, and I had to start an outside account, so nobody in the
bank would know what I was up to. I took eight thousand bucks,
and if you don't think that hurt, you never plastered your house.
Of course, it would be our luck that when the first of those books
came in, she was out to lunch, and I was on the window myself.
I took in the book, and receipted for it, but Church was only

three or four feet away, running a column on one of the adding machines. She heard what I said to the depositor, and was at my elbow before I even knew how she got there.

"I can do that for you, Mr. Bennett. I'll only be a minute, and there'll be no need for him to leave his book."

"Well—I'd rather Mrs. Brent handled it."

"Oh, *very* well, then."

She switched away then, in a huff, and I could feel the sweat in the palms of my hands. That night I warned Sheila. "That Church can bust it up."

"How?"

"Her damned apple-polishing. She horned in today, wanted to balance that book for me. I had to chase her."

"Leave her to me."

"For God's sake, don't let her suspect anything."

"I won't, don't worry."

From then on, we made a kind of routine out of it. She'd get in three or four books, ask the depositors to leave them with her till next day. She'd make out new cards, and tell me the exact amount she needed, that night. I'd hand her that much in cash. Next day, she'd slip it into her cash box, make out new cards for the depositors, slip them in the file, then make out new passbooks and have them ready when the depositors called. Every day we'd be that much nearer home, both praying that nothing would tip it before we got the whole replacement made. Most days I'd say we plugged about $400 into the cash, one or two days a little more.

One night, maybe a week after we started putting the money back, they had the big dinner dance for the whole organization. I guess about a thousand people were there, in the main ballroom of one of the Los Angeles hotels, and it was a pretty nice get-together. They don't make a pep meeting out of it. The Old Man doesn't like that kind of thing. He just has a kind of a family gathering, makes them a little speech, and then the dancing starts, and he stands around watching them enjoy themselves. I guess you've heard of A. R. Ferguson. He's founder of the bank, and the minute you look at him you know he's a big shot. He's not tall, but he's straight and stocky, with a little white moustache that makes him look like some kind of a military man.

Well, we all had to go, of course. I sat at the table with the others from the branch, Miss Church, and Helm, and Snelling, and Snelling's wife, and Sheila. I made it a point not to sit with Sheila. I was afraid to. So after the banquet, when the dancing started, I went over to shake hands with the Old Man. He always treated me fine, just like he treats everybody. He's got that natural courtesy that no little guy ever quite seems capable of. He asked how I was, and then: "How much longer do you think you'll be out there in Glendale? Are you nearly done?"

An icy feeling began to go over me. If he yanked me now, and returned me to the home office, there went all chance of covering that shortage, and God only knew what they would find out, if it was half covered and half not.

"Why, I tell you, Mr. Ferguson, if you can possibly arrange it, I'd like to stay out there till after the first of the month."

" . . . So long?"

"Well, I've found some things out there that are well worth making a thorough study of, it seems to me. Fact of the matter, I had thought of writing an article about them in addition to my report. I thought I'd send it to the *American Banker,* and if I could have a little more time—"

"In that case, take all the time you want."

"I thought it wouldn't hurt us any."

"I only wish more of our officials would write."

"Gives us a little prestige."

"—and makes them *think!*"

My mouth did it all. I was standing behind it, not knowing what was coming out from one minute to the next. I hadn't
thought of any article, up to that very second, and I give you one
guess how I felt. I felt like a heel, and all the worse on account of
the fine way he treated me. We stood there a few minutes, he telling me how he was leaving for Honolulu the next day, but he'd be
back within the month, and looked forward to reading what I had
to say as soon as he came back. Then he motioned in the direction
of the dance floor. "Who's the girl in blue?"

"Mrs. Brent."

"Oh yes, I want to speak to her."

We did some broken-floor dodging, and got over to where
Sheila was dancing with Helm. They stopped, and I introduced
the Old Man, and he asked how Brent was coming along after
the operation, and then cut in on Helm, and danced Sheila off. I
wasn't in much of a humor when I met her outside later and took
her home. "What's the matter, Dave?"

"Couldn't quite look the Old Man in the eye, that's all."

"Have you got cold feet?"

"Just feeling the strain."

"If you have got cold feet, and want to quit, there's nothing I
can say. Nothing at all."

"All I got to say is I'll be glad when we're clear of that heel, and
can kick him out of the bank and out of our lives."

"In two weeks it'll be done."

"How is he?"

"He's leaving the hospital Saturday."

"That's nice."

"He's not coming home yet. The doctor insists that he go up
to Arrowhead to get his strength back. He'll be there three or four
weeks. He has friends there."

"What have you told him, by the way?"

"Nothing."

"Just nothing?"

"Not one word."

"He had an ulcer, is that what you said?"

"Yes."

"I was reading in a medical magazine the other day what causes it. Do you know what it is?"

"No."

"Worry."

"So?"

"It might help the recuperating process if he knew it was O.K. about the shortage. Lying in a hospital, with a thing like that staring you in the face, that may not be so good. For his health anyway."

"What am I to tell him?"

"Why, I don't know. That you've fixed it up."

"If I tell him I've fixed it up, so nobody is going to know it, he knows I've got some kind of assistance in the bank. That'll terrify him, and I don't know what he's likely to do about it. He may speak to somebody, and the whole thing will come out. And who am I going to say has let me have the money, so I can put it back? You?"

"Do you have to say?"

"No. I don't have to say anything at all, and I'm not going to. The less you're involved in this the better. If he worries, he ought to be used to it by now. It won't hurt that young man to do quite a little suffering over what he's done to me—and to you."

"It's up to you."

"He knows something's cooking, all right, but he doesn't know what. I look forward to seeing his face when I tell him I'm off to—where did you say?"

" . . . I said Reno."

"Do you still say Reno?"

"I don't generally change my mind, once it's made up."

"You can, if you want to."

"Shut up."

"I don't want you to."

"Neither do I."

VI

We kept putting the money back, and I kept getting jitterier every day. I kept worrying that something would happen, that maybe the Old Man hadn't left a memo about me before he went away, and that I'd get a call to report to the home office; that maybe Sheila would get sick and somebody else would have to do her work; that some depositor might think it was funny, the slip he had got to bring his book in, and begin asking about it somewhere.

One day she asked me to drive her home from the bank. By that time I was so nervous I never went anywhere with her in the daytime, and even at night I never met her anywhere that somebody might see us. But she said one of the children was sick, and she wanted a ride in case she had to get stuff from the drugstore that the doctor had ordered, and that anyway nobody was there but the maid and she didn't matter. By that time Brent had gone to the lake, to get his strength back, and she had the house to herself.

So I went. It was the first time I'd ever been in her home, and it was fixed up nice, and smelled like her, and the kids were the sweetest little pair you ever saw. The oldest was named Anna, and the younger was named Charlotte. She was the one that was sick. She was in bed with a cold, and took it like a little soldier. Another

time, it would have tickled me to death to sit and watch her boss
Sheila around, and watch Sheila wait on her, and take the bossing
just like that was how it ought to be. But now I couldn't even keep
still that long. When I found out I wasn't needed I ducked, and
went home and filled up some more paper with the phoney article
I had to have ready for the Old Man when he got back. It was
called, "Building a Strong Savings Department."

We got to the last day before the monthly check on cash. Six
hundred dollars had to go into her box that day, over and above
the regular day's receipts. It was a lot, but it was a Wednesday, the
day the factories all around us paid off, and deposits were sure
to be heavy, so it looked like we could get away with it. We had
all the passbooks in. It had taken some strong-arm work to get
the last three we needed, and what she had done was go to those
people the night before, like Brent had always done, and ask where
they'd been, and why they hadn't put anything on savings. By sitting around a few minutes she managed to get their books, and
then I drove her over to my place and we checked it all up. Then I
gave her the cash she needed, and it looked like she was set.

But I kept wanting to know how she stood, whether it had
all gone through like we hoped. I couldn't catch her eye and I
couldn't get a word with her. They were lined up at her window
four and five deep all day long, and she didn't go out to lunch. She
had sandwiches and milk sent in. On Wednesday they send out
two extra tellers from the home office, to help handle the extra
business, and every time one of them would go to her for help on
something, and she'd have to leave her window for a minute, I'd
feel the sweat on the palms of my hands, and lose track of what I
was doing. I'm telling you it was a long day.

Along about two-thirty, though, it slacked off, and by five
minutes to three there was nobody in there, and at three sharp
Adler, the guard, locked the door. We went on finishing up. The

home office tellers got through first, because all they had to do was balance one day's deposits, and around three-thirty they turned in their sheets, asked me to give them a count, and left. I sat at my desk, staring at papers, doing anything to keep from marching around and tip it that I had something on my mind.

Around quarter to four there came a tap on the glass, and I didn't look up. There's always that late depositor trying to get in, and if he catches your eye you're sunk. I went right on staring at my papers, but I heard Adler open and then who should be there but Brent, with a grin on his face, a satchel in one hand, and a heavy coat of sunburn all over him. There was a chorus of "Hey's," and they all went out to shake hands, all except Sheila, and ask him how he was, and when he was coming back to work. He said he'd got home last night, and would be back any time now. There didn't seem to be much I could do but shake hands too, so I gritted my teeth and did it, but I didn't ask him when he was coming back to work.

Then he said he'd come in for some of his stuff, and on his way back to the lockers he spoke to Sheila, and she spoke, without looking up. Then the rest of them went back to work. "Gee, he sure looks good, don't he?"

"Different from when he left."

"He must have put on twenty pounds."

"They fixed him up all right."

Pretty soon he came out again, closing his grip, and there was some more talk, and he went. They all counted their cash, turned in their sheets, and put their cash boxes into the vault. Helm wheeled the trucks in, with the records on them, and then he went. Snelling went back to set the time lock.

That was when Church started some more of her apple-polishing. She was about as unappetizing a girl as I ever saw. She was thick, and dumpy, with a delivery like she was making a speech all the time. She sounded like a dietician demonstrating a range in a department store basement, and she started in on a wonderful new adding machine that had just come on the market, and didn't I think we ought to have one. I said it sounded good, but I wanted to think it over. So then she said it all over again, and just about when she got going good she gave a little squeal and began pointing at the floor.

Down there was about the evilest-looking thing you ever saw in your life. It was one of these ground spiders you see out here in California, about the size of a tarantula and just about as dangerous. It was about three inches long, I would say, and was walking toward me with a clumsy gait but getting there all the time. I raised my foot to step on it, and she gave another squeal and said if I squashed it she'd die. By that time they were all standing around—Snelling, Sheila, and Adler. Snelling said get a piece of paper and throw it out the door, and Sheila said yes, for heaven's sake do something about it quick. Adler took a piece of paper off my desk, and rolled it into a funnel, and then took a pen and pushed the thing into the paper, Then he folded the funnel shut and we all went out and watched him dump the spider into the gutter. Then a cop came along and borrowed the funnel and caught it again and said he was going to take it home to his wife, so they could take pictures of it with their home movie camera.

We went back in the bank, and Snelling and I closed the vault, and he went. Church went. Adler went back for his last tour around before closing. That left me alone with Sheila. I stepped back to where she was by the lockers, looking in the mirror while she put on her hat. "Well?"

"It's all done."

"You put back the cash."

"To the last cent."

"The cards are all in?"

"It all checks to the last decimal point."

That was what I'd been praying for, for the last month, and yet as soon as I had it, it took me about one-fifth of a second to get sore, about Brent.

"Is he driving you home?"

"If so, he didn't mention it."

"Suppose you wait in my car. There's a couple of things I want to talk to you about. It's just across the street."

She went, and Adler changed into his street clothes, and he and I locked up, and I bounced over to the car. I didn't head for her house, I headed for mine, but I didn't wait till we got there before I opened up.

"Why didn't you tell me he was back?"

"Were you interested?"

"Yeah, plenty."

"Well, since you ask me, I didn't know he was back—when I left you last night. He was there waiting for me when I got in. Today, I haven't had one minute to talk to you, or anybody."

"I thought he was due to spend a month up there."

"So did I."

"Then what's he doing back?"

"I haven't the faintest idea. Trying to find out what's going to happen to him, perhaps. Tomorrow, you may recall, you'll check the cash, and he knows it. That may account for why he cut his recuperation short."

"Are you sure he didn't have a date with you, now he's feeling better? To be waiting for you after you said goodnight to me?"

"I stayed with the children, if that's what you mean."

I don't know if I believed any of that or not. I think I told you I was nuts about her, and all the money she'd cost me, and all the trouble she'd brought, only seemed to make it worse. The idea that she'd spent a night in the same house with him, and hadn't said anything to me about it, left me with a prickly feeling all over. Since I'd been going around with her, it was the first time that part of it had come up. He'd been in the hospital, and from there he'd gone right up to the lake, so in a way up to then he hadn't seemed real. But he seemed real now, all right, and I was still as sore as a bear when we got to my house, and went in. Sam lit the fire, and she sat down, but I didn't. I kept marching around the room, and she smoked, and watched me.

"All right, this guy's got to be told."

"He will be."

"He's got to be told *everything.*"

"Dave, he'll be told, he'll be told everything, and a little more even than you know he's going to be told—when I'm ready to tell him."

"What's the matter with now?"

"I'm not equal to it."

"What's that—a stall?"

"Will you sit down for a moment?"

"All right, I'm sitting."

"Here—beside me."

I moved over beside her, and she took my hand and looked me in the eyes. "Dave, have you forgotten something?"

"Not that I know of."

"I think you have. . . . I think you've forgotten that today we finished what we started to do. That, thanks to you, I don't have to lie awake every night staring at the ceiling, wondering whether my father is going to be ruined, my children are going to be ruined— to say nothing of myself. That you've done something for me that was so dangerous to you I hate to think what would have happened if something had gone wrong. It would have wrecked your career, and it's such a nice, promising career. But it wasn't wrong, Dave. It was wonderfully right. It was decenter than any man I know of would have done, would even have thought of doing. And now it's done. There's not one card, one comma, one missing penny to show—and I can sleep, Dave. That's all that matters to me today."

"O.K.—then you're leaving him."

"Of course I am, but—"

"You're leaving him tonight. You're coming in here, with your two kids, and if that bothers you, then I'll move out. We're going over there now, and—"

"We're doing nothing of the kind."

"I'm telling you—"

"And I'm telling *you!* Do you think I'm going over there now, and starting a quarrel that's going to last until three o'clock in the morning and maybe until dawn? That's going to wander all over the earth, from how horribly he says I've treated him to who's going to have the children—the way I feel now? I certainly shall not. When I'm ready, when I know exactly what I'm going to say, when I've got the children safely over to my father's, when it's all planned and I can do it in one terrible half hour—then I'll do it. In the meantime, if he's biting his fingernails, if he's frightened to death over what's going to happen to him—that's perfectly all right with me. A little of that won't hurt him. When it's all done, then I go at once to Reno, if you still want me to, and then my life can go on. . . . Don't you know what I'm trying to tell you, Dave? What you're worried about just couldn't happen. Why—he hasn't even looked at me that way in over a year. Dave, tonight I want to be happy. With you. That's all."

I felt ashamed of myself at that, and took her in my arms, and that catch came in my throat again when she sighed, like some child, and relaxed, and closed her eyes.

"Sheila?"

"Yes?"

"We'll celebrate."

"All right."

So we celebrated. She phoned her maid, and said she'd be late, and we went to dinner at a downtown restaurant, and then we drove to a night club on Sunset Boulevard. We didn't talk about Brent, or the shortage, or anything but ourselves, and what we were going to do with our lives together. We stayed till about one o'clock. I didn't think of Brent again till we pulled up near her house, and then this same prickly feeling began to come over me. If she noticed anything she didn't say so. She kissed me good-night, and I started home.

VII

I turned in the drive, put the car away, closed the garage, and walked around to go in the front way. When I started for the door I heard my name called. Somebody got up from a bench under the trees and walked over. It was Helm. "Sorry to be bothering you this hour of night, Mr. Bennett, but I've got to talk to you."

"Well, come in."

He seemed nervous as I took him inside. I offered him a drink, but he said he didn't want anything. He sat down and lit a cigarette, and acted like he didn't know how to begin. Then: "Have you seen Sheila?"

" . . . Why?"

"I saw you drive off with her."

"Yes—I had some business with her. We had dinner together. I—just left her a little while ago."

"Did you see Brent?"

"No. It was late. I didn't go in."

"She say anything about him?"

"I guess so. Now and then. . . . What's this about?"

"Did you see him leave the bank? Today?"

"He left before you did."

"Did you see him leave the second time?"

" . . . He only came in once."

He kept looking at me, smoking and looking at me. He was a young fellow, twenty-four or -five, I would say, and had only been with us a couple of years. Little by little he was losing his nervousness at talking with me.

" . . . He went in there twice."

"He came in once. He rapped on the door, Adler let him in, he stood there talking a few minutes, then he went back to get some stuff out of his locker. Then he left. You were there. Except for the extra tellers, nobody had finished up yet. He must have left fifteen minutes before you did."

"That's right. Then I left. I finished up, put my cash box away, and left. I went over to the drugstore to get myself a malted milk, and was sitting there drinking it when he went in."

"He couldn't have. We were locked, and—"

"He used a key."

" . . . When was this?"

"A little after four. Couple of minutes before you all come out with that spider and dumped it in the gutter."

"So?"

"I didn't see him come out."

"Why didn't you tell me?"

"I haven't seen you. I've been looking for you."

"You saw me drive off with Sheila."

"Yeah, but it hadn't occurred to me, at the time. That cop, after he caught the spider, came in the drugstore to buy some film for his camera. I helped him put the spider in an ice-cream container, and punch holes in the top, and I wasn't watching the bank all that time. Later, it just happened to run through my head that I'd seen all the rest of you leave the bank, but I hadn't seen Brent. I kept telling myself to forget it, that I'd got a case of nerves from being around money too much, but then—"

"Yeah? What else?"

"I went to a picture tonight with the Snellings."

"Didn't Snelling see him leave?"

"I didn't say anything to Snelling. I don't know what he saw. But the picture had some Mexican stuff in it, and later, when we went to the Snellings' apartment, I started a bum argument, and got Snelling to call Charlie to settle it. Brent spent some time in Mexico once. That was about twelve o'clock."

"And?"

"The maid answered. Charlie wasn't there."

We looked at each other, and both knew that twelve o'clock was too late for a guy to be out that had just had a bad operation.

"Come on."

"You calling Sheila?"

"We're going to the bank."

The protection service watchman was due on the hour, and we caught him on his two o'clock round. He took it as a personal insult that we would think anybody could be in the bank without him knowing it, but I made him take us in there just the same, and we went through every part of it. We went upstairs, where the old records were stored, and I looked behind every pile. We went down in the basement and I looked behind every gas furnace. We went all around back of the windows and I looked under every counter. I even looked behind my desk, and under it. That seemed to be all. The watchman went up and punched his clock and we went out on the street again. Helm kind of fingered his chin.

"Well, I guess it was a false alarm."

"Looks like it."

"Sorry."

"It's all right. Report everything."

"Guess there's no use calling Sheila."

"Pretty late, I'm afraid."

What he meant was, we ought to call Sheila, but he wanted me to do it. He was just as suspicious as he ever was, I could tell that from the way he was acting. Only the watchman was sure we were a couple of nuts. We got in the car, and I took him home, and once more he mumbled something about Sheila, but I decided not to hear him. When I let him out I started for home, but as soon as I was out of sight I cut around the block and headed for Mountain Drive.

A light was on, and the screen door opened as soon as I set my foot on the porch. She was still dressed, and it was almost as though she had been expecting me. I followed her in the living room, and spoke low so nobody in the house could hear us, but I didn't waste any time on love and kisses.

"Where's Brent?"

" . . . He's in the vault."

She spoke in a whisper, and sank into a chair without looking at me, but every doubt I'd had about her in the beginning, I mean, every hunch that she'd been playing me for a sucker, swept back over me so even looking at her made me tremble. I had to lick my lips a couple of times before I could even talk. "Funny you didn't tell me."

"I didn't know it."

"What do you mean you didn't know it? If you know it now, why didn't you know it then? You trying to tell me he stepped out of there for a couple of minutes, borrowed my telephone, and called you up? He might as well be in a tomb as be in that place, till it opens at eight-thirty this morning."

"Are you done?"

"I'm still asking you why you didn't tell me."

"When I got in, and found he wasn't home, I went out looking for him. Or at any rate, for the car. I went to where he generally parks it—when he's out. It wasn't there. Coming home I had to go by the bank. As I went by, the red light winked, just once."

I don't know if you know how a vault works. There's two switches inside. One lights the overhead stuff that you turn on when somebody wants to get into his safe deposit box; the other works the red light that's always on over the door in the daytime. That's the danger signal, and any employee of the bank always looks to see that it's on whenever he goes inside. When the vault is closed the light's turned off, and I had turned it off myself that afternoon, when I locked the vault with Snelling. At night, all curtains are raised in the bank, so cops, watchman, and passersby can see inside. If the red light went on, it would show, but I didn't believe she'd seen it. I didn't believe she'd even been by the bank. "So the red light winked, hey? Funny it wasn't winking when I left there not ten minutes ago."

"I said it winked once. I don't think it was a signal. I think he bumped his shoulder against it, by accident. If he were signaling, he'd keep on winking it, wouldn't he?"

"How'd he get in there?"

"I don't know."

"I think you do know."

"I don't know, but the only way I can think of is that he slipped in there while we were all gathered around, looking at that spider."

"That you conveniently on purpose brought in there."

"Or that he did."

"What's he doing in there?"

"I don't know."

"Come on, come on, quit stalling me!"

She got up and began walking around. "Dave, it's easy to see

you think I know all about this. That I know more than I'm telling. That Charles and I are in some kind of plot. I don't know
anything I can say. I know a lot I could say if I wasn't—"

She stopped, came to life like some kind of a tiger, and began
hammering her fists against the wall.

"—bought! That was what was wrong! I ought to have cut
my heart out, suffered anything rather than let you give me that
money! Why did I ever take it? Why didn't I tell you to—"

"Why didn't you do what I begged you to do? Come over here
today and let him have it between the eyes—tell him the truth,
that you were through, and this was the end of it?"

"Because, God help me, I wanted to be happy!"

"No! . . . Because, God help you, you knew he wasn't over
here! Because you knew he was in that vault, and you were afraid
I'd find it out!"

"It isn't true! How can you say that?"

"Do you know what I think? I think you took that money
off me, day by day, and that not one penny of it ever found its
way into your cash box. And then I think you and he decided
on a little phoney hold-up, to cover that shortage, and that that's
what he's doing in the vault. And if Helm hadn't got into it, and
noticed that Brent didn't come out of the bank the second time
he went in, I don't see anything that was to stop you from getting away with it. You knew I didn't dare open my trap about
the dough *I* had put up. And if he came out of there masked,
and made a quick getaway, I don't know who was going to swear
it was him, if it hadn't been for Helm. Now it's in the soup. All
right, Mrs. Brent, that vault that don't take any messages till
eight-thirty, that works both ways. If he can't get any word to
you, you can't get any word to him. Just let him start that little
game that looked so good yesterday afternoon, and he's going to
get the surprise of his life, and so are you. There'll be a reception

committee waiting for him when he comes out of there, and maybe they'll include you in it too."

She looked straight at me the whole time I was talking, and the lamplight caught her eyes, so they shot fire. There was something catlike about her shape anyway, and with her eyes blazing like that, she looked like something out of the jungle. But all of a sudden that woman was gone, and she was crumpled up in front of me, on the sofa, crying in a queer, jerky way. Then I hated myself for what I had said, and had to dig in with my fingernails to keep from crying too.

After a while the phone rang. From what she said, I could tell it was her father, and that he'd been trying to reach her all afternoon and all night. She listened a long time, and when she hung up she lay back and closed her eyes. "He's in there to put the money back."

" . . . Where'd he get it?"

"He got it this morning. Yesterday morning. From my father."

"Your father had that much—*ready?*"

"He got it after I talked to him that night. Then when I told him I wouldn't need it, he kept it, in his safe deposit box—just in case. Charles went over there yesterday and said he had to have it—against the check-up on my cash. Papa went down to the Westwood bank with him, and got it out, and gave it to him. He was afraid to call me at the bank. He kept trying to reach me here. The maid left me a note, but it was so late when I got in I didn't call. . . . So, now I pay a price for not telling him. Charles, I mean. For letting him worry."

"I was for telling him, you may remember."

"Yes, I remember."

It was quite a while after that before either of us said anything. All that time my mind was going around like a squirrel cage, trying to reconstruct for myself what was going on in that vault. She must have been doing the same thing, because pretty soon she said, "Dave?"

"Yes?"

"Suppose he *does* put the money back?"

"Then—we're sunk."

"What, actually, will happen?"

"If I find him in there, the least I can do is hold him till I've checked every cent in that vault. I find nine thousand more cash than the books show. All right. What then?"

"You mean the whole thing comes out?"

"On what we've been doing, you can get away with it as long as nobody's got the least suspicion of it. Let a thing like this happen, let them really begin to check, and it'll come out so fast it'll make your head swim."

"And there goes your job?"

"Suppose you were the home office, how would you like it?"

" . . . I've brought you nothing but misery, Dave."

"I—asked for it."

"I can understand why you feel bitter."

"I said some things I didn't mean."

"Dave."

"Yes?"

"There's one chance, if you'll take it."

"What's that?"

"Charles."

"I don't get it."

"It may be a blessing, after all, that I told him nothing. He can't be sure what I've done while he's been away—whether I carried his false entries right along, whether I corrected them, and left the cash short—and it does look as though he'd check, before he did anything. He's a wizard at books, you know. And every record he needs is in there. Do you know what I'm getting at, Dave?"

"Not quite."

"You'll have to play dummy's hand, and let him lead."

"I don't want anything to do with him."

"I'd like to wring his neck. But if you just don't force things, if you just act natural, and let me have a few seconds with him, so we'll know just what he *has* done, then—maybe it'll all come out all right. He certainly would be a boob to put the money back when he finds out it's already been put back."

"*Has* it been?"

"Don't you know?"

I took her in my arms then, and for that long was able to forget what was staring us in the face, and I still felt close to her when I left.

VIII

For the second time that night I went home, and this time I turned out all the lights, and went upstairs, and took off my clothes, and went to bed. I tried to sleep, and couldn't. It was all running through my mind, and especially what I was going to do when I opened that vault at eight-thirty. How could I act natural about it? If I could guess he was in the vault, Helm must have guessed it. He'd be watching me, waiting for every move, and he'd be doing that even if he didn't have any suspicion of me, which by now he must have, on account of being out that late with Sheila. All that ran through my mind, and after a while I'd figured a way to cover it, by openly saying something to him, and telling him I was going to go along with it, just wait and see what Brent had to say for himself, in case he was really in there. Then I tried once more to go to sleep. But this time it wasn't the play at the vault that was bothering me, it was Sheila. I kept going over and over it, what was said between us, the dirty cracks I had made, how she had taken them, and all the rest of it. Just as day began to break I found myself sitting up in bed. How I knew it I don't know, what I had to go on I haven't any idea, but I knew perfectly well that she was holding out on me, that there was something back of it all that she wasn't telling.

I unhooked the phone and dialed. You don't stay around a bank very long before you know the number of your chief guard. I was calling Dyer, and in a minute or two he answered, pretty sour. "Hello?"

"Dyer?"

"Yeah, who is it?"

"Sorry to wake you up. This is Dave Bennett."

"What do you want?"

"I want some help."

"Well, what the hell is it?"

"I got reason to think there's a man in our vault. Out in the Anita Avenue branch in Glendale. What he's up to I don't know, but I want you out there when I open up. And I'd like you to bring a couple of men with you."

Up to then he'd been just a sleepy guy that used to be a city detective. Now he snapped out of it like something had hit him. "What do you mean you got reason to think? Who is this guy?"

"I'll give you that part when I see you. Can you meet me by seven o'clock? Is that too early?"

"Whenever you say, Mr. Bennett."

"Then be at my house at seven, and bring your men with you. I'll give you the dope, and I'll tell you how I want you to do it."

He took the address, and I went back to bed.

I went to bed, and lay there trying to figure out what it was I wanted him to do anyway. After a while I had it straightened out. I wanted him close enough to protect the bank, and myself as well, in case Sheila was lying to me, and I wanted him far enough away for her to have those few seconds with Brent, in case she wasn't. I mean, if Brent was really up to something, I wanted him covered every way there was, and by guys that would shoot. But if he came out with a foolish look on his face, and pretended he'd been locked in by mistake, and she found out we could still cover up that book-doctoring, I wanted to leave that open too. I figured on it, and after a while I thought I had it doped out so it would work.

Around six o'clock I got up, bathed, shaved, and dressed. I routed out Sam and had him make me some coffee, and fix up some bacon and eggs. I told him to stand by in case the men that were coming hadn't had any breakfast. Then I went in the living room and began to march around it. It was cold. I lit the fire. My head kept spinning around.

Bight on the tick of seven the doorbell rang and there they were, Dyer and his two mugs. Dyer's a tall, thin man with a bony face and eyes like gimlets. I'd say he was around fifty. The other two were around my own age, somewhere over thirty, with big shoulders, thick necks, and red faces. They looked exactly like what they were: ex-cops that had got jobs as guards in a bank. One was named Halligan, the other Lewis. They all said yes on breakfast, so we went in the dining room and Sam made it pretty quick with the service.

I gave it to Dyer, as quick as I could, about Brent being off for a couple of months, with his operation, and how he'd come in yesterday to get his stuff, and Helm had seen him go in the bank a second time, and not come out, and how Sheila had gone out looking for him late at night, and thought she saw the red light flash. I had to tell him that much, to protect myself afterward, because God only knew what was going to come out, and I didn't even feel I was safe on Sheila's end of it. I didn't say anything about the shortage, or Sheila's father, or any of that part. I told what I had to tell, and made it short.

"Now what I figure is, Brent got in there somehow just before we closed it up, maybe just looking around, and that he got locked in there by accident. However, I can't be sure. Maybe—it doesn't seem very likely—he's up to something. So what I'd like you guys to do is to be outside, just be where you can see what's going on. If it's all quiet, I'll give you the word, and you can go on home, If anything happens, you're there. Of course, a man spends a night in a vault, he may not feel so good by morning. We may need an ambulance. If so, I'll let you know."

I breathed a little easier. It had sounded all right, and Dyer kept on wolfing down his toast and eggs. When they were gone he put sugar and cream in his coffee, stirred it around, and lit a cigarette. "Well—that's how you got it figured out."

"I imagine I'm not far off."

"All I got to say, you got a trusting disposition."

"What do you make of it?"

"This guy's a regular employee, you say?"

"He's been head teller."

"Then he *couldn't* get locked in by mistake. He couldn't no more do that than a doctor could sew himself up in a man's belly by mistake. Furthermore, you couldn't lock him in by mistake. You take all the usual care, don't you, when you lock a vault?"

"I think so."

"And you done it regular, yesterday?"

"As well as I can recall."

"You looked around in there?"

"Yes, of course."

"And you didn't see nothing?"

"No, certainly not."

"Then he's in there on purpose."

The other two nodded, and looked at me like I must not be very bright.

Dyer went on: "It's possible for a man to hide hisself in a vault. I've thought of it, many a time, how it could be done. You think of a lot of things in my business. Once them trucks are wheeled in, with the records on them, if he once got in without being seen, he could stoop down behind them, and keep quiet, and when you come to close up you wouldn't see him. But not by accident. Never."

I was feeling funny in the stomach. I had to take a tack I didn't like.

"Of course, there's a human element in it. There's nothing in this man's record that gives any ground whatever for thinking he'd pull anything. Fact of the matter, that's what I'm doing in the branch. I was sent out there to study his methods in the savings department. I've been so much impressed by his work that I'm going to write an article about it."

"When did he get in there, do you think?"

"Well, we found a spider. A big one."

"One of them bad dreams with fur all over them?"

"That's it. And we were all gathered around looking at it. And arguing about how to get it out of there. I imagine he was standing there looking at it too. We all went out to throw it in the street, and he must have gone in the vault. Perhaps just looking around. Perhaps to open his box, I don't know. And—was in there when I closed it up."

"That don't hit you funny?"

"Not particularly."

"If you wanted to get everybody in one place in that bank, and everybody looking in one direction, so you could slip in the vault, you couldn't think of nothing better than one of them spiders, could you? Unless it was a rattlesnake."

"That strikes me as a little farfetched."

"Not if he's just back from the mountains. From Lake Arrow-head, I think you said. That's where they have them spiders. I never seen one around Glendale. If he happened to turn that spider loose the first time he come in, all he had to do was wait till you found it, and he could easy slip in."

"He'd be running an awful risk."

"No risk. Suppose you seen him? He was looking at the spider too, wasn't he? He come in with his key to see what all the fuss was about. Thought maybe there was trouble . . . Mr. Bennett, I'm telling you, he's not locked in by accident. It couldn't happen."

" . . . What would you suggest?"

"I'd suggest that me, and Halligan, and Lewis, are covering that vault with guns when you open the door, and that we take him right in custody and get it out of him what he was doing in there. If he's got dough on him, then we'll know. I'd treat him just like anybody else that hid hisself in a vault. I wouldn't take no chances whatever."

"I can't stand for that."

"Why not?"

For just a split second, I didn't know why not. All I knew was that if he was searched, even if he hadn't put his father-in-law's money back in the cash box, they'd find it on him, and a man with nine thousand dollars on him, unaccounted for, stepping out of a bank vault, was going to mean an investigation that was going to ruin me. But if you've got to think fast, you can do it. I acted like he ought to know why not. "Why—morale."

"What do you mean, morale?"

"I can't have those people out there, those other employees, I mean, see that at the first crack out of the box, for no reason whatever, I treat the senior member of the staff like some kind of a bandit. It just wouldn't do."

"I don't agree on that at all."

"Well, put yourself in their place."

"They work for a bank, don't they?"

"They're not criminals."

"Every person that works for a bank is automatically under suspicion from the minute he goes in until he comes out. Ain't nothing personal about it. They're just people that are entrusted with other people's money, and not nothing at all is taken for granted. That's why they're under bond. That's why they're checked all the time—they know it, they want it that way. And if he's got any sense, even when he sees our guns, supposing he is on the up-and-up, and he's in there by mistake, *he* knows it. But he's not on the up-and-up, and you owe it to them other people in there to give them the protection they're entitled to."

"I don't see it that way."

"It's up to you. But I want to be on record, in the presence of Halligan and Lewis, that I warned you. You hear what I say, Mr. Bennett?"

" . . . I hear what you say."

My stomach was feeling still worse, but I gave them their orders. They were to take positions outside. They weren't to come in unless they were needed. They were to wait him out.

I led, driving over to the bank, and they followed, in Dyer's car. When I went past the bank I touched the horn and Dyer waved at me, so I could catch him in the mirror. They had wanted me to show them the bank, because they were all from the home office and had never been there. A couple of blocks up Anita Avenue I turned the corner and stopped. They pulled in ahead of me and parked. Dyer looked out. "All right. I got it."

I drove on, turned another corner, kept on around the block and parked where I could see the bank. In a minute or two along came Helm, unlocked the door and went in. He's first in, every morning. In about five minutes Snelling drove up, and parked in front of the drugstore. Then Sheila came walking down the street, stopped at Snelling's car, and stood there talking to him.

The curtains on the bank door came down. This was all part of opening the bank, you understand, and didn't have anything to do with the vault. The first man in goes all through the bank. That's in case somebody got in there during the night. They've been known to chop holes in the roof even, to be there waiting with a gun when the vault is opened.

He goes all through the bank, then if everything's O.K. he goes to the front door and lowers the curtains. That's a signal to the man across the street, who's always there by that time. But even that's not all. The man across the street doesn't go in till the first man comes out of the bank, crosses over, and gives the word. That's also in case there's somebody in there with a gun. Maybe he knows all about those curtains. Maybe he tells the first man to go lower the curtains, and be quick about it. But if the first man doesn't come out as soon as he lowers the curtains, the man across the street knows there's something wrong, and puts in a call, quick.

The curtains were lowered, and Helm came out, and Snelling got out of his car, I climbed out and crossed over. Snelling and Helm went in, and Sheila dropped back with me.

"What are you going to do, Dave?"

"Give him his chance."

"If only he hasn't done something dumb."

"Get to him. Get to him and find out what's what. I'm going to take it as easy as I can. I'm going to stall, listen to what he has to say, tell him I'll have to ask him to stick around till we check—and then you get at it. Find out. And let me know."

"Do the others know?"

"No, but Helm's guessed it."

"Do you ever pray?"

"I prayed all I know."

Adler came up then and we went in. I looked at the clock. It was twenty after eight. Helm and Snelling had their dust cloths, polishing up their counters. Sheila went back and started to polish hers. Adler went back to the lockers to put on his uniform. I sat down at my desk, opened it, and took out some papers. They were the same papers I'd been stalling with the afternoon before. It seemed a long time ago, but I began stalling with them again. Don't ask me what they were. I don't know yet.

My phone rang. It was Church. She said she wasn't feeling well, and would it be all right if she didn't come in today? I said yeah, perfectly all right. She said she hated to miss a day, but she was afraid if she didn't take care of herself she'd really get sick. I said certainly, she ought to take care of herself. She said she certainly hoped I hadn't forgotten about the adding machine, that it was a wonderful value for the money, and would probably pay for itself in a year by what it would save. I said I hadn't forgotten it. She said it all over again about how bad she felt, and I said get well, that was the main thing. She hung up. I looked at the clock. It was twenty-five after eight.

Helm stepped over, and gave my desk a wipe with his cloth. As he leaned down he said: "There's a guy in front of the drugstore I don't like the looks of, and two more down the street."

I looked over. Dyer was there, reading a paper.

"Yeah, I know. I sent for them."

"O.K."

"Have you said anything, Helm? To the others?"

"No, sir, I haven't."

"I'd rather you didn't."

"No use starting anything, just on a hunch."

"That's it. I'll help you open the vault."

"Yes, sir."

"See the front door is open."

"I'll open it now."

At last the clock said eight-thirty, and the time lock clicked off. Adler came in from the lockers, strapping his belt on over his uniform. Snelling spoke to Helm, and went over to the vault. It takes two men to open a vault, even after the time lock goes off, one to each combination. I opened the second drawer of my desk, took out the automatic that was in there, threw off the catch, slipped it in my coat pocket, and went back there.

"I'll do that, Snelling."

"Oh, that's all right, Mr. Bennett. Helm and I have it down to a fine art. We've got so we can even do it to music."

"I'll try it, just once."

"O.K.—you spin and I'll whistle."

He grinned at Sheila, and began to whistle. He was hoping I'd forgotten the combination, and would have to ask help, and then he'd have a laugh on the boss. Helm looked at me, and I nodded. He spun his dial, I spun mine. I swung the door open.

At first, for one wild second, I thought there was nobody in there at all. I snapped on the switch, and couldn't see anything. But then my eye caught bright marks on the steel panels of the compartments that hold the safe deposit boxes. Then I saw the trucks had all been switched. They're steel frames, about four feet high, that hold the records. They run on rubber wheels, and when they're loaded they're plenty heavy. When they were put in there, they were all crosswise of the door. Now they were end to it, one jammed up against the other, and not three feet away from me. I dropped my hand in my gun pocket, and opened my mouth to call, and right that second the near truck hit me.

It hit me in the pit of the stomach. He must have been crouched behind it, like a runner, braced against the rear shelves and watching the time lock for the exact second we'd be in there. I went over backwards, still trying to get out the gun. The truck was right over me, like it had been shot out of a cannon. A roller went over my leg, and then I could see it crashing down on top of me.

I must have gone out for a split second when it hit my head, because the next thing I knew screams were ringing in my ears, and then I could see Adler and Snelling, against the wall, their hands over their heads.

But that wasn't the main thing I saw. It was this madman, this maniac, in front of the vault, waving an automatic, yelling that it was a stick-up, to put them up and keep them up, that whoever moved was going to get killed. If he had hoped to get away with it without being recognized, I can't say he didn't have a chance. He was dressed different from the way he was the day before. He must have brought the stuff in the grip. He had on a sweat shirt that made him look three times as big as he really was, a pair of rough pants and rough shoes, a black silk handkerchief over the lower part of his face, a felt hat pulled down over his eyes—and this horrible voice.

He was yelling, and the screaming was coming from Sheila. She seemed to be behind me, and was telling him to cut it out. I couldn't see Helm. The truck was on top of me, and I couldn't see anything clear, on account of the wallop on my head. Brent was standing right over me.

Then, right back of his head, a chip fell out of the wall. I didn't hear any shot at all, but he must have, because Dyer fired, from the street, right through the glass window. Brent turned, toward the street, and I saw Adler grab at his holster. I doubled up my legs and drove against the truck, straight at Brent. It missed him, and crashed against the wall, right beside Adler. Brent wheeled and fired. Adler fired. I fired. Brent fired again. Then he made one leap, and heaved the grip, which he had in his other hand, straight through the glass at the rear of the bank. You understand: The bank is on a corner, and on two sides there's glass. There's glass on half the third side too, at the rear, facing the parking lot. It was through that window that he heaved the grip. The glass broke with a crash, and left a hole the size of a door. He went right through it.

I jumped up, and dived after him, through the hole. I could hear Dyer and his two men coming up the street behind me, shooting as they came. They hadn't come in the bank at all. At the first yelp that Sheila let out they began shooting through the glass.

He was just grabbing up the grip as I got there and leveled his gun right at me. I dropped to the ground and shot. He shot. There was a volley of shots from Dyer and Halligan and Lewis. He ran about five steps, and jumped into the car. It was a blue sedan; the door was open and it was already moving when he landed on it. It shot ahead, straight across the parking lot and over to Grove Street. I raised my gun to shoot at the tires. Two kids came around the corner carrying school-books. They stopped and blinked. I didn't fire. The car was gone.

I turned around and stepped back through the hole in the glass. The place was full of smoke, from the shooting. Sheila, Helm, and Snelling were stooped down, around Adler. He was lying a little to one side of the vault, and a drop of blood was trickling down back of his ear. It was the look on their faces that told me. Adler was dead.

IX

I started for the telephone. It was on my desk, at the front of the bank, and my legs felt queer as I walked along toward it, back of the windows. Dyer was there ahead of me. He came through the brass gate, from the other side, and reached for it.

"I'm using that for a second, Dyer."

He didn't answer, and didn't look at me, just picked up the phone and started to dial. So far as he was concerned, I was the heel that was responsible for it all, by not doing what he said, and he was letting me know it. I felt that way about it too, but I wasn't taking anything off him. I grabbed him by the neck of his coat and jerked him back on his heels.

"Didn't you hear what I said?"

His face got white, and he stood there beside me, his nostrils fanning and his little gray eyes drawn down to points. I broke his connection and dialed the home office. When they came in I asked for Lou Frazier. His title is vice president, same as mine, but he's special assistant to the Old Man, and with the Old Man in Honolulu, he was in charge. His secretary said he wasn't there, but then she said wait a minute, he's just come in. She put him on.

"Lou?"

"Yeah?"

"Dave Bennett, in Glendale."

"What is it, Dave?"

"We've had some trouble. You better get out. And bring some money. There'll be a run."

"What kind of trouble?"

"Stick-up. Guard killed. I think we're cleaned."

"O.K.—how much do you need?"

"Twenty thousand, to start. If we need more, you can send for it later. And step on it."

"On my way."

While I was talking, the sirens were screeching, and now the place was full of cops. Outside, an ambulance was pulling in, and about five hundred people standing around, with more coming by the second. When I hung up, a drop of blood ran off the end of my nose on the blotter, and then it began to patter down in a stream. I put my hand to my head. My hair was all sticky and wet, and when I looked, my fingers were full of blood. I tried to think what caused it, then remembered the truck falling on me.

"Dyer?"

" . . . Yes, sir."

"Mr. Frazier is on his way out. He's bringing money to meet all demands. You're to stay here with Halligan and Lewis, and keep order, and hold yourself ready for anything he tells you. Let the police take care of Adler."

"They're taking him out now."

I looked, and two of them, with the ambulance crew, were carrying him out. They were going the front way. Halligan had opened the door. Lewis and five or six cops were already outside, keeping the people back. They put him in the ambulance. Helm started out there, but I called him.

"Get in the vault, check it up."

"We've been in. Snelling and I."

"What did he get?"

"He got it all. Forty-four thousand, cash. And that's not all. He got in the boxes. He left the little boxes alone. He went in the others with a chisel, the ones that had big valuables and securities in them, and he took it all from them, too. He knew which ones."

"Mr. Frazier is on his way out with cash for the depositors. As soon as that's under way, make a list of all the rifled boxes, get the box holders on the phone if you can, send them wires otherwise, and get them in here."

"I'll start on it now."

The ambulance crew came in, and started over toward me. I waved them away, and they went off with Adler. Sheila came over to me.

"Mr. Kaiser wants to speak to you."

He was right behind her, Bunny Kaiser, the guy she had brought in for the $100,000 loan the afternoon I had found the shortage.

I was just opening my mouth to tell him that all demands would be met, that he could take his turn with the other depositors as soon as we opened, when he motioned to the windows. Every window on one side was full of breaks and bullet holes, and the back window had the big hole in it where Brent had thrown his grip through it.

"Mr. Bennett, I just wanted to say, I've got my glaziers at work now, they're just starting on the plate glass windows for my building, they've got plenty of stock, and if you want, I'll send them over and they can get you fixed up here. Them breaks don't look so good."

"That would help, Mr. Kaiser."

"Right away."

"And—thanks."

I stuck out my left hand, the one that wasn't covered with blood, and he took it. I must have been pretty wrung up. For just that long it seemed to me I loved him more than anybody on earth. At a time like that, what it means to you, one kind word.

The glaziers were already ripping out the broken glass when Lou Frazier got there. He had a box of cash, four extra tellers, and one uniformed guard, all he could get into his car. He came over, and I gave it to him quick, what he needed to know. He stepped out on the sidewalk with his cash box, held it up, and made a speech:

"All demands will be met. In five minutes the windows will open, all depositors kindly fall in line, the tellers will identify you, and positively nobody but depositors will be admitted!"

He had Snelling with him, and Snelling began to pick depositors out of the crowd, and the cops and the new guard formed them in line, out on the sidewalk. He came in the bank again, and his tellers set the upset truck on its wheels again, and rolled the others out, and they and Helm started to get things ready to pay. Dyer was inside by now. Lou went over to him, and jerked his thumb toward me.

"Get him out of here."

It was the first time it had dawned on me that I must be an awful-looking thing, sitting there at my desk in the front of the bank, with blood all over me. Dyer came over and called another ambulance. Sheila took her handkerchief and started to wipe off my face. It was full of blood in a second. She took my own handkerchief out of my pocket, and did the best she could with it. From the way Lou looked away every time his eye fell on me, I figured she only made it worse.

Lou opened the doors, and forty or fifty depositors filed in. "Savings depositors on this side, please have your passbooks ready."

He split them up to four windows. There was a little wait, and then those at the head of the line began to get their money. Four or five went out, counting bills. Two or three that had been in line saw we were paying, and dropped out. A guy counting bills stopped, then fell in at the end of the line, to put his money back in.

The run was over.

My head began to go around, and I felt sick to my stomach. Next thing I knew, there was an ambulance siren, and then a doctor in a white coat was standing in front of me, with two orderlies beside him. "Think you can go, or you going to need a little help?"

"Oh, I can go."

"Better lean on me."

I leaned on him, and I must have looked pretty terrible, because Sheila turned away from me, and started to cry. It was the first she had broken down since it happened, and she couldn't fight it back. Her shoulders kept jerking and the doctor motioned to one of the orderlies.

"Guess we better take her along too."

"Guess we better."

They rode us in together, she on one stretcher, me on the other, the doctor riding backwards, between us. As we went he worked on my cut. He kept swabbing at it, and I could feel the sting of the antiseptic. But I wasn't thinking about that. Once out of the bank, Sheila broke down completely, and it was terrible to hear the sound in her voice, as the sobs came out of her. The doctors talked to her a little, but kept on working on me. It was a swell ride.

X

It was the same old hospital again, and they lifted her out, and wheeled her away somewhere, and then they took me out. They wheeled me in an elevator, and we went up, and they wheeled me out of the elevator to a room, and then two more doctors came and looked at me. One of them was an older man, and he didn't seem to be an intern. "Well, Mr. Bennett, you've got a bad head."

"Sew it up, it'll be all right."

"I'm putting you under an anesthetic, for that."

"No anesthetic, I've got things to do."

"Do you want to bear that scar the rest of your life?"

"What are you talking about, scar?"

"I'm telling you, you've got a bad head. Now if—"

"O.K.—but get at it."

He went, and an orderly came in and started to undress me, but I stopped him and made him call my house. When he had Sam on the line I talked, and told him to drop everything and get in there with another suit of clothes, a clean shirt, fresh necktie, and everything else clean. Then I slipped out of the rest of my clothes, and they put a hospital shirt on me, and a nurse came in and jabbed me with a hypodermic, and they took me up to the operating room. A doctor put a mask over my face and told me to breathe in a natural manner, and that was the last I knew for a while.

When I came out of it I was back in the room again, and the nurse was sitting there, and my head was all wrapped in bandages. They hadn't used ether, they had used some other stuff, so in about five minutes I was myself again, though I felt pretty sick. I asked for a paper. She had one on her lap, reading it, and handed it over. It was an early edition, and the robbery was smeared all over the front page, with Brent's picture, and Adler's picture, and my picture, one of my old football pictures. There was no trace of Brent yet, it said, but the preliminary estimate of what he got was put at $90,000. That included $44,000 from the bank, and around $46,000 taken from the private safe deposit boxes. The story made me the hero. I knew he was in the vault, it said, and although I brought guards with me, I insisted on being the first man in the vault, and suffered a serious head injury as a result. Adler got killed on the first exchange of shots, after I opened fire. He left a wife and one child, and the funeral would probably be held tomorrow.

There was a description of Brent's sedan, and the license number. Dyer had got that, as the car drove off, and it checked with the plates issued in Brent's name. There was quite a lot about the fact that the car was moving when he jumped aboard, and how that proved he had accomplices. There was nothing about Sheila, except that she had been taken to the hospital for nervous collapse, and nothing about the shortage at all. The nurse got up and came over to feed me some ice. "Well, how does it feel to be a hero?"

"Feels great."

"You had quite a time out there."

"Yeah, quite a time."

Pretty soon Sam got there with my clothes, and I told him to stand by. Then two detectives came in and began asking questions.

I told them as little as I could, but I had to tell them about Helm, and Sheila seeing the red light, and how I'd gone against Dyer's advice, and what happened at the bank. They dug in pretty hard, but I stalled as well as I could, and after a while they went.

Sam went out and got a later edition of the afternoon paper. They had a bigger layout now on the pictures. Brent's picture was still three columns, but my picture and Adler's picture were smaller, and in an inset there was a picture of Sheila. It said police had a talk with her, at the hospital, and that she was unable to give any clue as to why Brent had committed the crime, or as to his whereabouts. Then, at the end, it said: "It was intimated, however, that Mrs. Brent will be questioned further."

At that I hopped out of bed. The nurse jumped up and tried to stop me, but I knew I had to get away from where cops could get at me, anyway, until the thing broke enough that I knew what I was going to do.

"What are you doing, Mr. Bennett?"

"I'm going home."

"But you can't! You're to stay until—"

"I said I'm going home. Now if you want to stick around and watch me dress, that's O.K. by me, but if you're a nice girl, now is the time to beat it out in the hall."

While I was dressing they all tried to stop me, the nurse and the intern, and the head nurse, but I had Sam pitch the bloody clothes into the suitcase he had brought, and in about five minutes we were off. At the desk downstairs I wrote a check for my bill, and asked the woman how was Mrs. Brent.

"Oh, she'll be all right, but of course it was a terrible shock to her."

"She still here?"

"Well, they're questioning her, you know."

"Who?"

"The police. . . . If you ask me, she'll be held."

"You mean—arrested?"

"Apparently she knows something."

"Oh, I see."

"Don't say I told you."

"I won't, of course."

Sam had a taxi by then, and we got in. I had the driver go out to Glendale, and pull up beside my car, where I had left it on Anita Avenue. I had Sam take the wheel, and told him to drive around and keep on driving. He took Foothill, and went on up past San Fernando somewhere, I didn't pay any attention where.

Going past the bank, I saw the glass was all in place, and a gold-leafer was inside, putting on the lettering. I couldn't see who was in there. Late in the afternoon we came back through Los Angeles, and I bought a paper. My picture was gone now, and so was Adler's, and Brent's was smaller. Sheila's was four columns wide, and in an inset was a picture of her father, Dr. Henry W. Rollinson, of U.C.L.A. The headline stretched clear across the page, and called it a "cover-up robbery." I didn't bother to read any more. If Dr. Rollinson had told his story, the whole thing was in the soup.

Sam drove me home then, and fixed me something to eat. I went in the living room and lay down, expecting cops, and wondered what I was going to tell them.

Around eight o'clock the doorbell rang, and I answered myself. But it wasn't cops, it was Lou Frazier. He came in and I had Sam fix him a drink. He seemed to need it. I lay down on the sofa again, and held on to my head. It didn't ache, and I felt all right, but I was getting ready. I wanted an excuse not to talk any more than I had to. After he got part of his drink down he started in.

"You seen the afternoon papers?"

"Just the headlines."

"The guy was short in his accounts."

"Looks like it."

"She was in on it."

"Who?"

"The wife. That sexy-looking thing known as Sheila. She doctored the books for him. We just locked up a half hour ago. I've just come from there. Well boy, it's a crime what that dame got away with. That system in the savings department, all that stuff you went out there to make a report on—that was nothing but a cover. The laugh's on you, Bennett. Now you got a real article for the *American Banker.*"

"I doubt if she was in on it."

"I know she was in on it."

"If she was, why did she let him go to her father for the dough to cover up the shortage? Looks to me like that was putting it on a little too thick."

"O.K.—it's taken me all afternoon to figure that one out, and I had to question the father pretty sharp. He's plenty bitter against Brent. All right, take it from their point of view, hers and Brent's. They were short on the accounts, and they figured on a phoney hold-up that would cover their deficit, so nobody would even know there *had* been a shortage. The first thing to do was get the books in shape, and I'm telling you she made a slick job of that. She didn't leave a trace, and if it wasn't for her father, we'd never have known how much they were short. All right, she's got to get those books in shape, and do it before you next check on her cash. That was the tough part, they were up against time, but she was equal to it, I'll say that for her. All right, now she brings a spider in, and he slips in the vault and hides there. But they couldn't be sure what was going to happen next morning, could they? He might get away with it clean, with that handkerchief over his face nobody could identify him, and then later she could call the old man up and say please don't say anything, she'll explain to him later, that Charles is horribly upset, and when the cops go to his house, sure enough he is. He's in bed, still recovering from his operation, and all this and that—but no money anywhere around, and nothing to connect him with it.

"But look: They figure maybe he don't get away with it. Maybe he gets caught, and then what? All the money's there, isn't it? He's got five doctors to swear he's off his nut anyway, on account of illness—and he gets off light. With luck, he even gets a suspended sentence, and the only one that's out is her old man. She shuts him up, and they're not much worse off than they were before. Well, thanks to a guy named Helm it all went sour. None of it broke like they expected—he got away, but everybody knew who he was, and Adler got killed. So now he's wanted for murder—*and* robbery, and she's held for the same."

"Is she held?"

"You bet your sweet life she's held. She doesn't know it yet—she's down at that hospital, with a little dope in her arm to quiet her after the awful experience she had, but there's a cop outside the door right now, and tomorrow when she wakes up maybe she won't look quite so sexy."

I lay there with my eyes shut, wondering what I was going to do, but by that time my head was numb, so I didn't feel anything any more. After a while I heard myself speak to him, "Lou?"

"Yeah?"

"I knew about that shortage."

" . . . You mean you suspected it?"

"I knew—"

"You mean you suspected it!"

He fairly screamed it at me. When I opened my eyes he was standing in front of me, his eyes almost popping out of their sockets, his face all twisted and white. Lou is a pretty good-looking guy, big and thickset, with brown eyes and a golf tan all over him, but now he looked like some kind of a wild man.

"If you knew about it, and didn't report it, *there goes our bond! Don't you get it, Bennett? There goes our bond!*"

It was the first I had even thought of the bond. I could see it, though, the second he began to scream, that little line in fine type on the bond. We don't make our people give individual bond. We carry a group bond on them, ourselves, and that line reads: " . . . The assured shall report to the Corporation any shortage, embezzlement, defalcation, or theft on the part of any of their employees, within twenty-four hours of the time such shortage, embezzlement, defalcation, or theft shall be known to them, or to their officers, and failure to report such shortage, embezzlement, defalcation, or theft shall be deemed ground for the cancellation of this bond, and the release of the Corporation from liability for such shortage, embezzlement, defalcation, or shortage." I felt my lips go cold, and the sweat stand out on the palms of my hands, but I went on:

"You're accusing a woman of crimes I know damned well she didn't commit, and bond or no bond, I'm telling you—"

"You're not telling me anything, get that right now!"

He grabbed his hat and ran for the door. "And listen: If you know what's good for you, you're not telling anybody else either! If that comes out, there goes our fidelity bond and our burglary bond—we won't get a cent from the bonding company, we're hooked for the whole ninety thousand bucks, and—God, ninety thousand bucks! Ninety thousand bucks!"

He went, and I looked at my watch. It was nine o'clock. I called up a florist, and had them send flowers to Adler's funeral. Then I went upstairs and went to bed, and stared at the ceiling trying to get through my head what I had to face in the morning.

XI

Don't ask me about the next three days. They were the worst I ever spent in my life. First I went in to the Hall of Justice and talked to Mr. Gaudenzi, the assistant district attorney that was on the case. He listened to me, and took notes, and then things began to hit me.

First I was summoned to appear before the Grand Jury, to tell what I had to say there. I had to waive immunity for that, and boy, if you think it's fun to have those babies tearing at your throat, you try it once. There's no judge to help you, no lawyer to object to questions that make you look like a fool, nothing but you, the district attorney, the stenographer, and them. They kept me in there two hours. I squirmed and sweated and tried to get out of admitting why I put up the money for Sheila, but after a while they had it. I admitted I had asked her to divorce Brent and marry me, and that was all they wanted to know. I was hardly home before a long wire from Lou Frazier was delivered, telling me the bonding company had filed notice they denied liability for the money that was gone, and relieving me of duty until further notice. He would have fired me, if he could, but that had to wait till the Old Man got back from Honolulu, as I was an officer of the company, and couldn't be fired until the Old Man laid it before the directors.

But the worst was the newspapers. The story had been doing pretty well until I got in it. I mean it was on the front page, with pictures and all kinds of stuff about clues to Brent's whereabouts, one hot tip putting him in Mexico, another in Phoenix, and still another in Del Monte, where an auto-court man said he'd registered the night of the robbery. But when they had my stuff, they went hog wild with it. That gave it a love interest, and what they did to me was just plain murder. They called it the Loot Triangle, and went over to old Dr. Rollinson's, where Sheila's children were staying, and got pictures of them, and of him, and stole at least a dozen of her, and they ran every picture of me they could dig out of their files, and I cursed the day I ever posed in a bathing suit while I was in college, with a co-ed skinning the cat on each arm, in an "Adonis" picture for some football publicity.

And what I got for all that hell was that the day before I appeared before them, the Grand Jury indicted Sheila for alteration of a corporation's records, for embezzlement, and for accessory to robbery with a deadly weapon. The only thing they didn't indict her for was murder, and why they hadn't done that I couldn't understand. So it all went for nothing. I'd nailed myself to the cross, brought all my Federal mortgage notes to prove I'd put up the money, and that she couldn't have had anything to do with it, and she got indicted just the same. I got so I didn't have the heart to put my face outside the house, except when a newspaperman showed up, and then I'd go out to take a poke at him, if I could. I sat home and listened to the shortwave radio, tuned to the police broadcasts, wondering if I could pick up something that would mean they were closing in on Brent. That, and the news broadcasts. One of them said Sheila's bail had been set at $7,500 and that her father had put it up, and that she'd been released. It wouldn't have done any good for me to have gone down to put up bail. I'd given her all I had, already.

That day I got in the car and took a ride, just to keep from going nuts. Coming back I drove by the bank and peeped in. Snelling was at my desk. Church was at Sheila's window. Helm was at Snelling's place, and there were two tellers I'd never seen before.

When I tuned in on the news, after supper that night, for the first time there was some sign the story was slackening off. The guy said Brent hadn't been caught yet, but there was no more stuff about me, or about Sheila. I relaxed a little, but then after a

while something began to bore into me. Where was Brent? If she
was out on bail, was she meeting him? I'd done all I could to clear
her, but that didn't mean I was sure she was innocent, or felt any
different about her than I had before. The idea that she might be
meeting him somewhere, that she had played me for a sucker that
way, right from the start, set me to tramping around that living
room once more, and I tried to tell myself to forget it, to forget
her, to wipe the whole thing off the slate and be done with it, and
I couldn't. Around eight-thirty I did something I guess I'm not
proud of. I got in the car, drove over there, and parked down the
street about half a block, to see what I could see.

There was a light on, and I sat there a long time. You'd be
surprised what went on, the newspaper reporters that rang the
bell, and got kicked out, the cars that drove by, and slowed down
so fat women could rubber in there, the peeping that was going
on from upstairs windows of houses. After a while the light went
off. The door opened, and Sheila came out. She started down the
street, toward me. I felt if she saw me there I'd die of shame. I
dropped down behind the wheel, and bent over on one side so I
couldn't be seen from the pavement, and held my breath. I could
hear her footsteps coming on, quick, like she was in a hurry to get
somewhere. They went right on by the car, without stopping, but
through the window, almost in a whisper, I heard her say: "You're
being watched."

I knew in a flash then, why she hadn't been indicted for murder. If they'd done that, she wouldn't have been entitled to bail.
They indicted her, but they left it so she could get out, and then
they began doing the same thing I'd been doing: watching her, to
see if she'd make some break that would lead them to Brent.

Next day I made up my mind I had to see her. But how to see
her was tough. If they were watching her that close, they'd probably tapped in on her phone, and any wire I sent her would be read

before she got it, that was a cinch. I figured on it awhile, and then I went down in the kitchen to see Sam. "You got a basket here?"

"Yes sir, a big market basket."

"O.K., I tell you what you do. Put a couple of loaves of bread in it, put on your white coat, and get on over to this address on Mountain Drive. Co in the back way, knock, ask for Mrs. Brent. Make sure you're talking to her, and that nobody else is around. Tell her I want to see her, and will she meet me tonight at seven o'clock, at the same place she used to meet me downtown, after she came from the hospital. Tell her I'll be waiting in the car."

"Yes sir, seven o'clock."

"You got that all straight?"

"I have, sir."

"There's cops all around the house. If you're stopped, tell them nothing, and if possible, don't let them know who you are."

"Just leave it to me."

I took an hour that night shaking anybody that might be following me. I drove up to Saugus, and coming in to San Fernando I shoved up to ninety, and I knew nobody was back of me, because I could see everything behind. At San Fernando I cut over to Van Nuys, and drove in to the hospital from there. It was one minute after seven when I pulled in to the curb, but I hadn't even stopped rolling before the door opened and she jumped in. I kept right on.

"You're being followed."

"I think not. I shook them."

"I couldn't. I think my taxi driver had his instructions before he came to the house. They're about two hundred yards behind."

"I don't see anything."

"They're there."

We drove on, me trying to think what I wanted to say. But it was she that started it.

"Dave?"

"Yes?"

"We may never see each other again, after tonight. I think I'd better begin. You've—been on my mind, quite a lot. Among other things."

"All right, begin."

"I've done you a great wrong."

"I didn't say so."

"You didn't have to. I felt everything you were thinking in that terrible ride that morning in the ambulance. I've done you a great wrong, and I've done myself a great wrong. I forgot one thing a woman can never forget. I didn't forget it. But I—closed my eyes to it."

"Yeah, and what was that?"

"That a woman must come to a man, as they say in court, with clean hands. In some countries, she has to bring more than that. Something in her hand, something on her back, something on the ox cart—a dowry. In this country we waive that, but we don't waive the clean hands. I couldn't give you them. If I was going to come to you, I had to come with encumbrances, terrible encumbrances. I had to be bought."

"I suggested that."

"Dave, it can't be done. I've asked you to pay a price for me that no man can pay. I've cost you a shocking amount of money, I've cost you your career, I've cost you your good name. On account of me you've been pilloried in the newspapers, you've endured torture. You've stood by me beautifully, you did everything you could for me, before that awful morning and since—but I'm not worth it. No woman can be, and no woman has a right to think she is. Very well, then, you don't have to stand by me any longer. You can consider yourself released, and if it lies in my power, I'll make up to you what I've cost you. The career, the notoriety, I can't do anything about. The money, God willing, someday I shall repay

you. I guess that's what I wanted to say. I guess that's all I wanted
to say. That—and good-bye."

I thought that over for five or ten miles. It was no time for
lolly-gagging. She had said what she meant and I had to say what
I meant. And I wasn't kidding myself that a lot of it wasn't true.
The whole mess, from the time we had started doctoring those
books, and putting the money back, I had just hated, and they
weren't love scenes, those nights when we were getting ready for
the next day's skulduggery. They were nervous sessions, and she
never looked quite so pretty going home as she had coming over.
But it still wasn't what was on my mind. If I could be sure she was
on the up-and-up with me, I'd still feel she was worth it, and I'd
still stand by her, if she needed me and wanted me. I made up my
mind I was going to hit it on the nose. "Sheila?"

"Yes, Dave."

"I did feel that way in the ambulance."

"There's no need to tell me."

"Partly on account of what you've been talking about, maybe.
There's no use kidding ourselves. It was one awful morning, and
we've both had awful mornings since. But that wasn't the main
thing."

" . . . What was the main thing?"

"I wasn't sure, I haven't been sure from the beginning, and I'm
not sure now, that you haven't been two-timing me."

"What are you talking about? Two-timing you with whom?"

"Brent."

"With *Charles?* Are you crazy?"

"No, I'm not crazy. All right, now you get it. I've known from
the beginning, and I'm perfectly sure of it now, that you know
more about this than you've been telling, that you've held out on
me, that you've held out on the cops. All right, now you can put it
on the line. Were you in on this thing with Brent or not?"

"Dave, how can you ask such a thing?"

"Do you know where he is?"

" . . . Yes."

"That's all I want to know."

I said it mechanically, because to tell you the truth I'd about decided she was on the up-and-up all the way down the line, and when she said that it hit me between the eyes like a fist. I could feel my breath trembling as we drove along, and I could feel her looking at me too. Then she began to speak in a hard, strained voice, like she was forcing herself to talk, and measuring everything she said.

"I know where he is, and I've known a lot more about him than I ever told you. Before that morning, I didn't tell you because I didn't want to wash a lot of dirty linen, even before you. Since that morning I haven't told anybody because—*I want him to escape!*"

"Oh, you do!"

"I pulled you into it, when I discovered that shortage, for the reason I told you. So my children wouldn't grow up knowing their father was in prison. I'm shielding Charles now, I'm holding out on you, as you put it, because if I don't, they're going to grow up knowing their father was executed for murder. I won't have it! I don't care if the bank loses ninety thousand dollars, or a million dollars, I don't care if your career is ruined—I might as well tell you the truth, Dave—*if there's any way I can prevent it, my children are not going to have their lives blighted by that horrible disgrace.*"

That cleared it up at last. And then something came over me. I knew we were going through the same old thing again, that I'd be helping her cover up something, that I wasn't going to have any more of that. If she and I were to go on, it had to be a clean slate between us, and I felt myself tighten. "So far as I'm concerned I won't have that."

"I'm not asking you to."

"And not because of what you said about me. I'm not asking you to put me ahead of your children, or anything ahead of your children."

"I couldn't, even if you did ask me."

"It's because the game is up, and you may as well learn that your children aren't any better than anybody else."

"I'm sorry. To me they are."

"They'll learn, before they die, that they've got to play the cards God dealt them, and you'll learn it too, if I know anything about it. What you're doing, you're ruining other lives, to say nothing of your own life, and doing wrong, too—to save them. O.K., play it your own way. But that lets me out."

"Then it's good-bye?"

"I guess it is."

"It's what I've been trying to tell you."

She was crying now, and she took my hand and gave it a little jerky shake. I loved her more than I'd ever loved her, and I wanted to stop, and put my arms around her, and start all over again, but I didn't. I knew it wouldn't get us anywhere at all, and I kept right on driving. We'd got to the beach by then, by way of Pico Boulevard, and I ran up through Santa Monica to Wilshire, then turned back to take her home. We were done, and I could feel it that she had called the turn. We'd never see each other again.

How far we'd got I don't know, but we were somewhere coming in toward Westwood. She had quieted down, and was leaning against the window with her eyes closed, when all of a sudden she sat up and turned up the radio. I had got so I kept it in shortwave all the time now, and it was turned low, so you could hardly hear it, but it was on. A cop's voice was just finishing an order, and then it was repeated: "Car number forty-two, Car number forty-two. . . . Proceed to number six eight two five Sanborn Avenue,

Westwood, at once. . . . Two children missing from home of Dr.
Henry W. Rollinson . . . "

I stepped on it hard, but she grabbed me.

"Stop!"

"I'm taking you there!"

"Stop! I said stop—will you please stop!"

I couldn't make any sense out of her, but I pulled over and
we skidded to a stop. She jumped out. I jumped out, "Will you
kindly tell me what we're stopping here for? They're your kids,
don't you get it—?"

But she was on the curb, waving back the way we had come.
Just then a pair of headlights snapped on. I hadn't seen any car,
but it dawned on me this must be that car that had been following
us. She kept on waving, then started to run toward it. At that, the
car came up. A couple of detectives were inside. She didn't even
wait till she stopped before she screamed: "Did you get that call?"

"What call?"

"The Westwood call, about the children?"

"Baby, that was for Car forty-two."

"Will you wipe that grin off your face and listen to me? Those
are my children. They've been taken by my husband, and it means
he's getting ready to skip, to wherever he's going—"

She never even finished. Those cops hopped out and she gave
it to them as fast as she could. She said he'd be sure to stop at his
hideout before he blew, that they were to follow us there, that
we'd lead the way if they'd only stop talking and hurry. But the
cops had a different idea. They knew by now it was a question
of time, so they split the cars up. One of them went ahead in the
police car, after she gave him the address, the other took the wheel
of my car, and we jumped in on the back seat. Boy, if you think
you can drive, you ought to try it once with a pair of cops. We
went through Westwood with everything wide open, it wasn't five

minutes before we were in Hollywood, and we just kept on going. We didn't stop for any kind of a light, and I don't think we were under eighty the whole trip.

All the time she kept holding on to my hand and praying: "Oh God, if we're only in time! If we're only in time!"

XII

We pulled up in front of a little white apartment house in Glendale. Sheila jumped out, and the cops and myself were right beside her. She whispered for us to keep quiet. Then she stepped on the grass, went around to the side of the house, and looked up. A light was on in one window. Then she went back to the garage. It was open, and she peeped in. Then she came back to the front and went inside, still motioning to us to keep quiet. We followed her, and she went up to the second floor. She tiptoed to the third door on the right, stood there a minute, and listened. She tiptoed back to where we were. The cops had their guns out by now. Then she marched right up to the door, her heels clicking on the floor, and rapped. It opened right away, and a woman was standing there. She had a cigarette in one hand and her hat and coat on, like she was getting ready to go out. I had to look twice to make sure I wasn't seeing things. It was Church.

"Where are my children?"

"Well, Sheila, how should I know—?"

Sheila grabbed her and jerked her out into the hall. "Where are my children, I said."

"They're all right. He just wanted to see them a minute before he—"

She stopped when one of the cops walked up behind her, stepped through the open door with his gun ready, and went inside. The other cop stayed in the hall, right beside Sheila and Church, his gun in his hand, listening. After a minute or two the cop that went in came to the door and motioned us inside. Sheila and Church went in, then I went in, then the other cop stepped inside, but stood where he could cover the hall. It was a one-room furnished apartment, with a dining alcove to one side, and a bathroom. All doors were open; even the closet door, where the cop had opened them, ready to shoot if he had to. In the middle of the floor were a couple of suitcases strapped up tight. The cop that went in first walked over to Church.

"All right, Fats, spit it out."

"I don't even know what you're talking about."

"Where are those kids?"

"How should I know—?"

"You want that puss mashed in?"

" . . . He's bringing them here."

"When?"

"Now. He ought to be here by now."

"What for?"

"To take with us. We were going to blow."

"He using a car?"

"He's using his car."

"O.K.—open them suitcases."

"I have no key. He—"

"I said open them."

She stooped down and began to unstrap the suitcases. The cop poked her behind with the gun.

"Come on, step on it, step on it!"

When she had them unstrapped, she took keys from her handbag and unlocked them. The cop kicked them open. Then he whistled. From the larger of the two suitcases money began tumbling on the floor, some of it in bundles, with rubber bands around it, some of it with paper wrappers still on, showing the amounts. That was the new money we had had in the vault, stuff that had never even been touched. Church began to curse at Sheila.

"It's all there, and now you've got what you want, haven't you? You think I didn't know what you were doing? You think I didn't see you fixing those cards up so you could send him up when they found that shortage? All right, he beat you to it, and he took your old man for a ride too—that sanctimonious old fool! But you haven't got him yet, and you haven't got those brats! I'll—"

She made a dive for the door, but the cop was standing there and threw her back. Then he spoke to the other one, the one that was stooped down, fingering the money. "Jake!"

"Yeah?"

"He'll be here for that dough. You better put in a call. No use taking chances. We need more men."

"God, I never seen that much dough."

He stepped over to the phone and lifted the receiver to dial. Just then, from outside, I heard a car horn give a kind of a rattle, like they give when they're tapped three or four times quick. Church heard it too, and opened her mouth to scream. That scream never came out. Sheila leaped at her, caught her throat with one hand, and covered her mouth with the other. She turned her head around to the cops.

"Go on, hurry up, he's out there."

The cops dived out and piled down the stairs, and I was right after them. They no sooner reached the door than there was a shot, from a car parked out front, right behind my car. One cop ducked behind a big urn beside the door, the other ran behind a tree. The car was moving now, and I meant to get that guy if it was the last thing I did on earth. I ran off to the right, across the apartment house lawn and the lawn next to it and the lawn next to that, as hard as I could. There was no way he could turn. If he was going to get away, he had to pass me. I got to a car that was parked about fifty feet up the street, and crouched down in front of it, right on the front bumper, so that the car was between him and me. He was in second now, and giving her the gun, but I jumped and caught the door handle.

What happened in the next ten seconds I'm not sure I know myself. The speed of the car threw me back, so I lost my grip on the door handle, and I hit my head on the fender. I was still wearing a bandage, from the other cut, so that wasn't so good. But I caught the rear door handle, and hung on. All that happened quicker than I can tell it, but being thrown back that way, I guess that's what saved me. He must have thought I was still up front, because inside the car he began to shoot, and I saw holes appear in the front door, one by one. I had some crazy idea I had to count them, so I'd know when he'd shot his shells out. I saw three holes, one right after the other. But then I woke up that there were more shots than holes, that some of those shots were coming from behind. That meant the cops had got in it again. I was right in the line of fire, and I wanted to drop off and lay in the street, but I held on. Then these screams began coming from the back seat, and I remembered the kids. I yelled at the cops that the children were back there, but just then the car slacked and gave a yaw to the left, and we went crashing into the curb and stopped.

I got up, opened the front door, and jumped aside, quick. There was no need to jump. He was lying curled up on the front seat, with his head hanging down, and all over the upholstery was blood. But what I saw, when one of the cops ran up and opened the rear door, was just pitiful. The oldest of the kids, Anna, was down on the floor moaning, and her sister, the little three-year-old, Charlotte, was up on the seat, screaming at her father to look at Anna, that Anna was hurt.

Her father wasn't saying anything.

It seemed funny that the cop, the one that had treated Church so rough, could be so swell when it came to a couple of children. He kept calling them Sissy, and got the little one calmed down in just about a minute, and the other one too, the one that was shot. The other cop ran back to the apartment house, to phone for help, and to collar Church before she could run off with that dough, and he caught her just as she was beating it out the door. This one stayed right with the car, and he no sooner got the children quiet than he had Sheila on his hands, and about five hundred people that began collecting from every place there was.

Sheila was like a wild woman, but she didn't have a chance with that cop. He wouldn't let her touch Anna, and he wouldn't let Anna be moved till the doctors moved her. There on the floor of the car was where she was going to stay, he said, and nothing that Sheila said could change him. I figured he was right, and put my arms around her, and tried to get her quiet, and in a minute or two I felt her stiffen and knew she was going to do everything she could to keep herself under control.

The ambulances got there at last, and they put Brent in one, and the little girl in the other, and Sheila rode in with her. I took little Charlotte in my car. As she left me, Sheila touched my arm.

"More hospitals."

"You've had a dose."

"But this—Dave!"

It was one in the morning before they got through in the operating room, and long before that the nurses put little Charlotte to bed. From what she said to me on the way in, and what the cops and I were able to piece together, it wasn't one of the cop's shots that had hit Anna at all.

What happened was that the kids were asleep on the back seat, both of them, when Brent pulled up in front of the apartment house, and didn't know a thing till he started to shoot through the door at me. Then the oldest one jumped up and spoke to her father. When he didn't answer she stood up and tried to talk to him on his left side, back of where he was trying to shoot and drive at the same time. That must have been when he turned and let the cops have it over his shoulder. Except that instead of getting the cops, he got his own child.

When it was all over I took Sheila home. I didn't take her to Glendale. I took her to her father's house in Westwood. She had phoned him what had happened, and they were waiting for her. She looked like a ghost of herself, and leaned against the window with her eyes closed. "Did they tell you about Brent?"

She opened her eyes.

" . . . No. How is he?"

"He won't be executed for murder."

"You mean—?"

"He died. On the table."

She closed her eyes again, and didn't speak for a while, and when she did it was in a dull, lifeless way.

"Charles was all right, a fine man—until he met Church. I don't know what effect she had on him. He went completely insane about her, and then he began to go bad. What he did, I mean at the bank that morning, wasn't his think-up, it was hers."

"But *why*, will you tell me that?"

"To get back at me. At my father. At the world. At everything. You noticed what she said to me? With her that meant an obsession that I was set to ruin Charles, and if I was, then they would strike first, that's all. Charles was completely under her, and she's bad. Really, I'm not sure she's quite sane."

"What a thing to call a sweetie."

"I think that was part of the hold she had on him. He wasn't a very masculine man. With me, I think he felt on the defensive, though certainly I never gave him any reason to. But with her,

with that colorless, dietician nature that she had—I think he felt
like a man. I mean, she excited him. Because she is such a frump,
she gave him something I could never give him."

"I begin to get it now."

"Isn't that funny? He was my husband, and I don't care whether
he's alive or dead—I simply don't care. All I can think of is that
little thing down there—"

"What do the doctors say?"

"They don't know. It's entirely her constitution and how it
develops. It was through her abdomen, and there were eleven per-
forations, and there'll be peritonitis, and maybe other complica-
tions—and they can't even know what's going to happen for two
or three days yet. And the loss of blood was frightful."

"They'll give her transfusions."

"She had one, while they were operating. That was what they
were waiting for. They didn't dare start till the donor arrived."

"If blood's what it takes, I've got plenty."

She started to cry, and caught my arm. "Even blood, Dave? Is
there anything you haven't given me?"

"Forget it."

"Dave?"

"Yes?"

"If I'd played the cards that God dealt me, it wouldn't have happened. That's the awful part. If I'm to be punished—all right, it's
what I deserve. But if only the punishment—*doesn't fall on her!*"

XIII

The newspapers gave Sheila a break, I'll say that for them, once the
cops exonerated her. They played the story up big, but they made her
the heroine of it, and I can't complain of what they said about me,

except I'd rather they hadn't said anything. Church took a plea and got sent over to Tehachapi for a while. She even admitted she was the one that brought in the spider. All the money was there, so Dr. Rollinson got his stake back, and the bonding company had nothing to pay, which kind of eased off what had been keeping me awake nights.

But that wasn't what Sheila and I had to worry about. It was that poor kid down there in the hospital, and that was just awful. The doctors knew what was coming, all right. For two or three days she went along and you'd have thought she was doing fine, except that her temperature kept rising a little bit at a time, and her eyes kept getting brighter and her cheeks redder. Then the peritonitis broke, and broke plenty. For two weeks her temperature stayed up around 104, and then when it seemed she had that licked, pneumonia set in. She was in oxygen for three days, and when she came out of it she was so weak you couldn't believe she could live at all. Then, at last, she began to get better.

All that time I took Sheila in there twice a day, and we'd sit and watch the chart, and in between we'd talk about what we were going to do with our lives. I had no idea. The mess over the bond was all cleared up, but I hadn't been told to come back to work, and I didn't expect to be. And after the way my name had been plastered on the front pages all over the country, I didn't know where I could get a job, or whether I could get a job. I knew a little about banking, but in banking the first thing you've got to have is a good name.

Then one night we were sitting there, Sheila and myself, with the two kids on the bed, looking at a picture book, when the door opened, and the Old Man walked in. It was the first time we had seen him since the night he danced with Sheila, just before he sailed for Honolulu. He had a box of flowers, and handed them to Sheila with a bow. "Just dropped in to see how the little girl is getting along."

Sheila took the flowers and turned away quickly to hide how she felt, then rang for the nurse and sent them out to be put in water. Then she introduced him to the children, and he sat on the bed and kidded along with them, and they let him look at the pictures in the picture book. The flowers came back, and Sheila caught her breath, and they were jumbo chrysanthemums all right. She thanked him for them, and he said they came from his own garden in Beverly. The nurse went and the kids kind of quieted down again, and Sheila went over to him, and sat down beside him on the bed, and took his hand. "You think this is a surprise, don't you?"

"Well, I can do better."

He dug in his pocket and fished up a couple of little dolls. The kids went nuts over them, and that was the end of talk for about five minutes. But Sheila was still hanging on to the Old Man's hand, and went on: "It's no surprise at all. I've been expecting you."

"Oh, you have."

"I saw you were back."

"I got back yesterday."

"I knew you'd come."

The Old Man looked at me and grinned. "I must have done pretty well in that dance. I must have uncorked a pretty good rhumba."

"I'd say you did all right."

Sheik laughed, and kissed his hand, and got up and moved into a chair. He moved into a chair too, and looked at his chrysanthemums and said, "Well, when you like somebody you have to bring her flowers."

"And when you like somebody, you know they'll do it."

He sat there a minute, and then he said, "I think you two are about the silliest pair of fools I ever knew. Just about the silliest."

"We think so too."

"But not a pair of crooks. . . . I read a little about it, in

Honolulu, and when I got back I went into it from beginning to end, thoroughly. If I'd been here, I'd have let you have it right in the neck, just exactly where Lou Frazier let you have it, and I haven't one word of criticism to offer for what he did. But I wasn't here. I was away, I'm glad to say. Now that I'm back I can't find it in me to hold it against you. It was against all rules, all prudence, but it wasn't morally wrong. And—it was silly. But all of us, I suppose, are silly now and then. Even I feel the impulse—especially when dancing the rhumba."

He stopped and let his fingertips touch in front of his eyes, and stared through them for a minute or so. Then he went on:

"But—the official family is the official family, and while Frazier isn't quite as sore as he was, he's not exactly friendly, even yet. I don't think there's anything for you in the home office for some little time yet, Bennett—at any rate, until this blows over a little. However, I've about decided to open a branch in Honolulu. How would you like to take charge of *that?*"

Brother, does a cat like liver?

So Honolulu's where we are now, all five of us: Sheila, and myself, and Anna, and Charlotte, and Arthur, a little number you haven't heard about yet, that arrived about a year after we got here, and that was named after the Old Man. They're out there on the beach now, and I can see them from where I'm writing on the veranda, and my wife looks kind of pretty in a bathing suit, if anybody happens to ask you. The Old Man was in a few weeks ago, and told us that Frazier's been moved East, and any time I want to go back, it's all clear, and he'll find a spot for me. But I don't know. I like it here, and Sheila likes it here, and the kids like it here, and the branch is doing fine. And another thing: I'm not so sure I want to make it too handy for Sheila and the Old Man to dance the rhumba.

EBOOKS BY
JAMES M. CAIN

FROM MYSTERIOUSPRESS.COM
AND OPEN ROAD MEDIA

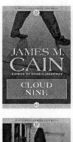    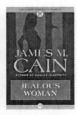

  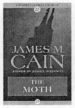  

These and more available wherever ebooks are sold

MYSTERIOUSPRESS.COM

MYSTERIOUSPRESS.COM

Otto Penzler, owner of the Mysterious Bookshop in Manhattan, founded the Mysterious Press in 1975. Penzler quickly became known for his outstanding selection of mystery, crime, and suspense books, both from his imprint and in his store. The imprint was devoted to printing the best books in these genres, using fine paper and top dust-jacket artists, as well as offering many limited, signed editions.

Now the Mysterious Press has gone digital, publishing ebooks through **MysteriousPress.com**.

MysteriousPress.com offers readers essential noir and suspense fiction, hard-boiled crime novels, and the latest thrillers from both debut authors and mystery masters. Discover classics and new voices, all from one legendary source.

FIND OUT MORE AT

WWW.MYSTERIOUSPRESS.COM

FOLLOW US:

@emysteries and Facebook.com/MysteriousPressCom

MysteriousPress.com is one of a select group of publishing partners of Open Road Integrated Media, Inc.

THE MYSTERIOUS BOOKSHOP, founded in 1979, is located in Manhattan's Tribeca neighborhood. It is the oldest and largest mystery-specialty bookstore in America.

The shop stocks the finest selection of new mystery hardcovers, paperbacks, and periodicals. It also features a superb collection of signed modern first editions, rare and collectable works, and Sherlock Holmes titles. The bookshop issues a free monthly newsletter highlighting its book clubs, new releases, events, and recently acquired books.

58 Warren Street
info@mysteriousbookshop.com
(212) 587-1011
Monday through Saturday
11:00 a.m. to 7:00 p.m.

FIND OUT MORE AT:

www.mysteriousbookshop.com

FOLLOW US:

@TheMysterious and Facebook.com/MysteriousBookshop

OPEN ROAD
INTEGRATED MEDIA

Open Road Integrated Media is a digital publisher and multimedia content company. Open Road creates connections between authors and their audiences by marketing its ebooks through a new proprietary online platform, which uses premium video content and social media.

Videos, Archival Documents, and New Releases

Sign up for the Open Road Media newsletter and get news delivered straight to your inbox.

Sign up now at
www.openroadmedia.com/newsletters

CPSIA information can be obtained at www.ICGtesting.com
Printed in the USA
BVOW02s1200231015

423870BV00004B/134/P